D0858462

Other Avon Books by
Pamela Morsi

THE LOVE CHARM

PAMELA MORSI

NO ORDINARY PRINCESS

AVON BOOKS ◆ NEW YORK

AVON BOOKS
A division of
The Hearst Corporation
1350 Avenue of the Americas
New York, New York 10019

Copyright © 1997 by Pamela Morsi
Inside cover author photo by Jennifer Jennings
Published by arrangement with the author
Visit our website at **http://AvonBooks.com**
Library of Congress Catalog Card Number: 96-95158
ISBN: 0-380-78643-5

First Avon Books Printing: June 1997

AVON TRADEMARK REG. U.S. PAT. OFF. AND IN OTHER COUNTRIES, MARCA REGISTRADA, HECHO EN U.S.A.

Printed in the U.S.A.

RA   10   9   8   7   6   5   4   3   2   1

For Janet,
who mothered me better than
any big sister ever.
And who pulled my ponytail so tight
I wore a startled expression all through grade school!

A man who marries for money earns every penny.

Oklahoma proverb

ONE

Burford Corners, Indian Territory
July 4, 1907

It was love at first sight for Princess Calhoun. Love, true love, pure love, totally consuming love, love that caught her heart in her throat and had her trembling, trembling from head to toe. He looked up and saw her. She felt the heat suffuse her cheeks. Then he looked at her, really looked at her as no man had ever looked at her. Seeing her, real and ordinary and imperfect, and finding pleasure in that gaze. She was stunned and struck dumb and screaming inside. Screaming for joy. Love at last, at long last, love.

"Someday, someday," she had confessed to her best friend, Muna. "Someday a man is going to come along and I am going to love him with all I am and everything I ever hope to be."

That someday was today. And that man stood fifty yards away looking at her. Not quite smiling, but looking, looking at her and watching her fall in love with him.

It was a day that had begun quite inauspiciously. Preparations for the Fourth of July picnic had kept her busy all morning. And her father's absence had been a nagging worry.

Last night, like most, he'd failed to return home. But she knew that he would make an appearance at his own party. If he didn't, Princess vowed, she would never forgive him.

"Any word from my father?" she had asked Howard, the young man who was part butler, part handyman.

He kept his full concentration upon his task as she spoke. "Nothin' yet, ma'am. For sure he'll be driving up in that noisy ol' thang any minute now."

"Naturally he will," Princess agreed with a certainty she didn't feel. "He must be delayed in a meeting. He wouldn't be late for his own Fourth of July party."

And if he was, she vowed silently to herself, she would cheerfully drag him out into the drive and choke him lifeless. Of course, she could never do that. Although she had once heard herself described by a neighbor as a hefty, strapping young woman, her father outweighed her by nearly a hundred pounds and had been considered quite a brawler in his day. But if he did not make it to this party she would certainly give him a piece of her mind. And she was just the woman to do so.

It was one of the truths of her life that Princess Calhoun knew what should be done and when to do it. And she could not fail to pass that knowledge on to others.

"Guests are arriving at the porte cochere, Miss."

Princess gave him a tight smile. "Thank you, Howard. I will be in the receiving room momentarily."

Princess Calhoun was not necessarily a willing pinion in the machinery of Burford Corners social life. In fact, if someone had asked her where she was from, she would have preferred to tell them that she was a resident of Topknot, the brand-new oil camp town that sat right on the city limits of Burford

Corners. The good people of the older community had not been welcoming to the wild oil field folks that flocked to their area. They had barred their doors, shuttered their windows, and crossed the street to avoid them at every opportunity. Princess was raised in the oil fields. She had friends among the people of Topknot, many of whom were more like family. They had moved together from boom town to boom town from here stretching back to West Virginia and Pennsylvania. But Topknot had no truly residential area and when her father chose to build her a house, he'd picked a lovely spot just north of Main Street in Burford Corners. Princess Calhoun realized instantly that as the wealthiest young woman in town, she was expected to become the purveyor of all that was polite and fashionable.

It was a duty that came to her easily. Her own mother, dead since Princess was a girl, had been shy and sickly. Demure in every way. But in all honesty, Princess was more her father's daughter. She needed work and purpose. She had little interest in idle chatter or the life of leisure. And the fine society of Burford Corners was as much in need of guidance and direction as the rest of the world.

Today the entire population of the two rather mutually disagreeable communities was to celebrate the birthday of the nation in the garden of her home.

For that reason alone, when Princess swept into the west receiving room, there was a smile on her face as she greeted the first arrivals.

"Oh, Daddy and I are so delighted that you came," she told first one and then another. "Mingle as you will, sample the food, and enjoy yourself."

It was a polite encouragement, not far different from one given from any hostess. But somehow when Princess said it, it sounded very much like a command.

She was never nervous or fretful. Determinedly she charged forward in life, doing what must be done in the manner most appropriate. Taking up the duties of the hostess with the same energy and vigor that might be employed in fighting battles or righting injustice. It was not something with which she was naturally at ease. But if there was anything that Princess Calhoun understood it was that hard work and organization were a strong substitute for natural talent. Of course, four years at Miss Thorogate's College, Saint Louis, Missouri had taught her much.

She had been an uninspired scholar, a fact that came as a great surprise to her father and his friends. It was one of the strange quirks of the human mind that people believed that a plain woman with a domineering nature would rightly possess exceptional intelligence. Princess knew herself to be neither bright nor beautiful. But she was practical and determined and had a strong sense of empathy for the unfortunate and downtrodden. If it could be said that she had a talent, it was for caring for other people in a deep and meaningful way. And transforming those feelings into actions and solutions.

Today those actions meant seeing that a hundred invited guests, many of them people she hardly knew, enjoyed themselves on this special occasion and got to know each other.

The food was prepared. The servants instructed. The production in order. Princess kept constant vigil on everyone and everything, all the while smiling and smiling and offering needed advice to anyone who came near. It was not, after all, simply a party. It was an important step in uniting the two communities.

"Good afternoon, Daddy and I are so glad you could join us."

The phrase was repeated dozens of times.

Princess smiled at all of them, welcomed all of them. Chatted with all of them. And wished desperately that she was elsewhere.

Howard ushered in more guests and Princess looked up once more, the polite smile still plastered upon her face. This time, however, her eyes lighted with genuine delight.

"We're here!" an attractive, dark-eyed young woman declared as she hurried through the door before her parents.

Princess grabbed her in a warm hug.

"Thank goodness," she said, chiding gently. "You are quite late. I was afraid I'd have to get out my surrey and go to get you soon. I simply could not make it through this afternoon without you."

Muna Nafee was the very best and truest friend of Princess Calhoun. And that had been the fact for some time. If people thought it strange that the strong-minded daughter of King Calhoun should take up with the soft-spoken and exotic offspring of Topknot's newly opened Emporium, then they just didn't understand the hearts of the two young ladies involved.

"I haven't seen you for a week. Where have you been?"

Muna looked momentarily uncomfortable. Whatever she intended to say, she didn't. Her mother moved up right behind her and quietly scolded her in their strange foreign tongue.

Muna nodded, clearly annoyed, but resigned. She turned to gesture toward the man that had entered with them. He was a short, balding fellow in his late thirties. He sidled up to her, grinning so broadly he appeared more foolish than friendly.

Princess gave the gentleman a polite nod. Undoubtedly he was one of Muna's numerous uncles. They showed up in the boomtowns from time to time. One by one, as his businesses grew, Mr. Nafee brought his family from the old country to work for him.

Eager to show welcome, Princess held out her hand even before Muna began the introduction.

"Prin, this is Mr. Maloof Bashara, newly arrived to our city."

The man began shaking her hand vigorously. "I speak English no good!" he declared heartily. "I speak English no good."

"It's a pleasure to meet you, sir," Princess said kindly. "Are you a member of the family?"

Mrs. Nafee was whispering furiously to her daughter. Muna spoke once more.

"Mr. Bashara is my fiancé," she said.

Princess turned to stare at her friend in disbelief. "What?"

Muna raised her chin a little higher. "Mr. Bashara and I plan to marry, Prin," she said. "I wanted you to be the first to know."

Princess stood, her jaw opened in shock for an instant before hugging Muna to her once more.

"I . . . I . . ." Her brow furrowed questioningly, Princess tried to ask the what, where, and why without words.

In reply, Muna merely rolled her eyes and gave a slight toss of her head in the direction of her father.

"We are so very happy," Mrs. Nafee declared in her heavily accented English. "Our little darling, to be married at last, and to such a fine man."

"I . . . I am so . . . so very delighted for you," Princess said finally, forcing the correct words from her lips. She continued looking questioningly at her friend and hugged her once more, but without the spontaneity of earlier. "I am just so . . . surprised and . . . so very happy for you."

There were more congratulations all around as the Nafees accepted the good wishes of the hostess.

Mr. Bashara declared once more that he didn't "speak English no good" and then to her surprise asked Princess, "How much you pay for this rug?"

"What?"

"How much you pay?" he asked, pointing to the Aubusson at their feet.

"I . . . I don't know, I . . ."

"This rug is no good," he stated flatly. "Friend of Muna, I get you better rug."

"Uh . . . ah . . . that's not necessary, I . . ."

"No trouble," Mr. Bashara declared. "I get you better rug."

Muna reached over and grabbed her fiancé's arm, almost protectively. "We do not discuss business at parties, Mr. Bashara," she told him.

"This is not business," he assured his intended with certainty. "I get friend a better rug . . . at cost."

Princess was still in shock as the Nafees and Mr. Bashara made their way out to the garden. Her friend's news was completely unfathomable, but her questions flew out of her head with the arrival, at last, of her father.

"Daddy, where have you been?" she demanded.

"Stayed up late with a sick friend," he answered. "Is everybody here?"

"Everybody but the host. You should have been here two hours ago. You've forced me to drastically rearrange the schedule of the day. That is so annoying."

Her father walked on past her, not even bothering to reply. He went through the French doors and had his arms outstretched and was laughing within a half minute.

"My God!" her father exclaimed loudly. "Is the whole damn territory here?"

His question brought hoots of laughter from every corner. King Calhoun loved a party. And the bigger, louder, gaudier, and more expensive, the better.

Princess had wanted the party to be a success. She was certain at this moment that it was. A grand, glorious success. She was rightly proud—and genuinely happy.

That happiness turned to full-fledged perfection not more than an hour later, when the sight of a man in a Rough Rider uniform changed Princess forever. True love descended upon her like a dove from heaven. She stood staring across the lawn, and then her heart stopped in stunned recognition. She saw for the very first time the only man she would ever love.

He was different than she had imagined him. He was far more handsome. Being a rather ordinary person, she had assumed that her true love would be also. But this man was far from ordinary. Even at this distance she could see that. Her heart was pounding. He was the most handsome man that she had ever seen.

His hair, a little long and showing from underneath his slouch hat, was jet black and straight as a razor. His bearing was tall and proud. And his uniform was tailored to fit him to perfection. He had wide shoulders and narrow hips, and his legs were long and muscular in the sturdy brown trousers that fit so snugly. He had a stance that said power and confidence. And his eyes . . . his eyes were compelling. They might be brown or green, or even blue, she didn't yet know, but the color was inconsequential. His eyes caught her, pinned her, held her. She couldn't have run from him if she had wanted to. And Princess Calhoun did not want to.

He was perfect, in every way perfect. And he was hers, her own true love, of that she was certain. And he was walking toward her.

Tom Walker had first surveyed the house described to him as "the Calhoun mansion" from the roof shade of the slapped-together barn that served as a stable. It was not a fine house. To Tom's mind it was only a middling house thrown together in such a way as to be merely a caricature of the grand palace it had obviously been meant to be. He'd only come here for the money.

There were two things that Tom truly hated in this world. One was the smell of manure. He'd spent nearly half his life shoveling horseshit.

And the other was being poor.

Tom Walker was born poor. He'd lived poor. And if something didn't happen pretty soon, he was probably going to die poor. But then, he doubted that anyone had ever expected any other fate for him.

He could almost hear old Reverend McAfee proclaiming to a group of summer visitors, "This unfortunate young man will be a contributing member of the community rather than a blight upon it."

A contributing member of the community. Tom snorted with disdain at the memory. That was the other thing he hated. Being a contributing member of a community created *by* the wealthy, *for* the wealthy. His contribution being service *to* the wealthy.

"Now listen up, Rough Riders."

The man who'd hired Tom two days before, when he was looking for work in Guthrie, spoke to him and the others standing around. All were dressed in the old slouch hats, blue flannel shirts, brown trousers, and kerchiefs recognizable as the uniform of the U.S.V.

"You aren't to have a drop to drink or cause any ruckus whatsoever," he said. "These people are having a party, but you're hired hands for the day."

"What exactly *are* we supposed to do?" a short, spindly-legged cowboy asked.

"Just look like what you are," he answered. "You're veterans of our victory in Cuba. It's the Fourth of July. King Calhoun wouldn't have a Fourth of July picnic without showing off some veterans."

The half-dozen men shrugged at each other and accepted the declaration. With President Roosevelt still so popular, even out of the White House, and his exploits in Cuba so well known, the American people had become fascinated with the breed of men that had made up the Rough Riders cavalry.

In the west this was especially true. Because of congressional restrictions, Roosevelt had been able to recruit his men only from the four U.S. territories: Oklahoma, Arizona, New Mexico, and Indian. Other than a few personal friends of Roosevelt and a handful of Ivy League athletes, it was the hometown boys who'd gone to war. And the people here in Indian Territory had a special sense of pride in their victory.

"You can eat all you want," the man continued. "You can laugh and joke and visit among yourselves. And if you don't cause no troubles, you'll each be paid ten American dollars at the end of the day."

"Easiest money I ever made," a burly fellow with a handlebar mustache commented.

"And if you're interested in long-term work, there are jobs to be had out on the drilling rigs. A man with mechanical experience can bring home twelve dollars a week."

One of the fellows whistled.

It sounded pretty good to Tom, too.

"Don't cause any embarrassment for Mr. Calhoun," the man continued. "And do whatever he or Miss Princess tell you, too."

"Miss Princess?" The question was Tom's.

"King Calhoun's daughter," the man answered.

Tom's brow furrowed in amusement. "Princess? What kind of name is Princess?"

The Calhoun employee appeared personally offended at the derision in Tom's tone. "It's the kind a man who calls himself *King* Calhoun would think up for his daughter," he answered disdainfully.

"Princess." Tom shook his head. "It sounds more like a name for dog than a woman."

The fellow with the mustache spoke up. "You've seen Miss Calhoun then."

His words brought hoots of laughter from the men in the wagon.

"She's plain?" Tom asked.

"Oh Lord, drag me screaming!" the mustached fellow exclaimed. "Princess Calhoun is not just plain, she's plain ugly!"

Tom laughed with the rest.

"Oh, she ain't so bad to look at," another piped in. "Better than your wife, I'd say."

That provoked a round of hoots and a few harsh words.

"She ain't hard-out ugly," a young cowboy suggested. "Really she's just built kind of like the rig named in her honor, narrow at the top, wide at the bottom."

Tom glanced at him in interest. "She's got a rig named after her."

The cowboy nodded. "It's one of those they're drilling out on the hill. The P. Calhoun Number One, the latest exploration well of King Calhoun's Royal Oil."

"A working oil well is one dang purty sight," he continued. "And Princess Calhoun ain't no dog."

"Oh no?"

"To an old ranch hand like myself, I'd describe her more as a little brown heifer."

"A heifer?"

"She's a heifer all right," the mustached man said. "Guess her name ought not to be Princess but *Bossy!*"

"She sure knows how to tell a man what to do," another fellow agreed. "I worked for her on this house, she about wore my ears out with her ideas and orders."

"Bossy, that's a good name for a heifer."

"But what a heifer," the cowboy declared. "Worth one million dollars on the hoof."

Beside him a man whistled in awe.

"A million dollars?"

Tom's throat went dry at the thought.

"The man who marries Princess Calhoun won't be breaking his back on a damned old oil rig," the lanky cowboy said with certainty. "And he won't be having to dress up in his old army uniform to earn an extra ten dollars on his day off, neither."

"You know, that gal ain't half so ugly as I was thinking!" the burly fellow with the mustache exclaimed.

The rest of the men laughed with him.

"Not so plain, maybe," the mustached man agreed. "But what kind of man would be wantin' to be told 'come here and sic 'em' for the rest of his life."

Tom shook his head. A million dollars. A woman worth a million dollars. It was almost more than a man could get his thoughts around.

Ambrose Dexter was probably worth a million dollars, he thought. But then, Ambrose's family owned a steel factory, a linen mill, and their own bank.

Rich people. He knew them, understood them, and sometimes despised them. And more than anything else, he was determined to become one of them.

The recruits were admonished once more. "Don't get drunk. Stay clean. And show up on the podium when Mr. Calhoun begins the festivities."

Tom barely listened. He had no intention of doing anything to muddy his uniform or risk losing the money he was to be paid. Ten dollars was a month's wages in most places he'd been. Here in the oil fields, it was about the cost of a fine steak dinner. But then, crackling meat was more what fellows like him were eating.

The men began to move away from the barn. Tom

wandered off by himself, content to go it alone. The area behind the mansion was barren and rough. There were no formal gardens with stone paths between an abundance of flowers and shrubs. There was merely a wide expanse of half-hewn prairie grass and a few hardy wildflowers, resistant to the mid-summer heat. In the center stood a raised wooden platform, shaded rather ineffectively with a tarpaulin roof, grandly referred to as "the gazebo."

"Pitiful," Tom whispered aloud and shook his head.

He reached the far end of the open area and leaned against the sturdy trunk of an aged cottonwood. He surveyed the area as a whole. The gardenless garden, the raw, unattractive barn and the rather small, ill-conceived house. With a million dollars, this was the best King Calhoun could do?

Tom shook his head derisively. It was all very raw, very new. Nothing looked like it really belonged there. Tom had seen the graceful gardens of the rich. He had seen the casual elegance that came with old money and the tasteful taming of nature by the finest families in the country. He had seen Ambrose Dexter's country house. In his mind he pictured the place—lush magnificence, understated elegance.

Poor King Calhoun, he thought to himself, *like a scrub brush set among the ornamental ferns.* No matter how long he grew there, he'd never cease to draw attention to himself.

Calhoun, like Tom himself, was up from nothing, and everybody knew it. The difference was that Calhoun could now buy off his detractors, but apparently the fellow didn't know how. Tom knew exactly what to do, but didn't have a nickel to his name.

His year in the Rough Riders had taught him much about life and the world. More than he could have ever learned in the Methodist Indian Home. Much of that knowledge, however, was about inequity and injustice. Life was a stacked deck, loaded dice, an unleveled wheel. A man born with name and fortune could find success at every turn. A man born with neither soon learned that even the mildest triumph would continually elude him. Some days Tom wished he didn't understand so much. Sometimes he wished he was still the silent, mixed-breed stable hand Reverend McAfee had intended him to be. But he had been Gerald Tarkington Crane. It was an experience a man didn't forget.

The French doors at the west end of the house were flung open and a steady stream of servants bustled in and out. The air seemed almost charged with the abundance of hectic activity. Everywhere he looked, tables were being set, flowers being arranged.

Servants. The word was a bitter taste in his mouth. Servants, those who serve. At least they knew who they were. They understood what they did. Most people were not so lucky. Tom had discovered that in the great America where all men were created equal, there existed only those who are served and the people who served them.

An argument broke out concerning spoons. Tom almost smiled at the resulting pandemonium. It might be a picnic, but it was obviously not an occasion for hiding the good silver. King Calhoun might be the unwashed, but he was definitely the wealthy. King Calhoun and the men like him were the examples to emulate, Tom thought. He was a servant who was now being served. That's what Tom wanted for himself.

A movement at the doors caught his eye. Talking a mile a minute, a young woman stepped from the doorway into the yard. She was regally gowned in a mustard silk trimmed with Irish lace, her waist was cinched fashionably narrow. Her hair was coiffed in the prevailing style made popular by the Gibson Girl, but the effect was spoiled by the bottle-thick lens of her spectacles. Tom looked her over head to foot and gave his personal nod of approval.

So this was King Calhoun's Princess. Tom eyed her assessingly. Neither dog nor heifer, this one million dollars on the hoof would win no blue ribbon at any county fair. Yet it was not that she had anything desperately wrong with her, Tom thought. She was burdened with no tragic limp, no frightening scars, no horrible disfigurement. She was tall, actually quite tall for a woman, although she was not particularly slim and lithe. Her hips were wide and Tom had always preferred dainty, delicate females. But he'd been around enough to appreciate a full-bodied voluptuous woman. She had a round, provocative backside. Unfortunately her bosom, though generously decorated with ruffles and lace, was decidedly boyish.

But it was not the physical appearance of Princess Calhoun that made a strong impression. It was the sound of her voice. It had a deep, almost masculine pitch, and the tone was brisk and strident.

As Tom watched her he was reminded of cavalry drill. The snapping of orders that men and animals obeyed without question. It was almost as if he could hear her calling cadence.

Fold those napkins, find those spoons
Serve the stuffed goose with the prunes

The imagined scene brought a grin to his face. Princess Calhoun, Tom decided, would have made an admirable drill sergeant. That was not a virtue generally found attractive to gentlemen.

Poor Princess, Tom thought to himself and then hastily discarded his sympathy. She was not poor. She was an heiress. She was the wealthy and undoubtedly spoiled daughter of a millionaire. She probably gave orders because she believed herself intrinsically superior to those around her. If she had a strident voice and a less than cuddly corset shape, well a man could suffer deafness by choice and any deficiency in bust measurement could more than be compensated for by the size of the young lady's pocketbook. A clever determined man could devote himself to following her orders and making her feel beautiful the rest of her life.

TWO

Tom watched the festivities with a skeptical eye. The great King Calhoun had not deigned to show up until things were well under way. Arrogance. Tom was certain that was it. Pure arrogance. He could admire that. He certainly had his own share of it.

"Who exactly do you think you are?" Cyril Upchurch had asked him angrily one evening in San Antonio.

"Whoever I damn well choose to be," Tom had answered.

In some ways that was true. In others it was the biggest lie of all. Tom had been pretending most of his life. He'd come into the world with no name at all. He therefore felt that whatever name he gave himself was just as valid as the one that Reverend McAfee had given him.

One summer he'd called himself John L. Sullivan and routinely bloodied the nose of any boy who dared refer to him as Tom. By the following winter he was Billy Sunday, holding tabernacle revival meetings every afternoon.

Tonight, he was completely anonymous. People moved around him, but they knew neither his face nor his name. He was nobody. He could be anybody.

17

The food was good, the people welcoming. The uniform had always commanded a great deal of respect, but it had been a long time since Tom had worn it.

He'd tossed a few horseshoes and listened to a few rowdy jokes. Somebody dragged a hundred length of two-inch jute rope across a bar ditch, and a tug of war between the rig builders and the tank builders ensued. The friendly competition between the two groups of workers was made lively by such derisive taunts as "chop down the pond gougers" and "set the flametorch to those sawdust sifters."

Tom clapped and cheered along with the others until the rig builders finally managed to pull the tank line into the ditch. There was some frustrated cursing from the losers, but the defeat was accepted with fairly good grace.

The gray of the evening was beginning to leaden the sky as the torches around the gazebo were lit. Calhoun stood on the dais joking and laughing with the crowd.

The man who'd hired him caught Tom's eye and motioned him toward the gazebo. The other uniformed Rough Riders were also headed that way.

Here's where I earn my dollar, Tom thought to himself, and made his way through the crowd. He joined the other men on the stage standing behind the host of the festivities.

The audience gazed up at them in undisguised admiration. Tom allowed his eyes to wander among them. Most were poor working folks, like himself. But there was money among this crowd.

The trappings of wealth and privilege, when not anointed by blood, could only be achieved in two ways, either hard work or underhanded means. In this place, in this time, with rich, black crude oil greasing the way, hard work had been the answer for these people. Tom Walker was not so particular about the method, only the outcome.

King Calhoun was energetic and long-winded. If stirring up shouts for the red, white, and blue was good enough for politicians, it was good enough for Royal Oil. He apparently loved hearing the sound of his own voice, and at length the rich oil man talked about another Fourth of July eight years earlier.

"The Rough Riders had taken heavy casualties on the charge up San Juan Hill," Calhoun told the crowd. "They would not march victorious into Santiago for two more weeks."

King, florid-faced and portly, shook his head dramatically. Not a sound was heard from those assembled. "We know that they were tired," he continued. "And we know that they were hurting, many dying on the bloody fields of Cuba."

Tom Walker had seen combat duty. He had killed men he never knew based merely upon the color of his uniform. He had watched young men die for a cause they couldn't quite articulate. And he'd saved Ambrose Dexter's life. He felt no pride or honor or glory for it. It had not been done bravely, but without thought at all. Tom was a man of action. And a man's actions can lie as surely as his words. His life in the Rough Riders had taught him that, too.

King Calhoun stepped back and motioned for a young man in a striped seersucker suit to step forward. Behind them the band began to play. The smiling fellow raised a megaphone to his lips and raised his soothing tenor voice in song.

"While the shot and shell were screaming
Upon the battlefield;
The boys were bravely fighting
Their noble flag to shield;
Came a cry from their brave captain,

'Look boys! our flag is down;
Who'll volunteer to save it from disgrace?'
'I will,' a young voice shouted.
'I'll bring it back or die.' "

Tom had heard the tune a thousand times. It was pure sap and sentiment. Written by a Tin Pan Alley scribbler with less knowledge of life or war than plow horse, the song was closely associated with the Rough Riders. It never failed to bring a tear to the eyes of a crowd.

"'Just break the news to mother,
She knows how dear I love her.
And tell her not to wait for me,
For I'm not coming home.' "

Tom observed the expressions on the faces before him. As the last strains of harmony faded, the emotion was almost palpable.

King Calhoun stepped forward once more and gestured to the men in uniform. "I give you, good people of Topknot and Burford Corners . . . true defenders of American freedom!"

A boisterous applause arose from the crowd. Cheers and whistles and long-forgotten calls to "Remember the *Maine!*" filled the air.

Deliberately Tom kept his face expressionless. The band struck up a faster, happier tune and Calhoun invited the crowd to shake the hands of the heroes. People surged onto the dais.

For twenty minutes, Tom and the others were slapped on the back, congratulated, and generally adored by strangers. It was not an unwelcome form of entertainment. Tom revelled in their attention even as he stoically maintained a demeanor of dignity.

"It's a privilege to meet you," the strangers said over and over. "Thank you." Tom almost had to bite his lip not to add, *But who do you think that you've met?*

He continued to shake hands, to speak politely, to accept the accolades that came his way. Then, as if he felt the gaze on the back of his neck, he turned to meet a pair of brown, bespectacled eyes staring at him from across the distance of the lawn. Princess Calhoun's expression was so openly adoring, Tom was momentarily taken aback.

He nodded slightly in recognition, only to see her look away hastily, a vivid blush staining her cheek. *Poor Princess,* he thought to himself. She'd obviously never learned the danger of wearing her heart on her sleeve.

Tom was, he'd been told, just about the most handsome fellow to ever don a pair of trousers. And he'd had sufficient luck with ladies over the years to have developed a confidence in his charm.

Deliberately he perused the young woman from head to toe. Then, keeping his lips perfectly still and noncommittal, he smiled from his eyes alone. It was a technique proven over and over to set the most hardened female heart aflutter. It felt as if he were giving a gift. The bossy drill sergeant in skirts would never be able to actually attract a man's eye in that fashion.

Then he remembered how attractive and desirable a million dollars could be. He began to walk in her direction.

It wasn't as if he'd planned it, he assured himself as he approached her. He'd never intended to approach her. It had been her eyes that had sought him out. And it wasn't as if things were all settled. If she turned out to be too small a catch, he'd ease her off the hook and throw her back.

He kept his eyes upon hers as each step brought them closer and closer. Her expression was awestruck, her hands clutched together over her heart.

Geez, almighty! he mentally exclaimed. She'd already swallowed hook, line, and sinker, and he had yet to even offer the bait.

He stood in front of her now, gazing down into wide brown eyes made inordinately large by thick, round spectacles, and complimented her in a way that he knew would be closest to her heart.

"It's a lovely party," he said.

The words came from his mouth, not in the slow, slightly nasal accent that came natural to him, but in the clipped Yankee tones that he had so carefully perfected.

Her mouth formed a big *O* of dumbstruck appreciation. He took her hand in both of his own, merely holding it gently without the merest hint of caress.

He glanced around and sighed with feigned exasperation. "As there is no one in proximity to formally introduce us, may I be so bold as to present myself to you?"

She remained wide-eyed and mute.

"I am Gerald Tarkington Crane," he said. "Late of Bedlington in the New Jersey and Yale University, class of '98."

"I . . . I . . . I . . ."

He squeezed her hand comfortingly. "You needn't speak," he assured her. "Standing within the mere presence of a lady such as yourself is quite enough."

"I . . . I'm Princess Calhoun," she managed finally.

"What a beautiful name," he answered. "And so suited to you."

"Oh no, not at all," she blurted out.

He smiled at her, this time using his whole face, flashing his pearly white grin with devastating effect.

"You don't think yourself a princess, Miss Calhoun?"

She was taking long, nervous breaths that had the effect of causing the abundance of ruffles upon her breast to rise and fall dramatically.

"You must call me Princess," she told him, her face flaming with her own boldness. "All my friends do."

Tom angled his head slightly and lowered his voice to a seductive timbre. "I don't think I care to be lumped in with *all* your friends. Perhaps I can give you a special name."

She was clutching his hand like a lifeline. He could feel her trembling.

"My best friend, Muna, calls me Prin," she admitted.

"Then I definitely don't want to do that," he said. "It sounds too much like prim, and doesn't suit you at all."

Princess looked momentarily surprised. Clearly she must have thought it a very apt description.

"I shall call you Cessy," he said.

"Cessy?"

"Yes, Cessy. May I?"

"It sounds strange."

He smiled down at her warmly as if she'd made some very clever little joke. "It doesn't sound strange to you and me." He leaned toward her once more. "And no one else need ever know."

"Cessy?" She whispered it as if it were already a secret between them.

"It's a sweet, happy, laughing name," he said. "And you certainly are sweet and happy. And you do have me laughing."

He looked down into those big, adoring eyes and momentarily he was stung by his conscience. Deliberately he stepped back, at least offering her a fighting chance.

"I am new to this your city, and as you can see," he indicated his uniform, "I'm a former cavalryman."

"You followed President Roosevelt to the West?" she asked.

"The colonel and I met on the tennis courts at Yale. He made horses and war sound so exhilarating and entertaining. I fairly begged to be included as a humble trooper."

Her gaze continued worshipful, but at least she had at last found her voice.

"And did you find Mr. Roosevelt's description of army life to be true?" she asked him.

"Absolutely," he answered with a wide grin and teasing humor. "Except for the mud, the mosquitoes, the horrendous living conditions, ill-tempered horses, bad food, and the danger of being killed— other than those few details it was gloriously perfect."

She giggled out loud at his words and then covered her mouth in embarrassment. Amazingly it was a warm and throaty sound, unexpected. Although he was not sure what *was* expected from a drill sergeant in skirts.

Back in the gazebo behind him the band struck up a boisterous tune.

"Ah, the dancing begins," he said. "Would you do me the honor?"

"Oh no, I rarely dance," she confessed quickly. "Actually you should be dancing with the young ladies. Perhaps if you—"

"You don't enjoy it?" he interrupted.

"Don't enjoy what?"

"Dancing."

"No, I mean yes, yes, actually I love to dance, though I don't often. Usually it is the young ladies who are partnered. I believe you will find . . ."

He raised a curious eyebrow. "And do you not consider yourself one of the *young ladies?*" he interrupted again.

"Well, of course I—" She was flustered. "I am twenty-four, sir," she blurted out. "Oh dear, I shouldn't have said that."

He laughed with delight.

"And a very charming twenty-four indeed," he answered. "Might I please have this dance, Miss Calhoun." He angled his head and gave her a little private grin. "Please, Cessy."

"Well, I do believe that rather than . . ."

Before she could protest further, he'd pulled her out onto the floor.

Princess Calhoun had stars in her eyes and butterflies in her stomach, but her head was amazingly clear as Gerald Crane escorted her to the dance floor and pulled her into his arms.

The area directly in front of the gazebo, illuminated by lanterns and drip gas torches, had been denuded of prairie grass and tamped down with a four-by-four until it was as even and hard as dancing on marble. Smudge fires were being lit at distances over the lawn. The greasy black smoke was a deterrent to mosquitoes and provided a dark, hazy cloud of mystery surrounding the guests.

She heard herself doing most of the talking, but she couldn't seem to stop. She offered him more advice in the space of five minutes than most men could accept good-naturedly in a week.

Gerald seemed perfectly confident and at ease with her suggestions as he spun her around the dance floor effortlessly. Princess had waltzed and one-stepped many times, but had never felt so graceful in another man's arms.

"It is considered quite out of the ordinary for a fine

gentleman to make an appearance in a boomtown," she explained to him.

"The West offers a man the adventure and challenge that is no longer available in the serene and civilized world of the East," he said. "Of course, the family wanted me to take my place in the business. Publishing, the Cranes have been in publishing since doing broadsides during the revolution. But Papa's still in fine health, and my brother really cares for the business more than me, so I've come out West to seek challenge and adventure."

Princess nodded. "It's what people have been doing for a hundred years, going west to seek their fortune."

Gerald smiled. "Luckily for me I needn't actually seek *fortune*. I have money from both my grandfather and one of my maiden aunts. And I shamefully confess that Papa and Mama worry inordinately about me and send me a monthly remittance to tide me over."

"You mustn't feel ashamed about it with me," Princess assured him. "My daddy has showered me with everything he could think of, ever since his first well came in."

"I'm sure he thinks the world of you," Gerald said softly. "But then how could he not?"

Princess raised her head to look directly into the eyes of the man with whom she had so easily fallen in love. A little sigh of pleasure escaped her. He was almost too handsome, she thought.

She had expected her true love to be disguised as a plain and uncomely man.

They continued to turn and dip and spin in time with the music. Her heart was light and frivolous and filled to overflowing. At that moment, that perfect moment, Princess believed that she had never been happier.

"Pure gold," he whispered.

"What?"

"Pure gold," he said. "The torchlight catches the glint of your hair and it shines like pure gold."

"My hair is just ordinary brown," she confessed.

"Oh, but you can't see it in this light," he said, softly. "I can see it, Cessy. It's so pretty and it shines like pure gold."

A little shiver of delight pulsed through her. He thought her hair was pretty. Of course, it was not, she knew that, but he thought so.

She glanced up at him again. Maybe he was seeing her through lover's eyes. The poet did claim that beauty was in the eye of the beholder. Perhaps he was seeing her as only his heart thought her to be.

Likewise, perhaps he was not as attractive as she imagined. Perhaps love was blinding her also. She gazed at him as critically as she could. His broad shoulders were powerful and masculine. The thick black hair had hardly a hint of wave except right in front where it curved along the edges of both brows, accentuating the heart shape of his face. His nose was narrow and straight, neither too long nor too short. His smooth-shaven jaw was strong and determined with high, well-sculpted cheek bones. And his eyes, those dark, compelling brown eyes, there was something about his eyes. They were slightly tilted at the edges, giving him a vaguely sleepy look that seemed exotic and yet familiar.

"You look part Indian!" she told him with some surprise.

"What?" He tensed up and seemed almost startled.

"Your eyes," she said. "They look like many of the Indians here in the Territory."

"No, no I'm not Indian," he assured her hastily.

He seemed so ill at ease, Princess wondered if she had insulted him. "We do a good deal of business with the tribes," she explained. "And with your dark hair and those eyes, I just thought . . ."

"I'm Italian."

"Italian?"

"Yes, it . . . it . . ." He lowered his voice to a whisper. "It was a dreadful scandal. The family never speaks about it."

"Oh dear, I'm sorry. I should never have mentioned . . ."

"Grandmama, my . . . ah . . . my maternal grandmother . . . she was taking a holiday on the Continent," he said. "She met him in Venice. He was a mere gondolier and her father just could not approve."

Princess tutted in sympathy.

"He cut her off without a penny."

"Heavens!"

"Grandmama loved her family, but she loved her gondolier so much more."

"Did her father ever reconcile?"

"Not until after it was too late."

"Too late?"

"The boat sank in one of the deep canals. The gondolier managed to get their baby daughter to safety, but then he went back for his wife." Gerald shook his head sadly. "At least they died together. I'm sure neither would have wanted to live without the other."

Tears welled up in her eyes as Princess thought of the young couple who loved so much.

"You're crying," he said softly.

"I . . ."

He danced her to the edge of the floor and then led her away from the lights.

"I'm so silly, I . . . I never cry," she stated firmly.

"Shhh," he whispered. "Sentiment requires no apology."

"It was just so beautiful and so sad."

They reached the relative privacy of the cottonwood shade and he turned her to him, gliding his hands around her waist as he pulled her gently into his arms.

"Love is always beautiful," he told her. "And those that have it should never be sad."

He angled his head and brought his lips down to capture her own. The touch of his mouth was light and warm and sweet and for Princess, utterly heart-stopping. It was a tiny kiss, just a taste of passion before he stepped back.

"Perfect," he breathed against her brow.

Her head spinning, Princess wrapped her arms more tightly around his neck and pressed herself against him. He'd offered her only a glimpse of heaven, she wanted more.

She plastered her lips clumsily upon his own. He responded more gently and when he opened his mouth, she did the same. She could taste him now, truly taste him and the persistent tugging had her insides cavorting and her pulse pounding.

"Easy, easy," he whispered as he pulled back slightly. "Not all the candy in one grab."

She was momentarily bereft, but he wrapped her more closely in his arms, the long length of their bodies touching from her wobbly knees to his chin against her brow.

"You are a passionate little princess, Cessy."

"I've never been kissed before," she confessed.

She felt his body suddenly become still. She looked up at him. His forehead was creased as if worried, and there was something troubling in his eyes.

"I . . . I'm sorry, I . . ."

"You're sorry you kissed me?"

"We just met, I shouldn't . . . I shouldn't take such liberties. And you are so innocent."

"Please don't feel bad about it," she interrupted. "I'm glad you were my first. If kissing is to be done, it should be done with someone very special, and you, sir, are that to me."

He looked at her for a long moment and his expression softened.

"Ah Cessy, I'm glad to be your first, too. And I want to be your hundredth, your thousandth, your millionth. But I . . . I must show a woman like you proper respect."

Princess felt daring, bold, almost powerful as she leaned against him seductively. "Respect is very nice, but I think I'd rather have another kiss."

Immediately he joined her mouth with his own. This time he was more intense, more demanding. Princess felt her body responding with feelings that were all new to her. As if compelled by some elemental force, she eased herself more tightly against him. His hands were stroking her shoulders and back, occasionally hesitating along her backbone to press her against the hard wall of his chest. She gasped with delight at the hot tingling sensation that suffused her bosom.

His kiss was all-encompassing, possessive and forceful. She was trembling in his arms, eager, urgent, willing.

"Geez almighty, darlin'," he moaned.

His voice sounded strangely unlike him and Princess was momentarily startled and stepped away. He held her at arm's length and the two stared at each other for long minutes as they recovered their breathing.

He was looking at her, looking at her as if he had something to say, something important to say. He never said it.

"Prin! Prin, is that you?"

Gerald immediately released her and Princess turned guiltily toward the sound. Muna and her fiancé were hurrying up beside them. Her friend's eyes were wide with curiosity. Clearly she had seen their embrace.

Princess held her chin high. She was, in retrospect,

a little surprised at her own behavior, but she had never been in love before and she was far too happy to be embarrassed about the fact.

"Muna, come meet Gerald," she said without apology.

As the two approached, Princess saw her friend's eyes narrow with suspicion as she stared at Gerald.

"Muna Nafee, this is my friend Gerald Tarkington Crane of Bedlington, New Jersey," she said. "Gerald this is Miss Muna Nafee, my best friend and this is her fiancé, Mr. . . . ah . . . I seem to have forgotten . . ."

Muna's escort stepped forward promptly and offered Gerald his hand. "I am Maloof Bashara, I speak English no good, yes?"

Gerald shook his hand and murmured a friendly reply. He nodded politely to Muna who continued to eye him warily.

"You are new around here, Mr. Crane. I don't believe I've seen you before. We have all known each other for years now," Muna said. "Princess and I met as girls in the drilling camps of West Virginia. We've been together in Jackson and Corsicana and Spindletop. All the people who follow the oil fields, the drillers, the merchants, the laborers, we all know and trust each other from way back."

"This is my first time to visit an oil field," Gerald admitted readily. "I find it very different and exciting." He offered a small, intimate glance to Princess. "And I find the people here much to my liking."

Princess couldn't help but smile back at him. Muna was being overly protective. That's what friends did for each other. But once Muna understood that Princess had found her true love, she would come to care for Gerald as her friend, too.

"Enough talking," Princess declared. "This is a dance and we must dance. Do you dance, Mr. Bashara?"

"Oh I am fine dancer," he declared. "In my country I am fine dancer. There men dance with men, women dance with women. But this dancing, dancing with the woman, it is different. I think I like it."

"Then you will dance with me," Princess said.

They hurried to the dance floor, with Gerald and Muna in their wake. Princess glanced back at them, walking uncomfortably together. She wanted to let the two of them get to know each other. She wanted to let Muna see what a fine, wonderful man he was. But only one dance, Princess decided. The night was too important, too perfect, too much a dream come true and she didn't want to spend it in the arms of any man but Gerald Tarkington Crane.

THREE

Queenie McCurtain awakened unexpectedly with the first light of dawn. Her stomach rolled unpleasantly as the strong odor of sweaty men, spilled beer, and stale tobacco drifted up from her place of business downstairs and assaulted her senses. The queasiness was unexpected. She rarely drank, thinking it poor business to consume anything that she could sell to somebody else. Maybe she was coming down with a fever, or perhaps it was just the earliness of the hour.

Through the thin wall at the far of her room she could hear Frenchie LaRue, still at work. Or rather she could hear the man Frenchie was at work upon. His wrenching, pleasurable groans clearly indicated another satisfied customer. At least Queenie hoped it was a customer and not that no-account Tommy Mathis, who paid for his pleasures with sketches and paintings until the whole place was a gallery of pictures.

Tommy was a favorite of Miss LaRue and although Queenie had made it clear to the painter that this was a cash business only, Frenchie might well have offered the fellow another barter deal.

It was said by fellows who might well know that Frenchie LaRue had the best mouth in three states.

That's why Queenie had her working out of the bar. Unfortunately, it was also true that Frenchie was extremely charitable and gave away for free almost as much business as she got paid for. She was one of those rare whores who truly enjoyed her work.

Queenie McCurtain was not. She'd begun whoring as a way to get by, to ward off starvation, to support herself in the wild new territory. She no longer did that kind of work. She no longer had to. Queenie's Palace was one of the most popular "joints" on the Topknot. A hard-working oil man could always find a mug of beer, a joint of beef, and a pretty girl at Queenie's. And if he knew Queenie and she thought he could be trusted, there was blackjack, poker, and craps in the back room.

Queenie was a successful businesswoman with enough money stashed away to insure that she would never have to entertain a sweaty roughneck or manure-stained rancher again. Any man found in her bed was there by invitation only. And the only man these days getting that invitation snored quietly beside her now.

In sleep, King Calhoun looked every one of his forty-nine years. He was ruddy, heavyset, and his hair was thick and curly only at the back and sides of his shiny head. His left hand lay splayed upon her naked breast. The wide gold band that encircled the third finger of his left hand glimmered in the morning sunlight. King Calhoun had been a widower for fourteen years. But he'd never removed his wedding ring. It was a symbol of the other world he lived in, the world that he wanted desperately, but within which he was not wholly comfortable.

Frenchie's customer was groaning louder now, his pleasure rising to a crescendo. Queenie should get a house, she thought. It was long past time that she quit living over the bar. But, in truth, she didn't trust anybody to look after her interests except herself.

She'd learned early that people could turn on you. They could let you down. They could throw you away. The only thing a woman could count on in this world was herself. That was Queenie's credo. A lot of people would have been surprised to hear that. A lot of people thought Queenie was owned lock, stock, and barrel by King Calhoun. A disenchanted cowboy had once asked her if she had ROYAL OIL tattooed on her backside.

Queenie had just smiled and flippantly reminded the cowboy that he would never know.

Certainly she'd done a few things to please Calhoun. She had followed him to the oil fields. And then from one strike to another. She'd kept herself as his exclusive property for the last five years. With her ear to the ground and her eye on business, she'd been able to give him a tip or two that had benefitted him.

And, of course, she'd changed her name. But then Hilda Prudence McCurtain was not a particularly good name for a scarlet woman. Undoubtedly when her parents had chosen it they had envisioned her as a quiet, pious farm wife with a half dozen well-scrubbed children on their way to church on Sunday. That was not at all how her life had turned out. She had become Queenie, King Calhoun's Queenie.

Frenchie's customer gave a loud holler that was indisputable evidence of salacious satisfaction. Beside her King Calhoun stirred restlessly.

He'd arrived at the Palace last night, having been host to a Fourth of July picnic all evening. He was in a tremendous temper. Queenie knew better than to question him about it. When Calhoun wanted to talk to her, he would. Talk was not what was immediately upon his mind. He'd hurried her upstairs, to the sounds of hoots and encouragement from the men in the bar.

When Calhoun was angry, when he felt the world out of his control, it was sex that he wanted, rough, fast, and aggressive sex. Queenie knew that mood well and she knew the blend of wantonness and passivity that suited him perfectly.

It had taken him the better part of an hour to work off his passion. Spent and exhausted, he'd apologized.

"Sorry, Queenie," he'd whispered as he rolled off of her and then pulled her into his arms. "I'll make it up to you tomorrow, darlin'."

In truth, though she preferred him gentle and tender with her, she was as satisfied as he was by an occasional wildness. And she knew this morning that he would be especially sweet and conciliatory.

"What time is it?" he groaned beside her.

"Still early," she answered. "Frenchie's got a customer, that's what woke us."

"Good Lord, does that woman never stop?"

"Let's hope not," Queenie answered. "She's a gold mine."

King chuckled and pulled her closer. "You okay this morning, Queenie? I didn't hurt you, did I?"

"I think I'm all right," she told him thoughtfully. Then she drew his hand down to the juncture of her thighs. "But maybe you ought to inspect me for damage."

He snorted with humor and did as she had bid him, his touch more caressing than clinical.

"Everything seems right and tight, darlin'," he said.

He kissed her then, slowly, leisurely. She loved his kisses. A lot of men never bothered to kiss a whore. King Calhoun seemed to want to taste her mouth as frequently as the rest of her.

The sweet, loving kisses and the caress of his hand continued pleasurably for several minutes. She reached between their bodies to stroke him and found him still flaccid.

He sighed and pulled away from her.

"You want to talk about it?" she asked.

He leaned up on one elbow and look down at her.

"Bankers! Damn all bankers!" he said, as he angled her a little differently and shook his head. "I don't know what I'm going to do."

Queenie nodded, her eyes full of concern. "You still haven't been able to find any financing." she said.

King sighed heavily. "We're drilling and it looks good, Queenie. It looks dang good. There's oil aplenty trapped in that salt dome and I can get it out of there. But what in the devil am I going to do with it? Build a hundred miles of pipeline? I've got to have a refinery. And I've got to have one here."

Queenie nodded sympathetically. She'd been a confidant of King Calhoun's aspirations and dreams for years.

"The dang bankers. They want their *safe* investments. Farmers, merchants. Oil's just pie in the sky to them. Or maybe a dream in the ground. I introduced that Kansas City fellow all around the party last night. He was laughing and joking and eating my food and drinking my beer. Then he says right to my face that he thinks I'm 'too risky.'"

Queenie rubbed his face comfortingly. "I'm so sorry. I bet you wished you could rearrange his teeth."

"I just kept on smiling," he admitted. "But honestly, I could have happily stomped him to a greasy spot."

"It's so hard to figure. They are all willing to let you put your money in their bank, but it's tough as nails to get them to loan you some out."

King nodded. "They'll take money from the devil himself, they just have preferences about where they lend it out," he said. "The oil business is new, it's speculative. And the truth of the matter is, the people making money in the oil business are not the fellows these bankers are used to dealing with."

She nodded sympathetically and began rubbing the thick tufts of hair on his chest.

"It takes money to make money," he continued. "And the folks that have got money are not so willing to take a chance on somebody who's not one of their own."

"But you've made millions of dollars, they should know that they can trust you."

"They don't trust anyone like us, darlin'," he said. "You know that firsthand, Queenie. When you started your own business would one of them puffed up, down-their-nose-at-you yahoos, would one of them have loaned you the money?"

She shook her head. "If I'd have asked, they'd have thrown me out of their fancy office on my backside," she said. "If you hadn't helped me, I'd probably still be setting up sweethearts in a camp tent."

King waved away her gratitude. "You're a good businesswoman, Queenie. Backing you was the best investment I ever made. You've made a damn fine return on a small stake. Most of these banker fellows couldn't hold a candle to you."

She snuggled up against him and closed her eyes, breathing in the scent that was him. She wanted to remember it always. For Queenie, loving King Calhoun was a complicated and dangerous avocation. They'd never spoken of love, nor a word of commitment. It was there. It was there between them. But Queenie was certain that if something happened, if something tipped their fragile little boat to the left or right, they'd be swamped in minutes. And he would be gone. He would be long gone without even a good-bye.

"It's not fair," she whispered, thinking about both him and herself. "It's really not fair."

"Darlin', if anybody told you that life was fair, they was just plain lying."

She huffed with appreciation and agreement.

Nothing in her life so far had seemed very fair. She'd had more than her share of troubles, sorrows, and sadness. Now she'd finally found success and had a man that she loved. She didn't want that or him to go away.

"Can I help?" she asked him. "I've got a pretty good nest egg laid by. I wouldn't be averse to investing it in the oil business."

He sat up a little and looked at her for a long minute before planting a kiss on the end of her nose.

"Queenie, refineries are big money. We could sell down to the shirt of every man in this town and it wouldn't be enough. If I don't get a bank to back me, I'm going to lose *my* shirt. There is not a soul in this world that I'd tell that to but you," he said. "I don't want to lose *my* shirt, but if you lose yours too . . ." He shook his head disagreeably and with the end of his finger gently flicked her nipple. "Well, darlin', let's just say I don't want the whole town to see you with your tits bare."

She smiled, accepting his judgement but remaining serious enough to add her own admonition.

"If you lose it, at least promise me that you'll look this direction for a new stake," she said.

"I can't promise nothing, darlin', but I'll keep it in mind," he agreed. "Right now, I just got to come up with a new banker and a new approach. We've got to find somebody to get us some cash."

"Where you going to start looking?"

"I thought I'd take a trip up to Saint Louis," he told her.

"Do you know somebody there?"

"Darlin', I done asked everybody I know and most that I know *of*," he said. "The crazy thing is, I *know* that the oil is there. But as far as we are from a refinery, it might as well be tomato juice. I can't build a refinery without capital. They got some up there in Saint Louis and I'm going to try to get it."

"When are you leaving?"

"Tomorrow, I suspect, or rather today, I guess. It is today already. I need to get up to the well this morning and make sure things are set up and under control while I'm gone. Then I'll catch the evening train. I'll be in Saint Louis in time for a steak-and-egg breakfast."

His words had a totally unexpected effect on Queenie. As the vision of steak and eggs flashed before her eyes, her stomach rumbled violently. With frantic haste she rolled out of bed and onto her feet.

"Queenie?"

All around her the world seemed to spin. Wave after wave of nausea coursed through her. Cold sweat popped out all over her skin. She dropped to her knees and barely managed to grab the chamber pot from beneath the bed before she vomited.

"Queenie? Queenie, are you all right?"

He was at her side immediately, solicitous.

"It must be something I ate," she said.

Naked, he hurried to the water basin where he dampened a towel and brought it to her.

"I heard there was an influenza spreading through the camp at Gladys City," he said.

Gratefully she pressed the cool towel against her brow. "I haven't heard a thing about that here," she told him.

"Still, maybe I shouldn't go off to Saint Louis," King suggested.

Queenie's eyes widened and she looked at him as if he had lost his mind.

"You have to go, King," she told him incredulously. "I'll be fine. Frenchie and the girls are here, and you know that I can take care of myself."

His brow furrowed, worried. "Even those who can take care of themselves sometimes need people to take care of them."

* * *

Although the annoyingly constant rhythm of drilling oil had kept Tom awake most of the night, he was up early the next morning, but not by his own choice. The oil camp "bunkhouse" where he was staying went by the auspicious name CLEAN CHEAP BEDS. All three words were an exaggeration. One long room was crowded with fifteen less-than-pristine cots crammed up against each other. To get out of bed, each man had to crawl to the end of his bunk and over the footrail. There was plenty of bumping, toe stubbing, and general mayhem as the morning shift prepared for work. After they'd finally left, Tom sighed with relief and snuggled down into the thin, straw-stuffed mattress that he'd rented for a dollar a day, only to shortly discover that most of the fellows in the bunkhouse were doubled up. They shared the rent on their cot with a fellow that worked nights. When the second round of noise and activity began, Tom simply gave up and roused himself out for the morning.

The day was bright and as warm as expected in Oklahoma in early July. With the morning tour already on the job and the evening one eager to take their rest, the camp was quiet and peaceful. A feeling of familiarity that was almost nostalgic welled up inside of him. He had grown up not very far from this place. The Methodist Indian Home was only a half day's walk away. The sky and clouds and the scent on the air around him were all as well known to him as his face in the mirror. He could go there. He could see Reverend McAfee again.

"It's all pride and it will be your downfall," he could almost hear the good man warning him. "Want less and work harder, that will better your life, young Tom."

Tom shook his head thoughtfully and sniffed in disagreement. He'd tried Reverend McAfee's way. He had tried working harder, he had tried wanting less.

But he'd seen too much to be satisfied; he'd learned too much to be content.

The Methodist Indian Home—warm and sweet and happy as those memories were for him—could not bring him his heart's desire. He pushed those thoughts aside. The life he had been trained for there was not at all the life that he wanted.

He had joined up with the Rough Riders at age seventeen. That, at least, was not a lie. He had been with Roosevelt in Cuba, but was no great friend of his. He was just a wild boy who could ride and shoot.

Colonel Teddy had a natural curiosity about him, about all of the Indians and part-breeds. They made up a significant number of the regiment and Roosevelt treated them as if they were strange, exotic animals that he was being allowed to observe in unnatural surroundings.

But Tom had been equally curious about Colonel Teddy and his friends. They were college men, athletes mostly, bent on living the manly life and having a grand time. At first they appeared as unnecessary as the two-headed calf at the traveling show. Later Tom had learned to appreciate them in many ways. And to envy them in many others.

Tom watched and listened and soon began to mimic "the cravats," the elegant eastern dudes who spurned the cotton neckerchiefs of the regiment for the same item made of silk. In the hot, tired aching boredom of military life, *cravat* watching quickly became a source of entertainment. Tom imitated the way they talked and walked and what they said. He did it as an amusement for the other fellows and could have a whole company of cowboy troopers clutching their sides and rolling on the ground with laughter.

Ultimately the inevitable happened. Ambrose Dexter, who answered to the nickname of Ambidextrous, had caught him in the act. Surprisingly there were no hard feelings. The fine eastern gentleman actually thought it great fun and suggested that Tom quit the army and take up the stage.

Ambi began to help him with what they all jokingly referred to as "Tom's vaudeville act." He taught him the things to say, the way to behave, the niceties of fine manners, and brought him to the attention of the other young men of his circle.

The character, life, and antecedents of Gerald Tarkington Crane came out of a barrel of Mexican beer that Ambi had confiscated for a night's encampment. They concocted the whole story. The man, his past, his family business, and his reasons for being in the U.S.V. It was just an hilarious way to pass the time.

Within a week, they were putting *Gerald* to the test. Since Colonel Teddy's friends were always welcome guests at parties and soirees, Ambi and the *cravats* took him along. They let him rub shoulders with the finest people in south Texas. It became sort of a game among them, laughing at the joke they played on the unfortunate locals who were unable to tell the difference between a real gentleman and a pretend one.

It was at that time that Tom had discovered the power Gerald had with women. Thanks to Reverend McAfee's diligence, Tom had been untutored in the ways of the feminine sex when he'd arrived in San Antone. He had, upon his first liberty, gone looking for female companionship. The women with painted lips standing around in saloons seemed to find him attractive enough. But the fine, fresh-faced ladies on the avenues looked through him as if he were invisible, and the pretty girls in their charge were as unapproachable as princesses.

"Princesses." He said the word aloud.

Amazingly, he'd learned that when he allowed "Gerald" to do the talking, both the girls and their mothers came after him almost panting.

Ladies, he discovered, much preferred the attentions of the very wealthy and sophisticated young man from Yale, rather than the ordinary attentions of Tom Walker, partbreed orphan.

As he slicked back his wet, black hair from his well-scrubbed face, he ruminated upon Miss Calhoun, who would undoubtedly feel the same.

This morning his uniform was safely stowed once more in his grip. He checked his belongings, not trusting any of his roommates further than he could see them. It was all there. Everything he owned. Two worn shirts, frayed at both collar and cuffs. A pair of blue denim overalls, the clothing typical of the working man, that he immediately put on over his underwear. There was a fairly presentable pair of black leather shoes, a deck of playing cards, and a paper of Doctor Joe's Miraculous Headache Powders. He got out his shaving gear, a bone-handled brush, a bent tin mug, a cake of shaving soap, and a hollow point razor. At the bottom of the traveling bag he spotted the slim, mother-of-pearl box that Ambrose had given him jokingly as a gift. It contained his business cards.

He checked the inside bib pocket of his overalls that was unobtrusively pinned shut. The ten dollar greenback was still there. Along with the forty-three cents he already had, it wasn't much of a stake. He needed clothes. His overalls were showing some wear and couldn't be expected to last much longer. But if he really intended to pursue Cessy Calhoun he'd need finer clothes than these. The ten dollars he'd made at the picnic could go as an investment in Gerald's pursuit. Or he could use it to tide him over until he managed to get another job.

He was thoughtful.

In his arms last night, she had been eager, willing. It would be almost too easy to seduce her. Then he could offer to do right by her and marry. It seemed like a reasonable plan.

"It will never work," he said aloud.

But it was the best idea he'd had. In the eight years since being mustered out he'd tramped around from one end of the country to the other. First he'd followed Ambi home. Tom had still been recovering from his wound and Ambi wanted his family to care for him. He'd liked Bedlington, he'd settled in nicely to the world there. Only to discover that among the wealthy an Army comrade, even one who had saved your life, was not truly fit company for your friends and neighbors. All he could reasonably be offered was a cast-off bit of condescending charity. Hurt and angry, he'd stormed out of Ambi's handsome, twelve-room cottage, never to return. Determined to make his way on his own.

He'd tried his hand at ranching and railroading. He'd sold pitcher pumps, tended poultry, and played poker. He'd seen the outside of the society life and the inside of the San Saba County Jail. There were only four ways to get the kind of money Tom wanted. He could beg it, borrow it, steal it, or he could marry it. Of all his schemes and dreams, Tom was sure that marrying for money was the quickest and maybe the most honorable way of becoming rich that he'd ever thought up.

He grabbed up his gear and began heading down the road. He'd rarely given a thought in his life to taking a wife. He was still young, he reminded himself. And life was often long. Binding himself to a woman, for better or worse, was not for the unrooted and unemployed. A man made a commitment to care and provide, not just to the bride, but to the inevitable children that followed. Tom had never thought himself settled enough for such responsibility. But what if the woman didn't need providing for? What if *she* could do the providing? Then all he'd be vowing to do would be love, honor, and cherish. That didn't seem like too big a price to pay.

He could love Cessy Calhoun, after a fashion. And as for honor and cherish, that wouldn't be much of a stretch. Who wouldn't honor a woman worth a million dollars? Her bank account was something any fellow would cherish.

"It will never work," he reminded himself once more. It just couldn't be as easy as it now seemed. Nothing ever was.

A wagoner passed him with a great load of pipe piled high. Tom hailed him.

"You need a lift, fella?" the driver asked, pulling up.

"Thanks," Tom answered, hurrying to find a seat on the top of the pipe stack.

"Where ye headed?"

There was only a moment's hesitation before Tom answered. "P. Calhoun Number One," he said.

FOUR

The Nafee Emporium was the only brick building along the raw, hastily constructed street that represented the commercial district of Topknot. It was adorned with long, covered porches along the front and side, where benches and rockers encouraged loitering. Bunkhouse men and drifters were to be found there any time of the day or night. It was said that the quickest way to hire a man or find a job was to spend a half day chomping crackers and chewing pickles on Nafee's porch. Mrs. Nafee fussed and fretted over the men and personally scrubbed the floorboards every day in her constant battle against fellows whose aim missed the spittoon.

An effusive welcome to strangers and the clean homeyness of the porches were the Nafees' chief ammunition against their competitor, J. M. Nell General Merchandise on Main Street in Burford Corners. Nell had founded his business twenty years earlier upon trade with the Creeks and Osage, who still patronized him faithfully. Later the cotton farmers became his patrons and the little town that grew up around the store was built upon land Nell had once owned.

Nafee was the upstart, the foreigner. But the oil men all knew him. He had followed the oil speculation, he had been a peddler in their camps back east to Corsicana, Jackson, and Gladys City. Several of those men paused in the middle of the stories they . were swapping to rise to their feet and nod deferentially to his daughter, Muna, as she passed them on her way inside.

She hardly noticed. For more than a week now her thoughts were a muddle and her mind was continually elsewhere.

It was not as if she had not known that one day she would marry. And it was not that her parents had not warned her that it would be they, and not her, who would choose the proper husband. But somehow she had thought it would be different. She'd thought that it would feel more romantic, more right.

The tiny bell tinkled over the doorway announcing her arrival. Her mind and heart full, Muna entered the store without so much as a hasty glance to the finery and fripperies in the locked glass case by the door, specifically intended to catch the attention of every female who passed beside it.

"Mama, I'm here," she called out, with little enthusiasm.

The Emporium was heavily stocked with everything from bathtubs to Brussels lace. With only three windows, all on the north side of the building, the big store was dark and gloomy. But the pine planking beneath her feet gleamed with devoted care and the white washed walls and shelving made things look spotless and new. Mrs. Nafee believed strongly in the selling power of cleanliness and had taught her daughter to do the same.

She located her mother busily demonstrating the ease of the new twist-off lid canning jars to a small circle of portly matrons. They shared a quick glance and the older woman gestured toward the back room.

"A shipment just arrived on the train," her mother

said. "There is much sorting to be done this morning."

Muna nodded. She hoped it was the ladies' wear. Just a few weeks past she had selected and ordered all the new summer styles. She could purchase, sort, organize, and price bolts, brass fittings, or bearshot. But the lacy confections of ladies' lingerie were her specialty and her weakness. She loved just looking at the latest offering and simply touching the fine, sleek fabrics gave her a cheerful lift. Of course, she had never worn any of it. Mama made up her underclothing in serviceable unbleached cotton. But in her naughty fantasies she could imagine herself in corset covers of delicate lawn and cambric, trimmed with dainty Brussels lace. She would wear pink tinted petticoats with a hundred glacé flounces. And beneath it all, French satin pantalettes cut close to conform to the body, not disguise it.

Her thoughts were so pleasantly distracted as she pushed past the curtain-covered doorway into the back room. Then her reality came crashing back. He was there.

Almost as startled to see her as she was to see him, he appeared to fumble for the correct words in English and greeted her in Arabic.

"Sabah elker."

"Good morning," she said.

Her words were less a reply than a reprimand. Her father insisted that Maloof learn English very quickly. The only way to do that was to completely forego speaking in Arabic.

He nodded, not taking offense. "Yes, good morning," he said. "It is good morning, yes?"

"Yes," Muna answered, not quite sure if he meant the words were correct or that he truly appreciated the day.

He was smiling at her. It was a big, broad smile. It

was open, friendly and somehow disconcerting. She never knew what he was thinking.

Her parents had told her that he had been sent for. A fine, worthy young man, he was to come to America, join the business and be her bridegroom. His father was a childhood friend of Nafee. Still Baba hadn't accepted him carelessly. He'd taken the train to greet Maloof in Kansas City and had spent a week with the man before he'd struck a bargain and brought him to the Indian Territory to meet his bride.

He had never asked her to wed him. It was all just handled by her father and assumed by everyone that she was well pleased. She was not unpleased. She was not anything, except perhaps confused.

"It is rude to stare," she told him sharply. "You must not stare."

Maloof's brow furrowed curiously. "What is stare?" he asked.

"To look at me so . . . so, to look at me like that," she answered.

Maloof shook his head, puzzled. "How can man be wrong to look at woman so beautiful."

Muna felt her cheeks suffuse with warmth.

"It is right word, yes? You are beautiful."

"I . . . it is an acceptable word, I suppose."

Embarrassed, she turned to the nearest packing crate, already opened, and began to peruse the contents. It contained her favorite goods: ladies' wear. She hardly noticed.

"I think you very beautiful," Maloof said.

Muna glanced nervously around for her father. But he was nowhere near.

"When I am in Tarablos and my father say the daughter of his friend need husband, I am angry. I think, ah poor Maloof, I must wed to loud American woman. She will be old, skinny, and with pig face. I am angry. I am disappointed. I bite my heart and take duty to family." He hesitated a moment and then

spoke more softly. "God rewards me. He give me
beautiful wife. I am not angry now. Not disappointed."

Gooseflesh skittered along Muna's arms and the
back of her neck. His words were halting, disturbing,
and somehow enticing. She could not even glance in
his direction. Determinedly she put her mind to her
task and efficiently sorted the finery in her hands
without one thought to the frilly styles or delicacy of
the fabrics.

She heard a gasp beside her and suddenly he was
right at her elbow.

"What is this?" he asked, picking up a pair of black
washing silk drawers trimmed with red ribbon and
Valenciennes lace. "I never see so fine thing. The
sewing, ah . . . look, it is tiny, perfect."

Muna had been embarrassed before. Now she was
horrified as he held the black drawers up for her
inspection, and waxed near poetic of their loveliness.
Then he looked over at her, smiling, friendly.

"You have like this?" he asked.

"Of course not!" she answered, shocked.

"Beautiful woman should have beautiful things. I
buy you," he declared.

"No! Absolutely not!"

"Absolutely yes," he insisted, apparently offended
by her response. "I have money. I have money, my
own. I can buy. I can buy retail."

Muna was too mortified and dumbfounded to even
speak. Fortunately she was saved from the necessity
of doing so.

"Maloof!" her father called from the outside doorway. "You must get the rest of the wagon loaded and
be on your way."

"Yes, I must go," he agreed respectfully.

It was then that her father apparently noticed what
he held in his hand.

"Don't spend your time going through the ladies'

wear," Nafee told him. "Muna just adores the pretty things and always takes care of the stock personally."

Maloof gave her one more questioning look before hurrying after her father.

Muna could still feel herself blushing; she was jittery and off balance. Surely he hadn't . . . he hadn't imagined her wearing the lingerie. When they married he would actually see her in her homesewn drawers. It didn't bear thinking about. But it seemed that she could think of nothing else. This strange, unfathomable man was going to be her husband.

Muna looked up startled as Princess Calhoun swept through the curtain-covered doorway and pulled her into a warm hug.

"Oh Muna, isn't it all so wonderful? Isn't *he* wonderful."

It was a statement not a question. For an instant Muna was bewildered, thinking her friend spoke of Maloof. Then she recalled vividly catching her in an indiscreet embrace with a stranger. Muna's expression momentarily turned stern and disapproving.

"I don't suppose you are talking about old man Wycoff out on the porch?" she said.

"Oh you!" Princess scolded with exasperation. "I mean Gerald, isn't he so . . . so perfect?"

"Well you seem to think so anyway," Muna replied, holding her friend at arm's length and looking at her.

"You don't?"

"I hardly spoke to the fellow," she answered. "He's certainly attractive. And he seems so taken with you."

The dreamy expression on her friend's face turned serious.

"Do you think so?" Princess asked. "Do you really think so?"

Muna shook her head. "It doesn't matter what I think. What do *you* think?"

"I think . . . oh Muna, I more than think." Her tone dropped to nearly a whisper. "I *know*, I know that I am in love. I am truly in love, at last."

Princess wrapped her arms across her chest as if needing to hold in the feelings of her heart.

"It was just as I thought it would be, Muna, just as I dreamed. I saw him across the distance of the lawn and I knew, I knew instantly that he was the one."

Princess closed her eyes as she pleasurably relived the moment.

"Gerald apparently felt exactly the same," she said with a soft sigh.

"Sometimes our feelings can be deceiving," Muna said, thinking of her own emotional confusion. "I don't think that we can always trust our initial impression of people."

"What? Don't be silly, Muna," she said. "If we can't trust ourselves to know people, what can we trust at all?"

Muna might have replied, nothing. But she held her tongue. She and Princess Calhoun were closer than sisters. They had grown up together in the half dozen oil boom towns between Pennsylvania and Topknot. They shared all and everything and swore to tell each other the truth.

"Oh Muna, it felt exactly as I always knew that it would," she said excitedly. "I love Gerald. I loved him that first minute and I will love him always."

"Oh Prin." Muna sighed.

"I saw him and I knew, I knew instantly."

"How did you know? How could you know?"

Princess laughed and shrugged. "I can't explain it," she admitted. "It was almost otherworldly. I just knew immediately. It was almost as if I recognized him."

"Like you recognized him?"

"Yes . . . but no, not really. In fact he didn't look at all as I expected."

"You were hoping for a blond man with blue eyes?"

"No, not really. I thought . . . well, I thought that he would not be so dreadfully handsome."

Muna nodded. "That's a good choice of words. He is dreadfully handsome."

"You know what I mean. I didn't expect such a man, such an attractive man, to be attracted to me."

"Oh Prin," Muna scolded.

"No Muna," she said determinedly. "If there is one thing I am clear about it is my plainness. To get one's bossy disposition *and* one's ordinary looks from King Calhoun is not a thing that young ladies would voluntarily line up for."

"You are beautiful on the inside, Prin," Muna insisted. "You have nice eyes and a friendly face."

"But the truth is, Muna, most men under the age of fifty don't even know that there is an *inside* to women. They know only what they see and that is all they expect or intend to get. But Gerald doesn't feel that way."

Muna sighed heavily. "Are you sure?" she asked.

Princess had been staring wistfully into space and was startled back into the present by her friend's words.

"What do you mean?" she asked.

"Oh Prin," Muna whispered, her voice concerned. "I don't think you should get your heart set on this one."

"What?"

"I'm not sure . . ." she hesitated. "I'm not sure, Prin, if he's truly the one for you."

"Why ever would you say that?"

Muna shook her head as if she was hesitant to answer. "I just think that he's . . . he's . . . well Prin, he's very good looking."

Princess laughed. "You say that as if it were a flaw in his character."

"No, no, I didn't mean that," she insisted quickly. "It's just . . . well Prin, if he is such a sophisticated gentlemen, so wealthy, so wonderful a catch, then why hasn't some other woman already got him?"

Princess looked at her friend as if she had lost her mind. "Because he was waiting for me," she said.

"Oh Prin, I just think . . ."

"You just think what?"

"Something about him just doesn't seem right," Muna answered. "I think maybe . . ."

"You think maybe what?"

Princess looked at her friend for a long moment. Muna's expression reflected worry and she bit nervously at her lower lip. Finally she shook her head and shrugged.

"I want you to be happy for me, Muna," Princess said.

"Oh well, I am so happy for you," Muna declared determinedly.

Princess appeared skeptical. "Okay, Muna, what's wrong?" she asked her. "What is it?"

"I *am* happy for you," Muna managed to get out. "I am so happy for you. I just worry, I suppose. You are so young."

"Young?" Princess was momentarily surprised. "Muna, we are the same age."

"Yes, I know but, but you . . . you still believe in love. You think you are in love."

"I'm in love," Princess said with certainty and then gazed at her friend, puzzled. "What do you mean *I* believe in love. You've gotten yourself engaged! I can't believe you didn't even tell me. You kept it all a secret and—"

"I'm engaged, yes," Muna interrupted her. "But I'm not in love."

Princess hesitated, disbelieving. "You don't love him?" The question was a whisper.

"I don't even know him," she answered.

"Then why . . ."

"He's my father's choice, not mine," Muna admitted. "Baba says that he is dependable and hardworking and that he will take good care of the business and always provide for me."

"But there has to be . . . there has to be love," Princess insisted.

"Baba says that security is more important than sentiment," Muna answered. "And Mama agrees with him. She says we will learn to love each other in time."

"Learn to love each other?" Princess was aghast. "That's not how it works, Muna. You know that. We've talked about this a million times. A person either loves somebody or they don't. You can't choose the *right* person for marriage and then fall in love with them later."

"I know that's what we always said," Muna agreed. "But then we were just children. We are women now, Prin, and it is not at all what we thought."

"Muna, it is exactly as we thought. Love is a . . . an elemental force, like lightning," Princess said. "We never know where it's going to strike, and there is no why. It just happens. The ancients thought of it as Cupid arbitrarily shooting an arrow through the heart. You can't choose when or who. You simply recognize when it happens and then live happily with the results."

Muna shook her head. "I felt nothing when I met Maloof," Muna admitted. "No arrow through my heart. Not even a tug of attraction. Nothing. And I'm sure it was the same for him."

"Then you cannot possibly marry him," Princess stated flatly.

Muna started to protest but Princess held up a hand to silence her.

"Choosing the person you should marry is serious," Princess said. "It is not a game for children. The decision is made soberly and with an eye toward the future. But love is an elemental part of it."

"Mama says all our talk about love is just girlish nonsense," Muna told her. "She says that Maloof and I will learn to love each other."

"Well, that shows clearly how little your mother knows," Princess assured her. "People *fall* in love, they don't *learn* to love."

Muna was thoughtfully mute for a long moment. "But I have to listen to Mama and Baba," she said. "They think he will be a wonderful husband for me."

"He seems like a nice man, Muna," Princess said firmly. "But I am telling you that if you don't love him you can't marry him."

"Our marriage will be based on mutual respect and understanding," Muna said. "Mama says that is much more important than love."

Princess looked at her sternly. "Do you believe that?"

"I don't know what I believe, Prin," Muna told her. "What I don't believe is that a man who never met you or talked to you can see you across the lawn and fall in love with you forevermore."

"That's a good deal more likely than marrying a man you don't love and learning to love him later," Princess said.

"I don't love Maloof Bashara," Muna told her. "But I do love my Mama and Baba. They love me and they trust him."

"But *he* doesn't love you," Princess pointed out.

"No," she said. "He doesn't. He is not pretending something he doesn't feel; he is honest with me so I'm going to marry him."

"What do you really even know about this man?" Princess asked.

"What do you know about this stranger you are going to marry?" Muna shot back. "I know that he's come all the way from Tarablos, half a world away to marry me. I know that his father and mine have been friends from boyhood. I know that Baba is making him a partner in the business. And I know that he wants the best for me. I know that he thinks . . . he thinks God has rewarded him by giving him to me."

"Oh, Muna," Princess said to her quietly. "You just can't marry this man if you don't love him."

"I can, Prin, and I will," she said firmly. "I know you enjoy telling me what to do, but this time I must decide for myself."

"We've talked about this so much," Princess continued. "We've giggled and daydreamed and speculated about how we would meet the man we were to love. How we would see him and know him."

"That's what I'm telling you, Prin," Muna insisted. "That was girlish fantasy. Women don't marry fantasies, they marry men. And they choose with their heads, not their hearts."

"Oh, I'm so angry at him," Princess told her.

"Who?"

"Why, at him, that Maloof," she answered. "A man who marries to better himself in the world. It's . . . it's despicable."

"Despicable?" Muna shook her head. "Oh Prin, he's only being sensible and smart. Those are qualities a woman wants in a husband. He's not at all despicable. Actually he is really rather nice."

"How can you say that?"

"Well, it's true. He is nice."

"He is about to marry you because it is a tremendous business opportunity," Princess said. "If that's not despicable, I don't know what is."

"Prin, don't call him names. He's going to be my husband."

Princess gave her friend a long look before nodding. "If you are going to marry him, Muna, then I'll never say a word against him. And I am going to marry . . . yes, I'm going to marry Gerald Crane. So don't you ever say another word against him."

The two gave each other a long look before simultaneously flying into each other's arms.

"I swear I will find some way to like your Mr. Bashara. I swear it as your best friend."

"And I'll give your Mr. Crane a chance," Muna whispered as she hugged her. "We are closer than sisters."

"Closer than sisters forever," Princess agreed.

The two pulled apart from their embrace and locked little fingers together in a secret handshake left over from childhood days. Then they both laughed at the silliness of it.

Then slowly their laughter faded to serious concern.

"Be careful, Prin," Muna told her. "I don't want you to get hurt."

Princess nodded agreement.

"Muna, make it a long engagement," she said. "And if you find that you can't love him, don't marry."

"Agreed."

"Agreed."

The P. Calhoun Number One stood at the top of a high bluff in a bend in the Arkansas River just south of the ferry crossing. Tom was certain that from its crown block a man could probably see Burford Corners and perhaps beyond. It was at least a hundred feet tall, but it was neither lonely nor alone. The wide hill, sloping gradually upward on the west and south, sported a forest of derricks rising tall in the sky, the noise of which certainly discouraged any type of conversation. The constant thud . . . chik . . . thud . . . that had kept him awake the previous night, was, upon closer examination, less an annoyance and more probably a cause of deafness.

The hill was sparsely greened by a thin covering of bluestem and sandburs. Deep, rutted walking paths were worn into the ground and Tom found that strolling beyond them was treacherous, as the thin shale beneath the grass tended to break off and shift.

Tom had been concerned that his presence at the drilling site might be noticed. But as he glanced around, he realized that it was very unlikely. There were men of every stripe moving in every direction. One more, dressed just like most, blended in without effort. Several were huddled upon the derrick floor in deep discussion about some sort of problem.

Beside the derrick itself, there were several other busy working areas around the site. He watched a group putting together a small building. They cut boards and hammered nails, but they were not like any carpenters Tom had ever seen. No measures, no levels, no square was being utilized. Every piece of lumber was eye-sighted and cut to fit. An obvious preference for fast buildings over sturdy ones.

Lengths of pipe in several diameters were being unloaded and stacked near the north side of the rig. Tom tried to imagine the tremendous depth of drilling that the piping, laid end to end, would represent.

Tom wandered around with his eyes watchful. If he did decide to woo Cessy Calhoun, this huge contraption of raw lumber and unattractive machinery might well be his very soon. He wanted to make absolutely certain that the prize was going to be worth the price.

"Is there really oil under there?" he wanted to ask someone, anyone. "How much oil will it be? Will the sale of it keep me in fine shoes and dress coats for the rest of my days? Is it worth enough to take on a wife to get it?"

He couldn't ask those questions. At least he couldn't ask them directly. Tom would have to watch and listen and learn. He'd take his time. He'd have to be quite certain. And when he knew the answer,

when he knew for sure, he'd be down on one knee
with a posy and a proposal for Miss Cessy Calhoun.

The thought of the plain little blusher had him
shaking his head thoughtfully. He wondered what
she was up to this morning. Had she lain awake all
night dreaming of his kiss? Had she whispered his
name into her pillow? Or rather, had she whispered
Gerald's name? He hoped so. He didn't have a lot of
greenbacks to spend on candy and gifts. He'd have to
win her with long looks and soulful sighs. And a few
more of those stolen kisses.

Tom had been, he admitted to himself, more than a
little surprised by her reaction to him. She'd held her
mouth pursed like a ten-year-old. He had known
before she told him that she was far from experienced
in courting ways. It had been her first kiss. And he
had meant it to be very romantic and chaste. But she
had not reacted with shock, fear, or embarrassment.
Cessy Calhoun had been, well, she had been really
quite passionate. She had pressed her body against
him without hesitation. Aggressive in her basic nature, she had been unrestrained in her openness to
him.

Too easy. That could be its own danger, Tom
reminded himself. If last night was any indication,
she'd probably be ordering him to marry her within a
week! He needed to keep his head. *He* was to do the
seduction here, at the right time and the right place.
And in secret, if at all possible. The last thing he
wanted was King Calhoun running him out of town
with a shotgun.

As if conjured up from Tom's thoughts, King
Calhoun came up over the rise in his Packard. The
well-worn and much abused automobile was blessed
with a wide body and high clearance that somehow
allowed it to traverse the slippery hill like a mountain
goat.

Tom watched as Calhoun and two others emerged

from the vehicle. They hailed the men at the derrick.
One of them, an older fellow with a decided limp,
moved forward to greet the portly, well-heeled owner
and his three-man entourage.

With some stealth, Tom made his way back behind
them. He wanted to hear what they were saying. But
he sure didn't want to get close enough to catch the
eye of Calhoun or his men. With great care, following
a crisscrossing path, he managed to come up behind
them on the far side of the car. A tall stand of
blooming pink dogbane offered relative privacy within earshot of Calhoun and the others. The noise from
the well had them conversing in shouts. Tom turned
away from them so that anyone glancing in his
direction would think his only interest was in reliev-
ing himself.

"I'm off to Saint Louis, Cedarleg," Calhoun said
loudly, addressing his remarks to the crippled fellow.
"I'm going to catch the Limited about seven. I'll be in
the Palmer House by morning."

"How long you going to be gone this time?"

"At least three days, but no more than a week," he
answered.

"You taking Miss Princess with you?"

"Nah, it's a business trip," he said. "Got to see one
of them numb-nut bankers. Lord, I hate those sorry
scum-suckers, but a man's got to do business where
business is being done. Ivel will have Friday's payroll
out here on time. And I'll be back before the next."

Tom felt a moment of pure elation. He almost
laughed aloud. With her father out of the way for at
least three days, Cessy would be easy prey. As soon
as he could beg or borrow a decent suit of clothes, he
could call on her at the Calhoun Mansion. Without
her father at home there would be no need for stealth
at all. Servants were notoriously bad chaperones. A
few evenings of spooning on the porch swing and

she'd be as malleable as territory clay. If Calhoun stayed away a whole week, he might even have time to get her to the "I do!"

"I'll keep the boys at it," the lame-legged fellow assured Calhoun. "We got some kind of back push this morning. Don't know yet if it's a gas pocket or more of that danged salt water."

There was a long moment in which, to Tom's surprise, Calhoun and Cedarleg moved away from the other three and in his direction. As he made a big production of doing up his fly, Tom could hear the hesitation in Calhoun's voice as he replied.

"It's down there, isn't it Cedarleg?" he asked.

The crippled man hooted with laughter. "You ain't thinking this could be a duster? It's there. I ain't saying it's going to be easy, the dome is old and the caprock goes way deep, but the oil is under this hill. I'd risk everything I have on that."

Calhoun snorted and then laughed out loud. "We've brought them in on a shoestring before, Lord knows."

He slapped the crippled man on the back heartily. "You'd best get back to your drilling crew, Cedarleg. No telling what those boys will be up to without you looking over their shoulders."

As Cedarleg headed for the derrick floor and Calhoun and his cohorts returned to the Packard, Tom made himself scarce.

There was oil down there. Those men knew it. And now Tom knew it too. If he married Cessy Calhoun it would all be his. Every beautiful, black, expensive drop of it.

Following a circuitous route once more, Tom made his way back toward the area around the derrick. He stopped next to a small group of men digging what appeared to be a large earthen pond.

"Any work to be had here?" Tom asked.

One of them raised his head, leaned momentarily upon his shovel, and gave Tom a long perusal. "We got a full crew of tank builders," he said. "The other gangs might need a hand. Ask the tool pusher."

"The tool pusher?"

The man glanced at his cohorts and gave a wide-eyed expression of disbelief. "Is this your first day in the oil fields?" he asked.

"My second," Tom answered. "I got into Topknot yesterday, but this is the first oil well I've seen up close."

"The tool pusher is the boss man on the derrick floor," he told Tom with a long-suffering look that indicated he was only barely tolerating Tom's ignorance. He pointed to the three men up on the rig. "The fellow on his right, he's the driller. He actually puts the tools, the bit and stem and cables to the hole. The other man is called the tool dresser. He keeps things ready, the bits honed and handy, and backs up the driller."

Tom nodded, deliberately committing the man's words to his memory.

"It only takes three men to drill an oil well?"

"Three at a time to drill the hole," the tank builder answered. "But there's better than two dozen that make up the whole crew."

"So they might need someone willing to learn?" Tom asked.

The man shrugged.

"Cedarleg!" he called out.

The crippled man at the rig looked up in his direction. The tank builder waved him over.

Tom raised his chin and put his thoughts in order. He needed a job. He'd have to spend the ten dollars he'd earned on courting clothes. If he could get work on the rig, he could learn about how it operated. If he was about to be an oil baron, it'd be a good thing to know which end of a well was up.

When the crippled man came within hearing distance, the tank builder spoke up once more.

"This one is looking for a job," he said, indicating Tom. "It's his first, no second, day in the oil fields."

The man couldn't resist a chuckle, and the rest of his cohorts joined in.

Tom ignored them and offered his handshake.

"Are you the boss here at the P. Calhoun Number One?" he asked.

The old man nodded. "We just call her the 'P,'" he said.

"I need a job," Tom told him. "And I'd like to work here on this rig."

Cedarleg looked at Tom assessingly.

"You look to have a strong back at least," the tool pusher said finally. "My name's Pease, but they call me Cedarleg. I don't suspect you know nothing about nothing."

"I'm a quick study," Tom assured him. "I've worked all over Texas and the territories. I know cattle, horses, farming."

"You know anything about machinery?"

Tom hesitated. He wasn't above lying, but there was no sense in making up something that would easily be found out to be untrue.

"No, sir," he said firmly. "I've never had much acquaintance with machines. I can shoot straight, ride well, and tend animals. But I'm hoping to learn something new."

Cedarleg continued to look at him thoughtfully. "That's a real good attitude, son," he said finally. "But I just ain't got the time to teach you nothing. This is a drilling rig. It's a dangerous place for anybody. It can be deadly for those who don't know their way around."

Tom opened his mouth to plead his case further when the consistent thud . . . chik . . . thud suddenly developed a strange, almost whirring sound.

Cedarleg obviously heard it, too, and turned, hurrying on his gimp leg toward the rig, calling out, "Slack in the line!"

Tom rushed forward with him, taking in the scene. One man knelt on the derrick floor, frantically jerking at the stove up drill stem.

"Turn it off!" he screamed. "Turn it off!"

The other man stood, pale and wide-eyed, frozen in place.

"Pull the brake!" Cedarleg called out to him as he raced forward, in eminent danger of falling over in his haste. "Pull the brake."

Clearly Tom saw that the frozen man could do nothing. He knew that look. He'd seen it in Cuba. A man too frightened to move was an easy target and the men around him usually suffered.

The heavy cable began pouring off the spool onto the kneeling man. It was going to kill him, Tom realized. Either the weight of it would crush him, or if he managed to pull loose the stuck drill stem he would be caught up in the line and ripped apart before their eyes.

The frozen man was not moving to save him and the crippled man was not going to have time. Tom leapt onto the derrick floor. He gave one glance at the driller contemplating his death and unerringly followed the direction of his eyes to the brake lever.

Tom pulled it downward with all his strength.

Silence.

Total silence.

Then Cedarleg was beside him, securing the chain that held the brake lever down.

All the men in the vicinity of the rig had rushed to the derrick floor. The tank builders were there first and dragged the driller out of the tangle of cable.

"He's all right!" one of them called out. "He's all right."

"Thank God."

Tom heard Cedarleg whisper under his breath only a moment before he turned toward the other fellow, the tool dresser, still frozen a few feet away.

"Git!" Cedarleg hollered at him.

The man stuttered, attempting some sort of reply.

"Git!" Cedarleg screamed more viciously. "Git away from this rig! Git off this hill! Git out of my sight!"

Cedarleg was walking toward the man threateningly. He picked up a greasy rag and threw it at the man.

"Git!" he hollered once more.

The fellow hurriedly backed off the rig, but it wasn't fast enough to suit Cedarleg. He followed. Stooping to grab a handful of dirt, he threw that at the man.

The fellow was killing mad. The tool dresser began hurrying away in earnest. And when a rock Cedarleg threw at him caught him square between the shoulder blades, he began running.

"Git outta here!" Cedarleg continued screaming and followed at as fast a pace as he could manage, throwing stones as he went.

Tom was right behind him. He grabbed the older fellow from behind, pinning his arms to his sides in a confining embrace.

"Let me go!" Cedarleg ordered.

"Let him go," Tom said quietly. "It's over. It's all over."

"I lost my leg 'cause of a sonuvabitch like him."

"It's over," Tom repeated calmly. "The driller is fine. Your leg is gone. And that fellow is, too."

After a long moment, Tom felt the tension go out of the old man.

"You can let me go now, son," Cedarleg said. "I'm all right now.

Tom released him and the two stood together silently as Cedarleg continued to look toward where the tool dresser had disappeared.

"I was driller on a rig up in Pennsylvania twelve years ago," he told Tom. "I lost my leg in a slack line accident a lot like this one."

The man turned to face Tom, his expression pensive, thoughtful.

"My dang leg got tangled in the line and when the drill bit popped through it ripped it off at the knee as easy as pulling a drumstick off a Sunday dinner chicken."

"I'm sorry," Tom told him.

Cedarleg nodded in response. "I always said that I was just grateful to be alive." He chuckled without humor. "I suspect sometimes I'm not as grateful as I pretend to be."

They turned and began walking back toward the rig.

"You're a dang hero, son," Cedarleg told him.

Tom scoffed. "If there's anything I learned in Cuba," he said, "it's that the only real heroes are dead ones. I intend to live a very long time."

Cedarleg laughed. "That's a good attitude. Surviving is a good motivator for working in the oil fields. What's your name, son?"

"My name?"

"All men with jobs have a name, I suspect."

Tom's brow furrowed. "I don't have a job."

Cedarleg raised an eyebrow. "I'm in dire need of a new tool dresser. I just run my last one off. If you want the position, it's yours."

Tom looked at him a moment and then gestured toward the rig. "I don't know anything about oil wells," he said.

Cedarleg shrugged. "You know where the brake is. That's a good start."

He held out his hand. "My name's Walker, Tom Walker," he said.

FIVE

He worked the rest of the shift beside Cedarleg. It was tough, hard work and somewhat confusing, but Tom kept at it.

The driller, who introduced himself as Bob Earlie, kept at it, too. After taking a few moments to collect himself after his near brush with death, Earlie started the rig up once more.

Over the constant pounding noise of the rig, Tom began learning the names of the clamps and sockets and joints, and which tools might be called on for what repairs. By midafternoon the July sun beat down upon them with such intensity that it slowed their movements to the rhythm of the rig and their bodies glistened with the sweat of honest work.

The constant drumming against solid rock dulled and warped the bits. Frequently they were removed and beaten back into shape. It was the tool dresser's job to keep the hot forge burning and to pound the heated bits upon the anvil into their proper dimensions.

The worst of the sun was just over when the evening tour, which Tom learned was pronounced "tower," arrived at six. There was some quick welcome, much talk of the accident, and nods of acceptance toward Tom. Each man had a few words with his night-shift counterpart. The evening tool dresser was a serious, sober fellow who accepted Tom's lack of knowledge or experience without any comment or change of expression.

Finally, the day crew began tramping back down the hill and along the riverside road to the ferry crossing.

Tom was exhausted. All he wanted was to get back to his narrow bunk at the CLEAN CHEAP BEDS and sleep until dawn.

"Walker!" he heard called out behind him.

He stopped and turned to see Cedarleg hurrying along after him in his awkward, unsightly gait.

"You trying to catch a train, boy?" he asked Tom. "I'm practically at what counts for me as a dead-out run to catch you."

Tom shook his head and shrugged. "I'm just so blamed tired," he admitted. "I guess I thought if I slowed down I might fall asleep at the side of the road."

The older fellow chuckled. "I hear ye," he said. "It's just a matter of getting used to it. The first day without so much as a bush to get under. That sun just saps it out of ye."

Tom nodded. "My bunk isn't much better than the side of this road," he said. "But it is sure looking pretty good to me now."

"That's what I wanted to ask you," Cedarleg said. "Where exactly are you bunking?"

When Tom told him, he shook his head and tutted with disapproval.

"You cain't bunk there, that's a roustabout place."

"Huh?"

"In the oil fields," Cedarleg explained, "we're kindy clannish. Each group of workers stays among their own kind. We eat together, sleep together, socialize together. We don't mix with others."

Tom raised an eyebrow in surprise.

"Now, it ain't what you're thinking," Cedarleg told him quickly. "It ain't like tank builders think they are better than rig builders or roughnecks think they are better than roustabouts, though they probably do. It's not even like where folks is from, though most of the rig builders hail from the mountains of Tennessee and Kentucky and the tool pushers usually got factory experience up north somewhere. What it is mostly, is that the way you get to be a good tool dresser is by listening to and talking with tool dressers that got more experience than you."

"That seems reasonable."

"You see how we work," he said. "The driller and I both dressed tools in our time. But the rigs and the way they're run changes ever' day. If you're really going to learn about it, you got to be around the men that's doing it."

"So I need to find a bunk among the tool dressers," Tom said.

Cedarleg nodded. "It's the best way. You can get your own tent in the tool dresser's part of the camp. You'll be one of them and they'll share what they know with ye."

Tom nodded thoughtfully. "How much does a tent in the tool dresser's part of the camp cost?"

Cedarleg didn't answer immediately. "I don't suspect that you got much money for stepping up in the world," he said.

The statement required no reply.

"I know what you can do," Cedarleg said. "You can stay with my woman and me for a week or so 'til ye get on your feet."

"I couldn't do that."

"Sure ye can," he assured him. "The pushers' camp ain't far from the dressers and I can take you around, introduce you to some fellers."

"I couldn't impose on you and your wife."

"You wouldn't be. Ma and me, we got us a nice, tight little place and she'll love you to death. We got a boy about your age working down in Baytown. His wife is going to make me a grandpa in the fall. Ain't that something?"

Tom laughed along with him.

It was impossible, he discovered, to refuse Cedarleg's invitation.

"Much appreciate it," Tom told him finally.

The older man clapped him on the back as if delighted. And he continued a steady stream of oil field explanation as they walked down the road.

The ferry across the Arkansas was obviously doing a steady business. The railroad crossing was fine for trains and men on foot, but there was no wagon bridge across the river. The area near the ferry docking was crowded with vehicles of all types, the drivers patiently awaiting their turn on the twenty-foot flat boat that was pulled across the river by ropes. The day tour workers made their way past a butcher's cart, around a lumber dray, and in front of a canvas-cooled milk truck. The ferrymen were just completing the loading of a heavy tanker. Already tied down in front was a brightly painted peddler's wagon. Tom stepped on board aside Cedarleg, hesitating only briefly to hold the head of a nervous horse as the ropes for the second vehicle were secured. As soon as they pushed off into the water, the two moved out of range of the tanker's disagreeable scent.

Leaning against the side rails, he drew in a deep breath of fresh air. Cedarleg had struck up a conversation with one of the boatmen and Tom was alone with his thoughts for a long moment.

He knew this river. He knew it well and today it was deceptively quiet, wide, and slow-moving. He had seen it wild and dangerous. It had tempted him to escape. Not far downstream was where Shemmy Creek flowed into it. And up that creek, six long miles, was the Methodist Indian Home. He remembered reading *Tom Sawyer* and dreaming of rafting down Shemmy Creek, making his way to the Arkansas and freedom forever. He'd even gone so far as trying to piece a raft together.

When Reverend McAfee had caught him, he'd blistered his backside. Years earlier three boys from the home had gone riding on logs down the flood-risen stream. All three had drowned.

"You'll be grown and heading downstream soon enough," he'd told Tom with great seriousness. "And I fear you will discover that it is far easier to begin the journey than to maneuver in the stream."

He pushed the memory away and turned from the river to admire the fashionable scene painted in an oval upon the side of the yellow-and-blue peddler's wagon. With the men on the rigs working twelve-hour shifts six days a week, most had little time to visit the stores and vendors in town. So the peddlers brought the merchandise to them.

Tom read the name above it and had only an instant to note the significance of NAFEE EMPORIUM before a familiar figure stepped out from behind the wagon. The two men recognized each other immediately.

"Mr. Crane! Ah, what surprise to meet soon again."

Tom stared, near dumbstruck at the sight of the strange foreign fiancé of Princess Calhoun's friend. He glanced quickly toward Cedarleg to see if he'd heard Tom addressed by another name. Gratefully he had not.

"Uh . . . uh . . . Mister uh . . ."

"Bashara," the fellow supplied. "Maloof Bashara, but you please call only Maloof, yes?"

He offered his hand. Tom took it mutely, his thoughts swirling with faster fury than a June tornado. He was caught, well and for sure caught. Here was a man who knew him as Gerald, but now met him dressed as Tom. He was grease-stained, dirty, and sweaty. It was obvious that he'd just put in a day's work on a rig. He had been introduced to the peddler as a gentleman, but now he stood before him clearly as a worker.

Tom was dumbstruck and uncertain. Should he offer some explanation? What sort of explanation could it be? How well-known was he to Cessy? Would he mention the chance meeting to her? Certainly he might speak of it to his young lady. Would she tell Miss Calhoun that he was seen heading back from the oil fields in worn, dirty overalls and work boots?

"It's . . . it's good to see you again . . . ah, Maloof," he managed to get out finally.

The foreign fellow pumped his hand with enthusiasm.

"You name Jarrett? Jarrod? Jerat?" Maloof struggled to remember correctly.

Tom ignored the implied question.

"What fun the party, yes?" Maloof said, chuckling. "We laugh, we dance, and then today . . ." He sighed dramatically. "We work again as if life is no pleasure."

Tom relaxed slightly. Apparently the foreigner didn't comprehend the disparity between Gerald Crane of last night and the man who stood before him now.

They had had fun at the party. The peddler had a keen sense of humor and the two young women were full of easy laughter. It had been a pleasant evening, but it had been Gerald's evening, not Tom's.

"Good to see you again, Maloof," he said assuming the cultured voice of Mr. Crane. "I didn't realize that you worked for Mr. Nafee." He gestured toward the wagon.

Maloof grinned, it was an expression that seemed

to come easy to his nature. "Yes, I peddle the wares of the father of my future bride. I think I am to prove myself worthy."

"Does he wonder if you are worthy of her?" Tom asked.

Maloof's eyes widened with mischief. "Oh no, he thinks I am fine for her. He wonders if I am worthy of his business."

The foreign fellow had a great laugh at that. Tom raised an eyebrow and chuckled with him.

"Who's yer friend, Tom?" the words came from Cedarleg who'd stepped up beside him.

With a lightning decision, Tom introduced Cedarleg to the peddler using Gerald's voice.

The tool pusher gave him a curious look but made no comment as he politely shook Maloof's hand.

"I am not friend," Bashara explained in his unusual way to the older man. "But not enemy for sure. We share ladies."

"You share ladies?" Cedarleg's question was incredulous.

Maloof laughed and shook his head. "No, no, I speak English no good. We do not share. We each have our own."

"Tom, you didn't tell me you had a lady," Cedarleg teased, with a well-aimed elbow poke to his ribs.

"Well, I . . . uh . . ."

"Our ladies are like sisters."

"Sisters?"

"Miss Muna and I are to be married," Maloof continued. "But just last night he met Miss Prin."

Cedarleg whistled with appreciation. "Just in town one day and already met you a gal."

"She's a very nice young lady," Tom said. "And I am of age."

"Of age to be courting for certain," Cedarleg agreed. "And I'm a great believer in it. Been married twenty-three years myself. I'm as happy about it this evening as I was on the first day. A feller gets himself the right woman, he cain't do no better in life."

Tom smiled in tacit agreement, but wanted a change in subject. He glanced at the wagon and figured he could kill two birds with one stone.

"I need a suit, Maloof," he said. "If a man is going courting, he's got to have a suit."

The peddler's eyes alighted with pleasure. "For you, the best I've got."

Tom gave a nervous glance toward Cedarleg. "Not the best you've got. Something . . . something fine, but thrifty."

Maloof grabbed Tom by the shoulders as if measuring their width and gave a little huff of approval.

"I have perfect, perfect. For you, fine big man, perfect suit."

Maloof hurried to the back of the wagon and began sorting his merchandise.

Cedarleg was grinning at him. "So this Miss Prin," he asked. "Does she have a first name?"

"Cessy," Tom answered without hesitation.

"Cessy Prin." He said the name over thoughtfully. "I don't think I heard that name before. Is her folks here among the oil people?"

"Ah . . . no," Tom answered. "Her father has a business in Burford Corners."

"Lord boy, be careful," Cedarleg cautioned. "Them town daddies don't take too kindly to us oil field men."

"I don't believe that her daddy knows about me yet," Tom told him in a conspiratorial whisper.

Cedarleg hooted with appreciation. "So you're hooking her good and true and will have her reeled into the boat before daddy knows it's fishing season."

"Something like that."

"Lord have mercy," Cedarleg said, pointing to the clothing that Maloof was carrying. "Look at the bait."

Tom was looking at it, concern in his expression.

Cedarleg already knew he had no cash, but Maloof obviously still thought him a wealthy gentlemen.

"I don't wish to spend a lot of money," he said firmly, embarrassed at the admission.

Maloof took up his words as a challenge. "I can see that you are a man who appreciates the pleasure of bargaining."

Princess Calhoun lay stretched out on the maroon velvet fainting couch in the sun parlor. It was only just sunset, but here on the east side of the house, the room was already dark and shadowless. With no lamp lit, it would have been impossible for her to see the book that she held in her hand. But it didn't matter. She had read Robert Hunter's *Poverty* many times and committed whole sections of his elegant words to heart. But tonight she hadn't even attempted to decipher one word.

She'd taken off her spectacles and laid them on the table beside her. She was very nearsighted and without the thick lenses that brought the world beyond the length of her arm into focus, she often felt disoriented and vulnerable. But somehow in the dim, blurry world of the sun parlor, she felt she could see into her own heart much more clearly.

She was lost in a dream, a very special dream, as familiar to her as the life she knew all around her. It was a fantasy that she had held close to her aching, lonely heart for a very long time.

In her mind's eye she saw a huge church crowded with people. All were dressed in their best finery and all looked back toward the door expectantly. She appeared there on her father's arm. Her dress was of the most delicate ivory silk, beaded and adorned with lace. As they walked to the front every eye was upon them, her father beside her was puffed up and smiling. And she, Princess Calhoun, was the bride beneath the long, frothy veil. She could not even see her own face, but she knew from the reactions all around her that she was, in her own way, beautiful.

Her father leaned down to whisper in her ear. "I am so proud of you, Princess," he said.

Her heart took wing over the clouds. She was beautiful. Daddy was proud of her. And today, today for the very first time, she could see the man standing at the front of the church.

She closed her eyes and hugged her book to her bosom.

"Gerald," she whispered to the dark, lonely room. "Oh Gerald, I love you."

Just hearing herself say the words brought a laugh of pure joy to her throat. She had never been in love before. Never, not once. But she had believed in it. She had known that it was there.

Many of the social reformers that she so admired were not as certain. Progressives of both genders were often quick to refer to love as a "trap" and marriage as "slavery." But Princess believed the very best about both and wanted each desperately.

She and Muna had carried a torch for Bennie Blakemon when they were sixteen and still in Corsicana. They had called it love at the time. But it was just a game. All the girls in that end of Texas were "in love" with Blakemon. He was a big old lonesome cowboy and every female heart sighed after him.

Neither she nor Muna had ever exchanged a word with the fellow and Princess seriously doubted that he even knew that either of them were alive.

But Gerald, Gerald seemed very much to know that she was alive. Vividly she remembered the sweet taste of his mouth and the warmth of his arms around her. Their eyes had met across a distance and they had known, obviously they had both known immediately that this was the love, the one true love, that they had been waiting for.

Her own reaction had vividly shocked her. She had never before been kissed and yet she responded to the touch of his lips with an ardor that was almost unladylike. It had been as if, the moment their eyes met, their hearts did also. She recognized him immediately and had loved him all her life. How then could she be expected to remain demure and distant?

Gerald Tarkington Crane. Gerald Tarkington Crane.

She was in love. With her heart so light, Princess could no longer sit still. She jumped to her feet and, holding out her arms as if embracing a partner, she began to waltz herself about the room as she sang in her high, nasal, slightly off-key manner:

> *"You had a dream, dear*
> *I had one, too.*
> *Mine was the best*
> *'Cause it was . . . of . . . you."*

He had danced with her. He had held her like this. Safe and protected in his arms. She had belonged there. And they had known it to be true. They had moved as one to the sweet strains of music. Together, as one.

"Miss Calhoun."

Princess gave a cry of startled dismay and dropped her arms in guilty embarrassment. She could feel the warm blush that stained her cheeks.

"Howard? You . . . you surprised me."

"My apologies, ma'am," he said. "There is a gentleman here to see you. I informed him that Mr. Calhoun was not at home and that you were not receiving visitors, but he insisted that I give you his card."

Princess hastily retrieved her spectacles and hooked them securely behind her ears before she picked up the card lying on the small silver tray. It was pure white, highly embossed with blue-black lettering and adorned with a thin gold border. It read simply: GERALD TARKINGTON CRANE, BEDLINGTON, NEW JERSEY.

"Oh!" Princess stared at the unexpected card. Her heart began to beat faster.

"Did you put him in the front parlor?" she asked as she hurried out into the hallway.

"Why no, ma'am. I left him standing on the porch."

"What?" Princess gazed at him horrified.

"It was at his own suggestion, since you are not receiving."

"Howard, I believe I am the one to decide whether I am receiving," she chided him gently. "I will, of course, see Mr. Crane."

She didn't even stop to glance at her hair, she simply smoothed the untidy strands that had escaped the chignon as she hurried past the stairway. It was as if she hadn't truly believed that it had happened, that she had truly met her true love and suddenly she was desperate to reassure herself that it was not just all part of the daydream that so enthralled her.

She rushed through the doorway and onto the porch.

"Mr. Crane." She spoke his name before she even saw him.

He was standing at the end of the porch on one of the garden steps. He was staring up at the house and the look on his face, caught unaware, was somehow guarded, critical. But when he glanced toward her he smiled so warmly, Princess wondered if she had imagined the other expression.

He was dressed elegantly in a pin-checked linen coat, dark alpaca vest and trousers, and a muslin shirt bedizened fashionably with large blue polka dots. Although the bowtie would have been the most typical neckwear for the costume, he wore a hem-stitched Windsor in a four-in-hand twist. No bill-board cigar advertisement could have looked more elegant or attractive.

"Mr. Crane," she repeated his name somewhat breathlessly and held out her hands to him.

He stepped forward immediately, his eyes devouring the sight of her. He took her fingers into his own and raised her knuckles to his lips, and then closed his eyes as if savoring the taste of her. When he opened them again to gaze at her once more, Princess wondered if he could feel her trembling.

"Mr. Crane?" he asked, in a soft, masculine whisper. "I thought we were on a first-name basis, Cessy."

Princess blushed and giggled. She heard herself and was momentarily chagrined at how young and silly she sounded. She pulled herself together. He was her true love, she felt certain. But she didn't want to discourage him in the leanings of his heart into thinking that she was a mindless nitwit.

"I also believed that we had progressed from the formalities," she told him. "But of course I wondered, as you felt it necessary to remain on the porch as if I might not see you."

He smiled down into her eyes. His own were so warm and brown and sparkling with inner fire as he teased her. "A gentleman can never be sure of the heart of a lady," he said. "To take such for granted is to court disaster. And I would much prefer to court *you*."

Princess felt the warmth stealing into her cheeks once more. But it was a heightened color brought on more by pleasure than discomfiture.

"I am so glad you came to visit this evening," she admitted to him. "I've . . . I've been thinking about you all day."

Gerald raised an eyebrow and gave her a long

perusal. "You have been much on my mind, too. But, dear Cessy, you must not tell a man such things."

"Why not? It's the truth."

"Young ladies do not often tell their suitors the truth," he said.

"That is totally ridiculous," Princess declared adamantly.

He nodded in tacit agreement. "Perhaps so, but it is how the game is played."

"I have no interest in playing games," she said firmly.

"Not even the game of the heart?" he asked, his tone smooth and alluring.

Princess found that her breathing was shallow and the blood was pounding in her veins.

"If I were to . . . care about someone, the very least that I can offer him is the truth," she told him, with as much directness and purpose as she could manage.

She watched a strange expression appear in his eyes. In an instant it was gone.

"Let's walk, shall we?" he suggested. "It seems so rude to keep a lady standing, and yet I do realize how untoward it would be for the two of us to sit on the porch unchaperoned."

Princess hadn't even realized that they *were* still standing. It was very difficult for her to keep her mind from running off into her fantasy. She knew that somehow he was her true love. But he had certainly not yet declared himself and she might well frighten him off if she continued to speak so boldly.

"A turn around the garden would be acceptable," she said, accepting his arm. Then with a light chuckle she added. "Although the term *garden* is not a particularly apt one."

He smiled politely and offered his arm. She laid her hand upon it formally and allowed herself to be led down the steps.

"It takes time to grow gardens," he told her. "One

must gauge their progress in years and seasons, rather than weeks and months."

"You are quite right," she agreed. "We've only just completed the house. The garden will be another matter entirely."

Princess caught Gerald glancing at the house critically once more.

"What do you think of the house?" she asked him.

Momentarily Gerald looked almost guilty, as if he had been caught at some horrible social faux pas. Then he visibly relaxed as he answered.

"In truth," he told her. "I am somewhat surprised at his choice of dwelling."

"Oh?"

"It's not particularly large," he pointed out.

"It has eight rooms," she told him. "And they are just for my father and me. The servants' quarters are separate."

"I only thought," Gerald said, "that a man of King Calhoun's wealth and position would want a mansion of the style of Mr. Rockefeller or Mr. Carnegie."

"Have you been to the camps?" she asked.

Gerald appeared momentarily taken aback. "Why, why yes, I've seen them."

"The workers, our workers, live mostly in tents. The best are half-walled with plank flooring," she said.

"Yes, they do live quite . . . modestly."

"I grew up in oil camps. I grew up living *modestly*. I cannot imagine that my father and I would ever have need to eat better, dress better, or require more room than we do now."

"But surely when building a house, one tends to think in terms of generations rather than the current requirements," Gerald said.

"I was thinking of the future," she assured him. "The house is small enough for me to take care of myself. It's nice having help, but when the boom

moves on, as it always does, there may not be many
wives who are interested in being day help. And in
terms of generations . . ."

Momentarily her thoughts turned dreamy.

"The house is big enough to raise a family," she
said with certainty. "Someday . . . someday I would
want a husband of my own. He will share this house
with me and . . . and our little ones."

She looked up at him then and saw something
indefinable in his eyes. Princess realized she had
spoken far too frankly. Most gentlemen would not be
at all appreciative of an unfashionably strong-minded
woman who could take complete charge of her own
life and those around her and who found it impossible to give over that duty to anyone, even the man she
hoped to marry.

Her cheeks flaming, Princess couldn't meet his
gaze. What must he think of her? Was that pity in his
gaze? Did she appear to him to be a mannish old
maid?

Suddenly she was wary. He laid his hand upon her
own and gave the knuckles just the slightest squeeze
of comfort. His action surprised her and warmed her.

"It is good for a woman to know what she wants
and go after it," he said. "I think it makes it more
likely that she will realize her dreams."

"They are frivolous dreams," she suggested with
some embarrassment.

"Not at all," he whispered. "I would envy such a
lucky man who would share this house and . . . little
ones with you."

She looked up into his eyes then. Her heart was
pounding like a drum. There was something so
compelling about this man, so forceful in his person-
ality. If he asked her to jump through hoops at a
traveling circus, she would immediately attempt to do
so. Such charisma could be as dangerous as drowning

water. Still, looking up at him, loving him, she waded right in.

"You don't have to envy anybody," she told him breathlessly.

He looked at her a long moment, obviously waiting, considering, as around Princess the treacherous waters of the heart swept ominously. Then with the very warmest of smiles, he threw her a life preserver.

"The style of the house is stark and simple," he said, adeptly changing the subject. "The current architectural fashion in the east is quite ornate."

Princess gratefully took the offered moment to regain control of herself. Without his intervention, she feared that in another moment she might well have been dropping to her knees and begging him to marry her.

"You mean all that busy gingerbread scrollwork? It's not for me," she said. "I always imagine that I would have to whitewash that ornamentation myself."

"Yourself?" he asked. "Certainly the lady of the house would never have cause to whitewash. Or are you one of the Janes?"

His reference to the social organization dedicated to the betterment of the lives of working women captured her attention.

"I am not a Jane, of course," she said. "But I believe strongly in the purpose they put forth. Even if women are allowed the vote, they can never achieve true freedom until they have viable options for employment in society."

"Oh? You would put women to work then?"

"Economic necessity puts women to work," she answered. "And they must have choices beyond domesticity and indecency."

Gerald nodded slowly as if taking it all in. It was important that he understand how she felt. She loved him already, but she needed for him to appreciate the causes that drew her.

"So you convinced your father to build a house as if his daughter must clean it herself?" he asked.

"I built my house in a way I thought would most benefit me and the people that I know," she said.

"You built your house?"

She nodded. "Daddy said that I could have whatever I wanted."

He looked up at the structure once more.

"I wanted something that the rig builders could put together," she explained.

"The rig builders?"

"The men who do carpentry work in the oil fields," she said. "Most are not skilled carpenters, but they are good with their hands and understand lumber."

"So these rig builders constructed your house?"

She nodded. "They put up the frame and I supervised the work. The pipe fitters installed the plumbing. Drilling crews and pumpers got running water into the house. And laborers of every stripe and trade helped inside and out to put it together. It is really a house built by Royal Oil."

Gerald eyed the house even more critically.

"Why not simply hire true carpenters and an architect?" he asked. "Didn't your father's workers have enough work to do out on those hundred rigs on the edge of town?"

"They came here on their off shift. No one was forced to come, although everyone who did was paid well. I felt that the workers will be wanting to build houses for their own families eventually. A house like this one will be within the realm of possibility for the most frugal and hardworking of our laborers. I thought that being a part of the construction of this house would give them some experience as well as some dream for which to aim."

"You sound almost socialist in your views, Cessy," he said.

She shook her head. "No, not really," she answered. "I am quite in step with Horatio Alger. I do believe that if you took all the Standard Oil millions and parceled them out to each and every man in the oil business, robber baron and rig worker alike, by the end of the year men like Rockefeller, my father, Josh Cosgen, and Harry Sinclair would have the bulk of it and the workers in the fields would continue to 'live modestly.'"

"So we are predestined to our financial state?"

"Not entirely," she explained. "A man born lame will never dance with greatness. Just as a child born into a family whose heritage is poverty and ignorance will not easily find the road to prosperity and privilege. But if the man has talent, drive, and interest he might choreograph the ballet. And if the poor child is given encouragement and direction he may ultimately be able to give to his parents some of those things that they were not able to give to him."

He looked at her with curiosity and interest.

"You have really thought about this, haven't you?"

Princess nodded. "I believe that we must do the best we can with the gifts and opportunities that we are given. If we do that, we often *will* move up in the world at least to some degree. It takes a great stroke of good fortune for a poor child like my father to become a wealthy man. It doesn't happen that often. Many of the workers on the rigs were once just as poor, and they will probably never become wealthy. But they can perhaps do better than they are doing now. I believe that they will do better than they are doing now. And if my modest house can give them some incentive to do so, then it suits me even better than a huge manse."

Gerald seemed to be marveling at her. "You are so

unexpected, Cessy," he told her. "So unlike I thought
you would be."

Princess bit her lip nervously. "I am strong-
minded, everyone says so. Are you disappointed?"
she asked quietly.

"Oh no," he said. "Not at all."

His words were so soft, so alluring, Princess felt the
undertow surging once more.

"Perhaps we should move back to the porch," she
suggested. "The sun is already set and it is far too
dark to see anything in the garden."

"But that is the point, isn't it?" Gerald asked. "If we
are walking in a garden so dark that nobody can see,
then we obviously are both hoping that I'll steal a
kiss."

Princess blushed, but honestly adored his teasing
repartee. It was such a new and exciting game, even if
she wasn't all that sure how to play it.

"I do not believe that larceny will be necessary,
Gerald," she told him. "I am only too happy to give
you all the kisses you desire."

"All the kisses I desire? Ooooh, Cessy, are you
becoming a temptress?"

"What a novel idea," she answered. "A temptress. I
like the sound of that. Among my classmates at Miss
Thorogate's College in St. Louis, I was voted Student
Most Likely to End up a Domineering Spinster."

Princess was embarrassed by her hasty confession.

Her years at school were not, to her mind, an
unqualified success. Young ladies of good family or
good fortune were taught the vagaries of proper
etiquette and basics of elegant conversation so they
could be appropriate wives for gentlemen of the
upper classes. The words had never been spoken
aloud, but it was her belief that her father had sent
her to St. Louis with the hope that she would find a
suitable young man to marry. It had simply never

happened. In a school of twenty-six well-heeled, privileged females, she had not been the plainest or the poorest. But she was without doubt the least concerned with the importance of elevating her social position. Each time a gentleman made her acquaintance, he was at the same time being introduced to twenty-five more preferable choices.

Princess had not felt disappointed. She had been waiting for her true love, and it was clear to her that he was not one of the gentlemen in St. Louis.

Gerald stopped walking and turned to her inquisitively. "You think of yourself as domineering, Cessy?"

His brow was furrowed and his gaze intense as he stared down at her. Princess felt the flush of embarrassment steal into her cheeks once more. She had made her peace with the reality of herself. Too many years of her youth had been wasted wanting to be someone else. She was exactly the woman that God had intended her to be. She was learning to accept that. She wanted her true love to be able to do the same.

"When I look in my mirror I see a very ordinary female looking back," she told him. "But, in truth, I do not believe that the mirror tells all. God gave me gifts of energy and leadership. I would be failing in my duty not to use them, and there is a whole world around me that seems to require my constant attention."

Gerald was silent for a long moment.

"The mirror is *not* the best judge of a woman," he agreed quietly. "It only reflects the most desultory observation."

"Many women would then ask how on earth are they to determine their worth," she pointed out, inflecting a tone of teasing into the question.

He stepped closer. So close that she need only lean slightly in his direction to press against his chest. The warmth of his nearness enveloped her. The scent of his shaving soap was masculine and enticing. She began to tremble.

"Look into my eyes, Cessy," he whispered. "Is the woman you see there not so very extraordinary?"

She did look up into those unfathomable dark eyes for an instant, but she saw no woman at all. And then he turned his head and brought his lips down upon her own.

SIX

Cedarleg was certainly right in his prediction about his wife. Sadie Pease, known by one and all simply as Ma, should have been extremely unhappy about sharing their living space with a young rig worker she'd never met. But in fact she did take Tom in like a son. She fussed over him. She nagged at him. And she kept his clothes clean and his food hot.

Ma was a short, round little woman. She had never met a stranger. And she loved a good joke. Once she heard one, she told it again and again. She worked with the efficiency of a dynamo. And she did it with a light heart.

The tool pusher's living quarters consisted of a canvas tarp that hung over a pitched frame. It had a pine plank floor and was half walled on three sides. Mosquito netting was hung in the "eaves" and across the front "door." It had an appearance reminiscent of a house, but without much of the protection from weather or privacy that such a structure usually afforded.

Tom's army camp in Cuba had not been quite as spartan or primitive, but Ma seemed to take it all in stride.

"I raised three children in places worse than this," she told Tom proudly. "They was ever' day clean and each one went to school through the sixth grade. I don't require much finery to live. My man's in the oil business and he's dragged me from pillar to post since the day we wed. And if there's anything that I've learned, it's that as soon as you've fixed up a place to really suit you, you're going to have to leave it behind."

Ma cackled at one of her favorite stories. "As soon as you've fixed up a place to really suit you, you're going to have to leave it behind," she repeated.

There was nothing temporary or campish about the way Ma and Cedarleg lived. She'd made a home under the tarp and it was in every way as warm and welcoming as any fine house Tom had ever visited. In many ways more so than the great mansions of Ambrose Dexter and his friends.

Each evening when they arrived from work her floor would be scrubbed to gleaming. Dishes would be set upon the plank table and heaping mounds of mouth-watering food would be hot and ready to eat.

She also kept Tom's courting clothes, as she called them, brushed and ready to go. But she made it clear that she had no high hopes for his future with a Miss Cessy Prin.

"A Burford Corners girl will never do for you," she told him plainly. "She'll be wanting you to settle here, and when a oil worker chooses to settle he's likely to starve."

"Ma," Cedarleg interrupted her. "You was once a town girl yourself."

"So I know what I'm talking about," she insisted. "If you think it's been easy learning to live with you, Winthrop Pease, then you're a fool!"

"Winthrop?" Tom asked, wide-eyed and teasing.

Cedarleg grinned at him. "That's the feller I used to be when I had two legs to my credit."

Ma continued her advice. "I'm just saying that

there are plenty of nice girls in Topknot without the
need for you to go looking over at Burford Corners."

Tom rather liked Ma's advice and attention, even
when she was nagging. There had never really been a
mother figure in his life. Reverend McAfee was the
closest thing to a parent he had ever had. He found
being treated like a son by the Peases to be a very
pleasurable and unexpected bonus.

"Please don't worry about me, Ma," Tom told her.
"I know what I'm doing."

But in truth he was no longer sure that he did.
Every evening he spent with Cessy, learning to like
and admire her as a person. A development that he
clearly had not planned for.

And every day he worked on the rig with Cedarleg.
As he became more skilled he earned the respect of
the men around him. He was learning a lot about the
tool dresser's trade, the oil business, and about the
viability of the well. And, he joked to Cedarleg, he
was learning about mud.

Mud, Tom discovered, was the lifeblood of the oil
drilling. A shallow, man-made pond next to the rig
was kept stirred up and oozing with the stuff. It was
pumped down the drill stem to cool and lubricate the
bit, to flush out the cuttings and create a counterpres-
sure that prevented both annoying cave-ins and dangerous blow outs. Keeping large quantities of the
easily obtainable brown viscous available was part of
Tom's job. And the most cursory glance at his work
clothing indicated as much.

Daily he worked, covered hairline to boot top in
mud. Occasionally he was so splattered with the stuff
that only his white-toothed grin was visible.

He saw Maloof one afternoon while he was in that
very condition. The peddler's eyes had widened at
the sight of him, but he made no comment except to
inquire about his satisfaction with his dress suit. Tom

was a bit disconcerted to be called Tom by the peddler to whom he had introduced himself as Gerald Crane. But the foreign fellow had obviously heard the other workers call him by that name and didn't seem to comprehend the discrepancy.

At the well Tom listened. He learned from the other men and profited from their experience. The Topknot was a salt dome geological formation underneath the ground. Because the salt was less dense than the sedimentary rock that surrounded it, it bulged up toward the top. The bulging created little traps, empty caverns between the rocks. Over time, as gas and oil moved upward through the natural passageways, it settled in these traps. And it was the oilman's business to find these hidden traps and to get the oil out.

Drilling was a new and still-developing technology. And it was fraught with unexpected difficulties. Yet Tom had begun to believe with all certainty, as did the men around him, that there was indeed oil beneath the ground of the Royal Oil field at Topknot. And he caught the fever that all the men seem to share of wanting to be the first to get at it.

For the next six evenings after supper, wearing his fine clothes and having scraped the mud and grease from beneath his nails, he made his way over to the Calhoun Mansion. His first night there had set up a precedent for the ones that followed. He would meet Cessy on the porch. They would take a walk in the sparse, unattractive garden in twilight. They would talk. She told him everything about her life, her parents, her friends, and her days at Miss Thorogate's College. He let her tell him everything about the oil business. He was surprised to discover a lively interest in her father's company and the labor in the fields. He deliberately showed no interest in it at all. He changed the subject every time it came up. Under no circumstances must she ever suspect that he was after a share of Royal Oil or that he spent his days pounding hot bits and backing a driller.

He told her nothing about himself. Nothing of the Methodist Indian Home or Cuba or any of the places in between. When the subject turned to him and his life, he let Gerald do all the talking. He discussed Gerald's views on politics and economics. Gerald's experiences with the family business and Gerald's successes at Yale. And he told her Gerald's hopes and dreams and aspirations.

As twilight turned to full night, he would find an opportunity to kiss her lips. Then they would return to the secluded darkness of the front porch, where they would sit in the swing, snuggle, and spoon.

"It feels so funny when you put your tongue in my mouth," she whispered.

"Funny? Like you're going to burst out laughing?"

"No, no, not like that. Like . . . like a tiny fluttering bird is somehow trapped in my chest trying to get out."

"A bird trapped in your chest? Where in your chest? Here?"

"Oh, Gerald," she answered him breathlessly.

They were sitting in the porch swing, or rather he was sitting in it. She was sitting atop his lap. They were both fully clothed. He had never so much as loosened a button at her collar. But he did allow his hands to follow their inclination, stroking and caressing her.

"When I put my tongue in your mouth I get some strange feelings, too," he admitted teasingly. "But it's not like a bird in my chest. It's more like a tentpole in my trousers."

"Oh!"

Cessy was clearly shocked by his implication. She might have a mannish stance, but her reactions to his enticements were completely feminine. She shifted uneasily upon the aforementioned tentpole and he groaned in pleasure that was near agony.

He stilled her with a hand on her derriere and kissed her again, allowing his tongue to trace the definition of her lips. He nipped her very lightly and she used her own tongue with equal effectiveness.

"You learn too quickly, Cessy Calhoun."

"You taught me everything I know," she replied. "I never imagined that people's mouths could do so many interesting things."

"You don't know the half," he told her as he ran his hand across her bosom. He could feel her nipples raised and stiffened through her clothes. "Wait until I put my mouth here."

Her sharp intake of breath was almost a cry of desperation. "Do it, do it Gerald. Put your mouth there."

"I can't, Cessy," he answered back in a hot, tempting whisper. "I won't. I won't compromise you. We must wait until . . . until . . . oh, Cessy, I'd better go before we do something that you'll regret."

"I would never regret anything with you," she breathed.

"I'd better go."

"Not yet, not yet," she insisted. "Kiss me, Gerald. Kiss me once more."

He did. He kissed her with all the seduction and expertise that he could manage. He kissed her with his whole body, his whole self. He kissed her wholly.

The moan of desire at the back of her throat was a sound akin to beautiful music. It had been like this every night. Every night from the first he had kissed, caressed, and conduced her toward the sensual pleasures. And every night she had been eager and willing to cooperate, even to offer instructions in her own seduction.

"We mustn't. We mustn't do this, Cessy," he told

her as he teased and tantalized the nipple between his fingers, and cupped and clutched the small, firm breast upon which it sat.

He felt her squeeze her thighs together tightly and momentarily he wished that his aching erection was buried firmly between them.

"It's not right, Cessy. It's grievous and I would not lead you astray," he insisted as he teasingly, tantalizingly did just that.

She was squirming atop his lap once more and Tom was enjoying it just a little too much. He clasped her around the waist and set her on her feet, only to stand beside her and pull her into his arms.

"I must leave," he whispered against her neck.

She made a soft sound and pressed her body more firmly against his own. Trailing hot kisses along her neck, interspersed with little love bites, he ran his hands down the length of her back and then clutched her buttocks in his hands and pulled her tightly against his erection.

"Oh, Cessy," he whispered against her ear. "I want you so much. I love you so much. I . . . I have to leave. I have to leave now."

He pulled away from her and stepped back.

"Gerald . . ."

Tom held up his hands as if to ward her off.

"We're playing with fire here, Cessy," he said. "We're playing with fire and I won't have you burned."

Even in the darkness, standing at a distance, he could see that she was trembling, bereft without his arms to hold her.

"I love you, Gerald," she said. "I love you so very much."

"And I love you, Cessy." He hurried down the garden steps and then turned back to blow her a kiss. "Tomorrow evening, Cessy, may I call upon you again tomorrow evening?"

"Yes, oh yes," she answered as she grasped the air, as if catching his kiss and bringing it to her lips. "You must call on me tomorrow."

Tom walked away from her, facing backward as if unable to tear his eyes from the sight of her. When he reached the darkness of the trees where she could no longer see him, he turned and gave a long-suffering sigh.

"Geez," he muttered to himself as he shook his head. "Hard as a brick and aching worse than a sore tooth. I can't keep going on like this."

He made his way with some haste through the edges of the dark, deserted downtown of Burford Corners and the rough noisy saloon district of Topknot and into the oil camp.

"I can't continue doing this," he repeated to himself.

In truth it had only been a week. King Calhoun lingered in St. Louis and Tom took advantage of the opportunity to see the young woman unchaperoned. Every evening after Ma's great meal, he hurried over to Cessy's front porch. He knew that he should make hay while the sun was shining. Of course, he could have made more hay than he had currently.

Cessy Calhoun was passionately in love with him. That was obvious. But even if he had not been able to tell by looking, the woman frankly told him so. She wanted him and seemed to have no compunction to wait for wedding vows. He could have bedded her a week ago. Truth to be told, he could have bedded her the night that he met her.

But something held him back. He wasn't at all sure yet if he should. It was all working out so perfectly. All just as he'd planned. Except she was not as he'd planned. She was not just an oil heiress. Cessy was a person. A person he found that he liked and admired. That should be good. That should be very good. But somehow it was not. He had a strong sense of foreboding. He was certain that there was some kind of trouble ahead.

If he bedded Cessy, then he would have to marry her—only a cad would do otherwise. And he liked her far too much to break her heart. But of course he *wanted* to marry her. And if he decided not to, whether he'd seduced her or not, her heart might well be irreparably broken nonetheless.

These nightly enticements were playing havoc with his sleep and his good humor. It had been a long while since he'd lain spent and satisfied in the arms of a woman. Normally that was no problem. He was fastidious enough to do without female companionship when there was none of the superior kind available. But he had never in his life allowed himself to become sexually aroused night after night with no relief.

"So the million-dollar drill sergeant in skirts is beginning to look good to you, Gerald?" Tom said to himself, snorting with self-disgust.

Tom reached the Pease camp tent, but he hesitated. It was dark and quiet inside. Cedarleg and Ma were both probably sleeping. Exhausted as he was, Tom knew that he was a long way from any rest. If he went in now, he'd toss and turn for another hour at least.

He decided that pacing was a better way to pass the time, and began thoughtfully to walk back and forth along the path in front of the tent.

He liked her. He had to admit that to himself. He actually liked her. She was smart. Not in the book sort of way, he concluded. But she was smart in the way that he was. Cessy was smart about people. Except, of course, about him. She was not at all smart about him. She'd fallen for Gerald like a sapling meeting a buzzsaw.

Yet she was different about that, too. She didn't hanker after Gerald's tales of Yale life and the finer things. She didn't seem impressed about Gerald's family or his social position. She didn't even seem to agree with some of Gerald's most strongly held beliefs about the importance of class structure in upholding the framework of civilization.

Cessy talked about real things. She talked about people's feelings and the way the world worked. She talked about the bright future she wanted, not just for herself and her family. The future she wanted for the folks that she knew, the folks in the oil fields. She talked about life in a way that self-involved Gerald could never understand. She deserved better than Gerald. Certainly she was a spoiled, rich woman with too much money and not enough good sense. But she deserved . . . she deserved . . . well, she deserved better than a deceitful fortune hunter.

"Son, is that you?"

Tom stopped pacing and turned to see Cedarleg emerge from the tent.

"I didn't mean to wake you," Tom said. "I was just not . . . not quite ready for sleep."

Cedarleg chuckled lightly. "That little gal sure keeps you stirred up. Don't you know a working man has got to get some sleep sometime?"

Tom shook his head. "I'll be awake and on the job come morning, don't you worry."

"Oh, I ain't worrying much about that," Cedarleg assured him. "I know you'll be there, but a tired man makes mistakes, and mistakes can be dangerous."

"You may be right," Tom told him. "But if a fellow can't sleep, he can't sleep."

"Oh, I know. It's been a while since I was courting that old gal inside there, but I remember it distinctly," he said. "That Ma'd kiss and cuddle 'til I was near crazy with wanting her. Then her old daddy would call out to her to get into the house. I'd wander home to stare at the ceiling all night and try not to think about the parts that ailed me."

Tom smiled at him. "With the kind of work I'm

doing daytime and seeing Cessy at night, *all* my parts are ailing me."

Cedarleg laughed and clapped him on the back. "Well son, the work is something you'll get used to. And the other, well . . . I suspect in the army you had some acquaintance of goodtime gals."

Tom folded his arms across his chest. "I met a couple," he admitted.

"Well, Mr. Calhoun's coming home on the train tomorrow evening. I'll be going over to meet with him at Queenie's Palace, the finest sporting place in Topknot."

Tom raised a curious eyebrow.

"You can come with me," Cedarleg told him. "I'll introduce you to Queenie and maybe she can set you up with one of her gals. Just to kindy take the edge off of things and get you a good night's sleep."

Tom nodded, but he was not thinking about Queenie or her gals. King Calhoun was returning tomorrow.

The awning striped surrey made slow and difficult passage through the narrow, uneven alleyways of the oil camp. Howard appeared unhappy and ill at ease in the primitive surroundings. Princess smiled and waved as she went calling out greetings to old friends that welcomed her.

Princess laughed and chatted with animation. She was so happy. So very happy, at last. She had waited all her life for that one man, that one man who could truly love her, and it had finally happened.

Discreetly she opened her alligator pocketbook and retrieved the card she carried inside it. Already it showed the wear of a hundred caresses and more than a few kisses. But once more Princess drew her fingers gently across the raised gold letters. GERALD TARKINGTON CRANE, BEDLINGTON, NEW JERSEY. It was all she could do not to shout her joy out to the world.

"I think this is it," she said as she directed Howard to the group of more spacious and better-constructed tents.

The sounds of the horses brought the "lady of the house" to the entrance, where she made an immediate declaration of delight.

"Princess! It's so good to see you. It's been an age."

Alighting from the vehicle, she was immediately wrapped in warm, loving arms.

"I've missed you, Ma," Princess told her. "I know how busy Cedarleg is on the rig, but *you* could come visit me."

"And I've been meaning to," Ma said. "I've really been meaning to. Cedarleg has brought a young feller home from the rig who's got no money nor no one and he's been staying with us. Tending for two men has kept me pretty busy."

"I certainly hope you're not letting some freeloader take advantage of you," Princess said.

"Don't you think I'm a little old to worry about fellahs takin' advantage?" Ma cackled at her own joke.

Princess shook her head. "You simply do not need to take on any more youngsters to raise," she pointed out.

Ma laughed. "Look who's talking. The little gal that finds employment for every sick or stuck or stray feller in the oil fields. And I hear you're wearing ruts in the road visiting out at that orphanage."

"I only try to help those that really deserve a chance," Princess insisted. "And I sure don't take anyone in and make them part of the family."

Ma's eyes widened. "Except maybe for Howard here."

They both looked up toward the driver who took his position much too seriously to join them in laughter, but nodded in agreement.

"I can return for you in an hour, Miss Calhoun," he said.

"That will be fine," Princess assured him. As he turned the team, she spoke to Ma once more. "I just don't want you to overwork yourself."

Ma laughed. "Oh, don't worry, this fellah is already grown and not long for this tent nohow. He's got him some little gal in Burford Corners that he goes to see every night. Love's done knocked him a blow straight to the head and that ringing in his ears is bound to be wedding bells."

Ma laughed again, enjoying the sound of that. "The ringing in his ears is bound to be wedding bells," she repeated.

Princess couldn't help but chuckle at the description.

"Come in, come in," Ma said. "I've got no coffee nor lemonade to offer you. But the springwater is cool and fine to drink. Remember that water in Gladys City?"

Princess wrinkled her nose in distaste. "Sulphur. It's awful living in a place where everybody and every living thing smells like rotten eggs."

Ma chuckled in agreement and held open the canvas door flap so that Princess could step inside. She looked around and nodded in undisguised approval.

"It looks great in here, Ma. I don't know how you do it. No matter where you are or what the place looks like, you always make it seem like home."

Ma made her way to the water bucket and dipped out two cups full. She set the cups upon a tray and served them at the table as if they were an elegant aperitif.

"This place seems like home because it is," she explained. "A woman can wait all her life for things to be different, for her circumstances to be better.

Then find out when she's old that her time was
simply wasted in waiting. Home for me is wherever
my man is. I ain't got no call for looking 'round and
whining, 'That woman over there is living finer than
me.' There's plenty that live finer. But they's a goodly
number that would think my tight little dry tent a
paradise on earth."

Princess smiled at her as she accepted the tin cup of
cool water.

"I think it's the love here inside that keeps it so
tight and dry," she said.

Ma laughed. "Well, some of that, some of that
indeed. But you keep a good place yourself," she said.
"Just naturally organized and intent on your ways. I
recall when you was no bigger than a minute and
doing for your daddy like you was full grown."

"Those were good times," Princess admitted. "But
I don't long for them. I wouldn't go back. I love my
little house. I love planting flowers and being able to
know that I'll be around when they come up to
bloom. I love the feeling of putting down roots and
stretching them out in the soil. And I love the school.
It's clean, it's new, it's modern. I feel like we're really
beginning to do important work there. When Daddy
moves on, as he always does, I'll be staying here."

Ma nodded thoughtfully. "Well, honey, we wish
you well and we'll surely miss you."

"You know I still want you to stay. I think it would
be a wonderful job for Cedarleg. He's so good with
the boys, and it's not nearly as dangerous as tool
pushing."

Ma shook her head. "It's hard for him to quit the
drilling rigs," she said. "Once getting oil out of the
ground gets in your blood, well it's hard to let go of it.
Even when you're getting a little too old and a little
too crippled to do it anymore."

Princess patted her hand lovingly. "I want you to

stay, but I do understand if you go. I will expect you to come and visit me from time to time."

"Of course we will," Ma assured her. "It can be a pretty lonely life for you, living all alone."

Princess's heart lifted and she felt a blush warm her cheeks. "I may not be alone," she said.

Ma nodded. "I heard that Muna is got her a man? Some foreign fellah her daddy done brought over," she said. "They going to settle down right here, you're thinking."

"Well, that would be wonderful," Princess admitted. "Although I can't say that I am really excited about her engagement. It's an arranged marriage."

Ma shook her head. "Them foreigners, they do that," she said. "But I've seen plenty of happy marriages among them."

"Well," Princess insisted. "It might be fine for people from other countries, but Muna has grown up here. She's an American woman. And she wants what every American woman wants. To marry the man of her own choosing. The man she loves."

"Did Muna tell you that?"

"No, of course not," Princess answered. "You know how she is with her parents. She would never go against their wishes."

"Then that *is* her choice, honey," Ma told her. "And you'd do well to stay out of it."

"But I can't bear to think of my dear Muna never knowing love," Princess lamented.

Ma waved away her tragic tone. "Love is all different kinds of things at all different times," she said. "We cain't never know what it is to someone else."

"I know what it is," Princess said quietly. "And it is the most wonderful feeling in the world. Nobody should ever have to live without it."

Ma raised an eyebrow and gave her a long look. "What's this?" she asked.

"I think . . . no . . . no, I am, I *am* in love, Ma."

"Land a-mercy and I'm just now hearing about it!" the older woman exclaimed. "Tell me, tell me. Who is this fellah and when do I get to meet him?"

"Oh Ma, he's . . . well he's every thing I ever dreamed about and nothing like I ever imagined."

"Where'd you meet him?"

"In my own backyard! He was at the Fourth of July picnic."

"Wouldn't you know it," Ma complained. "The first time I've missed that shindig in years and somebody interesting finally shows up."

Princess laughed. "I just saw him and, oh, Ma, I just knew, I just knew immediately that he was the one."

"Just like that?"

"Just like that. And he knew, too. It was, it was just so perfect, so wonderful."

"And he's wonderful?"

Princess nodded. "Yes, yes he is. I don't know how or why I even think so. The truth is the more I get to know him, the more I really wonder what we might ever have in common. But when we are together it just seems so right."

"Well, opposites can attract," Ma assured her. "Sometimes two very different kinds of people can make a pair that's much stronger together than two more alike persons could ever be."

"He's so very different from anyone I've ever known. He is far from ignorant. He's thoughtful and fair. Yet sometimes he says things that just seem positively wooden-headed."

Ma snorted good-naturedly. "I cain't imagine that you'd let him get away with that?"

Princess shook her head. "You know I can't. Daddy always says that my high opinion of my own opinions is my only vanity."

"So you tell him to his face that he's a woodenhead?"

"Pretty much. I openly disagree with him," she said.

"And how does he take it?"

"Very well," Princess answered. "In fact, almost too well. He doesn't take it personally at all. It's almost as if his opinions are not even his own."

"That is pretty curious."

"It is. It is curious," Princess agreed. "It's almost as if there is a shallowness to him. But somehow he is not shallow. Somehow there is depth to him and beneath that he's wonderful. I'm just sure of it."

Ma eyed her skeptically. "Well, tell me about him. I don't aim to let you take up with any old worthless roustabout."

"Oh you would definitely approve of him, Ma," Princess assured her. "And he's certainly no worthless roustabout. He's . . . well, he's . . . he's sort of a remittance man."

"A remittance man?"

Princess nodded. "His name is Gerald Crane and he's from back East. He's been raised in wealth and privilege. His family was in the publishing business back when Benjamin Franklin was their competitor."

"Land a-mercy, what's such a fellah doing here?"

"He came out West to join up with the Rough Riders, and he just stayed," Princess said.

"Rough Riders?" Ma looked thoughtful. "Tom was in the Rough Riders. Wonder if he knows this fellah?"

"Tom?"

"The young man that's staying here," she answered. "So what does this Gerald feller do now?"

"Well, honestly, Ma, I don't think that he does anything."

The older woman looked surprised.

"Everybody's got to do something."

Princess shook her head. "Rich people don't. If they don't need the money, well, they just take up some avocation like art or writing or some such."

"So what's this fellah's *avocation?*" she asked. "Top-knot ain't the kind of place where a person might take up writing or art. He's got to have some reason for being here."

"Why, honestly, I don't think he has one, Ma," Princess admitted. "He seems to just be wandering the country meeting people and seeing new things."

Ma tutted with disapproval. "I don't like the sound of that, honey."

"He just needs a direction. He just needs a little nudge," Princess assured her. "A woman can give that to a man. You know she can. And I am certainly the kind of woman to do it."

Ma nodded. "A woman *can* give a little nudge," she agreed. "And she can also spend her whole life pushing against a stubborn wall that ain't about to be moved. What makes you think this fellah is for you? Apart from that he don't seem to mind your ways?"

"I . . . well, I just knew."

"This is your ol' Ma Pease, Princess," the woman said. "Tell me the truth of it."

She hesitated a moment, partly embarrassed, partly unsure. "Well, I saw him and I . . . I just went all like jelly inside. Hot jelly, like just ready for the jars. He's . . . he's really handsome and I saw him and I thought, well, I guess I thought he would never notice me. But he did, Ma. He walked right over to me and wanted to talk to me and dance with me. Ma, he kissed me that very first night," she whispered.

Ma nodded sagely. "And a few times since then, I've no doubt. He's really handsome you say."

"Yes, he is handsome," Princess told her. "I was surprised at how handsome he was. I didn't expect . . . well, I didn't *require* that a man be quite so attractive to suit me."

"Good looks and money, too," Ma commented. "It's a miracle that some gal hadn't snagged onto him already."

"I know you don't believe in this, Ma, but I believe he and I were destined for each other."

"Oh, honey, when you're talking about men, don't ever even whisper the words *fate* or *destiny*," Ma scolded. "A woman can get herself into all kinds of trouble that way. You've got to make a choice with your head. Clear contemplation and far thinking will set a straighter course than relying on happenstance."

"But what about love?"

"People don't always love where they should."

"No, I don't guess they do," Princess agreed. "But they love wherever they can."

Ma laughed then. "So for all that you're given orders and directing your friends to and fro, when it comes to menfolk you're no smarter than the rest of us weak women," she said.

Princess shook her head.

"So where do you see this remittance man?" Ma asked.

"He comes to visit me every evening," Princess said.

Ma's brow furrowed. "With your daddy gone?"

"We stay on the porch," Princess assured her. "We just walk a little bit in the garden and then sit on the porch."

The older woman didn't appear pleased. "I don't suspect you're playing Parcheesi on that darkened porch," she said.

Princess blushed guiltily.

"How far has it gone?"

"We . . . well, we . . . Ma, I plan to marry him."

"Has he asked ye?"

"Well, no, not yet, but Ma I know—"

"Honey, I know a lot about men. And I'm telling

you that even the best ones are up to no good every chance they get."

"Gerald's not like that, Ma," she said. "I'm sure he's not like that. We love each other."

"Maybe so, but it wouldn't hurt to check this fellah out. If he really cares for you, he'll want to meet your daddy and court you properly."

"Of course that's what he wants," Princess assured her. "Daddy has just been out of town. Now that he's back, I'm sure Gerald will commence calling upon me in a more traditional manner."

"Well, I hope so," Ma said. "And if this Gerald feller is what you want, then I pray that he's everything that you want him to be."

"Thank you."

"I'm just sorry that you didn't get to meet Tom."

"Who?"

"Tom, the young fellah that we've taken on."

Princess nodded, recalling Ma's latest stray.

"He's a nice feller, fine looking, hard worker, got good manners. I thought to myself when I met him, this fellah would do right well for our Princess. But it's too late now, I suspect."

"Yes," Princess agreed. "I don't think I could ever care for anyone the way I care for Gerald."

SEVEN

The smell of stale beer and honest sweat permeated the dark, narrow clapboard building with the rather auspicious name of Queenie's Palace. Tom walked in by himself. He'd needed to find a boy to deliver a message to Cessy. He couldn't have her waiting all evening for him to arrive on her porch. But he couldn't afford to visit on her porch and ignore the information that he was undoubtedly to find out tonight.

The place was not busy since it was two nights before payday. Most of the oil field workers were already broke. There was no need to come out to a joint without money. The beer and bootleg were never sold on credit. And even if a fellow was not inclined to follow on the line upstairs, it took cold, hard cash to dance, drink, or even talk with one of the gals.

The walls and floor of the rough saloon were all raw planking, not even a covering of whitewash to brighten the place. More than a dozen brilliantly colored paintings of every size and subject hung on the walls. Tom glanced at the signature on the one nearest him. Tommy Mathis was apparently the favorite artist of the whorehouse/beer joint.

In the far corner an old man in a scraggly straw hat

banged out ragtime tunes on a upright player, as three or four couples weaved drunkenly on the floor to the rhythm of the music.

Cedarleg was having a word with a woman at the bar. As soon as he spotted Tom he waved him over and met him halfway, handing him a beer.

"Find a boy to send your message?"

Tom nodded. "A nickel the little fellow wanted. When I was a boy, I'd have run a note from here to Guthrie for five mils."

Cedarleg shrugged. "A half a penny don't go near as far as it used to." The older man directed him toward a table. "So you grew up around here, did ye?"

Tom momentarily blanched. He had not realized he'd admitted so much. "I . . . I grew up not far from here. Up on Shemmy Creek."

"The Methodist Indian Home?" Cedarleg asked.

"How'd you know that?"

"I know the place. You said you have no family," Cedarleg replied. "You got that Indian look about ye."

"Yes, I grew up there." He hesitated and then looked over at Cedarleg with pointed defiance.

The older man nodded. "You got a headright?"

"What? No," Tom answered. "My mother was white. She left me there when I was a baby. Guess she got herself mixed up with an Indian or maybe she was raped, I don't know. I don't even know her name, I just know that I should have never been born."

Tom heard the anger in his own voice and silently cursed himself for revealing so much. He never let it out, those feelings he kept very deeply buried.

"You should've never been born? Good Lord, where'd you get an idea like that?" Cedarleg asked, astounded.

"Isn't that what most people would believe about a part-breed bastard?" he asked.

Cedarleg shook his head. "If you'd not a-been born, poor old Bob Earlie'd be crippled or dead now. And Ma and I woulda missed getting to know ye."

"I'm not wishing I wasn't here," Tom assured him.

Cedarleg shook his head. "But you sure got a sad attitude as to why. It's like that old song they sing at church, 'Everybody's got a place in God's choir.'"

Tom shrugged. "But some people have better places than others."

"Son, you need to give up that kind of wrong thinking," Cedarleg told him. "You're a grown man now. You're near to marry up with that little town gal you got. And you'll have boys of your own soon. I believe every child deserves to think well of its daddy. I'm sorry for you that you can't. But if you don't think well of yourself, your younguns won't be able to, neither."

Tom looked over at his friend. His heart felt suddenly open, almost raw. He pushed the feeling away forcefully. When he answered, his voice was harsh with anger.

"Don't worry about me, old man," he said. "One of these days I'll have so much money the whole world will respect me."

Cedarleg's eyes widened and he gave a chuckle. "You planning to get rich, are ye? Well, I'm glad I met you now before you got too important for me to know."

Tom realized immediately how belligerent he sounded. He meant to smooth it over, but the arrival of King Calhoun precluded that.

The big man entered not from the street, but from the doorway at the back of the bar. Apparently he had been upstairs, and appeared casual in his shirt-sleeves. A very good-looking, buxom blonde was on his arm. She was brightly painted up with a big, welcoming smile, and everyone who nodded deferentially at Calhoun grinned warmly at her.

Tom watched as the two made their way to the table. They looked strangely right together. It was almost as if the image of the hard, portly businessman was improved by the fast-looking female at his side.

"I'll just move to this next table and leave you two alone," he told Cedarleg.

"I'll introduce you, you'll like Calhoun," Cedarleg said. "He's a straight-shooter and as down-to-earth a man as you'll ever know."

"No, I don't want to meet him," Tom said. "I'll just sit over here by myself, take no notice of me."

Cedarleg looked at him curiously. "Never realized you were shy, son," he said.

Tom didn't comment. He moved to a chair facing away from Cedarleg at the next table. He would still be able to hear, he hoped, but would not attract the attention of his employer

He could not meet King Calhoun as Tom Walker. Not if Gerald was to marry the man's daughter. As soon as he had Cessy saying "I do," Tom would have to disappear from the face of the earth. Certainly it would be risky. A lot of men who worked for Calhoun knew him as Walker. But maybe he and Cessy would not take an active interest in the business. He'd let Calhoun handle the day-to-day workings of the oil business and he would just bask in the wealth and luxury that it could provide. He regretted losing the chance to talk face-to-face with Calhoun. He was very intrigued with the oil business and wished he could have the opportunity to find out more. But marriage to Cessy was the most important part of his plan. And she was to marry Gerald Crane. So her father couldn't have so much as a passing word with Tom Walker.

"Evenin' Mr. Calhoun, Queenie." Tom heard Cedarleg's greeting and the scrape of his chair as the old man rose to his feet. "It's good to have you back in town, King."

"It's good to be back," Calhoun answered. "I hate them damned bankers with a passion."

Cedarleg made a noise that sounded like agreement. "Ye cain't trust 'em further than you can throw 'em. And an old fellah like me cain't throw 'em very far these days."

They all laughed. The sound of Cedarleg's humor was familiar. Calhoun's was a deep bass chuckle. And the woman's was a throaty little giggle that was somehow lush and feminine at the same time.

"You boys just go ahead and talk about business," she said to the men. "I know you're just dying to get your heads together about drill bits or limestone formations and I'll leave you to it. Besides I've got some introductions to make."

There was a light slapping sound that Tom interpreted as Calhoun patting the woman on the backside. He kept his eyes on his beer, all his concentration centered on listening to the conversation at the next table.

For that reason, he was startled when a female arm came around his shoulder and the woman he knew to be King Calhoun's Queenie leaned down beside him.

Up close, she was a bit older than he'd thought. She was probably in her mid-thirties. Her heavy face makeup was garish, but there was something about the genuineness of her person that was welcoming. In that second, Tom felt that in some way he'd known her all his life. That was undoubtedly how other people responded to her, also. It was a very fortunate trait for a woman in her business, or any business for that matter.

"Are you Cedarleg's tool dresser?" she asked.

He stared at her mutely, praying that Calhoun was not looking in their direction. He nodded slightly.

"Do you have a name?"

Tom hesitated. His face was still turned away from Calhoun, but he didn't want his future father-in-law to even hear of Tom Walker in passing.

"I'll just call you Tool Dresser," Queenie said with a warm smile, as if she was quite used to fellows who didn't wish to identify themselves.

She reached over and took Tom's hand.

"Let's go to the back," she said. "There's somebody I'd like you to meet."

He looked at her in disbelief.

"Come on, Tool Dresser," she said. "I don't bite. And even if I did, I wouldn't bite a good-looking young fellow like you."

She laughed that little throaty giggle at her own joke and continued to tug on his arm. Tom felt he had no option but to follow her.

He rose to his feet, deliberately keeping his back to the other table, and stepped sideways to avoid even giving a hint of his profile to the man behind him.

Queenie seemed to accept his strange behavior as reticence. As they made their way to the back, she took his arm and patted his hand as if offering comfort.

"Cedarleg tells me you've been on edge the last few days," she said.

Tom felt they'd covered a far enough distance that he could give a surreptitious glance back toward Calhoun's table. Neither he nor Cedarleg were paying any attention to him. That was good. But the two were going to discuss business, and he was not going to be there to hear it. He needed to get loose from the woman beside him and get back out there somehow.

She led him into the hallway next to the stairs.

"Ma'am, I really appreciate this but I don't think . . ."

"You got the dog, Tool Dresser?" she asked him casually.

"What?"

"You got the dog? It makes no difference. We got gals that got it and gals that don't. I just try to match people up."

"I . . . I don't have a venereal disease," Tom answered.

"Don't now, or didn't never?" Queenie asked.

"Never," he answered.

"Good, that's real good," she said. "Some of the young men straight from the farm, they think it makes them more manly to have it. But it ain't no bargain to my mind. I don't care how much spirit of niter or arsenicals you take, once you got it you pretty much always got it. And you only got to hear those poor fellows screaming while they piss to appreciate that it ain't something a man can much enjoy."

"Miss Queenie, I—"

"You just call me Queenie, everybody does," she interrupted. "I'm going to set you up with Frenchie. She's my best and I know she'll take a real shine to you."

"Queenie, I don't . . ."

"Don't worry about the money," she said. "I owe Cedarleg a couple of favors, and Ma would skin me alive if I was to try to fix him up with some of my gals."

"No, it's not the money, it's just that . . ."

Queenie paid no attention to him.

"Frenchie! Frenchie, come meet Tool Dresser."

Tom turned toward the woman who was hurrying down the stairs. She was too heavily made up for him to determine her age. She was short, a little stubby, and rather dark complexioned. Her very long and thick hair hung loose down her back and was the strangest color of red that Tom had ever seen. It obviously had its origins in a dye bottle.

When she reached the second stair on the landing, she leaned forward to grab Tom by the shoulders and gave him an exuberant kiss.

"Oh, precious!" she exclaimed. "You're so good-looking, I'd do you for free."

"Don't let that go to your head, Tool Dresser," Queenie said beside him. "Frenchie'd just about do everybody for free."

The young woman gave her boss an unhappy glare and wrinkled her nose mischievously.

"That's what she was up to when I found her," Queenie said.

"Oh, pooh, don't listen to her," Frenchie told him. "Come on up to my room and I'll make you feel like you're the only man for me in the whole wide world."

"Uh, Frenchie I . . ."

Tom turned back to Queenie to explain. She just grinned at him and patted him encouragingly upon the back. "Go ahead, you two. Have a big time. Cedarleg wants you to get a good night's rest, Tool Dresser. And Frenchie can sure make that possible. Just don't fall asleep in her bed. She's got a living to make."

Grabbing the fly button on his overalls, Frenchie led Tom, muttering and mostly mute, up the stairs and into the first doorway at the top. Safely inside, she shut the sounds of the barroom out and wrapped herself tightly against him.

"What was you hoping for, precious?" she asked. "You want a basic easyover, or maybe something a little more snappy?"

"There's been a little misunderstanding, Frenchie," he said. "I am not looking for any female companionship this evening."

"Oh, now, precious," she coaxed, rubbing her bosom up against him enticingly. "Don't get scared on me. Is it your first time? I love first timers. I always give 'em a two-for-one."

Tom ran his hand appreciatively through the strangely colored hair that hung down her back.

"It's not my first time," he said. "Although I have not had much experience with ladies on the line."

"With your good looks and sweet ways, I bet you never had to," she answered.

Tom didn't reply to that.

"You're very pretty and quite tempting, Frenchie," he told her. "But I'm . . . well, I'm involved with a young woman right now. And I just wouldn't feel right about . . . about enjoying your time."

"She'll never know," Frenchie assured him. "At Queenie's Palace we are very discreet."

"I would know," Tom said quietly.

"Well, I can get you off with my mouth. It's what I'm best at. They don't call me Frenchie cause I'm from France," she joked. "And the good girls don't do that, so it don't count as being unfaithful."

"For me it counts," Tom told her quietly.

Frenchie stepped back then and folded her arms across her chest with a look of disgust. "Well, damn," she complained good-naturedly. "And you're so pretty, too. I'll go downstairs and the ugliest old coot in town will have his money on the table asking for a double-dip, around-the-world with a topper."

Tom grinned at her, grateful not to be obliged to argue further. He dug into his pockets. For him it was two days until payday, also. And he'd given his last nickel to have the note delivered to Cessy.

"I've only got four cents," he told her.

"You don't owe me nothing," Frenchie said. "Worse luck that. Anyway, Queenie don't let me handle the money. She says I loan out more than I take in. You settle up with her. But be sure and tell her that I didn't even get your pants off."

"Thanks."

He opened the door and Frenchie called out to him. "If that gal of yours don't do you right, you come back this way now."

She ran the tip of her tongue around the line of her lips seductively and Tom paused momentarily at the sight, swallowing down purely physical desire.

"Good-bye, Frenchie," he said and left before the remnants of his better judgement deserted him.

He was genuinely surprised at himself. It had been a good long while since he'd enjoyed the pleasure of a woman. And it seemed almost stupid to turn down what was so generously offered. But somehow it did seem wrong. He'd been kissing and cuddling on Cessy's front porch every night for the last week. It would be wrong, very wrong to spend his first evening away from her in the arms of another woman.

At the bottom of the stairs one of the Palace's other girls spotted him and smiled hopefully.

"Where's Queenie?" he asked her.

The woman's face registered disappointment and she pointed mutely toward the back door.

As he made his way in that direction, he passed a huge, dangerous-looking cowboy who gave him a threatening perusal. Tom was momentarily taken aback until he heard the sounds coming from the doorway beneath the stairs, the click of the wheel, the rattle of dice. Queenie was running gambling in the back room. And this formidable man watching the door was the lookout.

"I'm just trying to find Queenie, I need to settle up," he said.

The fellow gave a jerky indication with his thumb toward the Palace's back door.

Tom made his way past the cowboy outside and into the dark, deserted alley behind the building. The noise from the joint was muted here. That was probably why he heard Queenie before he saw her.

She was bent over double, retching miserably. Tom hurried to her side.

"Are you all right, Queenie?" he asked.

She straightened with guilty haste.

"I'm fine!" she declared, one moment before she fainted.

Tom caught her. Immediately, surprised and scared, he turned to call back to the Palace, but knew that no one would hear him over the boisterous noise and the twangy piano. He slipped an arm under her knees and carried her over to the pump and water trough near the corner of the building.

She was already coming around as he dampened his handkerchief. He set the cool cloth against her forehead.

"Are you better now?" he asked.

She sat up, looking around curiously. "What happened?"

"You fainted."

Queenie laughed lightly, without humor. "A gal never has her smelling salts when she needs them."

She tried to get up. Tom was instantly at her side.

"You're ill," he said.

"It's just something I ate," she assured him. "What are you doing down here. Thought I left you with Frenchie. Didn't you like her?"

"I'm sure she's wonderful," Tom said. "A couple of years ago, I wouldn't have hesitated to enjoy her completely. But for all that I'm not sleeping too well, I . . . I am courting a young lady."

"Is that so? Courting ain't married, Tool Dresser. And most fellahs think that what the gal don't know won't hurt her."

"I'm not willing to risk it," Tom told her. "In some ways I think I've been given a chance to start over

again. And I would feel . . . well, I wouldn't feel right
about indulging myself."

"What do you mean you've been given a chance to
start over?" she asked.

"I guess I just got tired of the road I've been seeing
ahead of me, so I've decided to change my future."

"You make it sound like it's downright easy, Tool
Dresser," she said.

He snorted and chuckled lightly. "Well, it helps a
bit if you can just throw away your old past and start
out with a brand-new one, cut exactly to fit."

Queenie looked at him a long moment and smiled.

"What's your name, Tool Dresser?" she asked.

"Tom, Tom Walker," he answered.

"I'm going to remember you, Tom Walker," she
said. "You're going to make something of yourself in
this world."

"I certainly hope so, ma'am," he replied.

"And you are a genuinely decent fellow. I like that
in a man."

They had reached the back door. She handed his
wet handkerchief back to him.

"Are you going to be all right? Do you want me to
get someone for you?" he asked.

"No," she answered. "And Tool Dresser, keep
what you saw to yourself. I don't want anybody
worrying about me."

He raised his eyebrows. "What I saw? Why, I didn't
see anything. I just came back here to settle up with
you. I didn't take what Cedarleg set up for me, but I
did waste some of the young lady's time."

"I'd say we're square, Tool Dresser.

He nodded to her and headed back into the barroom alone. There were more people than before.
The music was louder, the dancers drunker.

Determinedly he began to work his way back
across the room to where he'd left Cedarleg and

Calhoun in deep discussion. He had missed sparking with Cessy tonight for a purpose. He was here to learn about Calhoun's business. Finally he could see the table where the two had been seated. Cedarleg sat there alone. Tom's heart sank and he sighed with momentary disappointment.

When he reached the table he dragged out a chair and sat down, offering a smile to his friend.

"That was damn quick, son," Cedarleg stated flatly. "As you get older, you might learn to make it last a while."

He chuckled at his little joke, and Tom laughed with him.

"I thank you for the offer, Cedarleg," he said. "But I just didn't feel right about it."

The old man nodded as if he understood. "You got lipstick on your mouth," he said.

Tom pulled out his damp handkerchief and wiped the evidence away.

It was Princess herself who hurried to the front door when the little boy pounded on the knocker. She was eagerly awaiting Gerald and disappointed that it wasn't him.

Her day had been busy. After her long, thought-provoking visit with Ma, she'd had Howard drive her out to the school to check on the construction of the machine shop building. It was nearly completed and looking as fine and functional as any such building she had ever seen. It was exciting to see it go up. And would be even more so when the machinery and the boiler engine arrived. Princess could hardly wait.

Of course, despite her protests, the dear old school-master had risen from his sickbed to greet her himself. He simply could not allow her to get away without a couple of bushels of fresh-picked sweet corn.

She and Howard had been helping the cook shuck sweet corn on the back step ever since they got home. Princess didn't have to help, but she always did. She loved the comradery of working on a task with other people and she didn't mind the work. But she hated picking up what would appear to be a perfect ear of corn and pulling down the outside husk to find one of those fat, awful, green corn worms hiding inside.

"Well, good evening, young man," she said to the child on her doorstep.

He held his grubby hand toward her, a piece of paper tucked securely in his fist.

"A fellah at the Palace in Topknot give me this."

Princess took the note from him, but looked disapproving.

"The Palace is not a nice part of Topknot for a little boy to see," she said sternly. "What would your mother think about you being in such a place?"

The little boy shrugged. "Mama does dime-a-dance at the Redhead Driller," he answered.

Princess didn't like the answer. She opened the door more widely. "Then you probably have not yet had supper," she said. Glancing up, she saw Howard hurrying in her direction.

"Take this young man back to the kitchen," she said. "And tell Mrs. Marin that he will have something to eat."

The boy's eyes were wide, but before he allowed himself to be led away he turned to her once more.

"That'll be a nickel for the delivery," he said, indicating the note.

Howard looked angry and ready to speak, but Princess forestalled him.

"The same price as Western Union?" she asked, tutting with disapproval. But she found a nickel in her pocketbook and gave it to him.

He bit down on it to insure himself that it was real

and then willingly followed Howard back to the kitchen.

Princess looked down at the note in her hand. She opened it, assuming it was from her father. He wired her earlier that he intended to return on the evening train. He was undoubtedly down at the saloon in Topknot visiting his . . . his female friend and was merely sending word that he would arrive home late.

When she saw Gerald's signature at the bottom, it set her heart to racing.

Deliberately she refolded it and clasped it against her chest.

Princess walked to the quiet solitude of the sun parlor. She seated herself in good light and then drew off her spectacles and methodically cleaned them of any film or dust. She had just, she decided, received her first love letter. It was the first written communication between herself and the man with whom she hoped to spend her life. At Miss Thorogate's she'd read some of the letters that John and Abigail Adams had exchanged. And the beautiful correspondence exchanged between Robert and Elizabeth Barrett Browning. Here in her hand were the words of her John Adams, her Robert Browning. And she was both elated and anxious that it would not live up to her expectations.

Finally she unfolded the note and held it open before her.

My own dear Cessy, it began. *I can not visit you this evenun as an herjent matter of business has come up. As I am sirten you know, I wood be there if I could.*

Her brow furrowed in curiosity.

"Yale?" she whispered aloud to herself.

I am hoping to see you on Sunday. Maybe we could go for a picknick on the river and spend the afternoon together.

The letter was poorly written and plagued with

spelling errors. Surely, a graduate of Yale, even one whose main interest was athletics, would be capable of composing a grammatical note.

I herd that your father is back in town. I think that you should not say inny thing about me to him yet.

That suggestion momentarily took her aback. She had never tried to conceal anything from her father. And she was quite certain that Daddy was going to just love Gerald. How could he not?

As always you hold my heart with your own. Gerald

Princess continued to stare at the letter for a long time, her original thoughts about love letters completely forgotten. A strange, niggling feeling of discomfort remained unsettled inside her.

Someone wrote it for him, she suggested to herself. He was busy with some . . . some undisclosed business and had to dictate the note to a less educated man. Some man in Topknot.

In truth, that was not an appealing thought either. That her beloved Gerald should have trusted words so personal to some other person was unthinkable.

But a graduate of Yale, a gentleman with apparent great interest in human nature and social concerns, who spoke as if he were widely read in those subjects as well as many others, would not, could not, be so uneducated as to create the note that she held in her hand.

Princess sat silent in the sun parlor. Her mind trying to fly in a hundred different directions. Her heart pounding as if she had just run up a hill. She pulled her thoughts tightly together, resisting panic.

"I love him," she whispered.

She glanced down, puzzled, at the note once more.

"That is all that matters."

EIGHT

Queenie was lying on the bed, staring at the ceiling, and thinking. She was wearing only the black washing silk chemise that King had brought her from St. Louis. Even without her corset, her body was still shapely and youthful. She ran her hands along her unbound bosom. Her breasts were somewhat swelled and slightly sore. She moved her hands downward, surveying her body. Her waist was still attractively narrow and her abdomen was firm and flat.

The door creaked as it opened and King Calhoun walked in as if he owned the place. He glanced down at her thoughtfully for a long moment.

"Darlin', is your man so distracted and worthless that you've got to touch yourself?"

Slowly, seductively, she grinned at him.

"If I remember correctly, mister," she said teasingly, "you used to like watching me touch myself."

"Queenie, darlin', I just like watching *you*," he said.

King dropped a knee beside her on the mussed sheeting and lay down full-length on top of her body. He was big and heavy and the weight of him pressed her deeply into the mattress.

So naturally her hands came up to caress his shoulders and then her arms wound around his neck.

"Ummm, darlin'," he said. "This is the most comfortable bed I ever owned."

She spread her legs slightly and wrapped her
ankles around his shanks.

"The most comfortable part of it, you don't own,"
she told him. "I'm just lending it to you."

"I hope it's a long-term lease," he said. "A man
could grow mighty fond of this."

She kissed him then. It was a long, lazy kiss. A
sublimely satisfying meeting of mouths, oft practiced
and mutually enjoyed.

When their lips parted, he looked down into her
eyes warmly. Queenie knew that in his own way, he
loved her.

"Am I smashing you?" he asked her.

She shook her head. "It feels good," she told him.
"I missed my King."

"I missed you, too, darlin'," he admitted, and then
grinned. "I suspect you figured that out from the five-
minute, not-so-fun you got earlier."

She shrugged with unconcern. "It was all right,"
she told him quietly. "You don't have to make it a
miracle for me every time, like I was some haughty
empress."

"You're not an empress," he answered. "You're a
queen, my queen, and I want to be good for you
whenever we're together."

"It takes two for that, King and I'm . . ." Queenie
hesitated. "I'm not quite myself."

"It's not you, darlin'," King insisted. "It's me.
Times are getting tough, Queenie. Those bankers in
Saint Louis wouldn't give me a thin dime."

"Oh, King, I'm so sorry."

"I talked to Cedarleg tonight," he continued.
"We'll be pumping oil from those rigs in the next
couple of weeks. Without a refinery it won't be worth
nothing."

"Two weeks? Are you sure?"

King shook his head. "You know the damned oil deposits. There ain't never nothing sure. But that oil is down there. I know it. We could hit it tomorrow or we might have to go down another hundred feet. But without a refinery to pump it to, we might as well just stop the work right now this minute."

"My offer to lend you what I have is still open," she said. "It's not much, King, but I'd bet every cent of it on you."

He made a tutting sound of disapproval. "I've been pretty clear on how I feel about that, darlin'," he said. "You've already invested your heart on me, there ain't no reason to throw your bank account in along with it."

Queenie said nothing, but held him to her breast comfortingly.

"I know that oil is there." King's frustration made his tone a little desperate. "Cedarleg agrees with me. It's a big field, maybe a million barrels a year, and it's all mine. But I can't afford to get it out of there if I can't have a way to refine it."

He sighed heavily. "I've just got to get me an investment stake from one of those down-your-nose, shoe-shined, my-shit-don't-stink, city bankers!"

King rolled off of her and threw an arm over his face. "I hate having to suck up to them, Queenie," he said. "I absolutely hate it."

She made sympathetic sounds and turned to her side to more easily caress his chest.

"It's like no matter how well I do, no matter how successful I am or how much money that I make, these men will always be treating me as if I'm something from the barnyard that got stuck on their boot."

"If they think that they're fools," Queenie told him.

"They may be fools, but they are rich ones," King said. "A lot of them come from inherited money.

Money that daddy or granddaddy got together and they've grown up with it all their lives, accepting it, believing it to be their birthright or some such."

He drew his arm away from his eyes and looked up at her. "I suppose I could stand it if I thought that *all* of them were that way. That *all* of them just have the misfortune not to understand that to have money some poor Joe somewhere has got to make it."

Queenie smiled at him.

"But the truth is that a lot of them know better. A lot of these bankers are smart and cagey and want to make a killing in the oil market. They don't see the future as clear as I do, but they do see the price of fuel oil going through the roof. And they see that the new internal combustion engines run on gasoline and that they can do lots of things that can't be done with steam boilers. They want to be a part of it all. They want a chance to get a piece of the newest pie. But it's me that they resist. It's me, Calhoun, that they are unsure about. A man whose name is King and calls his company *Royal* Oil. I thought it was a good idea, Queenie. I thought they'd respect something like that."

"It's a good name, King," she said. "It's a good name and it suits you and your company."

"But it doesn't suit the bankers. They'd rather loan money on a hardware store or a cotton crop, that's sure never going to make them only a tiny profit."

"They don't want to take the risk."

"But banking is meant to be risk," King said with certainty. "That's why it pays as well as it does. Essentially the banker is no different than the fellow that walks up to your wheel in the back room and puts ten dollars on twenty-three red."

Queenie nodded in agreement.

"It's something about me, something about the way I present myself to these money men that just doesn't work."

"Can you approach them differently?" she asked.

King sighed heavily.

"Lord knows, darlin', I've tried," he said. "Sometimes I go in like I think I'm the smartest, richest, most arrogant son-in-britches you ever met."

Queenie laughed.

"Then the next time, I'm all humble and bowing and treat them like they was the finest men I ever seen and I'm grateful for their attention. Either way, they just barely have time to see me and they never, *never*, have any money to throw my way."

"Why don't you try just being yourself?" she asked.

"Oh darlin', I do that, too," he admitted. "And that's what they like the very least."

He pulled her closer and laid his hand upon her breast, gently coaxing the nipple to harden.

"I just can't think about it anymore," King declared finally with a sigh. "I need to think about something else."

Queenie was silent for a long moment, then gave a long sigh.

"I've got something else for you to think about, King," she said. "Though I'm not sure that you'll enjoy pondering it anymore than the other."

She rolled away from him and sat up on the end of the bed. She'd thought and thought and thought about what she must do. She didn't have to tell him, of course. It was her and her life and he didn't even need to know. Their relationship was a good one, but any relationship between a man and his whore was by nature fragile. If things got too tough, Calhoun would simply cease stopping by. He already had more than enough on his mind, but somehow, Queenie had to share it with him. She had to tell him. Somehow he had to know.

"What is it, darlin'?" he asked, looking at her curiously.

"Well, King," she said. "We seem to have gotten me pregnant."

The silence was a long one and almost deafening.

King rolled off the bed and onto his feet. Immediately he began to pace the floor, his expression worried.

"I guess I don't need to ask if you're sure," he said.

In its own way it was a question.

"I haven't seen a doctor," she admitted. "But I didn't get the curse this month, I've been throwing up for a week, and my breasts are pretty tender. That's just the way it was last time."

He stopped pacing and turned to look at her. "Last time?"

"I got pregnant when I was seventeen," she said. "That's why I left home. I thought . . . I thought that the fellow loved me and wanted to marry me. I ran away from the farm with him. But at the very first big town he left me at the train station while he went to find a preacher, he said. I guess he's still looking for one. He never came back and I never saw him again."

King hesitated, staring at her. "I'm . . . I'm sorry," he said finally.

Queenie looked at him curiously. "Sorry because you made me pregnant?"

"Well, yes, I . . ." He looked extremely uncomfortable. "What I meant was that I am sorry that the man that you loved deserted you when you needed him."

"Oh, that." Queenie waved away his apology. "Truthfully, I don't think I loved him much at all." She sighed, thinking about the young girl that she had been. "And it was bound to happen. He was a fast-talking fellah selling grain shares. He was different, dressed fancy, I thought he was maybe the richest man in the world. I was naive then, very silly and naive. I believed in getting married and living happily ever after. But I also wanted more than a lifetime of hard work in a cotton field. I wanted money *and* marriage."

She shook her head and then looked up at him. Her smile carried no humor.

"Like most women I learned that I had to choose one or the other."

"What happened to your child?" he asked. "You never mentioned a child."

"I don't have one," she answered. "The old gal that gave me my first job in a saloon used a hay hook on me. After all these years I'd figured that she'd fixed me so well, I'd never be able to get pregnant again."

"Oh, Queenie," he whispered and sat down beside her on the bed, wrapping an arm around her waist.

She laid her head on his shoulder.

"I can see somebody next week and get it taken care of," she said.

"I'll find a doctor, Queenie, a good doctor. I won't have you risking your life at the hands of some clumsy barber. You mean too much to me."

She looked up at him and smiled.

"I shouldn't have worried you with this," she told him. "There is nothing in the world more guaranteed to set a man to packing than a girl telling him she's eating for two."

"Don't I know it," King replied. "I've been ruminating on the outbound train schedule for the last five minutes. And I could eagerly run from here to the station."

Queenie laughed. "You are always so danged honest, King," she said.

He planted a kiss on the top of her head.

"It's just with you, Queenie," he told her. "I was so dishonest with my wife, it made us both ill."

"Oh, I doubt that," Queenie said. "Maybe you were unfaithful, but you could never have been dishonest."

"I was, absolutely, I was," he insisted. "When she told me she was pregnant I felt just like I do now. I felt like running. But I always told her that I was so delighted."

"But you were delighted with Princess," Queenie reminded him.

"I am now," he said. "At the time I was just scared. We lost two before her to stillbirth and I lost count of the miscarriages. When she was pregnant I always felt more guilty and undeserving than I usually did."

"Guilty and undeserving?" Queenie looked at him, surprised. "I thought . . . I thought you loved your wife. You always wear your wedding ring."

"I wear it, I guess to remind me that *not* loving her is the thing for which I feel most guilty of all," he said. "She deserved better than me and she never had a clue about the kind of man she got."

King looked down and twirled it on his finger.

"I don't believe in wasting time with regrets," he told Queenie.

Queenie took his hand and squeezed it.

"You're right," she agreed. "We made the choices we made then and we live with them now."

"We can never change the past," King said. "We can never go back and start over."

Queenie's brow furrowed thoughtfully. The words of a handsome young man standing in the darkness beside her niggled at her memory. A young man who wasn't sleeping too well, but resisted the temptation to take an offered cure.

In some ways I think I've been given a chance to start over again.

Work on the "P" went on twenty-four hours a day and seven days a week, the understanding being that there would be plenty of days off once the well was drilled. With every pounding drop of the cable, the drill bit pushed deeper and deeper into the ground.

Closer and closer to the reservoir of oil that had been waiting there for them for a hundred generations.

"You're a natural," Bob Earlie told Tom one afternoon. "And I ain't saying that cause you saved my biscuits. Men work all their dang lives in this and never feel it. But some of us, we feel it, we hear it, we taste it. That oil down under that rock is ours and getting it out is personal."

"I couldn't a said it better myself," Cedarleg piped in. "And if I'd a said it you'd not believe me, 'cause I'm so partial to ye."

Tom was embarrassed, almost ashamed to bask in their praise.

"I . . . I like this work," he admitted. "I've always worked hard, I just never liked it before."

The other men laughed in agreement. But Tom knew that the words that he spoke were true. He did like the hard, hot work. He could smell the oil. Well maybe he couldn't quite *smell* it, but he knew somehow, just as Cedarleg and Calhoun knew, that there was oil beneath that ground.

After a hard day's effort, the worn table in Ma Pease's tent nearly groaned under the weight of good, hot food. Tom and Cedarleg managed to lighten the load by consuming a whole platter of ham and biscuits and at least a half gallon of red-eye gravy.

The two talked long and excitedly about the well. They'd hit a gas pocket early in the day. With great care and skill, Bob Earlie and Cedarleg had managed to expend the gas without blowing up everything from the top of the hill to Burford Corners. The gas pocket was frightening, but it was thrilling, too. More evidence that fine, wet, black petroleum was right below them.

Tom finally leaned back in his chair, almost moaning with fine satisfaction.

"I can't eat another bite, Ma," he declared. "What on earth makes you such a fine cook?"

"I just tried," she answered, then chuckled. "Did I tell you the story about the fellah that asked me if I could play the fiddle?"

"Yes, you did," Tom answered.

"I told him, 'I don't know, I never tried!'"

Ma laughed heartily at her own joke. Tom and Cedarleg just looked at each other and shook their heads.

Tom was feeling at peace. He'd spent part of his first paycheck on some dressgoods for Ma. He had meant his gift simply as a way to repay her for all her hard work, but the old woman had teared up as if it were the kindest thing anyone had ever done. It had made him feel good. He leaned back in his chair, utterly content. Perhaps that was why Ma's next question caught him so unaware.

"You ever hear of a fellah named Gerald Crane?" she asked.

Every muscle in Tom's body stilled and every fiber of nerve became alert. His face became a mask that revealed nothing as his mind raced with a thousand questions.

"Gerald Crane?"

"Yeah," she said. "He's a fellah here in Topknot supposed to have been in the Rough Riders. Did you know him?"

Tom remained noncommittal. "I don't suspect I know every man that was in the Rough Riders," he said.

"Where'd you hear of him, Ma?" Cedarleg asked.

"Princess mentioned him when she was here the other day," she answered.

"Princess?" Tom asked blankly.

"Princess Calhoun," Cedarleg answered. "King Calhoun's daughter."

"I didn't know you were friends with King Calhoun's daughter, Ma," Tom said. "What illustrious company you keep."

"Illustrious?" The old woman snorted. "I've known Princess since she was in diapers."

"Further back than then, Ma," Cedarleg argued. "We knew Calhoun and his wife before that little gal was even born."

"And what we know about her is that there ain't nothing illustrious about her," Ma said. "She's as levelheaded and down-to-earth as any gal I ever knowed. At least she used to be."

"What do you mean by that?" Cedarleg eyed her curiously.

"Why, it's this Gerald Crane fellah," the old woman answered. "She told me that she's in love with him. She says he's handsome, rich, and she talks like he's a saint among men. She says that she's in love and is thinking to marry him."

"What does King say about him?" Cedarleg asked.

"I don't think she's bothered to mention this fellah to her daddy," Ma answered.

Cedarleg's brow furrowed. "That don't sound good to me."

"It didn't set quite right against my ears, neither," Ma admitted. "So I began asking around about him."

"And?"

"And nothing. They ain't nobody knows him or even knows of him," she said. "And I swear I mentioned his name in front of every gossip in Topknot."

"Maybe he doesn't live in Topknot," Tom suggested.

"Maybe he don't live anywhere," she answered. "I asked Vella Murphy. She and her gals does laundry for nearly every single man in Burford Corners. He don't get his clothes washed. He ain't living in any of the hotels. Ain't nobody heard of him, except Princess."

"It don't sound right to me," Cedarleg said.

"Nor me either," his wife agreed.

"I'll mention it to Calhoun next time I see him. He's got a lot on his mind these days, but there ain't nothing as important to him as that little gal."

"That's the truth."

"If there's something amiss about this Gerald Crane, King will send the fellah packing faster than you can shake a stick," Cedarleg declared.

"What if she really does love him?" Tom asked. "If you really care about her, you wouldn't want to stand in the way of her happiness."

Ma considered the question for only an instant before she shook her head.

"I don't think this one is for her," she said. "He's some fancy man from back East. Slicker than silk, he sounds like. That's not for Princess. She needs a steady, hardworking kind of man. One that could match her energy and good sense."

"Princess needs someone like our Tom here," Cedarleg said.

Ma nodded. "That's what I was thinking. You two would just hang right and tight together."

" 'Course, Tom, the gal's a bit on the bossy side," he said. "Like as not she'd take to nagging you like ol' Ma here does me."

"She's not all that bossy," Tom piped in.

Both of them looked at him, surprised.

"You've met her?" Ma asked.

Tom hesitated only a moment. "Ah, no, no, I haven't actually met her. But of course I saw her at the Fourth of July picnic. She was the hostess after all. Everyone saw her."

"Oh, yeah, that's right," Cedarleg said. "I'd forgot that you went to that."

"That's where she met this Gerald Crane fellah," Ma pointed out. "Did you see him? She said they danced together most of the evening."

"Ah no, no, I don't believe I noticed her dancing partner," Tom lied.

Ma tutted. "I just wish somebody had," she said.

"Now quit worrying," Cedarleg told her. "I'll speak with King, he'll get the lowdown on this fellah and it'll be all settled before this thing goes one bit further."

NINE

His time was running out. With King Calhoun now home from St. Louis and Cedarleg determined to mention Gerald to him at their next meeting, Tom knew that his time was almost gone.

Never in his furthermost imaginings had he considered the idea that Cessy might know Ma and Cedarleg. After his time with Ambrose, Tom had learned all too well that the wealthy consorted with the wealthy. And even those who were new to money and position left their friends behind as they moved up.

It was going to become difficult, if not impossible, to meet Cessy alone. He had to get her hooked, tied, and completely his or he was going to lose out altogether.

He talked one of the other tool dressers into taking on his Sunday shift. A solitary picnic in a secluded romantic setting. A few kisses and caresses, maybe a little more. He'd get her to agree to a secret engagement. Or maybe they could even run off and wed. He'd asked Buddy Ruston, one of the roughnecks, recently wed, about what was required.

"Just find you a preacher, have him say the words, pay him the three dollars and he files the papers," the fellow answered. "You thinking of taking on another mouth to feed?"

Tom had only shrugged in answer. He wasn't taking on another mouth, he was going to marry a million-dollar oil well, with a really nice gal thrown into the bargain. A fellow couldn't ask for more than that.

Which was why on a bright Sunday, with a world of worry still on his mind, Tom was whistling happily as he made his way across town to meet Cessy. The livery stable made a deep dent in his weekly pay, but Tom felt that he had to hire the finest-looking team they had as well as the smartest rig. Gerald would expect nothing less. Even if Cessy had stars in her eyes, she couldn't help but notice the fancy turnout.

He'd driven by the back alley of the Palace, assuring himself that Calhoun's Packard was still parked there and that the old man was still snoring upstairs in the arms of the saloon's proprietor.

Feeling safe and certain, he'd pulled right up into the Calhouns' porte cochere, just as if he belonged.

He'd take her to the Shemmy Creek mouth, he decided. It was less than an hour's drive, but he doubted if many of the newcomers even knew that it existed. Shemmy Creek looked to be a small and inconsequential stream that meandered down Rough Tack Hill. In fact, just beneath the ground surface of the shallow stream ran a near torrent of cool, very drinkable water. The place where the streams—both aboveground and below—merged to flow into the river was quiet, private, and obscured by hundred-year-old oaks, shady willows, and blooming star grass.

It was close to the Methodist Indian Home. He certainly didn't want to take the chance of running into anyone he knew, but none of the students he knew when he lived there would still be around. And

Reverend McAfee had been too old and feeble to follow him to Shemmy Creek when he was a boy.

Yes, that's where he should take her, to his secret place. The place of sanctuary that he had run to the hundred times when he had run from the home. The one place in his childhood that he had somehow felt was his own.

He knew that Cessy would love it as much as he did. It was a part of him and although he could never tell her that, she would know. She would feel it. He would make love to her there, this very afternoon. Tom smiled to himself. In his own special place he would make love to the one woman who could give him everything that he had ever wanted. The idea was far from unpleasant. And then he would ask her to be his wife.

He ran his hand nervously over his breast pocket to assure himself that the tiny, gold-colored ring was still there. He'd paid two dollars for it at J.M. Nell General Merchandise. He probably could have gotten a better price bargaining with the foreign fellow who was engaged to Cessy's friend. But he couldn't risk Cessy finding out that it was not real gold. He intended to replace it as soon as he had control of his new wife's money. With any luck at all, that might be tomorrow.

Gerald Crane would marry Cessy. And Tom, poor Tom Walker, would simply disappear from the face of the earth.

Howard, the manservant whom he had seen on several occasions, hurried out to greet him as he secured the team.

"Good morning, sir," the man greeted him deferentially. "Miss Calhoun is receiving her guests in the sun parlor."

Guests? Tom thought to himself. Had she pretended that she was spending the day with more people than just him? That was probably a good idea. Servants did talk. Let them think she went out with a chaperone. It would give them more time, more privacy.

Tom followed the man's directions through the receiving room, the main hallway, and across the main sitting room to the sun parlor. He had never actually been inside the house and he looked around now in a leisurely way, and with pleasure. The high-ceilinged rooms gave a feeling of space and coolness that was welcome in the middle of July. The walls were covered in high-quality embossed paper with a raised leaf design. The moldings and mop boards were wide planks of dark walnut, stained just slightly lighter than the floorboards.

The halltree was mammoth, in gleaming cherry with marble inlay and a beveled mirror. But the parlor furniture was unfashionably overstuffed and looked comfortable and welcoming.

There was an unassumingly livable feeling about the place. It was a mansion, like many he'd seen, but it had none of the ostentatious and intimidating qualities that he usually so admired. This house was a home and felt very much that way. It was Cessy's house, she'd said. That meant it was to be his. The wonder of it struck him with awesome clarity.

With silent admiration he stopped to caress a walnut pillar that was part of the open front parlor entryway.

He, Tom Walker, the little part-breed orphan at the livery, would live in a house like this. Or rather Gerald, Gerald Crane would live here. He was well accustomed to such fine housing.

An unexpected bitterness swelled up in him. A man could work, struggle, save, and scrape all his life and never see the inside of a house like this. For others it was merely part of a birthright.

He remembered the first time he'd folded one of the *cravats'* silk neckties. The fabric so smooth and beautiful, it almost brought tears to his eyes just touching it. Later he saw Ambi cast it carelessly in the dust when it had become sweat-soaked and soiled on the parade grounds.

"I'll never take it for granted," he whispered to the walnut pillar. Silently he vowed to be a good husband, a decent fellow, and to thank heaven everyday for the good fortune that was about to befall him.

With those thoughts clearly in mind he hurried on to the sun parlor where his future wife, in point of fact his *entire* future, awaited him.

As he stepped across the threshold of the room, the smile froze upon his lips. Cessy was not alone.

Her friend, Muna Nafee, and the strange foreign fellow Maloof were in the room also.

Cessy jumped to her feet and hurried to greet him, her hands outstretched in welcome.

He took them into his own. In deference to the others in the room, he gave her fingers a slight squeeze of affection before raising her knuckles to his lips.

"Good afternoon, Cessy," he said softly. Deliberately he kept his eyes upon her as he speculated upon the presence of the other couple.

"Do you remember Muna and her fiancé?" Cessy asked.

"Of course, I do," Tom insisted with a warm smile toward the other young lady. "It is wonderful to see you again, Miss Nafee. Afternoon Maloof."

"You looking good today," the peddler commented. "Coat is perfect, like it just made for you."

"That's because it was," Cessy announced with a warm laugh. "He has a tailor in Boston and refuses to wear fashions cut or stitched by anyone else."

Tom's smile faltered. He tensed waiting for Maloof to show him to be a liar. He'd used the fib about the tailor to explain why a wealthy gentlemen like Gerald Crane would visit Cessy every evening in the same suit of clothes.

Maloof appeared momentarily confused, as if he didn't quite understand what Cessy was saying.

"It is fine, very fine," he said. "Some of the best I've seen."

Cessy nodded. "Gerald has a real eye for quality."

Tom smiled, schooling his expression, hoping he appeared modest. Not relieved. Thank heaven the peddler's command of the English language was so poor.

Gratefully Tom accepted the offered chair and began the task of making polite conversation by commenting to Miss Muna on the superior afternoon weather.

"Oh yes, it's perfect for a picnic," the young woman told him.

There was a way in which Miss Nafee looked at Tom, a way in which she looked too closely at him, that made him cautious. Cessy's best friend, it seemed, neither liked or trusted him. But she appeared to be trying to hide the fact.

"I've invited Muna and Maloof to go with us," Cessy said. "Two couples together is always fun."

"Always," Tom agreed with as much warmth as he could manage.

"Did you have a picnic spot in mind?" Muna asked him. Her tone suggested that she was not about to approve of his answer.

"No," Tom lied admirably. "A place by the river, I'd thought, with lots of tall trees and cool shade."

Cessy nodded. "I know just the place," she said. "I discovered it myself, and it is perfect for a July picnic."

Tom reached over to take her hand in his own. "Any place will be perfect as long as I am with you, Miss Calhoun," he said, softly.

To his surprise, Cessy laughed in his face. He glanced toward Muna and caught her rolling her eyes. Had he overplayed his hand? The young woman and her best friend were close as sisters, Maloof had told him. Would one sister advise against a suitor that she didn't trust?

"I told you he was dangerous," Cessy said, attempting to make a joke out of his compliment.

"Soft words and secret meetings." Muna tutted in disapproval. "I don't know how they do things back East, but here, Mr. Crane, a lady's reputation could be in jeopardy."

Tom had no reply to that. Muna Nafee was a threat, he decided. She had Cessy's ear. He could only hope that *he* had Cessy's loyalty.

With sophisticated ease, he changed the subject.

"I need to exchange the rig I've hired," he said. "It's a two-seater."

"Oh, we can just take the surrey," Cessy told. "It's very sturdy and my team is easy to handle."

Tom smiled pleasantly, thinking unpleasantly of the money he'd shelled out for the rented vehicle.

"Then all else required for this picnic is food," he said. "I trust you ladies have taken care of that."

"Overwhelmingly," Cessy assured him. "My cook has made up a basket large enough to feed all your Rough Riders, and Muna's mother has sent a veritable Syrian feast for us."

"Then shall we proceed to our picnic, Miss Calhoun."

Giggling, Cessy rose to her feet and accepted his arm. Laughing and exuberant, Tom and Cessy were a sharp contrast to the other couple. Muna still appeared suspicious and uneasy. And the peddler was keeping whatever thoughts he had to himself. The two couples made their way back through the house toward the porte cochere.

As if everything had been settled perfectly before his arrival, Tom found his own sleek, expensive rig moved aside and the striped-awning surrey hitched to a sleek, smoke-gray pair.

"I would be happy to return your rig to the livery, Mr. Crane," Howard offered.

Tom wished he could accept. He wanted his money back, but he'd hired the team as Tom Walker. He couldn't allow Miss Calhoun's employee to return them for Gerald Crane.

"Please don't concern yourself," Tom told him, feigning expansiveness.

With a good deal of feminine laughter, the baskets were loaded up and Tom found himself driving with Cessy at his side. She looked downright attractive, he thought, in a dark blue serge skirt and crisp linen blouse. Her high collar was modestly pinned with a carved ivory cameo. Her wide-brimmed straw hat was trimmed with only the thinnest braid of pink and blue ribbons. He smiled across at her, rapidly trying to reformulate his plan for the day. Obviously he had miscalculated. He'd thought her so enamored that she could be easily lured out alone. He must try never to underestimate her intelligence again.

Cessy responded jovially to a teasing comment from Muna. The young women apparently intended to chatter among themselves, ignoring their escorts. Tom was not about to let that happen.

He leaned close to Cessy, whispering so that only she would hear.

"I suppose it was very dastardly of me to try to get you alone, Miss Calhoun."

Cessy blushed in that way that he found so appealing. The young lady was incapable of coyness or deception.

"I . . . I thought that we . . ."

He grasped her hand in his own and squeezed it lovingly. "I know," he assured her in a whisper. "I have been rushing your fences. It is very good, perhaps that you force us to step back a bit."

"Oh Gerald, I didn't mean—" she began.

He hushed her with a look in the direction of the

silent couple in the seat behind them. And then he smiled at her, warmly.

"Just a fun picnic for four," he said. "As long as I am by your side, I will be content."

She laughed.

He would take it slow and easy today, he decided. If an opportunity for a more intimate situation presented itself, he would take it. But he wouldn't press her now. He'd let her make the next move.

The drive out of town was pleasant. Cessy seemed quite familiar with the local roads and in her no-nonsense way directed him away from the thorough-fares most consistently used by the trucks and wagons on their way to the oil fields.

The mid-July sun beat down on the deeply rutted, red dirt road before them. The prairie grass on either side of the road was so pale a green that it bordered on yellow, dotted here and there with purple paint-brush or dandelions. The rattling wheels of the surrey left dusty clouds in their wake as they drove.

The roads were familiar to Tom and became more so as they traveled. As each mile passed he became increasingly uncomfortable with the proximity of the Indian School. He couldn't quite shake his anxiety. Mentally he harangued himself. Did he think that Reverend McAfee was still looking for him after eight years? Was the old man going to run out to the road, grab him by the ear, and drag him back to that livery stable for the rest of his life? It was a foolish fear and he was foolish to waste a moment of his afternoon with such concern. McAfee was probably long dead and the school a splintery ruin filled with the ghosts of unhappy little orphan boys.

"Take this turn to the west up here," Cessy directed. "It looks like little more than a wagon track, but it's quite passable."

Tom was jolted. He swallowed his surprise and followed the road she'd indicated. He couldn't quite believe it, but he knew that Cessy was directing him down the little sparsely traveled path that led to the mouth of Shemmy Creek. She knew his secret place.

"Where on earth are we headed?" he heard Muna ask from the back.

"It's a beautiful place I found," Cessy answered. "There is a little creek over there along that tree line," she said, indicating the woods just ahead. "There is hardly any water in it at all, but it's wonderfully cool and very shady. I thought it would make a marvelous picnic spot."

"We trust your judgement in the matter completely," Tom assured her. "But how in the world did you ever find it?"

"I'm out this way quite a lot," she told him. "At least I usually am. Lately I . . ."

"Lately she's been spending too much time thinking about a certain young man," Muna finished for her.

Cessy appeared genuinely embarrassed by her friend's tone.

Tom decided to make her friend's ill-disguised displeasure work in his favor. He feigned comic surprise.

"A young man? So I have competition for your interest, Miss Calhoun? I am crushed."

She smiled at him as if to say that he needn't worry.

Tom followed her directions, although he didn't need them. He began to feel better. He was getting to take her to his special place and the quiet, apparently uninteresting couple with them might not prove to be as much a deterrent as a catalyst.

There were many sighs of appreciation and words of congratulation on Cessy's choice of location. Tom hobbled the horses in a shady spot with easy access to both water and the tall grass along the edges of the stream.

As Maloof watched, Cessy directed Muna to sweep

off the wide rock ledge that overlooked the river and lay out the tablecloth upon it.

Tom joined them as they began to unpack the food baskets. He and Maloof were ordered to take their places and allowed themselves to be served up a picnic lunch fit for royalty.

"The amazing thing about this place is that it's so cool," Cessy told him. "It's such a tiny little stream, and with all these trees and cattails there is barely a breeze, still it's inordinately cool even in the middle of July."

"It's the underground spring," Tom said. "That water is coming from so deep down that it cools the whole area.

"What?"

Cessy was staring at him.

He hesitated only a fraction of a second. One could be thoughtful when telling the truth, but lies were most convincing when presented quickly and concisely.

"I think that it must be an underground spring," he said. "There is a place much like this upon my family's country estate in Connecticut. A virtual river of very cool water runs underneath it and keeps the temperature moderate all summer long."

"I didn't know your family had an estate in Connecticut," Cessy said.

"Oh, it is Grandmama's place," he answered. "My cousins and I used to wander the grounds like gypsies when we were boys."

"Is this the grandmama that married the gondolier?"

"Ah, no . . . no, this is the other one. What is this wonderful delicacy?" he turned to ask Muna.

"It's simply a cabbage roll," she answered.

"We call it *maashi*," the young peddler piped in. Tom had thought he wasn't listening to the conversation. "It is my most favorite and this very good."

"It is wonderful," Tom agreed. "Maloof, you are a lucky fellow to find a beautiful woman who can also cook."

"It is my mother who cooks so well," Muna told him, unwilling to accept the compliment. "And how one looks is simply a quirk of nature and nothing in which a person can take pride."

Deliberately he relaxed his shoulders and plastered a wide, winning grin across his mouth.

"How right you are," he agreed, turning his full attention upon the woman who was apparently out to discredit him. "Our appearance, fine or ill, *is* a happenstance. But thankfully the eyes heaven gives to a man or a woman see with love, less critically perhaps, but more clearly for all that."

He felt Cessy's hand slip into his own and turned to look at her. His smile was gone now, his expression soft and serious.

Her eyes were wide with wonder.

"That's what I thought," she told him. "It's exactly what I thought the night that we met."

Their gazes held for a long moment. Tom felt almost frightened, almost desperate as he looked into her face. But he knew that it was something that he'd never felt before and something that he was not ready to confront today.

He glanced away first, regarding his plate and making a hasty comment about the food.

"You have a good appetite," Cessy commented. "That is your second cabbage roll and I haven't noticed you ignoring the cook's fried chicken."

Tom delicately wiped his mouth with the snowy white napkin in that way that was so naturally elegant for Gerald.

"A man who has gone without meals learns to appreciate the wonders of food when it is presented to him."

The words had barely passed his lips when he was

desperate to call them back. Gerald had never known hunger or want. It was Tom whose world was always at risk.

A strange expression came across Cessy's face and for a moment he thought that she'd found him out. Then she reached over and took his hand.

"You needn't try to shelter me from the unpleasantness of your military service," she told him. "I want to share your life, Gerald, all of it."

Their eyes met and the look that passed between them was so intense, Tom felt as if all the air had been stolen from his lungs. This had to stop, this strange heart stopping power she had over him. It simply had to stop. If he didn't win her soon, he'd confess all and throw himself upon her mercy.

"More bread, Mr. Crane?" Muna's voice interrupted.

He glanced at the other young woman, grateful for the fateful reprieve. "No thank you, Miss Nafee, I believe I could not eat another bite."

"Then you must be ready for some dessert," she continued. "Prin's cook makes the best pies in the oil field and my mother has packed some pastries like nothing you have ever tasted before."

"It sounds tempting, but perhaps later," he said. "Truly, I must take a bit of exercise before I attempt to enjoy any more of this fine cooking."

He rose to his feet and turned toward Princess, offering his hand.

"Shall we explore this place, Cessy?" he asked. "To see if I am correct about the underground spring."

Immediately she placed her palm in his own and would have walked away without another word if Muna's voice hadn't injected a moment of reality.

"Don't worry about this, Prin," Muna said, gesturing toward the empty plates and the remainders of their repast.

The woman on his arm hesitated. It was she, of course, who was the hostess of the picnic. She should be the one to take care of the clean up. Or at least suggest that it be done.

"Oh no, Muna, I can't leave all this mess for you," Cessy said guiltily.

Tom could wait no longer to be alone with her and determinedly wrapped her arm more firmly around his own. "Maloof will help her," he said, grinning at the peddler who looked up at him in surprise. "It will give you a fine opportunity to show your betrothed what a helpful husband you hope to be. And with us out of the way, it will give you a good chance to steal a kiss."

His words brought a little "Oh" of shock from Muna, whose cheeks immediately sported two bright red spots.

Maloof seemed as embarrassed as she was. "Later I brew coffee for you, Turkish coffee with the sweets," he said. "You go with Tom, friend of Muna. I have no sisters, I know to help Muna. I am very helpful."

"Good, good," Tom said and led Cessy away from the picnic spot and into the cool shade of the woods. "I'm going to try to steal a kiss myself."

With Princess and Gerald off in the woods, Muna found herself sitting in silence with Maloof on the opposite corners of the tablecloth. She gave him a surreptitious glance from beneath her lashes. His brow was furrowed and he looked concerned. Muna assumed that all the talk of kissing had embarrassed him as much as her.

Maloof had never made any attempt to actually kiss her. But then he didn't need to. They would be married soon. There was no need to spark and spoon a woman who was already committed to be your wife.

He caught her looking at him and smiled.

Muna felt a strange fluttering in her heart.

"Tom is very brave man," he said.

"Tom?"

He gestured toward the woods. "Tom, the man friend of Miss Princess."

"Gerald," Muna told him. "His name is Gerald."

He shrugged as if he couldn't accept her words but was unwilling to argue them.

"He is brave man," Maloof repeated.

"Why would you say that?" she asked him.

"He goes to steal kiss," he said.

Muna blushed. "That's just an expression," she assured him.

"Ah . . . good," Maloof replied as if a huge worry had been taken from his shoulders. "I like him and would not want him in pain or prison."

"Pain or prison? What on earth are you talking about?" Muna asked him.

"Your father has explained to me," he said.

"Explained what?"

"The customs of America," he answered. "It is different here for couple unwed and has much danger."

"Danger?" she asked, puzzled at his words.

He looked at her for a long moment and then, to her surprise, moved closer to her side of the table-cloth.

"I am not afraid of danger," he assured her, his voice surprisingly low and strangely seductive.

Muna felt gooseflesh raise upon her skin.

"I would risk much," he whispered as he eased himself next to her. "I would endure much. The danger is much, but I face it bravely."

Her heart was pounding now, his nearness over-whelming. He leaned slightly toward her, supporting his body with one tanned brown hand only inches from her own. He was not touching her anywhere, but the warmth of him, the scent of him, embraced her as certainly as any arms ever would.

Muna swallowed, determined to keep her head. "Romance is a powerful emotion," she admitted, "and is certainly the risk of a painful broken heart. But I have already agreed to wed you, sir. You needn't fear I shall reject your affection."

Maloof seemed momentarily taken aback. His brow furrowed in confusion.

"I do not fear you," he said. "I fear police."

"The police?" Muna sat up straight and looked him squarely in the eye, befuddled. "What on earth do the police have to do with it?"

Maloof tilted his head slightly, considering her words.

"It no good to go prison in my new country," he said.

"What on earth are you thinking to do that could send you to prison?" she asked.

"Kiss you," he replied.

"You think that if you kiss me you will go to prison?"

Maloof nodded. "Your father explain," he told her. "In America it is much free, not like Tarablos. In Tarablos man and bride meet with parents, sit with parents, get married."

Muna nodded. "Here we don't have arranged marriages," she agreed. "But what has that to do with prison?"

"In America young man and woman have much time alone, yes?"

Muna agreed.

"There is much privacy, much time for . . . kisses but family no worry."

"Well, I think sometimes they do," she said.

"Your father say to me, 'In America law is clear. Touch bride before wedding and go to jail, face torture.'"

"What?"

"Go to jail, face torture," he repeated. "Steal a kiss very dangerous."

Muna stared at him in disbelief for a long moment and then burst into laughter.

"Baba told you that if you try to . . . to touch me you'll go to jail and be tortured?"

Maloof looked puzzled.

"It is not true?"

"No, of course it's not true," Muna told him. "Couples in America touch and kiss and . . . well they touch and kiss."

Maloof was incredulous. "Your father lies to me!"

"Yes, yes, I'm afraid he did lie to you," she said.

"He lies to me." Maloof shook his head with disbelief. "He lies to me." After a long thoughtful sigh, a trace of a smile niggled at the corner of his mouth and then pulled into a full-fledged grin. "There is much to respect about your father," he said.

Not for one moment, Princess Calhoun assured herself, had she allowed the nagging worry of the note to intrude upon her good judgement. She was so glad that she hadn't confided her strange doubts.

Just for a moment, she had lost her nerve. She had doubted. It had been in that instance of uncertainty that she had contacted Muna and asked that she and her fiancé attend the picnic.

Gerald, being the true gentleman that he was, chose not to take offense at her bad nature.

Princess glanced toward the man beside her. He patted her arm.

"I've been waiting all day for a moment alone with you, Cessy," he said.

She looked up at his warm, honest, loving expression and she smiled.

"I've been waiting to be alone with you, too," she said.

He smiled, obviously delighted at her candor. As soon as they were well hidden among the trees he released her to take off his pin-checked linen coat.

"It's far too warm to be so formal," he told her.

Princess didn't complain. She relished the sight of him in his snowy white shirt and slate-colored lisle web bretelles. He used a nearby tree branch as a coat rack, and when they continued on, he didn't escort her formally, but wrapped his arm with familiarity around her waist.

They walked among the dark umbrella of towering oaks and through the open field in the direction of the river. They stopped for a moment to stand and admire a growth of blooming milkweed, its pink flowers so dark they were almost lavender. Princess wanted to linger but he hurried her on.

"You must see this," he insisted.

And when he pointed out to her the Queen Anne's lace with its feathery, delicate tops and tiny, brilliant flower in the center, it was worth the hurry.

"It is so beautiful," she told him. "Do you think people would think me strange if I took to growing weeds in my flower garden?"

She made the statement as a joke, but his eyes softened. "People mostly do favor the traditional beauty of garden flowers," he said gently. "But I will always appreciate the special loveliness of a blossom uncultivated."

Princess felt for a moment like crying. She wasn't sure exactly why and she pushed the emotion away from her, deliberately choosing to remain in good humor.

"So you are comparing me to a weed?" she teased.

"Be careful," he warned, tweaking her nose. "When we besotted suitors wax poetic you could end up being a sandbur in my heart."

She managed a bit of genuine laughter.

He carefully plucked the blooming flower and led

her on further. It was almost as if he knew his way around the area. He seemed so much at home and so anxious for her to see it all. Princess was a little surprised at his obvious love of and familiarity with the out-of-doors. It was unusual, she thought, for a city man. And infinitely endearing.

As they got closer to the river, he spotted a flat rock embedded in the ground.

"Put your hand on that," he urged.

"Why?"

"I want you to prove that I am right," he answered.

Looking at him curiously, Princess laid her palm against the smooth brown stone. The chilly temperature was so startling, she gave a little cry of alarm.

"It's so cold!" she said.

Gerald nodded. "The underground spring is just below here, I think," he said. "And the rock holds the temperature of it better than the ground."

"It's amazing," she said.

He smiled down at her. "I think so, too. This is just an amazing place."

When they finally made it all the way to the river, he found her a pleasant seat on the bank with a broad view downstream.

"It's lovely," she told him.

Gerald nodded. "Let me get you a cattail to go with your Queen Anne's lace."

He made such a vaudeville production of hacking through the tall, marshy growth that Princess found herself laughing with delight at his antics, which appeared to spur him on to more zany behavior. She realized that usually he was more than a bit stuffy, but this place, this magical place, somehow made Gerald Crane appear more like a regular fellow. She was grateful. She loved him, of that she was certain, but it would be difficult being wife to a man who lived so far above her. She had glimpsed the heights of culture and fashion and found no place for herself there. She was a simple woman.

But she wasn't willing to give Gerald up either. And she'd already learned that wealthy spinsterhood did not equal freedom. She'd decided to marry him. Nothing less, no star-crossed love nor illicit liaison would ever be enough.

Princess watched as he fought his way back out of the tall grass. He hurried up the bank bearing a long, soft brown cattail. He dropped to his knees in front of her and held it out as if offering a fancy bouquet.

Princess laughed lightly as she accepted it. She gently ran the down against her cheek.

"It's so soft," she said.

Gerald reached over and with one finger caressed the opposite side of her face.

"Yes, it is so very soft," he whispered.

She warmed to his touch and the tenderness of his words. He cupped her chin in his hand and leaned forward to press his lips all too fleetingly against her own.

Princess sighed.

Gerald smiled. "Oh, I like to hear you make that sound," he said.

"Do you?"

He nodded. "It makes me think I should go on kissing you for a lifetime."

"That sounds nice," she said.

Taking her words as invitation, he brought his lips to hers once more. It was a sweet, chaste kiss. But as usual, it sparked a fire. Princess ran her palms up the snowy sleeves of his shirt and along the wide expanse of his shoulders before wrapping them around his neck.

His own hands oh-so-very-gently caressed her midriff as he deepened the kiss, using his tongue to tease the corners of her mouth.

She was trembling with pleasure at the taste and feel of him. He was warm and solid and she was so protected in his embrace. His fingers fleetingly teased the curve of her breast. She gave a little whine of impatience as she tried to press her bosom more firmly against his hand. He resisted, seemingly unwilling to allow things to go too far.

"Your friend Muna may come strolling out from the trees at any moment," he warned. "She would be scandalized."

Princess agreed with a little giggle. "You're probably right. Then she'd send for my father, who would bring his shotgun and you would be mine forever!" she teased.

Gerald leaned closer and whispered warm, soft words in her ear. "Too late, Cessy. I am already yours forever."

She pulled back to look up into his eyes, marveling at her good fortune. How could it be that this wonderful, sweet, sophisticated gentleman loved *her*? It was almost too much to be fathomed.

Deliberately she changed the subject. "I worry about Muna," she said. "I only wish she could be as happy as I."

"Don't worry too much," Gerald reassured her, caressing her shoulders. "Her fellow may be a bit slow for spooning, but he'll most likely get the idea."

"You shouldn't joke about it," she said. "And you really shouldn't encourage him."

"You're seriously concerned about Muna?"

Princess nodded. "Yes, I doubt if Maloof has ever kissed her, and I don't think it's good to give him such an idea."

"They are engaged to be married," Gerald pointed out. "Please don't tell me you disapprove of a couple kissing. It's something *we* seem to be so good at."

As if to prove his point, he brushed his lips once more against hers.

Princess giggled as she felt the blush sweep into her cheeks. "Oh, you silly," she said. "I just . . . I just don't want Muna to marry that fellow."

"You disapprove of Maloof?"

"No, no, I don't disapprove of him," she insisted. "It's just that Muna deserves better."

"You don't like him," Gerald said.

"No, it's not that either. In fact I do rather like him. He seems very sweet, but he doesn't love Muna," she said.

"How do you know that?"

"Her father arranged the marriage," Princess told him. "He wanted Maloof for a business partner, so he just brought him into the family."

Gerald made a sound that was noncommittal.

"Muna is going to have to live with a future devoid of love. He's only marrying her to improve himself financially," she explained.

Beside her she felt Gerald stiffen.

"You're shocked," she said. "I was, too, when I heard it. I know that it's not uncommon for foreigners, but I just find that kind of thing despicable."

"Perhaps we are too hard on him," Gerald said evenly.

"Oh, I don't think so," Princess assured him. "Believe me I've seen these greedy fortune-hunter types. A man would have to be lower than dirt to do such a thing. Luring a woman into a marriage devoid of love."

"Cessy, we have no idea what led him to this pass," Gerald pointed out. "He, also, is choosing to forego love. Maybe there are extenuating circumstances."

"You mean an excuse," she said unkindly.

"I mean that people sometimes do things for reasons they would rather not," he said. "Surely my heroine of social justice believes that."

Princess considered his words.

"Well, of course, he is a stranger here and it's a great advantage to immigrants to have established family connections," she said.

Gerald nodded as Princess continued thoughtfully. "And I understand from Muna that the situation under the Ottoman Empire is very difficult for the Christians of western Syria. With the stagnant economic conditions and religious prejudice, a younger son with any ambition is almost forced to seek his fortune on foreign soil."

"He seems to genuinely care for Muna," Gerald said quietly.

Princess nodded. "Yes, I suppose that is so. And her parents approve of him completely. I don't believe they would ever deliberately do anything to risk her happiness."

Gerald pulled her into an embrace. "That is one of the things that I truly love about you, Cessy," he said. "You are always fair and empathetic, even when you don't wish to be."

She looked up into the handsome eyes of the man she loved. "And *that* is one of the things that I love about you," she said. "That you would take the side of this man as if he were your closest friend, when he can't even remember your name."

"My name?"

"Didn't you hear him back there," she said. "He called you Tom."

"Tom? I . . . ah . . . I guess I didn't notice," he said.

"I can only wonder where he got that," she said.

Gerald shrugged and gave a rather boisterous laugh. "Well, he . . . what is it he says, 'I speck Inglush no good,'" he mimicked.

She giggled. "Oh, you sound just like him," she said with delight.

He pulled her deeply into his arms. "But I am not at all like him," he said. "Because when I am given a chance to be alone with my sweetheart, nobody will have to remind me that it might be a good opportunity to steal a kiss."

His firm, warm mouth came down upon her own, not with teasing brevity like before, but with serious romantic intent. Princess parted her lips to give him full access to whatever sweetness he sought there. With the delicate touch of his tongue he made a sensitive trace of her lips that brought a soft moan from deep inside her.

The sound seemed to entice him. He ran his hand along the length of her back, pressing her bosom into the hardness of his chest. She loved the feeling of it. Her breasts were tight, the nipples taut. The bodily contact made that worse, and yet somehow oh-so-much better.

He broke the contact of their mouths only to press his lips a dozen times against the length of her jaw and the sensitive skin at her throat.

"I love you, Cessy," he whispered into her ear. "Have I told you yet that I love you?"

The breathy warmth of the welcome words sent shivers of delight down her flesh.

"Oh, Gerald, I love you, too," she answered.

He pulled away slightly to look down at her. "You really do, don't you," he said. "You really do love me."

"Was there ever any doubt about it?" she asked.

"Then say you will marry me, Cessy," he said. "Here, in this very special place, today, say that you will marry me."

She swallowed with difficulty and looked up into his eyes. All her life she knew that she'd waited for this moment.

Momentarily the dream image was in her mind. She, in the white dress and upon her father's arm, walked down the church aisle toward the man she loved, toward this man. A man to whom her commitment was total. It was the sanctification of an earthly love that symbolized the union of mankind with its creator.

"If that is what you want, Gerald," she said. "Then it is what I want, too. Yes, Gerald Crane, I will marry you."

TEN

Tom nearly shouted in triumph at Cessy's answer. He had begun to feel almost desperate to win her. If he slipped up and revealed himself as Tom, or if Calhoun found him out, everything would be for nothing. Cessy might love him, but she would surely turn from him if the truth became known. Her obvious distaste for the financial motives of Maloof had made him genuinely uneasy. Tom had had schemes fall through before, but somehow this one had taken on a life of its own. Maloof already knew he was Tom. All the men at the "P" did as well. Topknot and Burford Corners might be two places, but even together they were far too small for a man to maintain separate identities for long.

He couldn't, wouldn't give it up. Gerald Crane was going to marry Princess Calhoun, and Tom Walker was going to disappear. He was determined. Cessy was exactly perfect, he'd decided. She was kind and caring and he even found her bossy ways rather intriguing. She loved him and believed him to be wonderful. That made the million dollars almost a bonus.

"I want it to be soon," he said, voicing his plans aloud as he made them. "I can't wait forever, Cessy.

And I already feel that this last week has been the
longest in my life. I want to marry soon and I want it
secret."

"Secret?" Cessy was startled at the suggestion.

"I think it would be best, don't you," he told her.
"If we notify my family or even tell your father, then
most certainly there will be a huge wedding party
that might take months to plan."

"Well, surely it wouldn't be that big," she hedged.

"Your father's Fourth of July picnic is an extrava-
ganza," Tom pointed out. "How much bigger celebration is he going to want for his only daughter's
wedding."

"Yes, you are probably right," she admitted.

"And my family!" Tom rolled his eyes deliberately.
"They'd arrive in an entire trainload of private cars.
If they allowed us to be wed out here at all."

"What do you mean?"

"Why, the Cranes are always married in Saint
Andrew's, right in the heart of Bedlington. I can
almost read those insistent telegrams now."

"Oh!" Cessy sounded genuinely alarmed. "I would
not want to travel back East to wed."

"Nor I," he assured her. "But if they know in
advance, they will almost certainly ask us to do so.
And it would not be good to start our marriage
disappointing them."

"No," she agreed. "That really wouldn't be good."

"But," Tom went on, "if we could find a nice,
private place that suited us and a discreet preacher,
we could be husband and wife and completely settled
in our ways before anyone has time to come up with
any party plans for us."

Princess was thoughtful for a long moment. He
could almost see her mentally giving up any dreams
she'd probably had for a big church wedding with all
her friends and family there to share it. Tom hated to
deny her that, but he couldn't risk it. Too many truths

were bound to come out. He couldn't have that happen before they were legally man and wife.

"I know exactly," she said suddenly. "I know exactly the place and the person to marry us."

Tom was momentarily surprised at her easy capitulation.

"He is the sweetest man and he is so caring," she said. "He's given his whole life to helping the less fortunate."

"Can he be trusted?" Tom asked.

"Absolutely," Cessy assured him and giggled joyously. "And he always says that he owes me more favors than he can ever repay. I'll tell him that I am collecting."

"So how soon can we say 'I do'?" Tom asked.

"Anytime that we want, I'd think," she answered. "The place is not far from here. We could stop by on the way home and see when it is convenient."

"Today would be very convenient for me," Tom said.

Cessy's eyes widened. "Today?"

"It would be perfect, Cessy," he coaxed her. "We could marry this afternoon. Maloof and Muna could stand up with us. We'd be man and wife, at last."

"Today?" She spoke the word almost breathlessly.

Tom pulled her into his arms once more. "Today, Cessy, we could be married," he said planting a gentle kiss upon her brow. Then he nuzzled her neck and whispered in her ear. "And tonight we could be man and wife."

"Oh! Oh, yes," she agreed as he began laying a path of kisses from her jaw to her throat.

Tom heard her sigh with pleasure and pushed his advantage. He brought his mouth to her own once more and laid her back against the surface of the rock. Covering her soft, warm body with his own, he wedged one thigh between her own, opening her legs as easily as he'd opened her heart. She eagerly wrapped her arms around his neck, lovingly sifting her fingers through his hair and caressing his shoulders.

He was hard now and pressed himself commandingly against the soft juncture of her thighs as he whispered sweet promises.

"Cessy, I can show you such pleasure," he declared as he lustily rocked his pelvis against her. "Pleasure like you've never dreamed."

She moaned a low, hot sound in her throat that was infinitely enticing.

"Knowing that you love me is all the pleasure I can imagine," she replied.

It was barely an hour later that they gathered up all of their picnic paraphernalia and loaded the surrey.

Maloof and Muna were both stunned into silence at their impromptu announcement. Neither seemed particularly approving, but Tom was grateful that they said little. And Cessy seemed too starry-eyed to notice.

It was all going to work out perfectly, he assured himself. He would be a good, loyal, and faithful husband to his plain little bride. She would never, by any word or deed, ever suspect that he did not love her passionately.

Actually, passion was to be no problem at all. Cessy Calhoun was hotter than a Cuban chili pepper, and the two of them were so physically well-suited that breaking off their impromptu engagement celebration on the big river rock had been difficult.

Clearly, he would be acquiring a worthy bed partner as well as a loving, giving wife and a million-dollar fortune. It was all that a man could ask. Tom didn't truly believe in love, he assured himself. It was just all a mix of romance and passion. His Cessy, he vowed silently to himself, would never be stinted by him on either.

He helped her into the front seat and then, taking up the reins, seated himself beside her.

"Where is this wonderful wedding spot that I will hold fondly in my memories forever as the place where all my dreams came true?"

Cessy giggled beside him and wrapped her arm around his own, laying her head fondly against his shoulder.

"It's right up this road, only about three miles," she said.

Tom felt his heart still.

"That close is it?" he said, deliberately trying to make his voice calm as the blood pounded through his veins in fearful anxiety.

"It's a lovely place," she said. "I've wanted to take you out there and introduce you. And what a wonderful opportunity to do so."

"It's some kind of a church?" he asked.

"There's a little church there," Cessy answered. "That's where we'll be wed. But the place is a school, an orphanage really, where young Indian boys who have no other place to go are given love and care and education and shelter."

"Oh?"

"It's the Methodist Indian Home and it's really my favorite charity. There is this wonderful kind old man, Reverend McAfee. He's devoted his whole life to being a father to the fatherless."

She continued to talk, but Tom didn't hear anymore. His stomach was rolling like he'd eaten something rotten. It was all going to blow up in his face. He was so close, so very close, and it was all going to blow up in his face.

He wanted to scream and curse the heavens. What uncanny twist of fate would introduce Cessy, his Cessy, to Reverend McAfee?

Desperately Tom tried to puzzle out what to do. He

could call a halt to the horses right now and claim a remembered errand in town. But what possible kind of errand could distract a man on the way to take his wedding vows? Snidely, he thought he was perhaps not the first man to seek such a distraction.

Perhaps he could simply brazen it out. When the old man pointed an accusing finger at him and declared him an imposter, he could simply deny it. People found ways to believe what they wanted to believe, often in complete contradiction to all evidence. Cessy would be the same. She loved him and she would take his part, willing enough to assume that poor old Reverend McAfee had lost his mind.

Tom relaxed slightly, his natural optimism rebounding. And Tom had certainly changed a lot in the last eight years. The old man very well might not even recognize him. He was the only father that Tom had ever known. But the good teacher had undoubtedly raised several dozen young boys from infancy. There was certainly no reason why he would remember one nameless, part-breed orphan.

He had almost convinced himself when they came to the top of the hill. The only real home he had ever had was in sight. It was changed, irrevocably changed. Large new buildings dotted the grounds and the trees and shrubs were mightily grown. It was all changed and yet the same as it had ever been. It was as familiar to him as the face in his shaving mirror.

The wide-spreading black walnut had a child's swing hanging from every long limb. The brown rock building stones shone clean and new with the diligent labor of a dozen pairs of young strong hands. The outbuildings gleamed with fresh whitewash, the color relieved only by the occasional twisting vine of morning glories or four-o'clocks. It was beautiful, homey, welcoming. It had been, Tom thought, a prison. And he had been grateful that he had finally made his escape.

He forced himself to remain calm as he drove the team beneath the entrance gate. The arched sign above it read, as it always had, METHODIST INDIAN HOME: *Inasmuch as ye have done it unto one of the least of these my brethren, ye have done it unto me.*

The least of these my brethren. That was Tom, of course. One evening as he was pretending to be Captain Rourke O'Donnell, Union spy, behind Confederate lines, he'd overheard Reverend McAfee describing him to the visiting bishop.

"Young Tom is an unfortunate little fellow, illegitimate and of mixed race. He was undoubtedly destined for a life of dissipation and drunkenness. Because of his sojourn here with us, he is learning an honest trade and we have every hope that he will be a contributing member of the community rather than a blight upon it."

The words were a revelation. He knew at long last who he actually was. An illegitimate, mixed-race unfortunate who by birth was destined for the dregs of existence.

But that was not going to happen to him. Today, he made sure that any chance of that happening would be stifled forever.

The boys, the young students of the school, were everywhere. To Tom's eyes it appeared there were closer to three dozen than the twenty-some-odd that had lived here when he did. They were spread out among the grounds, each by himself, none speaking to another. It was "quiet time." Tom remembered the Sunday afternoon ritual distinctly. The longest hour in the week. One in which it was expected for a boy to be alone with his own thoughts. Tom's thoughts had, as often as not, driven him to make another run for the world outside.

Beside him Cessy was still chattering. Her words seemed more intended for Muna and Maloof than for himself. And those two were as silent as he was. She was nervous, Tom assumed. But he was so personally shaken, he was hardly in condition to reassure her.

It wasn't until he had unerringly driven up to the front of Reverend McAfee's cabin that he reminded himself that Gerald would not know which building to enter. He had to be careful, he reminded himself. He still had to be very careful. It would serve no purpose to fool Reverend McAfee and then give the truth away himself.

Tom set the brake on the surrey and jumped to the ground to help Muna and Cessy.

Muna appeared suspicious and concerned, clearly worried about the unexpected outcome of the day. Cessy was falsely bright and overcheerful.

"I have a friend in the oil business who is really nearing the age to retire," she was saying. "I keep bringing him out here and talking with him. This would be a great place for a couple to spend the later years of their lives. And it would be so wonderful to have a man about who could teach the boys about machinery and modern technology."

"Yes, I suppose so," Tom agreed.

"Reverend McAfee is a clergyman and a scholar. Beyond that he knows only a little about farming and tending horses. The young men who show no great aptitude for schooling must either be trained as farm hands or for working in a livery stable."

Tom nodded, stifling the surge of feeling that swept all around him.

"There are always jobs for livery hands and cotton pickers," he said.

"Yes," Cessy agreed. "But there is so much more in the world and so much more in the future. I want these boys to at least know what exists in the world outside."

That's what Tom had wanted, so much more. He let his eyes wander the familiar grounds, awash with emotions both nostalgic and abhorrent. He had vowed never to come back. He had pledged to leave it all behind him. Now he was here. Or rather, Gerald was, and everything, *everything* that he'd planned could just go up in a puff of smoke.

"This is Reverend McAfee's cabin," Cessy said beside him. "He usually takes a nap on Sunday afternoon."

"Yes," Tom agreed, nodding, and then added, "I hate to disturb the old fellow."

When she didn't answer, Tom turned to look at Cessy. Her brow was furrowed in concern. She glanced back at Muna and Maloof and then grasped Tom's arm.

"Walk with me," she said simply.

Surprised, Tom followed her lead. They moved around the corner of the building out of earshot of her friends. The fields in the distance were bright with thousands of rows of knee-high cotton.

Cessy took his big brown hand in her own two smaller ones and brought his knuckles to her lips. Tom's heart did a somersault at the gesture.

"Cessy?"

"If you've changed your mind, I understand," she said evenly.

"What?"

"I understand," she said. "It was just the . . . the emotion of the moment and now you are . . . regretting, but you are too much the gentleman to bow out. I won't have you do that, Gerald. I'll understand if you've changed your mind."

Tom shook his head, inwardly cursing himself. Of course she would think his strange behavior to be the evidence of reluctance.

"Oh, Cessy," he said, pulling her into his arms and setting his cheek against her brow. "It *was* the emotion of the moment, and I want a hundred million moments just like that for the rest of my life."

She pulled away from his embrace, unconvinced.

"I can tell that you are upset, Gerald. The truth is, and everybody knows it, I push people into things. I am . . . bossy and demanding and sometimes I just do not . . ."

Tom placed a finger upon her lips to hush her words.

"Cessy, I want to marry you," he said honestly. "It's not something that just occurred to me this afternoon. The truth is, I've been thinking about it since the night we met."

"You, too!" She smiled with such warmth, the coldest heart in the world would have melted. "I loved you then, right then," she admitted. "I knew that very first moment that you were the man I'd been waiting for all my life. The special man that God had made to suit me just perfectly."

Guilt stung Tom as he looked down into her bright blue eyes, made so large by the thick lenses of her spectacles.

"Cessy, I'm not perfect," he said quietly.

She laughed with genuine delight. "Well, it's a good thing," she answered. "I'd hate to marry myself to a true paragon."

"I am no paragon," Tom said. "In fact, Cessy, there are things about me, things that you may find out about me that you may not like at all."

His words were excruciatingly serious, but Cessy seemed unable to take them as anything but humor. Once he'd assured her that he did want to marry, nothing else had the power to evoke her concern.

"Things I don't know about you?" She tutted dramatically. "That does sound ominous, Mr. Crane. Are you suggesting that you are a former bank robber? Or that you sleep with your boots on?"

"I'm serious now, Cessy," he said. "I want to marry you. I will spend my life trying to make you happy. But I want you to understand, going in, that there are things about me that you do not know."

Her expression softened and she raised up on her tiptoes to press her lips against his own.

"Do you think I am sweet and demure?" she asked.

Tom was momentarily mute.

"I . . . ah . . ."

"It's a simple question, Gerald," she said. "Do you think I am sweet and demure?"

"Cessy, you . . . ah . . . those are probably not the first words I would have come up with to describe you. You . . . you . . ." He chose his words with great care. "You have an inner strength that shines out from your soul that I find very beautiful."

"Exactly," she interrupted. "You love me for what you perceive is the person that I am. The person I am in my heart. I am not insulted by that. I am overjoyed. You see, that's how I love you, too, Gerald. I love you for the man inside you. I don't know him that well, yet. But I know that he is a good man. I can perceive that much. Whatever I learn about him later will never alter that feeling."

"But what if . . ." Tom began.

"Hallo!" A voice hailed them from the corner of the house. "I didn't expect to see you here today, Missy."

"Reverend McAfee!" Cessy ran toward the old man and gave him a hug. "I have the most wonderful news. Come here, there is someone that I want you to meet."

Tom stood rooted to the spot. The old man had changed. He had changed a lot. The bushy black beard that he remembered hung gray and uncut to the middle of his shirt. The sharp eyes that had never missed anything were now cloudy with age. Momentarily Tom remembered a long-ago moment when he'd been small and frightened and had clung to the old man's pantleg. Today Reverend McAfee was so stooped, the top of his balding head came barely to the height of Tom's rib cage.

"Reverend McAfee," Cessy said formally. "I would like you to meet Gerald Tarkington Crane."

Tom held his breath as the old man appeared to scrutinize him. His brow furrowed thoughtfully.

"I didn't quite catch your name, son," he said.

"Crane," Tom answered in Gerald's crispest eastern intonation. "Gerald Tarkington Crane of Bedlington in the New Jersey, at your service, sir."

Tom extended his hand graciously. The old man hesitated only a fraction of a second before he accepted it, his grasp unexpectedly strong.

"What brings you to visit us today, Mr. Crane," he said.

"Gerald is my intended," Cessy piped in, almost gushing.

The old man seemed taken aback. "You're getting married, Missy? When did this happen?"

"This afternoon," she answered with a laugh of delight. "He asked me, or perhaps I asked him, you know how difficult it is for me wait for others to take action. Anyway, I did not say no."

Reverend McAfee gave a small chuckle at her little joke, but clearly his heart was not in it.

"Marriage is a fine thing," the old man said. "I was wed myself many years ago. We had two little girls."

Tom was startled by this revelation.

"I lost them all to the yellow jack," he finished.

"Oh, Reverend McAfee, I am so sorry," Cessy told him as she lay a comforting hand on his shoulder.

He shook his head with unconcern and patted her hand. "Heaven has seen fit to compensate me. With the young fellow we got last Christmas from the Arapaho, it makes sixty-eight sons that I've been sent to raise. Not many men are so fortunate."

The old man turned to offer a glance toward Tom.

"And each one as dear to my heart as if he were my own flesh and blood."

Tom felt his words as if they were almost a slap. Did the old man recognize him? Surely he could not. If he did, he would speak up.

"Maybe some of your happiness and good fortune will rub off on us," Cessy said. "We want you to marry us, Reverend McAfee."

He gave a little startled sigh of pleasure. "I would be delighted to do so, Missy," he said. "You have been such a friend to the school and a comfort in my old age, but these old bones don't take to the buggy much anymore. I'd never be able to stand the ride into town."

"Oh, but we want to marry here," she said. "In your chapel, today."

"Today!"

"Yes," she told him. "Our families will make such a fuss if we go back and announce our engagement. My father will want to put on some grand show. And all of Gerald's relatives will have to come from back East and well, we just want to be married without all the *fixings*."

"But surely you want your father there, Missy," he said. "And your friends."

"My best friend is with me," she answered. "With her, and you, and Gerald, I will be surrounded by people who love me."

As if on cue, Muna and Maloof came around the corner and further introductions were made.

"So you two want to stand up with this couple?" Reverend McAfee asked. "Then you must know them pretty well."

"I've known Princess forever," Muna said with great certainty. "We've all just met Gerald."

Her words held an almost palpable air of distrust.

"Ah . . . but you no need time for sure a man can trust," Maloof interjected. "My friend is such man, good man."

His words clearly surprised his fiancé and Muna looked at him askance.

"Mr. Bashara," she snapped. "You do not know this man at all. You can't even remember his name."

Cessy laughed. "Mr. Bashara doesn't speak very good English," she explained to Reverend McAfee. "But I agree with him totally. I trust Gerald completely and there is nothing I want more in the world than to be his wife."

The old man looked concerned. He glanced at Tom once more. But nodded affirmatively.

"Do you have a license?" he asked.

"No," Tom replied quietly. "We just became engaged an hour ago."

"Oh, dear!" Cessy exclaimed. "I didn't even think. I hope it doesn't mean we can't get married."

"Well . . ." the old man began.

"We have thirty days to get one?" Tom replied for him. "Isn't that how it often works, Reverend McAfee? A couple marries and then the officiant has a month to file the papers with the state court."

"Why yes, that is often the way," he admitted.

"Then we *can* get married today!" Cessy exclaimed, delighted. "Gerald, you are so smart. You know so much about everything. Did you study the law when you were at Yale?"

"No," he answered.

"Yale?" Reverend McAfee's eyes widened with surprise. "A fine and venerated institution of higher learning," he said.

There was something in his tone that Tom recognized as dangerous.

"Yes, the oldest in the country," he replied, raising his chin almost in challenge. "The men of my family have always attended Yale."

It was not at all as she had imagined it would be. It was no grand church crowded with fancy dressed people. Only the young schoolboys, fidgeting and curious, were seated in the pews. She did not have the arm of her father as she made her way down the aisle. He was not there smiling down at her, looking proud of her. She wore no beautiful gown of beaded silk and no long frothy veil partially obscuring her face. She was dressed as if for an afternoon picnic and she carried a Queen Anne's lace and a cattail surrounded by buttercups for her bouquet.

No, none of that was as she had imagined, as she had hoped and dreamed. But as she walked slowly, unerringly to the side of the man who was to be her husband, Princess could not fathom a happier or more beautiful wedding.

As she stepped up and accepted Gerald's hand she had to stifle the urge to giggle. The marriage ceremony was supposed to be solemn and serene, but Princess had the nearly uncontrollable desire to laugh out loud, to shriek with joy, to climb to the rooftop and cry out to the whole world that she was the luckiest woman ever born.

Her exuberance was not shared by the other members of the wedding party. Muna stood beside her, still and vaguely disapproving. Maloof, at Gerald's right, seemed to be as puzzled with her mood as he was curious about the occasion. Reverend McAfee was positively morose, she thought. His words about the responsibilities of wedlock and the sanctity of marriage were stern enough to sound almost angry and threatening.

And Gerald, her beloved Gerald, looked so pale and shaken, it seemed questionable whether he would make it through the vows without fainting.

Perhaps she should not have pushed to have the wedding today. Could she not, even on her wedding day, stop trying to manage everything? Clearly, despite what he'd said, Gerald had second thoughts about his offer. Of course he was afraid. What man would not be? Giving up his freedom to take on the responsibility of a wife and, hopefully soon, a family.

And Princess was quite sure that *she* was not at all what his family would have expected for him. Undoubtedly they had in mind an attractive and fashionable young woman from a family they knew well and approved of. They would find the plain, brusque, and domineering daughter of a brash oil baron quite a dismay. But she was not going to worry about that. Gerald was hers. And clearly Gerald was never the type of man to be happy in the very closed, rigid life of the five hundred. It was almost as if he were as much a part of the world of the west as she was herself.

Gerald turned to face her. He was making his vows to her. Promising to love and cherish her, to guard and keep her, to give himself only to her for the rest of his life.

"I do," he said.

Her heart fluttered inside like a bird taking flight.

Reverend McAfee addressed her next.

"Do you, Princess Calhoun, take this man to be your lawful wedded husband? To honor and obey him. To keep yourself unto him for better or worse, for richer or poorer, in sickness or in health, 'til death do you part?"

"I do," she answered, a bit too loudly, and then blushed at her unseemly enthusiasm.

Brides were supposed to be shy and scared. Princess felt only elated and eager.

Gerald was holding her hand now and placing a wide gold band upon it. She was momentarily surprised at the ring. It was fashionable enough and very traditional, but it was a strange color gold. Perhaps it was mixed with some worthy alloy, something very modern and up-to-the-minute. It was not at all what she would have picked out herself. But Gerald apparently liked it. If it made him happy, then just having it made her happy.

He was speaking to her again now, but gazing up into his dark, handsome eyes had turned her momen-

tarily deaf to his voice. She caught only the last words
of his utterance.

". . . and with all my worldly goods I thee endow."

Reverend McAfee pronounced them man and wife.
Princess raised her chin, eager for the kiss of the man
that she loved.

Gerald appeared momentarily embarrassed and
only pressed his lips against hers for the slightest
moment.

Princess was puzzled at his strange behavior and
looked at him curiously. He leaned close as if to
whisper another vow for her ears alone.

"I will do everything in my power to see that you
are never sorry about this day," he said.

She almost laughed aloud as she wrapped her arms
around his neck. "Nothing, nothing in the world,
could ever make me sorry about becoming your wife."

Then *she* kissed him. Not the prim little peck that
he'd offered, but a kiss of real passion and ardor. She
kissed him until the sounds of snickering by youngsters in the pews penetrated her thoughts and caused
her to pull away from the embrace with embarrassment.

There was enthusiastic applause from the boys.
The congratulations of Muna and Maloof were more
subdued. And Reverend McAfee quietly encouraged
her to come to him with any troubles or difficulties
that she might have to face.

Determinedly, Princess refused to allow the long
faces to cast a shadow of gloom upon her wedding
day. She laughed and hugged her friends and gently
tossed her bouquet for Muna to catch.

Maloof brewed his Turkish coffee and they served it,
along with Mrs. Nafee's pastries and Mrs. Marin's pies
for the wedding party. There was much laughter and
well wishes from the boys. The youngsters, as always,
were well-scrubbed, genuine, and unfailingly polite.

It was only a short time later when, seated upon

the front seat of the awning-striped surrey, she wrapped her arm around her husband's and leaned her head upon his shoulder.

"Mrs. Gerald Tarkington Crane," she said, trying it out. "What do you think?"

Gerald smiled wanly.

"What do you think, Muna?" she asked.

"It . . . it sounds fine, Prin," Muna answered.

"Princess Crane?" the new bride suggested and then wrinkled her nose. "Sounds like too much, don't you think? I'll just be Cessy Crane, just plain Cessy Crane. That will be positively perfect for me."

"You don't want to be a princess anymore?" Gerald asked.

She shook her head. "When I was the daughter of the king, I didn't mind it. But now I am a simple wife, first and foremost."

It was true. It was really, finally true. She had found the man of her dreams and she had married him. It was wonderful, magical, even a little frightening.

She glanced over at the strong arm entwined in her own, the big, brown hands that held the reins with such certainty and control and the sturdy, muscular thigh that were part of the man that was now her husband, for better or worse, hers only forever.

In her mind she could taste once more his passionate kisses, feel the touch of his hands on her body, and tremble with the desire to join her flesh with his own.

Tonight. Tonight. Tonight all the mysteries of married life would be revealed. Tonight all the stoked fires of their formerly forbidden passions would be allowed to blaze at last. Tonight he'd see her with her hair down. He'd see her in her nightgown! Would he wear a plaid nightshirt like Papa's?

She snickered a little at the thought of Gerald dressed that way. When he glanced over at her questioningly, she laughed out loud.

"What is so funny to my new bride?" he asked her.

. She shrugged, unwilling to answer.

"I'm just happy," she said. "I'm just very, very happy."

Gerald's answering tone was much more serious.

"I'm happy, too, Cessy," he said. "Happier than I'd ever imagined."

His words warmed her, thrilled her, charmed her. She was delighted with herself and all the world. It was perfect, all of it was just so perfect.

"I am positively giddy," she announced. "I swear if I could carry a tune in a bucket, I'd just start singing."

Gerald looked down at her warmly.

"I'm sure you sing beautifully," he told her.

Still giggling, she glanced back at Muna.

"Remember that song leader at the church in Jackson? We were standing right behind him when he said to the pastor, 'Miss Calhoun doesn't sing any sweeter than she talks.'"

Princess shook her head, laughing at the memory. "Daddy was so angry, I thought he was going to punch that fellow in the face right there on the church steps."

"Well, I should think so!" Gerald's jaw was set with such angry affront that Princess couldn't help but smile.

"What a lucky woman I am," she stated. "The men in my life stand ready to defend me at any moment from the absolute truth."

She grasped his hand, lacing her fingers through his own. "I am not and cannot be offended by the truth," she said.

Her words caused his brow to furrow once more. They had already reached the edge of town and it was all she could do not to hug him right in public.

"I never wanted too much for myself," she told him, quietly. "Only to be loved."

It was nearing sunset as they dropped Muna and Maloof at the Emporium. Princess exacted a promise from her friend not to tell Mr. and Mrs. Nafee until after her father had heard the news.

"Be happy for me, Muna," she whispered to her friend as she said goodbye.

"I am," Muna insisted. "I am, it's just . . . oh, it's just something strange. I'm too suspicious, I suppose."

"There is nothing to be suspicious about," Princess assured her. "I love him, he loves me, we're married now and plan on living happily ever after."

"Of course you will," Muna said with almost too much conviction. "I . . . I am very happy for you, Prin. Maybe I'm just jealous that you got to marry first."

They laughed together at that and then kissed each other on the cheek.

Gerald helped her back into the surrey and they headed for home.

"I don't want you to worry about meeting my father," she told him. "Believe me, his bark is much worse than his bite."

"Is he going to bark at me?" Gerald asked.

"Probably," she admitted. "He's probably going to bark at both of us. But we're just not going to pay any attention."

"It's a good plan," he agreed.

To her disappointment, Princess realized as they pulled into the porte cochere, her father's Packard, and therefore her father, was not at home.

"Oh, dear," she complained. "I hadn't thought about that and I should have. He . . . he stays out many nights, on business, of course."

"Of course."

Howard hurried out to take charge of the horses. Gerald leapt down from the seat and raised his arms to her. He didn't help her down in the genteel fashion of a courtier, but rather grabbed her waist like a loving husband and lifted her to the ground. She loved it and smiled up at him, her heart in her eyes.

"Well, perhaps it's better that Papa isn't here," she said. "I'm not sure what to do. Do you think that we should send for him? I'm not sure exactly where he goes. But somehow Howard always seems able to find him."

Gerald looked down in her eyes and smiled as he shook his head. "I think tomorrow will be soon enough for him to know."

"Do you think we can . . . we can stay in the house together before we tell him?" she asked.

"We are man and wife," Gerald answered. "Didn't Reverend McAfee say that what God has joined together let not man put asunder."

Cessy nodded. "Then you think that it's all right," she said.

Gerald smiled, leaned closer, and whispered softly to her. "I think that we'll have this whole big house to ourselves this evening."

Cessy blushed, suddenly unable to meet his gaze. "I'm sure Mrs. Marin has prepared a wonderful meal, and there is always more than enough for two. We—"

"We will certainly need to eat a hearty supper," he agreed, his voice sultry and teasing. "Something to keep up our strength."

Then he slipped his arm under her knees and lifted her up into her arms.

"Oh dear! You needn't carry me," she exclaimed. "I can walk."

He raised an eyebrow. "I will try to make that as easy to say tomorrow as tonight."

"What?"

"Never mind," he answered and carried her across the threshold of the porte cochere doorway.

ELEVEN

Queenie's Palace was quiet since Sundays were typically slow. There were a couple of games still running in the back room. A few patrons sat at the bar. The bartender had strict orders to cut them off at three drinks. Queenie didn't believe in appearing to have too a good time on the day the townspeople would find it most objectionable. In the legal vacuum between the dissolution of the territory and the brand-new state, the laws regulating drink and vice had become murky and unenforceable. But community groups were already beginning to petition the legislature to come down hard on businesses like the Palace. The wild, free-for-all territory days were quickly becoming a thing of the past. The good people of the future Oklahoma now wanted churches and schools and the quiet pleasures of home.

Home. Queenie sat in the silence of the upstairs room that was her home, staring out the back window at the sunset just beyond the alley.

In the distance she saw a well-sprung buggy driving slowly through the streets of town on a late Sunday drive. What was that like, she wondered. What was it like to be a Sunday-drive kind of person? What was it like to be a decent person with an ordinary life? To be a wife, a mother, an accepted member of a community.

King always said that he didn't believe in regretting. She'd always agreed with him. Nothing could change the past. And given the same set of circumstances, Queenie believed that most folks, certainly she herself, would make exactly the same choices a second time.

No, she didn't believe in ruing the past. But she did believe in planning for the future.

Queenie laid a hand upon her stomach. She felt nothing there, no life, no mystery, no anticipation. There was a new beginning there, but all it brought to her life was an intermittent nausea.

She could never change the past. She could never again be a young girl, green and foolish, picking cotton and listening to a sweet-talking man's lies. She didn't even want to.

The road she'd traveled had taught her a lot. She wouldn't give up what she'd learned about life and about people. And she wouldn't have wanted to miss King. If she'd married some hardworking, respectable farmer, if she'd worked his land and raised his children, she would never have found King, the love of her life. That alone was worth all the dues that she'd paid.

She continued to silently watch the sunset from her window. It was amazing that as it got closer to the earth, closer to the end of the day, it seemed to grow larger and brighter as if daring the land to try to extinguish it. All day it had shone yellow against a pale-blue sky. But now, after all of that, it was vivid orange against an horizon of pink and magenta.

Was life like that? Could people live one way, easily recognizable and familiar, and then dramatically change to an entirely different life?

What had the young tool dresser said? *It helps a bit*

if you can just throw away your old past and start out with a brand-new one, cut exactly to fit.

Queenie closed her eyes and a yearning welled up in her. A yearning so strong and sweet and powerful it choked her throat and became an ache in her breast.

Unexpectedly the door burst open and King Calhoun entered the room.

"What you doing sitting here in the dark, darlin'?"

"Don't you ever knock?" Queenie snapped, hurriedly drying the dampness at the corners of her eyes.

King gave her a long look. "Didn't know I needed to," he replied. "You want me to light the lamp?"

"I'm watching the sunset," she told him, still waspish in her tone. "I don't need a lamp for that."

"No, I suspect not," King agreed.

He came up to stand behind her, following her gaze through the back-alley window. He lay his hands on her tired shoulders and began to gently knead the tightness in her neck and rub out all the pain and cares of her day.

"It is kinda pretty, ain't it?" he said finally. "That sunset, I mean. A fellow like me don't get too many chances to just sit and watch the world turn around. Seems like I'm always busy trying to get it to spin in my direction."

Queenie sighed under the machinations of his hands and regained her good humor.

"Is it spinning your way today?" she asked him.

"Nope," he said. "Not yet. I don't have so much as a trail to follow on a lending banker. We're hitting oil up there on the hill, any minute now, I can almost smell it. Without a pipeline or a refinery, we might as well let the buffalo grass soak it up and put a match to it."

"I'm sorry, King," she said. "The offer of a loan is still open."

"It wouldn't be enough, not even if I sold the house

I gave Princess and stole the money I put for her in trust. It takes bank money to build a refinery. A man can't do it on his own fortune alone."

There was nothing more that Queenie could say.

"I just wish I'd made some provisions for you," King told her. "I'm real sorry about that, Queenie. I truly am."

"What do you mean provisions for me?"

"If the field goes belly-up there'll be nothing here but the stinking little Burford Corners that we started with," he said. "It'll be no place for a fine Palace like this."

"It's just a building," Queenie said with a shrug. "It's the people that make a business, we can always do as well one place as another."

King shook his head. "Still, darlin', I regret getting you messed up in this."

"I thought you didn't believe in regrets, King," she pointed out.

The big man shrugged thoughtfully. "Maybe I've been wrong," he said.

He pulled up a chair and took her hand in his own. He chose his words carefully as if for once he was hesitant to speak his mind.

"Queenie, this is a real nice place you've got here," he said. "It's a clean and honest business. There ain't nothing here that a person would have to be ashamed of."

"Thank you," she answered.

"It ain't . . . well . . . it ain't bad like . . . I mean, Queenie, I've seen worse."

Queenie couldn't imagine what he was getting at and snorted, shaking her head.

"I imagine you have," she said. "There's worse up and down both sides of the street outside."

"Queenie, I mean I've seen a lot worse."

Beads of sweat popped out on King's forehead, yet the evening breeze through the back-alley window was cool. He looked over at her, his expression weary, worried, torn. He cleared his throat as if steeling his determination before he spoke.

"My mama was a whore, Queenie," he stated bluntly. "She was more than a whore. She was a gin-crawler with her hands out and her legs open."

"Oh, King," Queenie whispered.

"It's true, too true. This joint *is* a palace compared to the way we lived."

Queenie watched him, waiting.

"We never had no place," he continued. "From time to time she'd have a crib, but mostly we lived on the streets. She hardly knew and never cared. Why would she? She was never sober. Philadelphia looks mighty fine from the avenues, but it's an ugly view from the street."

"King, you don't have to—"

"Queenie, I want to tell you," he interrupted. "I've been keeping it inside me for a lifetime now, hiding it, running away from it. It's time I said it out loud and heard it myself."

The pain in his heart was reflected upon his face.

"I learned to steal and lie and cheat. I learned to do things for money that most men wouldn't have done to save their life."

There was no emotion in his voice. He spoke the words almost dispassionately, as if he were reading them from the story of someone else's life.

"I learned to sell my mama, Queenie. I went out and sold her body myself. When she'd be too drunk to get herself a Joe Poke I'd go around to the bars and hustle her business. I was about eight or ten, I guess."

He raised his eyes to Queenie's, his voice mimicking that he'd once had as a child.

"'Hey fellah, you wanna meet my sister?' I'd say. It was always best to pretend she was my sister. To make the fellahs think she was younger than she was. 'My sister, she likes it all; suck, pull, or pump and you're guaranteed to fire, sure as a gun.' That's what my boyhood was like, Queenie. That was what I did with my childhood."

Queenie squeezed his hand, wanting to offer whatever comfort she could. "I'm sorry, King," she whispered. "I'm very, very sorry."

"It was a long time ago," he said. "It was a very long time ago. She's dead and I'm . . . I'm the King Calhoun."

"You are the most wonderful man that I have ever met," Queenie assured him. "And the things you been through only make me love you more."

He nodded. "That's my point, Queenie. I had a terrible mother, no father at all, and a really bad start in life. I've lived things I don't want to remember and done things that I can't forget. But I'm not ashamed to be who I am. Even with all of that, I've turned out all right. I've worked hard, made something of my life. Maybe this child, our child, could, too."

She looked at him questioningly.

"This Palace is not such a bad place for a boy to grow up. It's warm and dry and . . . and he would know that he was loved. You'd be a wonderful mama for any boy."

Queenie eyed him suspiciously. "You want me to have this baby, King? Even after what you just told me about your own life, your own shame."

"But it wouldn't be like that for him."

"He or she might well think it is," she said. "No matter how clean and legal the saloon is, King, it's still a saloon. And I may not be a gin-crawler, but I'm as much a whore as your mother."

"You haven't whored in ten years, I'd swear it."

"What do you call last night?" she asked.

"Last night?" King was momentarily nonplussed.

"Last night you made love with me."

"Is that what you'd call it?" she asked.

"I certainly would."

"Well, our child might hear it called otherwise. Every decent soul in Burford Corners would be quick to tell him that his mother is a barroom prostitute and his daddy a whoremonger."

"Queenie . . ."

"You're not the only one who's been trying to see a way out," she told him. "I've hardly been able to put my mind to anything else. But what you're thinking just won't do. You've turned out to be a good man, King, a fine, gentle, tender man, despite who your mother was and what kind of life you were born into. But I've seen otherwise, King. I've seen boys and girls who could break my heart. Innocent children jerked into the world and left to fend for themselves in the shadow of the bar or the bordello. Hungry, dirty, beaten, and broken, all they get from life is a harsh word and a slap in the face. I won't do that to a child, King, not even one that I want as much as I want yours."

His expression was immediately crestfallen.

"Then there is no way?"

Queenie looked into his eyes, loving him, wanting him, wanting his child.

"I wish . . . I wish . . . hell, I've even *prayed* for a way, but I just can't see one, King. I just can't see one."

The quiet evening at home on her wedding night was one of the longest and most nerve-racking that Princess could ever remember. Gerald had taken the team back to the livery and she was jumpy as a cat the whole time he was gone. She tried to organize a lovely dinner for two, but she was so nervous and almost giddy that she simply could not think straight. Mrs. Marin had graciously taken up the challenge of their wedding feast as if a gauntlet had been thrown. They sat in the dining room for what must have been hours.

Princess was so anxious and edgy she had no appetite at all. Still, it was an impressive display of culinary excellence. The formal dining table was set with the snowy handloomed linen table dressings. The rose china was hastily unpacked and washed. And a simple pork roast dinner miraculously blossomed into a veritable feast of a thousand courses.

Cessy had no idea what she ate, but she was extremely aware of every bite that Gerald took. She sat at the far end of the table from him and barely a word passed between them during the meal. Yet she was aware of every movement he made. Every breath he took. Strangely, it made her tremble.

Howard had managed to unearth a dusty bottle of wine. Although Cessy had never cared for spirits, she found herself nervously bringing the rim of the glass to her lips time and time again. Gerald drank very little, but as they rose finally to leave the table, he drained the contents of his glass and urged her to do the same.

"Shall we withdraw to the sitting room, Cessy?" he suggested.

She agreed, and they spent a very long, uncomfortable evening making stilted conversation as they sat next to each other on the silk damask tête-a-tête. They had always talked so easily together and been so in tune. Why now that they were man and wife could they not seem to find one interesting thing to say to each other?

Cessy knew the answer. They couldn't enjoy a pleasant evening together without thinking about the inevitable night that followed it. She had felt so free, so alive and cheerful in their ride home from the school. But now, looking at the man that was now her husband, the niggling doubts that she had deliberately refused to give credence to had begun to creep into her thoughts.

Muna clearly did not trust him. And Reverend

McAfee seemed disturbed by her choice as well. Ma suggested that it was very strange for such a man to live in town for no reason. And then there was the letter, the strange, nearly illiterate letter from a Yale graduate.

"Cessy, I believe that it is time for us to retire for the evening."

Gerald had leaned his head down more closely to her own to speak quietly in her ear. Princess was startled at his unexpected nearness. His voice broke into her rumination and she felt momentarily guilty and disloyal for her thoughts. It was simply nerves, she assured herself. Wedding jitters was what they were called.

"Are you ready to go upstairs?" Gerald asked with more concern.

"Oh! Whatever you think," she assured him hastily.

He stood and formally offered his arm. Princess took it.

"You are a bit fidgety tonight," he said.

"Yes, it's really quite natural. I'm . . . I'm not used to being alone with you," she admitted.

"What about all those dark nights on your front porch?" he asked.

Cessy blushed, remembering. She knew she had allowed him an inordinate amount of liberty with her person, but tonight somehow she was ill at ease and shy. As they climbed the wide staircase with its sharp angles and sturdy, austere design, she deliberately steeled herself against her fears.

"Tell me what to do and I will do it," she said.

Gerald's brow raised in question. "Has marriage turned my lovely lady who gives orders into such a biddable bride?" he asked.

"I . . . why yes, I suppose," she answered him, somewhat flustered.

"Then perhaps I shall be unscrupulous in what I ask of you," he said.

"Unscrupulous?" she repeated the word. Her heart was in her throat. He had spoken in jest, she assured herself. It was only a silly joke. So why were her hands shaking and her heart pounding as they stepped into the privacy of her bedroom?

Gerald set the lamp he carried on the bedside table, illuminating the room that had been hers alone since the day that they built the house.

Her room, which she'd always thought of as basically Spartan and practical, suddenly appeared to her as a girl's room. The wallpaper was pink roses and the window shades were trimmed in lace. Gweneth, her doll, sat gussied up and ready for play upon the highboy. The gleaming four-poster captured most of her attention. It was not an overly large bed. Certainly it might accommodate two people, but when she had purchased it, she'd had no such thought in mind. This was her room, her things, her bed. And this . . . this stranger was here with her now.

Gerald moved behind to pull the heavy, ceiling-height walnut door closed. The metallic snap of the lock being engaged was inordinately loud. Cessy's throat went dry.

"We're all alone now," he said, a little too softly.

"Yes," she agreed.

"The two of us, man and wife, all alone," he continued. "And you, Cessy, you just promised to be my obedient bride."

"Well, I . . . I . . . of course, I just meant that . . ."

He was walking around her. Slowly walking around her as if she were some sort of specimen being examined. It was fear, genuine fear that welled up in her now. She didn't know him, not really. Her mind quickly ran through the stories he'd told about himself and his life. They were only pieces, tiny pieces, of what surely must have been a long and complicated life. She should have asked him more. More about himself and his past. They'd spent far too much time talking about life and the world and philosophy. She should never have married a man she didn't know.

Gerald continued to walk around her, looking her up and down as if she were something that he owned.

"I just meant," she continued more forcefully, "that I wish to be a good wife to you. I . . . I have not said that I would do anything that you ask."

He stopped in front of her then. He folded his arms across his chest and regarded her critically.

"Cessy," he asked, "what is it that you think I might ask of you that you would not be willing to do?"

"What?"

"What is it? Tell me. What would you say no to?"

"I . . . I don't know."

He continued to stare at her for a long moment.

"All right, then, what is it that you would say yes to?" he asked.

She clasped her hands together tightly to keep them from trembling. "I don't know that either," she admitted.

"I think perhaps you know more than you admit," he said.

His words surprised her, indeed shocked her. Did he think that she was not a virgin? Did he believe that she had been alone like this with another man? How could she tell him it wasn't so? She could never bring herself to utter the words of explanation.

"I've never . . ." she began.

He waved his hand to hush her.

"I'm not saying that you are experienced in love, Cessy. I'm saying that you understand more about it than you think you do."

Her brow furrowed curiously, unsure.

"Kiss me," he said.

With little hesitation she stepped forward to put her mouth against his own. It was a warm and sweet kiss. Not as intimate as some they had shared that afternoon, but very pleasurable.

"That was nice, Cessy," he told her. "That was very nice."

She smiled back at him, a little less hesitantly.

"Now," he said. "Please remove all your clothing and bend over the edge of the bed there. I plan to take you heifer style and we've wasted enough time on the pleasantries already."

"What?"

"You did hear me, didn't you?"

Her eyes widened in embarrassment. Cessy was totally scandalized. "I . . . I . . . you . . . we can't . . . it's not . . . and . . . and . . ."

"And what, my biddable bride?" he asked.

"And . . . and I am not a heifer. And no, I will not!" she said, nearly choking with outrage.

Slowly, very slowly, he smiled.

"Are you laughing at me?" she asked, infuriated.

"No, Cessy, I'm listening to you prove me right."

She frowned.

"You do know what you do and what you don't want to do," he said. "And I hear you telling me so very plainly."

Her fear fading, her confusion magnified. "I . . . it's not that I don't . . . don't want to be intimate with you," she tried explaining. "But that . . . it's so unseemly and embarrassing and I could not simply just . . . just disrobe."

"Of course not," he agreed.

He reached out to take her hand in his own. She was still trembling, but the warmth of his touch reassured her somehow.

"Cessy," he said. "I am your husband. I have

promised to love and honor you. As a husband, I will make demands upon you. But I don't want you to ever feel afraid of me. Cessy, you can always tell me no. About anything at anytime."

"Gerald I . . . I am . . . I am a little afraid," she said. "It's just all so fast and I'm not sure. I'm not sure that I . . . that I really know you."

"All you need to know, Cessy," he told her, "is that I am your husband and that I will cherish you."

"I'm sorry, Gerald," she said. "I suppose that I am hopelessly unsophisticated."

He grinned at her, seemingly delighted.

"Cessy, a person does not need sophistication to have good sex. This is one activity that is not at all confined to class."

He reached for her then, pulling her into his arms lovingly. "Romance is free and equal for everyone."

She nodded. "Yes, I suppose so."

"Then you will trust me on this, won't you."

"Yes," she said a little more easily. He was still looking at her in that very disconcerting way. But somehow it was as thrilling as it was unsettling. "Yes, I love you and I will trust you."

"Then perhaps you can change into your night-clothes," he suggested. "Please make use of the dressing screen if you like. I have no wish to inordinately embarrass you."

"Thank you," she said. Cessy forced herself not to race to the partial privacy behind the dressing screen. She was still nervous, but the shocking fright he'd given her had somehow calmed her worst fears. He was tonight the same gentleman she had been so eager to wed today. He was Gerald Tarkington Crane, her husband and the man she loved.

"Oh!" she exclaimed, turning back in time to catch him removing his coat. "I forgot that you have no nightclothes. I will get you one of my father's night-shirts."

He shook his head. "Don't," he told her. "I never wear them."

Wide-eyed once more, Cessy slipped behind the screen. He didn't wear any nightclothes? Was she going to step out to find him totally naked and exposed? The very idea of it took her breath away.

With nervous fingers and a bit of clumsy contortion she managed to undo the buttons at the back of her dress and to get it off over her head. She divested herself of her petticoat and ruffle-laden camisole and removed her corset. Seated upon the dainty little dressing stool, she unhooked the laces on her shoes and rolled down her stockings.

Stripped down to only her chemise and pantalettes, Cessy eyed herself critically. Her figure had never been one to turn heads, but she had long since given up worrying about it. Her failure to develop a curvaceous bosom had led her to purchase her camisoles heavily ruffled. And her backside was effectively augmented with a horsehair bustle.

Tonight, without the enhancements of the fashion arts, the man she loved would see her as she truly was. It was daunting. She was not ashamed of how she looked. She looked exactly as God had made her, but on this one special night she couldn't help but wish that heaven had been a little more generous with those physical traits that men seemed to so appreciate.

Determinedly she rose to her feet and unhooked her spectacles. If there was ever a time when near-sightedness could be an advantage, the wedding night must be it.

Princess discarded her remaining "frillies" and pulled on her prettiest nightgown. It was sleeveless gauze with a profusion of delicate blue ribbon hanging from the shoulders. She began taking down her hair, but she had neither her brush nor her pin box. She bit her lip, considering her options. Should she step out from behind the screen with her hair half up and half down and go sit at her dressing table? Should she wind it back up as best she could and repin it? Or should she let it all down and comb it the best she could with her fingers?

She decided on the latter course, but then stood unsure because she had no mirror in which to judge her success or failure. Finally, raising her chin high and mustering her courage, Cessy walked out from behind the screen, determined to be unintimidated.

Gerald sat on the edge of her bed wearing only his gray, knee-length cotton trunks. He stood immediately, observing the refined amenities even in this very awkward private moment.

Even with her faulty vision, Cessy could see that his shoulders were tremendously broad for a gentleman. And his bare chest heavily muscled. Princess thought that he must be very athletic indeed to develop and keep such a splendid physique. His abdomen was as rigid and defined as a washboard. And his waist was trim and his hips narrow. Beneath the covering of his trunks, a pair of long, sturdy thighs and masculine hindquarters were evident.

Cessy's eyes were drawn to five small buttons on the front placard of his trunks. Five small buttons were all that remained of modesty. And the manner in which the gray cotton clung to him in that area revealed more than she was ready to allow herself to imagine.

"I must tend my hair," she announced in almost a frantic tone, turning from him to hurry to the dressing table.

She seated herself hastily. Her hands were shaking as she fumbled for her delicate silver hairpin box, causing her to spill most of the ones she carried.

A creaking of the floorboard behind her caught her attention and she glanced into her mirror to see

Gerald had come up behind her. Wordlessly he took the round, plateback brush from her and began to draw it through her mess of tangles.

"Oh, you needn't do that," she told him. "I'm sure you're not familiar with ladies' hair."

"I'm familiar enough," he answered. "And I want to be very familiar with you."

His words soothed and skittered across her heart with much the same sensation as the Russian bristles that raised gooseflesh at the nape of her neck.

Cessy watched him in the mirror. He was intent in his task. Not overly gentle, but not hurting her either as he patiently unsnarled the length of her hair.

"It's pretty, you know," he said in a manner quite matter-of-fact.

"Is it?"

He held a handful up for her inspection. "It's thick and shiny and the color is nice."

"But it doesn't grow very long," Cessy told him. "I never cut it, but it continues to hang only to the middle of my back. Muna can sit on hers."

Slowly, sweetly he smiled at her.

"Why would she want to?" he asked. "Do her family's chairs lack upholstery? Perhaps we can speak to Maloof about it. I'm sure he will get them a very good deal."

Princess laughed then. That seemed to please him a lot. Gerald laid down the brush and she turned to face him.

He squatted beside her at eye level.

"Any more rituals that must be taken care of before we go to bed?" he asked.

"Aren't you . . . c-cold without a shirt on," she managed to choke out.

He took her hand and placed it against the bare skin of his chest.

"Do I feel cold?"

"No, not at all."

"Are you cold?" he asked as he took her chin in his hand and then allowed his palm to ease along the entire length of her throat.

"It's July," she answered.

"So it is."

His big brown hand continued to caress her, tracing her collarbone and easing under the lace of her neckline.

"What are you doing?"

"Just being friendly, Cessy," he told her.

"It . . . this doesn't seem very friendly," she said.

"You don't like it?"

"No, no, I . . . do like it," she admitted somewhat breathlessly.

"I know you do," he said.

"How could you know?"

"From these," he said, using both thumbs to oh-so-gently pluck at her nipples.

Cessy looked down at the turgid points visible through her nightgown and gasped. She raised her hands to cover herself, but he took her wrists in his own and held them fast.

"Don't cover up," he begged. "I like looking at you."

Princess felt the flames in her cheeks. She could not look at him. She could not meet his eyes.

"Can't you tell that I like it?" he asked. "Look at me, see if you can tell that I like it."

He cupped her chin in his hand and forced her to face him.

"Look at me, Cessy," he told her. "Mine are as hard as your own."

She did look at him. His bare, masculine nipples were beaded up to tiny points. He drew her hand to them. He closed his eyes, swallowed deliberately, and gave a long sigh as she touched him.

Princess felt a surge of unexpected power with the reaction that she had provoked.

"Feel how tight they are," he said.

"Yes," she answered, her own voice a faraway whisper.

"They are much like yours. Just by touching each other here we can always tell if the other partner likes what we are doing."

Cessy nodded, nearly entranced by the strange, pleasurable sensation of simply stroking his skin.

"But it's much easier for you to tell," she said. "Because mine are so much bigger."

He opened his eyes then, his gaze sultry and enticing.

"Well, if there is ever a question in your mind about it," he said with silky softness. He grasped her wrist once more and eased it downward. "Then you can just bring your hand down here for a verification."

A tiny squeal escaped from the back of Cessy's throat as she touched Gerald. Only a thin layer of cotton separated her hand from the most private parts of his body.

"Is that hard enough for you?" he asked.

She sat frozen and immobile for a thousand hurried heartbeats before she realized that he no longer pressed her hand against him. It was she herself who clutched him so intimately.

Cessy jerked her hand away and jumped to her feet. She tried to step around him, but he was right there. He wrapped his hands around her from behind and held her fast.

"Don't run from me," he whispered against her hair. "Don't run from me and don't be afraid. I'm going to make it wonderful for you, Cessy. I promise it will be as fine and sweet as any wedding night any woman ever had. You deserve nothing less. And I can give you that."

"I'm being so silly," she said, attempting to regain control of herself. "I . . . I want this, I want you. It's just all so strange and so . . . scary."

He nuzzled the hair away from her neck and teased her with little nips and kisses.

"Maybe that is because there is something inherently scary in seduction."

The last word was spoken in a whisper and it nearly took her breath away.

She raised her hand, perhaps instinctively, to protect herself from the sensual assault that his mouth made upon her flesh. But ultimately she buried her fingers in his hair, reveling in his touch and urging him on.

"I'm your wife, Gerald," she told him, as calmly as she could manage. "I don't have to be seduced."

As an answer he turned her to face him and brought his mouth to hers. But he did not kiss her, he allowed his tongue to trace the definition of her lips. His words were a soft, warm whisper, so close and intimate.

"Perhaps a bride on her wedding night does not, by necessity, require being wooed and won," he told her. "But my Cessy, I want you to have the whole experience, all of it. I want you to never be able to imagine that our first night together could have been more exciting."

"I don't really want excitement," she assured him. "It's the excitement that is so frightening. I just want some . . . some tenderness."

"Oh, Cessy," he promised. "I will be so tender with you."

As if to prove it, he kissed her then, sweetly and civilly. And it was oh-so-seductive.

"Lay down on the bed, Cessy," he said softly. "Lay down and let me lay down with you."

Cessy would have been happy to comply if she had retained the strength to move. Somehow her limbs

had turned to jelly and her brain to mush. It was
Gerald who lifted her to the bed and eased her down
on pressed cotton sheets. And it was Gerald who
stretched full-length atop her.

"Oh! Oh dear!"

"Am I too heavy for you, Cessy?" he asked.

"No . . . no."

"Do you want the light out?"

"No . . . I mean yes, yes, please," she said.

"Whatever you want," he told her.

But he kissed her instead of turning to the lamp. It
was a kiss like none other he'd given her. It was a kiss
of more than his lips, it was his mouth, his arms, his
hands, his whole body.

The nearness of him was familiar and welcome, yet
the feelings he evoked were new and enticing. His
hands moved along her body with ease and comfort.
But in the wake of their touch her skin began to tingle
and her insides to quiver.

He teased and tasted her from the corner of her
mouth, along her jawline, to the flesh of her throat
and beyond.

He nuzzled his face against her thinly clad bosom.
And then showed her, by toying her nipples with his
teeth and tongue, that he was aware of her pleasure
in his touch.

She bit down on her lower lip to stifle the moan
that rose from her throat.

His hands were not idle, one moment stroking her
thigh, the next caressing her breast.

Cessy wrapped her own arms around his bare
shoulders, burying her fingers lovingly into his thick,
dark hair.

Between her legs there was growing a strange,
aching emptiness, that somehow could not be ignored. She squirmed beneath him, attempting to
assuage the craving.

As if he understood her distress, he clasped her leg

behind the knee and bent it, parting her legs around his hips.

She was closer to him then, much closer, and she could feel the hardness of his body against the softness of her own. Cessy needed to press against him. Somehow she needed very much just to press against him.

Her nightgown constrained her and she jerked at it in frustration.

"Easy, easy sweet bride," he whispered against her neck. "We'll get this thing off of you and it won't be in the way."

She heard his words but when he moved away from her she tried to hold on to him.

"Don't leave," she pleaded.

"I'm putting out the lamp," he said. "And I'm getting rid of this blasted nightgown."

He dispensed with the light with one energetic puff of breath into the top of its chimney. The room was immediately pitch black. Cessy heard him fiddling with the window shade.

"What are you doing?"

"Moonlight, Cessy," he said as he finally got it to retract into its roller. "I think they must call it honeymoon because couples see each other for the first time in moonlight."

He was standing in that stream of glorious silver moonlight as she watched him peel off the thin cotton trunks and cast them carelessly to the floor.

She could see him only in silhouette, but clearly he was as differently made as ever she had imagined a man to be.

He pressed one knee on the mattress tick.

"Let's get rid of this nightgown," he suggested softly.

Cessy remained mute as he firmly grasped the hem of the last remnant of her maidenly modesty and slowly eased it up. Her body was prickling with thrills and quaking with anxiety.

"Up," he ordered simply as he reached the top of her thighs.

Like a trained pony she braced herself upon his strong shoulders and raised her bottom so that the gown slid under easily. A second later it was over her head and Gerald threw it behind him as if he never cared to see it again.

She was half sitting, half lying on the bed. And she was naked. She tried to cover her breasts, but he held her back. Propping her up on her elbows, giving himself unrestricted access to her body.

He explored her slowly, almost curiously. His hands left a trail of tingling sensation upon her skin. With one finger he made a circle around her right breast, as if staking out a claim. Then he took it into his hand, weighing it, sizing it.

"You have pretty breasts," he said.

"They are too small," she answered quickly.

"No, I don't think so," he disagreed, exploring them in a seemingly dispassionate manner that somehow took Cessy's breath away.

"They are firm and high and they have very long nipples," he said. "I like the very long nipples."

To prove his words, he first placed a delicate kiss upon the very tip of one. Then he took it between his lips. With insistent pressure, gentle at first and then more lustily, his mouth pulled at the keenly aroused nipple.

Cessy, overwhelmed by the sensation, threw back her head and cried out in gratification.

"So you like this, my Cessy," he whispered to her as he moved his attention from the right breast to the left. "You like it when I lavish attention on your bosom. I suppose, dear wife, that we'll have to make it part of your evening routine. You brush your hair one hundred strokes and then I suckle you until you cry out my name.''

He did not need to help her a second time to get close to him. Deliberately, she parted her legs around him, pressing herself as closely as nature would allow.

Gerald turned on his side and slid one strong thigh firmly between her own. That was better, it was much better. But it wasn't nearly enough. Cessy almost immediately began to squirm and wiggle against him. He allowed her freely to do so and even aided as he caressed the curve of her buttocks and urged her even closer.

"This is my Cessy," he whispered against her neck. "This is my own, determined, aggressive Cessy. And I think that she wants me."

"I want you," she replied, aching. "Oh please, please, I want you."

He rolled her onto her back and got up on his knees. The loss of his body was tangible. Cessy whined and reached for him.

"Wait, Cessy, I'm going to kiss you."

"Yes, but . . ." She couldn't quite voice her need. But she scooted way down in the bed, attempting to capture his knee between her own.

He resisted.

"Oh, no, no more of that," he said, clasping one large hand upon each buttock and sliding her back away from him.

"But . . . please . . ."

"I said I am going to kiss you," he told her. "And you've got to trust me, Cessy, to know what is right for when."

Her whole body was on fire. She was trembling from the need to be touched. But she did trust him. He had given her so much pleasure, and if this was almost pain, Cessy vowed that she could stand it.

"Kiss me," she said, raising her arms to accept his embrace.

He took her hands and held them in his own as he bent down and placed his lips upon that part of her that so instinctively craved him.

Cessy cried out in shock and momentary shame as she tried to pull her knees together decently. He would not allow it and held her open as he used his mouth and tongue upon her.

It was wonderful, it was thrilling, it was almost frightening. Cessy tried to clamp down upon the feelings that swamped her. It was a wild abandon that began to override all her conceptions of sensuality and propriety.

Her hands, which only moments earlier she had sought to use for her own protection, were now buried in his thick dark hair, urging him on.

When he raised himself to embrace her once more, every nerve in her body was at attention and she was as malleable as a wet dishrag.

He kissed her and she tasted herself upon his mouth. It was startling, strange, and without any precedence in her experience.

His hand replaced his lips in exploration. She could feel his fingers inside her, searching her, stretching her. His thumb intermittently working the small stiff nubbin partially hidden in her curls.

"I think you're ready now," he told her. "I don't wish to hurt you, not a little, not at all."

"I'm not afraid," she told him. "Hurt me anytime if it feels this good."

He gave a very light chuckle and positioned himself above her. Guiding her hand to his erection, his words were demanding but tender.

"Put me inside you, Cessy," he said. "This is not something I do to you. It's something we do together."

His body was warm and smooth and Princess wanted him very much. She wanted to join with him, be part of him, to be bonded for life, to bear his children.

A little clumsily she eased him into her entrance. He pushed forward, gently, firmly. His hands were everywhere, soothing, caressing as he pressed inward with slow, smooth strokes.

"This is it," he said softly. "I'll be easy . . . I'll be easy . . ."

She felt something give inside her. But there was no pain, not even a sting. Having overcome a tremendous obstacle, he began moving forward at a more rapid pace. Kissing, caressing, and cooing to her as he went.

Then he was completely inside her. He filled her and was part of her, as deeply embedded in her body as he was in her heart.

Inexplicably tears began to flow down her cheeks.

"Cessy?" His tone was rife with concern. "Oh, sweetheart, did I hurt you? I'm so sorry. I didn't think I hurt you."

"I love you," she said to him in answer. "I'm not hurt, I'm in love. I love you and I love your body in mine."

"Oh, sweetheart," he whispered, relieved and almost jubilant. "Oh, Cessy, I haven't even showed you the fun part yet."

"You mean it's not over?"

"Not by half," he answered, holding her face in his hands and smiling down at her. "And the best half is yet to come."

As he began to withdraw, Cessy clasped her hands upon his naked buttocks.

"Don't take it out yet," she pleaded.

"Trust me, Cessy," he told her once more as he thrust back inside her, only to begin withdrawing once more. "Trust me."

She intended to do just that, but the effect his rocking movement was having upon her prevented her from any further coherent speech.

He was certain and sure, adjusting his rhythm to that which seemed easiest for Cessy. She began meeting and matching his pace. More and more sure of herself and her part in this dance of bodies and hearts.

Her legs became restless as she sought to get herself nearer and him deeper. Understanding her need, he grasped her knees and wrapped her legs around his waist. It gave him more access and her more of him.

The pace accelerated until she could not move at all. He thrust into her more and more rapidly and within minutes had her quaking, shaking, shrieking. As if the whole of her physical sensation was coalescing into an ever-tightening spiral. Further. And further. And further. Until her body went for an instant totally rigid. Then the deep recesses of her female anatomy grasped and spasmed and clenched around him, pleasure filling and sparkling through her entire body as his essence spilled into her.

"Gerald!"

She screamed out his name in wondrous gratification and complete, earth-tilting satisfaction.

TWELVE

Cessy Calhoun, Tom thought to himself as he tiredly observed his sleeping wife in the faint light of early dawn, *had the finest twachel he had ever encountered in his entire life.*

He quietly pulled down the window shade so that the rising sun would not awaken her.

Many women were beautiful. Some had curvaceous bodies. Some had pretty eyes. Some were charming and witty. Some could sing so beautifully, they put the birds to shame.

But of all those traits and talents a woman might have, Tom could not imagine one more sure to please a husband than the natural ability that his new bride had shown last night.

He leaned over the bed and gave her a tiny kiss on the forehead. He didn't want to wake her, but somehow he couldn't leave without the gesture. Sweet, the thought came to him. She was so sweet. And she was such pleasure.

And he had to leave. Cedarleg would be expecting him at the rig. He couldn't just not show up. He'd have to tell him something, make some sort of explanation.

Tom Walker had to very permanently disappear. But he couldn't just vanish without a word. There

would be too many questions. The path of sophisticated Gerald Crane would surely never cross the
acquaintances of ordinary Tom.

So he quietly made his way out of her room and
down the stairs into rooms that were wallpapered in
fine silk and trimmed with polished walnut. There
were sounds of breakfast preparation and conversation emanating from the back part of the house.
Practicing amazing stealth, Tom managed to attract
the attention of no one. The front door was too
accessible and the porte cochere too close to the
kitchen. So he eased out the little-used French door in
the sun parlor. The exit put him in a completely
private part of the garden. With no windows to
observe the area, it was a perfect place for a thoughtful person to contemplate the nature of the universe.
Or for a wily person to enter or exit the house
without notice.

Once he cleared the danger of the yard, he put the
white picket fence behind him in a single leap. He
could walk more quickly through the awakening
town and think more clearly about his new wife and
his unexpectedly fabulous wedding night.

Tom was whistling happily. She'd been nervous,
what bride was not? But her strong-minded nature
helped her. She was willing to take charge and not be
afraid of her sensual appetites.

Tom shook his head almost disbelievingly at the
strangeness of life and fate. Princess Calhoun was not
favored in many ways to catch the attention of
gentlemen. Except the one guaranteed to make her
husband inordinately content.

She was, of course, completely unaware of her
talent. And clearly there was no way for him to tell
her. No polite language existed for such attributes.
And a husband couldn't even suggest that she was
beyond the compare of his former bedmates, since a

husband could never admit there had *ever been*
former bedmates.

Tom thought of all the foolish men who had passed
over Cessy Calhoun, never giving the drill sergeant in
skirts a second look.

"Stupid fools," he said aloud. Though he was
honest enough to number himself among that way-
ward number.

He, like all the others, was more nearsighted than
Cessy would ever be. Cessy Calhoun was not only
totally lovely in heart and mind, she was more
sexually satisfying to him than any innocent bride
should be expected to be.

He grinned broadly. And she was no longer Cessy
Calhoun. Now her name was Walker, or rather it was
Crane, he corrected his thoughts hurriedly. His Cessy
had married Gerald Crane. His brow furrowing, Tom
found that reality did not sit as well with him as he
thought that it would.

Still, she was his wife and after today he would
forever more be Gerald Crane. Tom Walker was going
to cease to exist altogether and completely.

By the time he made it to Pusher's Camp, his good
humor had returned and he was whistling once
again. But his song abruptly faded when he saw Ma
Pease standing outside her living quarters and got a
glimpse of her concerned face.

"Oh, thank God!" she called out when she saw
him. "He's home, Winthrop!"

Tom rushed forward with concern. The old woman
hugged him as if he were the prodigal son.

"What's wrong?" he asked.

Ma wasn't given an opportunity to answer.

"Where in the devil have you been all night?"
Cedarleg demanded as he came charging out of the
tent. The tool pusher's expression was livid. "Don't
ye know you about scared poor Ma to death!"

"I . . . ah . . . ." Tom was at a loss for an answer.

The interior of the Pease tent was lit by the faint golden light of a kerosene lantern. Dawn was well upon them now, and Tom was certain that Cedarleg should be at the well already. But the old man showed no hint of preparing to go.

"When we awakened and realized you hadn't come home," Ma began, "well . . . you must know what kind of thoughts went through my head."

Tom honestly had no idea what kind of thoughts went through her head. Except for his boyhood with Reverend McAfee, no one had ever cared where he went or how long he stayed.

"Why didn't you come home?" Cedarleg asked. "We pictured you lying crippled or killed on one of those hills out there."

"No, I . . . I . . . well, I got married yesterday."

"What!" two astonished voices exclaimed in unison.

"The girl that I've been seeing, well, I told you I was thinking about asking her, and she said yes. So we eloped."

"Just like that?" Ma sounded somewhat affronted. "Without even your family and kin to stand up with you?"

"I haven't any family," Tom answered.

"Well, by God, you got us, don't you?" Cedarleg said. "Did you think we wouldn't want to be there to wish you happy?"

"And to get a look at your gal," Ma said. "Make sure she's healthy and fit enough for being a wife."

"She's a fine wife, Ma," Tom assured her. "I'm sure that you would like her."

"Well, we'll see if we do," she answered. "Where is she now?"

"Why . . . she's at home," he said. "At her family's home. In Burford Corners."

"Is she packing up her things?"

"Ah, no," Tom answered. "We're going to live there."

The momentary anger the two had obviously felt about his failure to return home faded as Ma and Cedarleg enthusiastically began to accept the news that Tom had gotten married.

"So when she said yes, you just made a run for the preacher?" Cedarleg asked, chuckling at the image that created.

"Poor girl," Ma said with sympathy. "Once you'd set your heart on her, she didn't have a chance."

Tom didn't feel it necessary to respond to that, and only managed to escape by hurrying inside the tent to change into his work clothes.

Ma had saved him a slab of ham and a half-dozen biscuits. He was very grateful and thanked her effusively.

"I'm starving this morning," he admitted.

"Worked up an appetite last night, did ye?" Cedarleg teased.

Tom chuckled, not deigning to reply. Ma sharply scolded her husband for his teasing.

"So you're going to set up housekeeping there with her family," Ma said as she poured him the last of the coffee.

"Why, yes," Tom answered.

Ma nodded thoughtfully at his words. "I'm not a believer much in young couples living with their kin, but I can see that it might be necessary for a while. Until you get some money saved up and get on your feet."

"Her family has a nice house and plenty of room," Tom assured her.

"Well, that is probably better than one of these tents," Ma said. "Especially for a new bride who is still trying to find her way around things."

"Yes, I'm sure you're right," Tom agreed.

"After your shift is finished you can bring her over," Ma said. "I'll fix the best supper the two of you ever ate and we'll all get to know each other better."

Tom blanched at her words. "Oh, no, Ma, I can't," he said quickly.

"Why ever not?" Cedarleg asked.

"Because . . . because this is my last shift. I've come to quit my job."

Cedarleg stared at him as if he'd lost his mind.

"Quit your job? What are you thinking of, son?" he asked. "Now that you've got a wife to support, you're going to need it more than ever."

"I'll work today," Tom said. " 'Cause I know you can't get a replacement that quick. But then I'm done. I'm . . . I'm going into her family's business."

"What kind of business is it?" Ma asked.

Tom was momentarily struck dumb. Always he planned his lies and his excuses with great care. But he'd made no provisions for what to tell Ma and Cedarleg. He'd not thought he'd have to tell them anything. He had gotten to know them and actually begun to care about them. Still, he planned merely to walk out of their lives and never look back. Obviously that was not going to work.

"Yeah, son? What kind of business is it?"

He couldn't answer oil. The only family in the oil business in this part of the state was King Calhoun. It had to be something respectable. Something that paid good wages. Something that a man would give up the drilling rig for.

The laughing face of Ambrose Dexter swirled into his memory unexpected.

"Banking," Tom answered. "Her family is in banking."

"Banking?" Cedarleg looked genuinely astonished. "In Burford Corners?"

"Yes . . . ah, yes, her family owns a bank there," he said.

"Which one?"

Tom stared at him mutely for a long moment, mentally trying to reconstruct the Main Street of Burford Corners and banks located there. He could not think of a single name.

"Which one? Ah . . . Citizens Savings," he answered finally, grasping a name from thin air.

Cedarleg shook his head. "Never heard of it," he admitted.

Tom was grateful that he didn't dispute its existence.

"Well, my, my, Tom," Ma teased. "You are really moving up in the world. They are really going to miss you out on the rig. I know Cedarleg would never tell you, but the men like and respect you and we've both been so proud of what a hard worker you've turned out to be."

Tom was surprised and uncomfortable with her adulation. He'd worked hard, he'd enjoyed the work. But he'd never thought to win the praise of these two people.

"I . . . I can put in a shift and then I have to go," he said firmly. "Tomorrow I'll be a banker, not an oil man."

Cedarleg offered his hand. "I don't know whether to wish you well or offer my sympathy. I ain't got much use for bankers, but I guess I'll make an exception for you."

Tom smiled wanly.

"Well, if you can't congratulate him for being a banker," Ma said, "at least congratulate him on his new bride."

She threw her arms around Tom's neck and hugged him to her. "I am very proud and happy for you," she told him. "If you say that she's wonderful, then I know she must be. I can hardly wait to meet her."

"Well I . . . I don't know when you'll be able to meet her," Tom said. "We're going to be very busy and I don't know if . . ."

"You certainly won't be too busy to stop by for supper one night," Ma insisted.

"Well, we may be, Ma," he said. "We may be just so busy that we can't make any promises to come by at all."

"Why, that's the most foolish thing I ever heard," Ma said. "Of course you can come by and see us."

"No . . . I just don't think . . ."

Tom was stumbling along badly.

"I don't think I can bring her over here."

"What on earth . . ." Ma began, and then gasped as understanding dawned upon her.

Cedarleg simultaneously came to the same conclusion. His words spoke a volume of hurt.

"So now you've flown so high, married up so well, that you can't associate with oil-patch trash like Ma and me."

"I never said that," Tom insisted.

"It's the truth, though, ain't it?" Cedarleg asked.

"Well, no, it's not exactly," Tom began.

The expression on Ma's face was as if he had slapped her. It was a perfect way to break it off. A perfect way to never have to see them again. Still, Tom couldn't bear the pain that he was causing these two people who had treated him so kindly.

"I . . . I don't think that you would have anything in common with her," he said.

It was no explanation.

"She is not familiar with oil people and . . . and . . ."

Ma raised her hand as if to hush him.

"Not another word need be said," she told him. She raised her chin bravely, determined not to take offense at the unkindness so obviously done to her.

"You two better get to work, the evening tour is going to be hopping mad already at how late you are."

Cedarleg nodded in agreement.

"We'd best get out there," he said. "You put in a full day and then draw your pay at the end of it. Ma and I won't be bothering ye or intruding on yer life for one more moment."

Cessy awakened slowly and with a smile on her face. She rolled to her side and reached out for Gerald, the man of her dreams, the love of her life, her husband whom she had reached out for several times during their long, lingering wedding night.

He wasn't there. The sheets beside her were cold. That opened her eyes.

"Gerald?" she called out, even though it was clear that she was alone in the room. It was a vague blur. Without her glasses, she could not distinguish objects at a distance.

She could see that the window shade was pulled closed and the full sunlight of midday was slanting in through the edges. It was undoubtedly much later than she thought. Gerald, her husband, had probably already gone down to breakfast. In truth she was ravenously hungry herself.

When she sat up in bed the sheet fell to her waist and she realized that she was naked. In broad daylight, Cessy Calhoun was naked!

She blushed and giggled, embarrassed and also delighted. She was somebody's wife. But not just any somebody's wife. She was the wife of the most wonderful, romantic man in the universe. And he could do things with his hands and his mouth that she had never imagined possible.

As she climbed out of bed she felt a little twinge. She was stretched and sore *down there*. But then, how could she not be? He had warned her after the first time that perhaps she needed to allow herself to grow accustomed to the new duty. Cessy had been unwilling to forego further activity. Nothing in her life had prepared her for the sheer pleasure of sex. And having once discovered it, she found her appetite for it insatiable.

She also decided that she was in very great need of a bath. It was one of life's surprises that the marriage act, solemn and sacred, was also sticky.

Cessy found her spectacles, donned her Mother Hubbard housedress, and sneaked down the stairs. She didn't see Gerald and was both disappointed and grateful. He was undoubtedly in one of the parlors, reading or thinking . . . or . . . whatever he did all day.

She did encounter Howard, who greeted her politely. Cessy found it difficult to meet his gaze. Did he know what married people did? Did he have any idea how her night had been spent? It didn't bear thinking.

"Are you ready for breakfast, ma'am?" he asked. "Or would you prefer to wait for Mr. Crane."

"Mr. Crane has not yet eaten?"

Howard's brow furrowed. "Mr. Crane has not come downstairs," he replied.

"I believe you are mistaken," she told him. "He is undoubtedly in one of the parlors. Please find him for me, Howard, and tell him that I will have breakfast with him as soon as I complete my bath."

Howard nodded. "Very well, ma'am," he said.

Cessy slipped into the small room beside the kitchen and realized immediately, to her dismay, that it was Monday, washday. The housekeeper, Mrs. Marin, and the washerwoman, Daisy Pilgrim, were busily engaged in the scrubbing, rinsing, and wringing of the household laundry.

"Good morning, Miss Princess," they said in unison.

"Good morning," Cessy answered. "I was . . . I was hoping to take a bath."

"You won't bother us one bit," the housekeeper told her. "I just filled up that hot water contraption. Don't know if it's had time to get to boiling."

Cessy tested the side of the galvanized oil-burning water heater. It was hot to the touch. She turned the valve to the direction of the bathtub and opened the spigot. As the water poured out, Cessy gathered up her soap, towel, and fleshbrush.

The women were not paying her any attention, still it was a little disappointing not to be able to take a private bath. By necessity, the bathtub was located near the plumbing. So that meant either the kitchen or the washroom. Since laundry was done only twice a week, the washroom seemed the better idea. She chided herself that she should be grateful for the indoor plumbing and the luxury of automatic hot water. Not too many years ago she had to haul water from the well and heat it on the stove to stay clean.

The spigot began to spit and sputter as the last of its twelve gallons emptied into the tub. Cessy turned off the spigot, reset the valve, and then began pumping the hot water tank full once more. The washerwoman came to her assistance.

"Go on and have your bath before the water gets cold," she said. "I can do this for you."

"Thank you, Daisy."

Cessy walked over to the tub and checked the temperature of the water. Had it been hot enough, she could have added cold to it, filling the tub nicely. As it was only fairly warm, she chose to bathe in the three-inch depth that the small tank provided.

With as much modesty as possible she discarded her outer clothing. She lowered herself into the tub still wearing her chemise. Soaping up her brush first, she relinquished her final sodden garment reluctantly and hurriedly covered her exposed flesh with a sudsy lather.

"I hear that you married up with some fellow yesterday," Mrs. Pilgrim said.

Cessy continued scrubbing, unwilling to even glance in the woman's direction until she was certain that the film of soap preserved her modesty.

"Why, yes, I did," she said. "We were wed yesterday afternoon."

"Eloped," Mrs. Marin said.

The housekeeper made the word sound positively sinful.

"Oh, no, not an elopement exactly," she assured them both hastily.

"Did you have your daddy's permission?" Mrs. Marin asked.

"Well, no, I . . ."

"Then that's an elopement," the washerwoman stated.

"Mrs. Pilgrim, I am of age," Cessy said with as much dignity as she could master.

The two women shared wild-eyed looks, as if such a small point was lost upon them.

They continued their washing. Cessy was grateful that at least they were turned away from her.

"Who is this fellow anyway?" Mrs. Pilgrim asked.

"Oh, he's a very wonderful man," Cessy told her. "I met him at the Fourth of July picnic, and he's charming and witty and very easy to talk to. He's a veteran of the Rough Riders. He's been so many places and done so many things."

"What's his name?" she asked. "We can't continue to call you Miss Princess if you are a married woman."

"Oh, it's Crane, Cessy Crane. I mean that's my name. He calls me Cessy, so I've decided to go by that. It's nice, don't you think?"

The housekeeper nodded. Mrs. Pilgrim was non-committal.

"His name is Gerald," she told them. "Gerald Tarkington Crane."

"Never heard of him," Mrs. Pilgrim announced.

"He's not from here," Mrs. Marin told her.

"A Topknot feller, I'm guessing," Mrs. Pilgrim said.

"No, he's actually from New Jersey," Cessy explained. "Bedlington, New Jersey."

"Never heard of it."

"Well, there is probably a lot of the world that you've never heard of," Cessy pointed out with as much grace as possible.

Mrs. Pilgrim shrugged. "That's why I wouldn't marry no man that I ain't knowed him and his kin all me life. Marriage is strange enough without trying it with a stranger."

Cessy resisted the temptation to give sour old Mrs. Pilgrim a piece of her mind. She didn't want to waste the first day of her married life in a bad humor.

"Gerald, Mr. Crane, and I are far from strangers," she said firmly.

It was irritating that people would think merely because she had known Gerald only two weeks and that the introductions between families had not been made, that their marriage was impulsive or unconsidered. Certainly Cessy had not meant to elope with him yesterday. But she had meant to be his wife since the moment she'd laid eyes upon him.

With no hope for privacy or even the solitude of her own thoughts, Cessy finished her bath quickly. In her Mother Hubbard once more she headed back to her room. She met Howard coming from the porch.

"Mr. Crane is not in the house," he said.

"Oh. Well, look in the garden," she suggested.

Back in her room she dressed and planned. She and Gerald would need to get their heads together about meeting her father. King Calhoun would probably not return to the house before afternoon, but they needed to plan his introduction to Gerald. He was a good and loving father, but he *was* a father and one who'd in the past shown evidence of temper where his daughter was concerned.

She dressed for the day in a starched white shirtwaist with leg-of-mutton sleeves and a narrow ascot tie at her throat. Her four-gore skirt was black serge and sported a ruffle at the hem. A quick glance in her mirror assured her that her hair was neat and her appearance presentable.

She closed her eyes and felt in memory his body atop her own, the warmth of his breath against her skin, the tender touch of his hands upon her.

Cessy sighed heavily and trembled with delight. She was going to love being married. If this was what it was like between a man and a woman, she could almost understand why her father spent so much time at the illicit places in Topknot.

But, of course, that was different. Her father's illicit pleasures were not at all like marriage. Marriage was about love and trust, honesty and commitment.

Smiling at that thought, Cessy hurried down the stairs, more eager for the nearness of her new husband than for the morning meal. She had expected Howard to have laid out the impressive dining table as he had the night before. But her own modest breakfast was awaiting her on the kitchen table, exactly as it had been every other morning since she'd moved into this house.

"My husband isn't eating with me?" she asked.

Howard appeared ill at ease and Mrs. Marin was positively livid.

"Mr. Crane is not in the house nor on the grounds," he said.

"Where is he?"

"It appears that he has left, ma'am," Howard said.

"Left? Well, where did he say that he was going?" she asked.

"He did not say, ma'am. He spoke to no one, departed with no note or word of intent."

"He's probably taking a morning constitutional," she said. "Health walks are very popular back East."

"Yes, ma'am," Howard replied. His tone was almost conciliatory.

"For heaven's sake Howard," Cessy told him with a little chuckle of disbelief. "You sound as if you believe he has abandoned me."

The silence that followed, from both Howard and Mrs. Marin, was telling.

Cessy stared at both of them, stunned and exasperated. They were as bad as the washerwoman, seeing something sinister in a singular walk. Refusing to lose her good humor, Cessy ate her food in silence. This was the first day of her married life. She was in love and desperately happy. She was resolved to feel no other way.

That steely determination lasted through the morning. Having broken her fast late, she put off the noon meal interminably. But by then her appetite had deserted her anyway. Perhaps he had been hit by a cart or collapsed from the heat.

She sent Howard to town for any news of accidents or mishaps that morning. He returned with no news. There had been a little trouble up at the well sites, but life was peaceful and uncomplicated in Burford Corners.

By midafternoon she'd begun to feel a strange aching in her heart. A feeling that was despondent, downcast. She sat at her desk in the sun parlor. From the depths of the tiny, secret compartment within the scrolled door, she withdrew the note.

My own dear Cessy,

I can not visit you this evenun as an herjent mat-

*ter of business has come up. As I am sirten you
know, I wood be there if I could. I am hoping to
see you on Sunday. Maybe we could go for a
picknick on the river and spend the afternoon together. I herd that your father is back in town. I
think that you should not say inny thing about me
to him yet. As always you hold my heart with your
own.*

                                        Gerald

Why was his spelling so atrocious? What kind of
business did he have to take care of? Why had he
wanted their growing friendship kept secret from her
father?

In that moment, that frightening, heart-wrenching
moment, she doubted. Immediately she was angry
and disappointed, not with Gerald but with herself.
How flimsy were her vows of undying love and trust
that they could so easily be called into question?
Gerald was her husband and he loved her. She knew
in her heart that it was true. She had been certain of it
yesterday. And surely his care and tenderness last
night more than expressed it.

That man could not have cast her off and abandoned her this morning. It was not possible. And as
his wife it was her *duty* to have faith that it was not so.

She heard a step and looked hopefully toward the
doorway. She almost called out his name, but was
grateful that she did not. It was Howard. Hastily she
glanced away, not wanting him to see the unwanted
tears that filled her eyes. She raised her chin and
forced a smile to her face. She refused to feel sad or
scared. He was her husband and she believed in him.

"Miss Princess, you have visitors in the front
parlor," he said, his voice almost too quiet.

"Who is it?" she asked him.

"Miss Nafee and her gentleman friend," Howard replied.

She didn't want to see them. She didn't want to see anyone but Gerald. But Muna was her best friend. She never refused to see Muna. If she turned her away today, it would be the same as saying that something was wrong. And despite the pitying looks of the servants, Cessy was deliberately adamant that nothing was wrong.

Pasting a welcoming smile upon her face, Cessy made her way to the front parlor.

"Hello and hello!" she greeted them effusively. "Is this not the most beautiful day that you have ever seen in your life?"

Muna hugged her warmly.

Maloof nodded to her. "I bring you wedding present," he said, indicating a rolled rug in the corner. "It is better than rug you have. I get good rug for good friends, yes."

He rolled it open on the floor for Cessy to admire. It was beautiful and she thanked him.

"I couldn't stay away," Muna admitted. "I knew I should let you two have this first day alone together. But my curiosity just got the better of me."

"You're always welcome here, Muna," Cessy assured her.

"How did it go with your father?" she asked. "Did he take the news well?"

Cessy was momentarily confused, but recovered quickly. Of course, Muna would think that the announcement of their elopement would be the primary news of the day.

"Daddy hasn't come home yet," she said.

"He hasn't been home since yesterday?" Muna asked.

"He often has meetings late into the night," Cessy said. "And I would suppose that this morning he must be out checking the wells. We haven't seen him."

"Oh my heavens, then it is still ahead of you," she said. "You must be a bundle of nerves having to wait like this."

"Oh I'm fine," Cessy assured her. "Truly I am fine. I'm . . . I'm sure that Daddy is just going to love Gerald."

"Where is he?"

"Daddy?"

"Gerald?"

"Oh, Gerald. He's not here."

"He's not here? Where is he?"

"He had . . . something to do," she said.

"When will he be back?" Muna asked.

"When? Ah . . . later, he'll be back later," Cessy said uncertainly.

"Oh, well, we are sorry to miss him," she said.

Cessy nodded politely and was momentarily grateful that Muna and Maloof did not know. Then she realized that keeping the truth from them was the same as lying. And the truth, she had already decided, was not that she was abandoned, but merely that her husband was temporarily absent.

"When I awakened this morning, Gerald was gone," she said, her expression almost challenging.

"Gone?"

"Yes, he had already left for the day," Cessy told her.

"Wherever did he go?"

"I have no idea," Cessy answered.

"Oh, you poor thing," Muna wailed, coming forward to enfold her friend in a comforting embrace. "How could he do this? How could he . . ."

"Do what?" Cessy asked. "Go about his business as any man would without mentioning what that business might be to his wife."

"But what on earth . . ."

"He is my husband, Muna," she said. "Yesterday you promised to try to like him for my sake. Now at the very first crossroad you are eager to believe the worst of him."

Muna looked embarrassed. "I don't want to believe the worst of him, Prin," she insisted. "But I could never bear to see you hurt."

"Your lack of faith in my husband hurts me as dearly as if you refused to believe in me myself."

Muna sighed heavily and nodded, but she still looked very worried.

"But where on earth can the man be?" she asked.

"It is Monday," Maloof interjected. "He is gone to the work."

Muna eyed him curiously.

"What on earth are you talking about?" she asked him.

"It is Monday," the young foreigner tried again. "He has job to go to on Monday."

"Oh, Gerald doesn't work, Maloof," Cessy explained to him. "Not everyone in America has a job. Many men from wealthy families do not participate in business, they just pursue interests and avocations."

Maloof listened to her thoughtfully, nodding as if he understood, but apparently he did not.

"Tom has job," he assured her.

"Maloof, his name is Gerald," Muna said patiently. "And he does not have any kind of job."

"*Gerald* has job," he insisted, emphasizing the name. "On the wells of King Calhoun."

The two women shared a momentary puzzled glance. Then Cessy began nodding with understanding.

"Oh," she said to Maloof. "You mean that now that he's my husband, he will be working with my father."

"Yes, of course that's what you mean," Muna agreed.

"And you are undoubtedly right," Cessy told him. "Gerald probably will be a great help to my father. But first they have to meet each other."

Maloof's expression was puzzled. He opened his mouth as if intending to say more, but Muna interrupted him.

"First your husband has to return to you," she said.

"Muna, Gerald has not left me," Cessy insisted. "He is simply not here right now. If you are my friend then you must learn to trust him and believe in him as I do."

Muna didn't appear convinced, but she did have the good grace to change the subject.

"So do you like the rug that Maloof picked out for you?" she asked.

"It's perfect," Cessy assured Muna and then directed her words to Maloof. "It's a beautiful rug," she said. "And I know that Gerald will be equally as pleased with it."

THIRTEEN

It was barely half-past six when Tom slipped unnoticed through the sun parlor doorway as he had that morning. He had cleaned up and changed clothes in record-setting time. And he'd pushed a brisk pace from the Pusher's Camp in Topknot to residential Burford Corners. He was weary, worried, and anxious as if waiting for the other shoe to drop. His last day at work had not gone at all as he would have wished.

Just after ten o'clock, the Sixteen, one of the wells upwind from the "P," hit a pocket of noxious fumes. Every man on the Topknot scrambled for safety. A similar blow had hit a well in Baston three years earlier. The bad air had killed five men, plus several horses, hogs, and chickens.

Fortunately today none of the men were seriously poisoned, but many were sick and vomiting and the work stopped for hours as everyone waited at a safe distance for the wind to carry the dangerous gas away.

Calhoun was on the scene within minutes and stayed all day. Fortunately most of the attention went to the Sixteen, but King consulted with Cedarleg several times. Each time he came over, Tom either wandered away or got busy with some task that required keeping his head down. He was very concerned that Cedarleg might try to introduce him. If Calhoun met him as Tom, all would be lost when he attempted to pass himself off as his son-in-law Gerald.

With that in mind, toward midday, Tom approached Cedarleg and asked to leave.

"It's my last day, and you're not going to need me for any work, so I might as well get on **out** of here and save Royal Oil the money they have to pay me for standing here."

"You can hardly wait to see the last of us, eh?" Cedarleg said unkindly.

"That's not it at all."

"Well, you owe me a full day and I expect you to work it," the old man insisted. "If the wind comes up it'll blow that bad air out of here in no time and we'll be restarting the rig."

Tom didn't argue. He stood around with the other men for most of the afternoon waiting for the wind to come up. It was time for Tom Walker to disappear. He wanted Tom to disappear.

But he just couldn't, not yet.

Gerald was his new life. Gerald was who he was going to be from here on out. But somehow he hated to leave Tom behind. Tom had made friends, found a trade he liked, and was loved by a smart and generous old cripple and his wife. But the necessity of being Gerald was the end of Tom's existence.

"Cedarleg, I'm sorry about this morning," he said by way of apology. "Believe me, things are not at all the way you think them to be."

"It don't matter to me a bit," he insisted, his chin up in challenge. "But you hurt Ma's feelings. I ain't so forgiving of that. I ain't so forgiving at all."

Tom wasn't very forgiving of himself either. He *had* hurt Ma. It had seemed necessary at the time, but surely he could have planned better. He should have been able to see how things were going to turn out.

But he hadn't. He'd simply done what was good for himself without thinking about what that meant for Ma and Cedarleg. And now they were paying for it with hurt feelings and broken hearts.

The sun parlor was dim and fortunately empty. Tom walked through the house, listening for the sound of Cessy's voice. The place was extremely quiet, inordinately quiet. Almost as if there had been a death in the family.

The parlors were all empty. Tom made his way upstairs. Cessy was not in her bedroom. He'd almost wished that she had been. He wished that she still lay warm and sweet as she had been when he'd left that morning. She'd undoubtedly been busy all day long. But she'd thought about him, after their night together, of that he was certain. Tom stowed his duffle beneath the bed, discarded his panama hat, and went to find his new bride.

He walked through the empty, silent house, ill at ease. The place needed noise and laughter and, well, it needed children. Tom was surprised to find himself pleased by the prospect. A whole house full of bright and curious little faces, endless giggles and loud enthusiasm. The Walker children, all well-scrubbed, well-heeled and unfailingly well-mannered.

Of course, they wouldn't be the Walker children, he remembered. They would be the Cranes, of the Bedlington, New Jersey Cranes. Tom's brow furrowed with displeasure at the thought. Then he determinedly pushed it away. They would be his children, his and Cessy's. It didn't matter what they were called or who they were thought to be related to, the children would eternally and inalterably belong to them.

There was no china laid out in the dining room, but Tom heard the clatter of dishes in the kitchen and could smell dinner cooking. He had never been in that part of the house, but perhaps Cessy was there.

He made his way down the back hall, past the washroom, and through a spring-hinged door.

She was seated at a long table. A huge dishpan of fresh picked okra set in front of her. She was busily engaged in cutting, cleaning, and preparing it for the frying pan.

She glanced up hurriedly and Tom was privileged to watch the most beautiful change of expression he had ever seen on a human face. Like the blooming of one of the flowers in her garden, the stern and determined visage was transformed into joyous happiness.

"Gerald!" she called out to him, rising from her seat so hastily that the chair clattered unheeded to the floor.

Cessy raced to him, throwing her arms around his neck and hugging him to her tightly.

Tom was delighted by the effusive greeting and a little embarrassed, as he noted the presence of the housekeeper and butler, by her obvious display of affection.

"Where the devil have you been?" Mrs. Marin demanded.

Tom, who had barely set eyes upon the woman the day before, was astonished at the vehemence in her tone.

"What?" he asked.

"Left the girl in the morning without so much as a by-your-leave and then waltz back in here as if it's nothing in the world!"

"Mrs. Marin, please," Cessy scolded. "I told you he would be back."

"Of course I'm back," Tom said, confused.

"They—" Cessy said, indicating the servants. "They thought that you had abandoned me."

Her statement was offered as a joke, but it was obviously not as far from the truth as she attempted to make it seem.

"Abandoned?" Tom was incredulous. "Why, I would never . . . surely you know . . ."

"How are we supposed to know that?" Mrs. Marin asked. "Never even heard of you until a week ago, you run off and marry Miss Princess and then sneak out of here like a thief."

"I didn't . . ." Tom began to defend himself and then remembered that he did actually slip out unnoticed on purpose. "I didn't . . . I didn't imagine that you would worry about me," he said finally. "I had some business to attend to today and I didn't want to wake you before I left."

"I knew it was something like that," Cessy told him.

"I never meant to worry you," he told her sincerely. "I am new to being a husband. It just didn't occur to me to say anything."

Cessy nodded lovingly and hugged him tightly, obviously forgiving him completely.

"You are just accustomed to doing things on your own. Now you know that when you leave without a word, your wife might worry."

"Yes," he said. "I am sorry, Cessy."

She smiled up at him. "We both must get used to our new roles. But the good thing is, we have the rest of our lives."

She encouraged him to take a seat at the kitchen table beside her. Mrs. Marin and Howard were still not particularly pleased with him. But Cessy seemed totally happy and at ease with him.

"Did you get your things from your bachelor quarters?" she asked.

"Yes, yes I did."

"Mrs. Marin and I will make some room in the wardrobe for your things," she told him.

"Oh, I don't have much," Tom assured her. "I . . . I travel light."

Cessy nodded with understanding. "Yes, I do suppose that would be necessary. But now that you have a home, well, you can send back East for your things."

"Ah . . . yes, yes, I guess I can."

"Did you wire them?" she asked.

"Who?"

"Your family? Did you send them a telegram about our marriage?"

Tom had not thought of this. Of course, he would have to start some story about his family. Cessy would naturally expect him to want them to know.

"Why . . . why yes, yes, of course I did. It was the most important thing that I had to do all day," he told her.

"And did they send a reply?"

"Ah . . . not yet," he said, hoping to buy time.

Cessy giggled and feigned biting her fingernails. "I'll be on pins and needles until we hear if they approve."

"How could they not approve of you, Cessy?" he said. "You are wonderful."

"But I'm not at all the kind of woman that should have married Gerald Tarkington Crane," she said with a shake of her head.

Tom was surprised at her words. She was exactly the kind of woman to suit Gerald. And she certainly suited him.

"Cessy," he said evenly. "I am just glad that *you* are married to *me*."

A blush stole into her cheeks and she lowered her eyes. His words obviously pleased her and he was glad that he said them.

She gave a hasty glance to see if Howard or Mrs. Marin was looking, and when she found they were not, she kissed him quickly and hurried away.

"You must be starving," she said. "Why don't we eat in here, it is so much more friendly."

Cessy fixed him a glass of sweetened lemonade

and began bustling around, setting the table in the kitchen as the servants finished up the dinner preparations. She was jovial and teasing and her mood was positively infectious. She told him about her day. She made taking a bath while the laundry was being done sound like an adventure. And her description of Maloof's pleasure at presenting them with a new rug was as entertaining as any vaudeville skit. Tom just sat back in his chair, relaxed, and watched her.

This was the life, this was what he wanted. A fine, clean home, nice clothes, plenty of good food and a woman who loved and respected and worried about him. It was perfect. It was everything that Tom Walker had ever dreamed for himself and he basked in it.

Dinner was placed before him. It was simple fare, but tasty and hot. Tom was very content.

"I don't want you to be nervous about meeting my father," Cessy told him. "His bark is very much worse than his bite. Once he gets to know you, he will see just how perfect a son-in-law you are."

Tom shook his head. "I don't know about perfect, Cessy, but I am going to try to do my best."

"Of course you will," she said.

"And I won't be going anywhere without letting you know," he assured her.

"Don't give it another thought," Cessy insisted. "It was just something that happened. Years from now we'll look back at today and laugh."

"I love to hear you laugh, Cessy," he told her.

She did then, just for him.

"And besides, you are not the only one who has been gone all day," Cessy told him. "My father still hasn't shown up and I worry about him, too."

"Don't be anxious about King Calhoun," Tom told her as he finished his last bite of okra. "The Sixteen blew into a gas pocket and he's been up on the Topknot with the men all day."

Tom dipped his fork in his potatoes before the stillness of the woman across from him caught his attention. He raised his head.

"You know Daddy?" she asked.

"No, oh no, but well, everybody knows King Calhoun," he said.

She nodded slowly.

"How did you find out about the blowout?"

"I . . . ah . . . it's what everybody is talking about down at the saloons in Topknot. I . . . ah . . . stopped by to get a beer before I came home . . . ah . . . from the bank. All the men in there were talking about it. They said Calhoun was up there with his men all day."

"Oh," Cessy said, shrugging acceptance. "What were you doing at the bank?"

It was an innocent question. Unfortunately, Tom had no reasonable answer.

"I was . . . I was . . . well, when I sent the telegram to my family I also wired my banker that since I'm going to be here, I'd . . . ah . . . need a transfer of funds."

"Oh, yes," Cessy agreed. "I would imagine that's so. Then you stopped into one of the saloons." She hesitated. "Why would you go all the way over to Topknot to get a beer? They have a beer garden in Burford Corners."

"I . . . ah . . . I have a favorite saloon over there that I prefer to do business with," he answered.

"A favorite? Which one?"

Tom searched his mind for the names of just one of the rows of saloons that were the part and parcel of downtown Topknot. Only one came to mind.

"Queenie's Palace," he answered.

Glass shattered noisily on the floor and lemonade splashed everywhere as Howard dropped the decanter that he carried.

FOURTEEN

Cessy Crane knew herself to be the happiest young woman on the planet. Others may have doubted, they may have tempted her to doubt, but she'd believed in him. And he'd proven her true.

After dinner the two sat cuddled up on the sofa together. Between occasional kisses they made plans.

"I have been considering the best way to break the news to Daddy, and I want you to follow my lead," she told him. "I think that we should let the truth come out rather gradually," she told him.

"That sounds like a good plan," Gerald agreed. "It is likely to be a shock to him. And he may even get angry that I have so propitiously stolen your heart."

She grinned at him. "Such a charming robber, you are," she teased.

"King Calhoun may not find me so," Gerald admitted.

Cessy nodded. "It will be fine, I'm certain of it," she said. "He will be surprised, but he's not the kind of father who would deny me anything that I desire."

"And do you desire me, Cessy," he whispered close to her ear.

"Whatever do you mean, Mr. Crane?" she asked him, batting her eyelashes like a coquette.

Gerald laughed at her performance and rewarded

her with a hasty peck upon the end of her nose. It was no passionate kiss, but it was so dear and familiar and so ordinary it made her feel very married. And Cessy found that she liked that feeling very much indeed.

"When Daddy gets home," she said, "I will introduce you. We can sit around for a few moments chatting and getting to know each other."

Gerald nodded.

"When he's warmed up to you a bit, we'll mention that we've been seeing each other," she said. "Now, Gerald, that may surprise him a bit because, honestly, I haven't been keeping company with any gentleman."

Cessy was a little self-conscious about this admission. It was no great shame to have lived so long devoid of willing suitors. She had a husband now, the most wonderful husband she could imagine, and he was well worth the wait. So she was determined not to be embarrassed by the truth.

Gerald reached over and ran one long brown finger down the side of her face to her jawline and gently raised her chin.

"You were just waiting on me," he told her.

She smiled at him, admitting the truth of his words.

"Once Daddy has gotten to know you and learns that we've been seeing each other for almost two whole weeks," she said, "I'm sure it won't seem quite as impetuous to admit that we've eloped."

Gerald held her chin in his hand and lovingly stroked her bottom lip with his thumb.

"Cessy, I think that you need to expect that your father may not be too pleased to find that you've married me," he said.

"He may be a little upset at first," she admitted. "But he would never stand in the way of my happiness, Gerald. You can be certain of that. He has always wanted only the best for me."

"Then he and I have a good deal in common already," he said.

"I believe that ultimately you two will get along very well," Cessy assured him. "He'll probably want to make an oil man out of you."

She giggled at the idea of always clean, always perfectly pressed Gerald covered with the muck and mire of working on a rig.

"Can you imagine yourself on a work gang?" she asked.

Gerald looked displeased at the prospect. "Not really," he said. "Surely he will not expect that of me."

"Oh, certainly not rig work," Cessy agreed. "Although I have to tell you that you do look strong enough for it."

She punctuated her little joking comment with a squeeze of his biceps.

"But Maloof is right, Daddy will probably take you into the business."

"Maloof?"

"When you weren't here today, he assumed that, as my husband, Daddy would have you out working already," she said. "I suppose that's what he would expect, since Mr. Nafee has him working day and night already and he and Muna are not yet even wed."

"How droll," Gerald suggested.

"Don't worry, it won't be all work and no play," Cessy said. "Daddy has his business and I have my interests, but we both enjoy giving entertainments and having guests to visit."

"I'm sure our life will be quite diverting," Gerald said. "Any life with you, my Cessy, would be that."

The compliment pleased her.

"Daddy and I will, of course, want to introduce you to all our friends," she told him.

"That would be nice," he replied.

"We know a lot of people here in Burford Corners," she explained. "And we know everybody in Topknot. It's Daddy's field, and most of the folks working there were handpicked and have been friends of ours since way back in Pennsylvania."

"How nice," he commented.

"It really is," Cessy agreed. "Most of those people are like family. Many of them helped raise me. Mama died so young and Daddy was always working out on the wells."

"It must have been a very difficult life," he said, taking her hand in his own.

"It was hard, I suppose," she told him. "But it was a wonderful life, too. We were all working together and sticking through the tough times by leaning on each other." Cessy shook her head. "Wait until you meet Ma."

"Ma?"

"That's what everybody calls her. Her name is actually Sadie Pease, but she's like a mother to all of us that grew up in the oilpatch."

"How nice."

"She and Cedarleg, that's her husband, have been as dear to me as my own parents. I've tried to get the two of them to retire here and work at Reverend McAfee's school. Ma would be so good for the boys and Cedarleg could expand the teaching there to include mechanics and industrial training."

Gerald's brow was furrowed as if he was worried. "It sounds as if these people are very important to you," he said.

"They are. I love them dearly," she said.

He was looking very worried now and Cessy was momentarily puzzled. Then she wrapped her arms around his neck and offered a reassuring kiss.

"Don't worry, my darling," she told him. "Ma and Cedarleg are just going to love you, I'm certain of it," Cessy said.

He didn't look so sure.

"Cedarleg will take a bit of winning over, I suppose," she said. "But once he gives somebody his trust, he never falters. Ma won't even need to be won. She's a very generous soul, always. And she has a real sense about people. It's almost as if she can see straight to the heart of a person the minute they meet."

"A worthwhile talent," Gerald observed.

"And such a sense of humor," Cessy added. "She's always got some funny story to tell and she tells it over and over."

"I will try to remember to be amused," he said. "So that she will like me."

"Of course, she usually finds something to like in just about everybody," Cessy pointed out. "But I think she would see you as I do, honest and fair and true all the way to the heart."

He nodded thoughtfully for a long moment. Then to Cessy's surprise he abruptly changed the subject.

"Where do you want to go on your wedding trip?" he asked.

"Wedding trip? Why I hadn't even thought about one," she said. "Do you want to take a wedding trip?"

"Isn't that what newly married couples do?" he asked. "Niagara Falls or perhaps Europe."

"Europe?"

"If it's good enough for Teddy Roosevelt, it's good enough for my bride and me," Gerald assured her.

"I don't know," she said. "I really hadn't considered Europe."

"Then we could stay bound to American soil," he said. "We could take the train to Chicago for a few weeks, it's a wonderfully exciting city."

"I haven't been there since I was a girl," she admitted. "Daddy took me to the Exposition."

"So we see Chicago and then on to New York," he said. "You do like New York, don't you?"

Cessy nodded.

"We could see stage plays, eat at restaurants, peruse the cabarets and the dancing palaces, enjoy ourselves until we are totally exhausted with our leisure."

"Oh, that would be wonderful," she agreed.

"Then let's do it," he said. "Neither time nor money need concern us, why not enjoy ourselves to the fullest."

"I enjoy every moment that we are together," she told him honestly.

Gerald smiled at her. "We'll get away alone together," he whispered seductively in her ear. "Just the two of us in a pullman berth, our bodies rocking against each other in every state from here to the Atlantic Ocean."

His words sizzled through her, setting her heart to pacing rapidly, and stirring up vivid memories of the previous night that had her squirming restlessly upon the sofa beside him.

Gerald pulled her into his lap and began kissing her. That very special kind of kissing where he stroked her mouth with his tongue and nipped her lips with his teeth. Cessy wrapped her arms around his neck and pressed her body closely against his own.

"Mmmm, you taste so good," he whispered.

"Oh, it feels so good," she answered.

"If we can get some of these clothes off you," he promised. "I can make it feel even better."

He undid the buttons on her shirtwaist and helped himself to the linen-covered roundness that spilled above the top of her corset.

Gerald ran a fiery trail of kisses from the base of her throat to the valley between her breasts. His tongue snaked out to taste that very tender flesh.

Cessy buried her fingers in his hair and pressed him more closely to her as she threw her head back, eagerly offering him whatever he desired to take.

The parlor doors opened and slammed startlingly into their pockets.

Cessy squealed and jumped to her feet to find herself facing her father. Hastily she covered her exposed bosom. King Calhoun was glaring at them like the wrath of God.

"We're married!" she cried out by way of announcement.

Tom would have hoped for a more auspicious introduction to his father-in-law. But they had come to an understanding, at least. Tiredly Tom trudged up the stairway to Cessy's room. She'd gone to bed over an hour earlier, while Tom had been questioned and cross-examined in the library by his new father-in-law.

Having the man catch them spooning in the front parlor had not been Tom's finest moment. Inelegantly, he had kept his seat, but it seemed the easiest way to cover his lap. He met King Calhoun's furious glare with as much raw courage as he had mustered against the Cubans.

"Married! By God, you'd better not be married without asking me!"

Cessy attempted to make her careful, well-thought-out explanation into a quick and concise excuse. And she was not doing particularly well.

"We met at the Fourth of July picnic," she said. "And we knew right then, the night that we met, that we were meant for each other. Gerald and I have been keeping company on the porch for the past week and a half, and yesterday we went for an outing with Muna and her fiancé and we got married."

King Calhoun had not been easily won over.

"Have you lost your wits!" he had screamed at one point. "You *must* be addled in the brain," he suggested at another. "Has this fancy talking fellow lured you into something against your will?"

It took the better part of an hour to convince Cessy's father that she was sane, in her right mind and of her own free will, married to Gerald Crane.

"It can't be true," Calhoun insisted.

"Well, it is," she had assured him. "Reverend McAfee performed the ceremony in his little church yesterday afternoon."

King Calhoun paced the length of the parlor like a caged lion. Tom stood protectively at Cessy's side. She held on to his arm as if it were a lifeline as her father bellowed and complained.

"I've always tried to watch over you, protect you," Calhoun ranted. "I've tried to do for you the things that I thought best."

"I know that, Daddy."

"I sent you to that fancy, highbutton school of Miss Thorogate's. I thought you'd be happy among the females there. That you'd go to parties and gala entertainments and make friends. But you were more interested in falling-down tenements than coming out parties."

"I know you were disappointed in me," she agreed.

"Disappointed! Sweet Mother Magee!" he bellowed. "I wasn't disappointed, I was mystified. You come back to the oil fields and I watch you get on with your life and I'm thinking that you are happy and content. I build you this house in Burford Corners. You involve yourself with social obligations of the community, with the Library Committee, that Indian School. But in all this time, not by even the smallest word have you ever indicated that you wished to marry."

"Daddy, it's not that I *wished* to marry," Cessy

insisted. "And you make it sound as if I've kept
something from you. There was nothing to tell so I
didn't tell you."

"Well, I dang well wish that you had," he told her.
"If I'd had one inkling that you wanted to marry up,
I'd a found you somebody to wed. You didn't say a
word."

"I don't want *somebody* to wed," she countered. "I
. . . met Gerald and I fell in love with him, Daddy."

She'd glanced up at Tom. He nodded at her to give
her courage and wrapped his arm protectively
around her waist.

"I met this man and I fell in love," she said. "So I
just had to marry him."

King Calhoun had not been impressed.

"That's the stupidest thinking I've ever heard in my
life," he stated flatly. "Good Lord, Princess, I thought
you had more sense. You fell in love," Calhoun
repeated her words in near disbelief and exasperation. "Well, there isn't even no such thing. Love
between a man and a woman is just something
written about in storybooks."

"Daddy, that's not true," Cessy told him, aghast. "I
love Gerald. I truly love him with all my heart."

"There is no such thing as love between a man
and a woman. There is mutual respect and there is
sex," King Calhoun declared. "Princess, you just met
the man, so you can't possibly know anything about
respect. But from what I see, he's already given you a
bit of an education about sex."

Tom could hardly allow Cessy's father to continue
to berate her. And he certainly was not willing to
allow the older man to tell her that she was not in
love with Gerald.

"Mr. Calhoun," he began.

Cessy's father continued as if Tom had not spoken
at all.

"I always thought you were like your mother," he said. "She was Presbyterian clear to the bone, never had an earthy desire in her whole life."

The cheeks of Tom's young bride were flushed bright red.

"Mr. Calhoun," he tried again.

King ignored him and continued walking as if still unable to face his daughter. "Lord knows, it's my fault."

"Your fault?" Cessy's question was incredulous.

"It is not a thing I would ever wish my daughter to know about me," he said. "But the truth is, Princess, your daddy has a very physical nature and I suspect that along with your looks and your good health, you've inherited it."

Cessy appeared nearly rigid with her own embarrassment.

"*Mister* Calhoun!" Tom practically bellowed his name.

The big man stopped his pacing to turn and give Tom a long, perusing once-over from head to toe.

"Have I directed a question to *you*?" Calhoun asked sarcastically.

Tom's eyes narrowed. "Perhaps you should," he had answered, blatantly refusing to be intimidated.

"Oh, I should? Why in the devil would I do that?"

Tom took a step forward, putting Cessy slightly behind him, not so much for her protection as for illustrating his point.

"Because I am your daughter's husband and this is our home," Tom told him smoothly.

He heard Cessy's small intake of breath behind him, but it was nothing compared to the sheer red-faced rage of his father-in-law.

Tom continued, his words quiet but firm.

"I am of age, your daughter is of age. We have been united in marriage before God and in the eyes of this territory. You have raised a very loving and dutiful daughter, Mr. Calhoun. And one of the things that you have taught her so well is to trust her own mind and her own judgement. I think you are now mistaken in calling that judgement into question."

"It was not judgement," Calhoun insisted. "It was an impulsive decision."

"That is your opinion, sir. But Cessy and I are very happy with our marriage. We have every hope that you will be happy with us. You will be a very welcomed guest in our house."

Finally it had sunk into Calhoun's brain. The power had shifted. Cessy owed her loyalty to her husband and if her father wanted any influence with her at all, he would have to deal with Gerald. Cessy's father was up to the challenge.

He had ceased his pacing, and the three of them sat in the front parlor for a more polite and civil discussion of the facts.

Cessy had spoken with gushing sincerity of how much she loved Gerald and how happy she was to be married.

Clearly Calhoun had not liked it, but he kept his opinion to himself, at least until she went up to bed.

The two had shared a glass of port in the library. Tom had barely touched his. He was certain that he would need a clear head for any discussion with his new father-in-law and he was not wrong.

"I don't like fancy men and I don't like fancy ways," King Calhoun had stated flatly. "I suppose you could interpret that as, *I don't like you.*"

Tom had smiled without warmth.

"Yes, I suppose I could," he agreed.

"I've seen your kind all my life," he said. "Soft, slithery snakes you are. Thinking you're better than the rest of the world, but couldn't earn an honest dollar if your good name depended on it."

"One never knows when one's good name might

depend upon it," Tom replied, fastidiously picking a tiny piece of lint from his trousers.

"My Princess is a sweet and loving girl, honest and kind-hearted clear to the bone."

"Yes, I know," Tom replied.

"She's tough and strong-minded though," Calhoun said. "She ain't a bit missish at all. And it don't seem quite right that such a fine-faced feller like you would take up with her."

Tom shrugged elegantly.

"I am curious about this business of falling in love at first sight," he went on. "Was this like a spiritual attraction, like the merging of two celibate souls?"

The man's tone was disagreeable.

"Certainly there was a physical aspect to it also," Tom replied.

"A physical aspect also," Calhoun repeated. "Tell me, Mr. Back-East, Better-Than-Everyone-Else, what was it about my daughter that stiffened your pecker? Her frying-pan figure or those bottle-thick spectacles?"

Tom straightened his shoulders and deliberately glared at his father-in-law as if he were a worm.

"Crudities about my wife, Mr. Calhoun, even from her own father, will not be tolerated."

The two men glared at each other.

It was King Calhoun who relaxed first, almost chuckling as if he admired Tom's defense of his daughter.

"Princess likens you to one of those English remittance men that come out to adventure in the West, while being supported by their families back home," he said.

Tom nodded. He'd heard Cessy's explanation.

"What I'm wondering is if you are actually more like those impoverished aristocrats who broker their honor and titles to marry into the fortunes of the five hundred."

Tom's only answer had been to take a generous sip of port.

"Gerald," a sleepy voice called out to him.

"I didn't mean to wake you," he said as he followed the sound to her bedside.

He sat down and she raised her arms for his embrace. In the darkness she was warm and soft and scented with soap. She was dearly familiar and innocently seductive.

"You smell good," he told her.

"And you taste good," she replied. "Daddy broke out the port for you. That's a good sign."

Tom's response was noncommittal as he nuzzled her face and neck and gathered up a generous handful of her hair.

"Oooh, sweet Cessy," he whispered. "I want to be with you, inside you, tonight again. But perhaps you are . . . ah . . . sore. Remember, you can tell me no."

"Yes!" she said, teasingly pulling at his necktie. "Yes, yes, yes. I want to be with you inside me tonight, too."

He kissed her long and lingeringly, but with lots of good humor and loud sucking noises until she was giggling rather than passionate.

Tom stood in the darkness and began removing his clothes. From the darkness of the bed, he knew that she watched him and he made the task as seductive and sensuous as possible.

"What on earth did Daddy keep you talking about for so long?" she asked.

"He's doing just what you wanted. He's trying to get to know me," Tom told her.

"Oh, I'm so glad," she said

In fact, he was trying to get to know more than Tom had bargained for. The old man had brazenly asked to see his financial statement, his war records, and his bank balance.

Tom had agreed easily, knowing that any hesitation would be viewed as an attempt to conceal. Tom had *nothing* to conceal. He had no financial statement and no bank balance. And the war records were all in the name of Thomas T. Walker. Even the most casual glance at the Muster-Out Roll for the U.S.V. would reveal that no person named Gerald Tarkington Crane had ever been a Rough Rider.

"At least it is over," Cessy told him. "Daddy was a little angry at first, but I think he's accepted you."

"I don't know what your scheme is," Calhoun had told Tom in the library, his eyes narrowing to slits. "But if you hurt my little girl, if you break her heart or misuse her trust, I'll stomp you 'til there is nothing but a greasy spot left on the floor."

As Tom removed the last vestiges of his clothing and eased himself into the comfort of the bed and the embrace of his wife, he hoped that Calhoun would never be called upon to fulfill his threat. Like Calhoun, Tom didn't want to see Cessy hurt. But the whole plan was looking more and more like a house of cards, and the wind was picking up.

With movements in tune, as if this were their thousandth night of love instead of their second, he divested her of her nightgown and luxuriated in the feel of her flesh against his own as he ran his hands down the length of her body.

"Oh, Cessy, I love you," he said.

The words coming from his mouth surprised him. But she was his wife. And as such, of course he loved her, he assured himself. And it felt so good to say so. It felt as if he had waited all his life to say those words. And this was the woman he wanted to say them to.

"Cessy, I love you," he repeated, taking pleasure in hearing the phrase a second time. "I love you. I love you. I love you. Forever."

She sighed so prettily, alive and eager against his touch.

"I love you too, Gerald."

The sound of another's man name on her lips momentarily startled him. His hands stilled and his shoulders stiffened.

She felt it.

"What's wrong?" she asked him.

Tom swallowed. Unsettled by the wave of sadness that had so unexpectedly engulfed him. She loved Gerald. Of course she did. All the women loved Gerald.

"What is it?" she asked again.

He kissed her forhead and hushed her question. It was not her fault. His pain was very much a self-inflicted wound.

"Nothing, nothing my Cessy," he told her as he parted her legs and settled himself between them. "Just a little twinge, I guess."

'Are you in pain?" she asked.

"I have perhaps been a little too enthusiastic a lover," he said.

He could hear her concerns slip away as he stroked and caressed her.

"Have I been overworking you?" she asked, teasing. She ran her hand enticingly up the inside of his thigh before tentatively touching him. "I thought it was the bride who was supposed to be sore."

Kissing and coaxing, he eased himself inside her fully and then set her ankles up on his shoulders so that he might delve even deeper.

She gave a startled "Oh!" of exclamation and appreciation.

"Be gentle with me, my darling," Tom told her in the same playful tone. "I've never been a husband before."

FIFTEEN

"I tell you, Queenie," King Calhoun complained as he paced her back room, empty this morning of both games and gamblers. "There is something strange about that fellow and I just can't like him at all."

Queenie had listened to the man rant and rave for the better part of a half an hour.

It was the middle of the afternoon, but the windowless room was locked and lamplight illuminated the week's worth of Palace receipts that lay spread out on a poker table. Queenie had counted them all in neat stacks and was totaling them in her folio ledger.

"King, she married him," she stated flatly, hardly pausing to look up from her work. "Princess is of age and she is certainly a young lady who knows her own mind. It's completely out of your control."

"It may be out of my control," he answered her. "But it still feels like she is my responsibility."

Queenie didn't deign to answer. King had come in madder than a hornet in a rainstorm. He stomped and threatened and slammed his fist on the table. He was furious at his new son-in-law, annoyed with his daughter, and upset with himself. But he'd come to the Palace for the express purpose of picking a fight

with Queenie. It might have made him feel better, but
Queenie had neither the time nor inclination to
humor him. She had her own situation to think
about.

She'd contacted a barber in Ponca. For the right
amount of money he was willing to take care of her
problem. Queenie was to take the train up Thursday
morning, have it over with and return home Thursday night. She had decided that she wasn't going to
tell King anything more about it. He obviously
wanted her to try to bring an unwanted, unlawful
child into the evil world that she lived in. She was not
going to do that. But it was her decision, not King's.
He was her lover, not her husband. And lovers, she
decided, could have no more say in her life than
strangers.

Besides, King had enough on his mind already.
The bankers weren't being cooperative, his oil field
was about to come in with no place to refine the oil,
and now his daughter had eloped with a fellow she
hardly knew. King's troubles and his anger would
pass as it always did. As hard as he was huffing and
puffing, she fully expected him to run out of steam
very soon.

"What do you know about him, Queenie?" King
asked her. "What can you tell me about him?"

"Me?" She looked at him dumbfounded. "Why
would I know anything about him?"

"Howard overheard him say that Queenie's Palace
is his favorite saloon," King told her.

"Now you've got Howard spying on the fellow?"
she said, shaking her head. "It's no wonder that
Princess eloped with him. She didn't trust her daddy
to stay out of business that didn't concern him."

"Get off my back, Queenie," King told her. "I'm
just looking out for my daughter. You don't know
what it's like to be a parent."

There was a long silence. Queenie didn't look up

from her work. She held herself still, her body, her mind, her emotions, were all held still for that protracted moment. When she spoke her words were calm and civil, almost cold. "No, I don't," she said. "I don't know what it is like to be a parent."

"Oh, Lord, honey, I'm sorry," King said, ceasing his pacing immediately. "It was a dang poor choice of words. I . . . I would never say nothing to hurt you like that. I'm just piss-poor company today."

"Don't worry about it," she said, waving away his concern as if it were nothing. "So the Palace is his favorite saloon. What's this fellow's name again?"

"His name is Crane, Gerald Tarkington Crane. He's so fancy born he thinks he's got to have three names instead of two."

She gave a half smile, acknowledging his attempt at humor. "What does he look like?"

"Oh you can't miss him," King assured her. "He's a tall fellow, over six feet, I'd expect. Got an impressive physique, dark hair and eyes. He's handsome, I suppose, and a dandy, tight and true. All dressed up in fancy clothes, pale polka dot shirts, and silk suspenders. I'd like to see him up to his eyeballs in muck, that's what I'd like to see."

"Now that's the most childish thing I've ever heard you say," Queenie told him.

"I can't help it, Queenie. I don't like his kind and I never have."

"Well, you'd better get to liking him cause he is family," she said. "You can have some choice with which friends you associate, but your family is whatever they happen to be."

"I just want it to be some other fellow," King said, throwing himself down in a chair with a long sigh.

Queenie gave up on the bookkeeping and rose from her chair to go to him.

"I sure am annoying for a fun-time fellow, I suppose," he commented with a sigh.

She grinned at him. "I'm glad you said it instead of me."

Queenie stepped behind him and lovingly began to massage his shoulders.

"Oh, that feels good darlin'," he told her with a little moan of appreciation. "It almost lets me forget that frilly pants blueblood calling my Princess's little house 'our home.'"

"He said that?"

King nodded.

Queenie tutted in appreciation. "He was out to tweak your beak, Mr. Calhoun, and that's a fact."

"It worked, too," he admitted. "I just can't like the man. I know his kind and I've got no use for them at all."

"What kind of man were you thinking about for Princess?" she asked. "You do want her to have a man, don't you?"

King was thoughtful for a long moment. "Yes, I do," he said finally. "Truthfully, I'd about given up on her, Queenie. I thought she was like my wife. I thought maybe she just didn't need affection or sex or even the touch of another person."

He reached back to take her hand in his own. Absently, he rubbed her palm against the side of his face and then lovingly kissed her fingers.

"But I guess I just thought . . ."

He hesitated as if embarrassed to speak his thoughts aloud.

"Well, I thought that . . . Princess has always . . . well, she's always looked up to me and thought better of me than I ever deserved. I just thought that . . . that when she married, she'd marry someone like me."

King shook his head and huffed in self-depreciation. "I sound like an old fool, don't I?"

Queenie leaned down and planted a kiss on the side of his forehead. "You sound like a daddy whose baby girl is all grown up. And what makes you think this fellow *isn't* a lot like you?"

"I told you, Queenie, he's a blueblood eastern dandy and sharpie if I don't miss my guess," King told her.

"A sharpie?" Queenie rolled her eyes. "Then I know he hasn't been around my place. I can't abide those types. Except for you, of course, I make an exception in your case."

"Woman, I'm taking you to the woodshed if you backtalk me once more." His tone was more amused than threatening.

Queenie came around his chair and seated herself upon his lap. "Promise?"

He kissed her then and clasped her tightly in his arms in a manner that was more a friendly bear hug than an embrace of passion.

"Queenie, I don't know what I'd do without you, darlin'," he said. "If I couldn't talk to you, I guess I'd never talk to no one."

"Then honey, if I can offer one more piece of advice, it would be better to talk to no one than to talk badly about your new son-in-law behind your daughter's back."

He nodded.

"I know you're right. In a way, what I'm feeling is jealousy, I suppose," Calhoun admitted. "Her bride-groom is and has everything I ever worked for in my life. And it was just handed to him. Handed to him as if somehow he deserved it just for being born to the people he was."

"That's sure not fair, King," Queenie said. "But I don't guess you could say that it's the man's fault."

"I know," he agreed with a sigh. "I just feel like if that's the kind of man my Princess really admires and wants for a husband, then maybe she didn't think as well of her daddy as I thought she did."

"King Calhoun!" Queenie exclaimed, shaking her

head. "You are far from the finest fellow alive, and I would be the first one to say so. But you've been a good father to that girl and she loves you for it. She always has and she always will."

"I didn't have no idea about how to be a father to her," King said sadly. "I never had one of my own, nor even had much expectation to be one. I thought the mother would raise the child. All I'd have to do is keep a roof over our heads and bread on our table."

"Well, you did that well enough," Queenie told him. "And she grew up to be kind and good and fair-minded. I know where she got those qualities."

"I just love her, Queenie," he said finally. "I want her to be happy and I hope he doesn't make her life a misery."

"I don't think you need to worry about it," Queenie told him. "Princess seems to make her own happiness as she goes along. If she don't like the way things are, she just insists on them being rearranged."

A knock on the door ended their conversation. Queenie walked over and opened a tiny peephole.

"It's Cedarleg," she called back over her shoulder.

King motioned to let him come in.

"Good afternoon, Miss Queenie," the man said as he entered the room. "How you been keeping yourself?"

"Very well, thank you," she answered, then feigned a whisper. "Watch yourself, the big man's in a foul mood."

"I heard that," King complained. "And I most certainly am not. Foul mood's almost all over."

The older man limped over to where King waited. The two shook hands and took seats.

Cedarleg scooted up a second chair and gave a little moan as raised his bad leg to rest upon it.

"Are you having more trouble with that leg?" King asked.

The old man snorted. "It's the rheumatiz, Ma

says," he answered. "I think she's right, but I tell her that she ain't never was nor will be no doctor."

King chuckled. "It sounds like me and Queenie aren't the only couple that annoys each other."

Cedarleg smiled. "Oh, Ma and me get into a tiff from time to time. Course it's not like you and Queenie. With us, it's usually Ma's fault. But I'm thinking with you two, the blame would be mostly on your side."

"Try to remember who you work for," Calhoun warned.

Cedarleg only chuckled.

"So what's eating you today," he asked. "Them bankers still givin' ye indigestion?"

"Worse than that," King answered. "I guess you and Ma haven't heard the news yet. Princess has got married."

"Oh, my Lord-a-mercy!" Cedarleg exclaimed. "Ma'll be having a fit when she hears. Did she marry up with that fancy feller?"

King's eyes widened and he sat up straighter. "You've met him? What can you tell me about him, Cedarleg?"

"Ain't met him," the old man admitted. "Just heard what she told Ma about him. He's wonderful, from what Princess says. But he didn't sound like our kind of folks to me."

"See, just like I said," King called out to Queenie, who was attempting to resume her bookkeeping duties.

"Nope, he just don't seem quite right for her," Cedarleg continued. "But I guess if he suits Princess, he ought to suit the rest of us."

"Just like I said," Queenie pointed out with a patronizing grin.

King gave her an impudent look but made no comment.

"Cedarleg, if you could kind of keep your ear to the

ground about this fellow," King suggested. "Anything you hear, good or bad, I want to know."

Cedarleg nodded.

"And you and Ma have got to come over and meet him," King continued. "Maybe being the father I'm not quite fair, I want to get an idea of what you think of him."

"We can stop by anytime," he said.

"Why don't we make it a dinner toward the end of the week," he said. "Howard and Mrs. Marin think you're family anyway and I'm sure there won't be any problem for Princess. She'll be eager for you to meet her new husband."

"Sounds good to me," he said. "Give Ma an excuse to wear her new dress."

"So you bought Ma a new dress, did you?" King said. "Thought that woman wouldn't let you spend money on her."

"I didn't buy it, Tom did," Cedarleg told him.

"Who's Tom?"

"That new tool dresser I hired," he said. "The one that was living with us for a while. He just up and bought her the prettiest piece of dark green brilliantine you ever saw. She sewed it up lickety-split and ain't had no chance to wear it yet."

"Is that the young tool dresser that I met?" Queenie asked him.

"Yes, ma'am," he answered.

"He is a very fine young man, an honorable fellow," Queenie said. "I liked him a lot."

"High praise indeed from a gal who's been watching men behave at their worst for years," King pointed out. "So is he working out pretty well as tool dresser?"

"Well, the truth is, Mr. Calhoun, he was turning out to be a dang fine worker. I was thinking to putting him to drilling within a year at the latest. But he done quit me," Cedarleg said.

"He quit you? Already? There aren't very many who think to quit this close to bringing it in," King said. "Did he head out to another oil field?"

"Nope, he married up some gal in Burford Corners," Cedarleg answered.

"He went ahead and married her," Queenie said, delighted. "I'm really glad for him."

King gave her an exasperated look.

"What does getting married have to do with it? Most fellows husband at night and hold a job during the day."

"And most fellows don't work half hard enough at either," Cedarleg joked. "No, Tom has done moved up in the world. Married a banker's daughter. So he's quit the oil business to become a banker."

"A banker!" King exclaimed. "Sounds like a sheriff taking up train robbery!"

Cedarleg laughed. "I suspect most folks would think it to be more like a vile sinner getting salvation and taking up preaching the word."

King shook his head, appreciating the dark humor. "I guess you're right. But I hate to think of a good oil man wasted in one of those stinking banks."

"Well maybe that's just what the oil business needs," Queenie said.

"Huh?"

"Maybe if you had more bankers that knew the oil business, then you've have more bankers willing to loan money to finance it," she said.

King nodded thoughtfully. "Queenie's got a point," he said.

"It sure makes sense," Cedarleg agreed.

"This Tom, how long did he work out on the rig?"

"Couple of weeks, I guess," Cedarleg answered. "It seemed like more 'cause he was such a quick study."

"And do you think that he knows that there's oil down there?" King asked.

"He knows, all right," Cedarleg said. "And he was as antsy and eager about it as the rest of us."

"So," King said, nodding slowly. "We know a banker that got a little bit of oil in his blood. If I don't get the money for that refinery, we might as well just plug those wells and let the oil lie there another million years."

"That's so."

"What do you think, Cedarleg," he asked. "Will this Tom of yours loan me the money to build a refinery?"

"I couldn't tell you," the old man answered. "I suspect that he'd want to, but he just got married on Sunday. I doubt if he's going to have a whole lot of pull at that bank."

"But if the bank belongs to his father-in-law, maybe he could talk him into it," King said.

"Maybe," Cedarleg agreed. "Course you can't count on that. You got a new son-in-law yourself, and I doubt very much that you'd let him talk you into anything."

King waved away the comparison. "That's talking apples and oranges," he said.

"Well, it sure wouldn't hurt to try," Cedarleg agreed.

"Not one bit," King said. "I've done asked half the bankers in this part of the country. Now what is this fellow's name again?"

"It's Tom Walker," Cedarleg answered. "He a tall, good looking man, part Indian, raised right around here."

King Calhoun smiled broadly.

"Look at him," Queenie said, shaking her head. "He looks happier than he's been all day."

"I'm going out and find this Tom Walker," he told her. "And I'm going to get him to loan me a refinery."

* * *

Cessy discovered that she rather liked married life. She had made such a strong independent life for herself, she worried that perhaps she would bridle under the demands of a husband. And the idea that one must, of necessity, consider the schedule and inclination of another person in deciding everything, from when to go to the market to what to buy there, was a little unsettling. But the first days of her marriage were such total bliss that Cessy could not imagine that it could ever be anything but wonderful.

Gerald was attentive and sweet. And he was most always right there beside her. He did not again leave the house early or without telling her where he was to go. In fact he rarely left the house at all, telling her that he preferred her company to that of anyone else in town.

They worked together in the garden. Gerald appeared to have a real aptitude for growing things and Cessy gratefully let him carry forward with it. He even teased her that he was going to grow the wildflower garden that he had threatened.

They spent long hours in the quiet of the sun parlor together. Gerald was not, it seemed, much of a lover of books. But he enjoyed hearing Cessy read aloud. And amazingly, he had apparently missed many of the classics during his education.

They played lawn tennis. Cessy had never much enjoyed games that required great athletic prowess, being a bit clumsy on the best of occasions. But Gerald was an enthusiastic player and experienced from his days at Yale. He generously sent the volleys deliberately in her direction. Her favorite aspect, however, was when it was necessary to wrap his arms around her in the interest of improving her backhand.

But what they mostly did in those first few days of wedded bliss was to talk together, laugh together, and make love.

It was, Cessy thought to herself, *perfect.* Or rather, it was nearly so. They had not as yet heard from the Cranes of Bedlington, New Jersey. Cessy looked for a telegram constantly and became very concerned that it never arrived.

"They are aghast that you have married me," she told him finally. They were sitting in the quiet coolness of the porch at evening. Gerald had removed his coat and had wrapped his arm around her shoulder.

"Don't be foolish," he said. "They probably didn't get my wire."

She had not considered that at all. "Do you think that maybe they didn't get it?"

"Cessy, it happens all the time," he said.

"But everyone says that Western Union is so reliable," she told him. In her whole life she had never heard anyone complain that telegrams were not being delivered.

Gerald shook his head. "If you only knew how many important messages were lost, you'd not be surprised at this one being mislaid at all," he said.

Cessy nodded hopefully. Thinking the wire mislaid *was* better than thinking that his family was furious. But they still had to be notified, and as far as she was concerned, the sooner the better.

"Well, if it's mislaid, then don't you think you should send another one?"

"Ah . . . ah, absolutely," he replied. "I'll do it the next time I am in town."

"Perhaps we should make a special trip," Cessy suggested. "I can go with you."

"Oh, no, it's far too much trouble," he said. "I . . . I was going to go out and . . . and consult with my banker this afternoon anyway. I'll send the wire on my way."

Cessy nodded, mollified. Still she couldn't quite understand Gerald's cavalier attitude about it. Perhaps he had simply gotten accustomed to living his life as he saw fit without the advice and interference of relatives. But a man only married once. It was an occasion of consequence and his family must be duly informed.

Cessy fully expected a certain degree of disapproval from the Cranes. Even her own father had been less than pleased that they had eloped. Once they were notified and were able to voice their disfavor, then the acceptance could begin.

Cessy was determined to win them over. She had learned over the last few days that family meant so much to Gerald. He spoke of it all the time. He wanted a house full of children and all the noise and hectic activity that went with it.

Strangely, however, he was not interested in the children at Reverend McAfee's school.

"I think the boys would really be thrilled to get to know you," she told him. "You could tell them about all the places you've been and the things that you've seen. Most of them have never been farther than Burford Corners. And I don't know a boy who ever lived that wouldn't be enthralled to hear about your adventures with Teddy Roosevelt and the Rough Riders."

Gerald shook his head. "No, Cessy, I don't really want to get too involved in your charity work. It's yours, something you can rightfully claim as your own, and I think it best if a husband keep his distance."

His logic seemed flawed, but Cessy didn't press him. When she was at Miss Thorogate's school, she'd seen plenty of uninterested young misses forced to perform charitable service that rather went against their nature. It was clear to Cessy that the recipients of such grudging largess were no more happy about it than the givers.

Many people believed that poverty was as repulsive to fine society as sin and that orphans were somehow to blame for their own condition. Talking with Gerald, it did not appear that he was one of that number, but he certainly had an aversion to the Methodist Indian Home.

He had a similiar aversion to the oil business. The Topknot was coming closer and closer to fruition and the excitement was building, but Gerald didn't want to hear a word, or make a comment, about it. Even when her father talked over dinner, it was almost as if Gerald tried deliberately not to listen.

He was also not very keen on meeting Cessy's friends.

"Remember the couple who are like second parents to me?" she asked.

Gerald's reply was vague.

"Well, Daddy talked to Cedarleg," she told him. "And he and Ma would like to come to dinner and meet you. The end of the week seems perfectly timed to me. Which would be best for you, Friday or Saturday?"

He seemed startled by the question. The gentle movement of the swing had stopped abruptly as he put his foot down. Clearly he was struggling for an answer.

"Neither," he answered finally.

"Neither?"

"I . . . we have other plans, I believe," he said.

"Other plans? I don't know of any other plans," Cessy said.

"Well, I . . . well, if we don't have some we should definitely make some. Saturday night we should go out together, don't you think? We should make it a tradition in our marriage to go out together for some entertainment on Saturdays."

"Out?" Cessy looked at him, puzzled. "Where? This is Burford Corners, not Kansas City. Except for the occasional traveling circus or medicine show, there *is* no entertainment."

"I . . . ah . . . I saw a bill that indicated a lecture at the Chautauqua House this Saturday," he said. "We could attend that."

Cessy's brow furrowed. "You want to hear Maizie Prinzwhite speak on *Demon Rum the Destroyer of Families?* I had no idea that you held temperance views."

Gerald flushed slightly. "Well, actually I don't but . . . it's a lecture, Cessy, a person should always be willing to listen and learn."

"All right, then," she agreed. "Then we'll invite Cedarleg and Ma for Friday."

"No!"

"Friday is not convenient either?"

"No, no, I don't believe that Friday will do at all," he said. "I . . . ah . . . just as I think that Saturdays should be an evening of outside entertainment, I think Fridays should be kept specifically for the two of us at home. It will be a night for our family. You and me and our children when we have them. We will spend time together. Do you play five hundred? Or perhaps seven-up?"

"Well, certainly, but . . ."

"And maybe we can . . . we can sing," he suggested. "That beautiful piano in the music room should not be allowed to go to waste."

"I told you that I don't sing very well," she said.

"Then it's perfect that it will be just us only, every Friday." He punctuated his statement with a gentle kiss that was more winning than his words.

Cessy acquiesced, wondering in silence if this was to be typical of their married life. Certain activities for certain days of the week. It was a very efficient way to live, she supposed. But it did feel a bit wanting in spontaneity.

"I'm sure your friends will understand that we are

just wed and getting used to our time together," he said. "We can surely have them over at some later date."

"Well, yes, I suppose so," Cessy admitted. "But I really want you to meet them, Gerald."

"And I will, I will, sweet Cessy," he assured her. "Just not this week."

"All right then, I'll put them off if that's what you want," she said.

"Thank you," he said with a depth of sincerity that felt to Cessy somehow inordinate. She glanced up to question him, but he quickly changed the subject.

"Then let's not talk about it anymore," Gerald said. "Let's talk about what I really want to talk about."

He was lightly tickling her throat and grinning at her in a manner that was hard to resist.

"And what is that?" she asked him.

"Our wedding trip," he said. "I'm ready to leave tomorrow, if you are."

"Leave tomorrow!" Cessy nearly fell out of the swing. "Oh, you are joking aren't you," she said.

"Yes, I suppose that I am," he said with a sigh. "But I do wish that we could get away for a while. That we could spend some time getting to know each other without anyone else around."

Cessy giggled and shook her head. "Now you are being silly. We've hardly seen a soul since we wed."

"Yes, but they are all here," he said. "Your father could come popping in at any time and Howard and Mrs. Marin are scandalized every time I close the door to the room we're in."

"Oh, they are not that bad," she said.

"Just about. Cessy, I want to get away from here for a while. I want to take you places like we talked about."

"All right, Gerald," she told him. "I did marry you, I don't think that it's too far a step to be willing to go to the ends of the earth with you."

"Not all the way to the ends of the earth," he assured her. "Just Chicago and New York."

"All right, not the ends of the earth, although Chicago and New York seem almost that far away from here," she said.

He leaned down to whisper teasingly in her ear. "I told you about that train, that pullman train."

Cessy was grateful for the darkness that hid her blush.

"While we are in New York we can take the excursion to Ocean Grove," he told her. "It's on the New Jersey shore, which should be lovely this time of year. We can take a spin along the boardwalk in one of those rolling chairs."

"Do you mean like the ones in the 'Why Don't You Try' song?"

"Those are the ones," Gerald told her.

"Oh, wouldn't we look elegant," Cessy said, feigning a haughty accent. "We simply *must* have someone photograph us."

"Indubitably, madam," he replied.

"Oh, Gerald!" she exclaimed with sudden excitement. "If we're to be in New Jersey, then we could take the train out to see your parents."

"Ah, well, I don't know, Cessy," he said. "Bedlington is not that near, nor is it on our way," he said.

"But it's ever so much closer than Burford Corners," she said, laughing. "It would be silly to go all that way and not go by and see them. Perhaps I will make a better impression in the flesh than I do by way of telegram."

"Cessy, of course my family will love you, but . . ."

"Then we can go to see them," she said. "Oh, please, Gerald, say yes that we can."

There was a strange hesitation in him as if he wished to say something else, and then he sighed smoothly.

"Of course we will go to see them, Cessy," he said.

"I am so proud of my new bride and I want my whole
family to know her and love her as much as I do."

The Nafees lived in a large, sparsely-furnished
apartment built over the store. The appearance of the
store downstairs was of prime importance to customers and could mean success or failure of the business.
The comfort of the family living quarters was not a
vital concern. Ever diligent against dirt, Mrs. Nafee
kept the rooms spotless.

The evening meal was partaken later than in most
households. The store was first cleaned and closed
and the peddlar wagon, having made rounds through
the oil camp, was returned to the carriage house.
Muna and her mother usually shared the cooking
chores, but tonight her parents were double-checking
a freight bill that her father believed was in error.

The odor of hot, steaming *bamia*—stewed lamb
with okra and tomatoes—filled the air. It was not
Muna's best dish. No matter how many times she
cooked it or how careful and conscientious she tried
to be, it was never as good as her mother's. And
worse yet, her father never failed to mention that fact
as he ate it.

Determinedly she attempted to concentrate upon
her task, but her thoughts were in a whirl. Ever since
the day of the picnic, Muna's life had become increasingly exhilarating. And for one reason alone. Maloof
had made it so.

He had not kissed her. She had thought that he
would. Perhaps, when she explained how her father
had deceived him, she had hoped that he would.

They were interrupted by Prin and Gerald. And
with the surprise engagement and the ensuing excitement of the hasty wedding, it was natural that he had
not found time to kiss her that day. Although that
evening as they walked up the stairs he had taken her
hand. Maybe that was merely meant to steady her.

But when they reached the top, he pressed it against his cheek and closed his eyes as if savoring the touch of her flesh against him.

He looked at her before as a cousin or a brother might. But now he gazed at her with longing and with passion. It was almost more of a thrill than a young woman could endure.

How had she not realized how handsome he was? she asked herself. Certainly he was not as tall or muscular as some men and his hair was thinning on top. But his eyes, those dark, luminous eyes, were so alluring. And his smile was so easy and genuine. How lucky a woman would be to have that man smiling at her.

She sighed and raised her eyes dreamily, only to find the man of her vision standing in the doorway.

"Oh!"

Her startled cry was as much guilt at being caught in such a pleasant fantasy as it was authentic surprise.

"Good evening, my little bride," he said.

Muna covered her flustered reaction and raised her chin undaunted. "I am not your bride as yet, sir," she replied.

He grinned broadly as if he approved of her reply. "No, not yet," he agreed. "You are not yet bride. I do not think of you as bride."

"How do you think of me?"

He was thoughtful for a moment, then shrugged. "I do not have English for what I think," he admitted. "In my thought, you are my *entee batata*."

Muna's jaw dropped. She was astounded. "You call me your sweet potato?"

"Sweet potato," Maloof considered the English words, nodding. "It is good on ear. I like in English, too."

"Why on earth would you think of me as such a thing?" she asked.

"Because it is like you," he insisted. "Sweet potato is so ordinary, so familiar, so plainly pleasant with meat or fish."

As he spoke he moved farther into the room and closer, so that he was standing only inches from her, the warmth of his body permeating her own.

"So simple, so ordinary, the sweet potato," he said. His voice lowered to a whisper. "But when I heat it up, add a bit of cinnamon, a clove, some sugar, it makes my mouth wet with longing for it is more tasty than any candy or delight."

He was right next to her then, his chest only a breath away from her own, his mouth open, eager, urging.

"Maloof?" Muna's heart was pounding and she was trembling with passion.

"Kiss me, sweet potato," he begged her. "I have been tortured enough."

She did.

SIXTEEN

Tom had little idea what to do with himself. He wandered the Main Street in Burford Corners for the specific purpose of sending a mythical telegram to a group of people who didn't exist.

Tom felt the noose of lies grow tighter and tighter at his neck. He was going to be found out. He had thought somehow that his old life as Tom Walker could just cease to exist. But there were far too many people who knew about it.

Maloof was one. He called him Tom on more than one occasion and even told Cessy that he worked on the oil wells. It was only the man's shaky grasp of the language that kept him from being believed.

But Cedarleg and Ma had no problem with language. All it was going to take for them to unmask the scheme was to lay eyes on Gerald Crane.

Tom had lain awake the previous night attempting to concoct a story of explanation. The best he could come up with being that Tom and Gerald were identical twins separated as children when his parents came West on a tour of the plains and their conveyance was attacked by wild Indians. The Crane family believed the lost brother dead until the two had discovered each other in the Rough Riders.

It sounded more like the plot of a two-penny

adventure novel than an explanation of why Gerald
Crane appeared to be exactly the same man as Tom
Walker. He was loathe to attempt to use it. Worse,
Tom was sure, being found out a liar would put Cessy
in the position of choosing to believe him against all
evidence and the advice of her friends. He didn't
want that to happen.

But avoiding the good people of Topknot and
Burford Corners was not going to be as easy as he'd
supposed. Truly, the only solution was to take Cessy
away on that wedding trip.

That was easier to get her to agree to than to get
done. Tom was down to four dollars and change.
That would get the two of them about as far as Joplin.
To provide Cessy with a month-long, first-class
honeymoon of the type that he'd envisioned, he
would need nearly a hundred dollars. A paltry sum
from the fortune of King Calhoun, but Tom was not
yet able to get his hands upon one thin dime of
Calhoun's money. He couldn't even work up the
nerve or think up an excuse to ask Cessy about it.
Certainly there had to be household accounts. And
undoubtedly his wife had money in trust.

Perhaps the best answer was simply to mention the
funds transfer again. Simply tell her that his funds
had not arrived—another blow to the efficiency of
Western Union—and that she needed to advance him
the money to purchase the fare. That would undoubtedly work. She trusted him completely. Maybe that
was why he was so hesitant to abuse that faith.

Still, he had to. If he did not get Cessy out of town,
his marriage was over. He had to get her away from
here, away from people that could identify him.

He wasn't sure how well that would really work.
Unless he kept her away, the threat of meeting up
with Ma and Cedarleg would always be there. And
what about his supposed parents? She was extremely
keen on meeting them. Even if he convinced her that

they dropped dead sometime between now and when they arrived back East, he was certain that he would be obliged to escort her to visit his ancestral home in Bedlington, the country house in Connecticut. She would want to be introduced to all of the myriad siblings, cousins, aunts, uncles and etcetera that he'd made up stories about for her entertainment.

Not even on the wedding trip, unless they ventured to Timbuktu, would he find any real refuge from his tangled web of deceit.

But perhaps if they went away, he could gain some time with her. If he were able to prove himself dependable and honorable, if she were given time to get to know him as the real person that he was, if he could have a chance to show her how much he truly loved her, then . . .

Tom's thoughts halted abruptly in midsentence. *That he truly loved her.* Was that what he thought? *That he truly loved her.* It was impossible, of course. He didn't really believe in love. And even if he did, certainly he would have chosen someone delicate and pretty, quiet and shy. Cessy was . . . Cessy was . . . well, Cessy was wonderful. She was kindhearted and genuine, she was sweet and funny, practical, determined, always smiling and, of course, she was in love with him. It was a combination that created a powerful love potion.

Did he really love her? Was that why the pack of lies that he'd created sat so sourly upon his stomach? He really loved her and he didn't want to hurt her. And somehow there was not going to be any way not to do that.

The far end of Main Street brought Tom to the railroad track. He gazed up and down the long length of galvanized steel and wondered if heading out of here in one direction or another would help.

But he couldn't desert her, she surely didn't de-

serve that. Better that he throw his body in front of
the train and make her a grieving widow than an
abandoned bride. Tom shook his head. With the way
his luck was going these days, somebody would
probably recognize him as he lay dead in his coffin.

He gave up the idea completely when he noticed
the signal was up. Burford Corners was a jerkwater
town. A huge trough of water was kept filled between
the tracks. The train merely scooped up the water as
it went by, not bothering to stop unless it was
unloading a passenger or was signaled to pick one
up.

Tom gave a casual glance in the direction of the
platform. Sure enough, a lone woman in gray serge
sat waiting upon one of the benches.

He tipped his hat politely and meant to pass on by
when he realized who the rather dowdily clad woman was.

"Miss Queenie," he said. "How are you this morning, ma'am?"

She looked up, startled as if her thoughts had been
very far away, and then smiled at him.

"Tool Dresser," she said. "I've been thinking about
you."

"Thinking about me, ma'am? I am flattered."

"Well, don't be," she said chuckling suggestively.
"I wasn't thinking that you were the best-looking
man I ever laid eyes on. I was just thinking about
what you told me the other night about starting
over."

"Ummm, yes," Tom said nodding. "Starting over."

He was no longer so sure that it was going to be as
easy as he had believed.

"King Calhoun is looking for you," she said.

Tom stilled inside and out. "King Calhoun is
looking for me?"

"You're Tom Walker, aren't you?"

He nodded slowly.

"Cedarleg speaks very highly of you. He told King that you'd left the oil business for a banking opportunity," she said. "Now King is wanting to get you involved in a business venture."

Tom cleared his throat nervously.

"I don't know that I'd be interested," he said.

"Well, of course you don't know until you hear him out," Queenie said. "You can trust King. He may not know a lot of things, but that man knows how to make money."

"It's a fine skill to have," Tom agreed, and then deftly changed the subject. "So you are traveling today, ma'am."

"Just a short trip," she said. "I'll . . . I'll be back by evening, back to work, back to my life."

"Is this a pleasure jaunt or business?" he asked.

"Neither," she replied. "What about you? Are you here to take a train?"

"No, not really," he said. "I'm just walking, walking and thinking. A typical pastime for a new husband, no doubt."

Queenie nodded thoughtfully.

"May I join you?" Tom asked, indicating the empty space next to her on the bench.

"Should you?"

He raised his eyebrows at her question.

"I understand that you recently wed that young woman that you wanted," Queenie said. "I may be dressed here in disguise, so to speak, but people still know who I am. I'd hate for your new bride to think we were making an assignation."

Tom seated himself with unconcern. "Cessy would never believe me unfaithful to her," he said.

"Why is that?"

"Because I never would be," he answered. "There is a whole world of things I am guilty of, but that is not now nor ever will be one of them. I think she knows that."

"She must love you then, very much," she said.

Tom nodded.

"And amazingly I believe that I love her, too. Isn't that funny? I went after her, deliberately making her fall in love with me, only to find myself in love as well."

She smiled at him. "It sounds as if this is destined to end happily ever after."

Tom sighed heavily. "No, I don't really think so."

"Why not?"

"Truthfully?"

"Would a woman ever want to hear a lie?" she asked.

"I used to think so," he answered. "I used to believe that the ladies greatly preferred pretty lies to unpleasant truths. But I'm beginning to revise my judgement."

"Experience often does bring wisdom," she agreed. "And marriage, I understand, is an experience famous for that."

Tom laughed at her clever bit of humor. "In honesty, I have never been happier in my life," he told her. "Nor have I ever been so miserable."

"Well, that certainly sounds like a typical marriage."

"There is nothing typical about mine," he said.

Tom turned to look at Queenie for a long moment. She was a strong, sensible woman. Not necessarily the type to whom a man should choose to divulge his secrets, but somehow Tom knew he could trust her.

"You know when you tell a doctor personal things about your body, he's got to keep it to himself," Tom said. "And when you tell a lawyer about your business dealings, he can't tell anyone, either."

Queenie nodded.

"What about your profession, Miss Queenie?" he asked. "You must hear plenty of stories that shouldn't be spread around. Are you obliged to keep quiet about them, too?"

"Are you asking me if I'll keep a confidence for you, Tool Dresser?"

"Yes, ma'am, I guess that I am."

Queenie nodded slowly. "You've kept one for me," she told him. "I believe that I can return the favor."

Tom leaned back more comfortably on the bench and stretched his long legs out in front of him.

"I told you that I created a whole new life for myself. That I left everything behind and began as a new person."

"Yes, I remember that. The idea intrigued me," she admitted. "I . . . I've occasionally thought of doing the same thing myself. And for you, at least, it has obviously worked."

"I suppose that it has," he said. "But the new person I've become is a pack of lies. There is nothing about him that is familiar or genuine or even honorable."

Queenie raised an eyebrow. "That doesn't sound good," she said.

"No, it's not," Tom agreed. "I thought it would be, but it's not."

Tom rubbed his beardless chin thoughtfully.

"I guess that all my life I've wanted to be somebody else. Always I've pretended to be somebody else," he said. "Now I have even created another whole person with a history and friends and family. All of it just made up."

Queenie shook her head in admiration.

"It sounds like a grand scheme to me," she said.

"I thought it was fun and I . . . well, I hated being who I was. I wanted to be somebody different," he said. "Now I truly have become a different person, I've taken on a completely new identity and I find I do not like it at all."

"Why did you do it?" she asked him.

"I felt that to survive, to get ahead in the world, I had to change. I had to be a different man than the man I was born to be. So that is what I did. I became someone else," he said.

"And was it true? Do you need to be a different man to survive in the world?" she asked.

Tom shook his head. "I'm not sure," he said. "I can do a job. I can work hard. I can earn the respect of other men. But I won't get rich that way. I'll never be . . . I'll never be King Calhoun."

Queenie was thoughtful for a long moment before she replied. "King Calhoun is a good man. He's been a good friend to me and I admire him a lot. But King would have never turned down a free sample from Frenchie. He might not have sought it out, but if it were offered he wouldn't have had the constancy to resist. Perhaps you will never be as rich as he is, you may never own your own oil company or buy and sell in millions of dollars. But in this one thing you are the better man. Do you really want to give up that superiority?"

"No, Miss Queenie, I don't think I would," Tom admitted finally. "Now that I find myself wholly taken over by the man I pretended to be, all I really desire is to be once more that fellow that I once was."

"Then you should go back to being him," Queenie said. "And you should go back now, without delay. Over time the distance gets further and further, until you are certain that you can not go back at all."

"I want to, but there is so much to lose," he said. "Like the woman that I'm in love with."

"You said that she loves you?" Queenie asked. "Does she love the man that you really are? Or does she love the pretender that you've claimed yourself to be?"

"I . . . I'm honestly not sure," he answered.

"Well, you need to find out," she said. "You need to find out for sure. And the only way to do that is to give her the chance to choose between the two."

Tom sat for a long moment, then slowly nodded. "I guess you're right. I have to lay my past before her and let her decide if she cares for me or if what she really wanted was him. And I'd better do it before she hears the truth from someone else."

The sound of a train whistle could be heard in the distance. Tom turned to look in that direction and could barely make out the puff of smoke on the horizon.

"Looks like your train is coming in, Miss Queenie," he said.

"Yes, yes, it's my train," she said.

Her words sounded so forlorn that Tom turned to glance at her.

She'd planted a brave smile on her face, but it was evident that she was upset.

"What's wrong, Miss Queenie?" he asked. "Are you feeling ill again?"

"No, no, I'm fine," she assured him. But she didn't look it.

She had no real luggage, just a small club satchel, still Tom picked it up to carry for her.

"This is another way that I'm better than King Calhoun," he told her.

"Carrying luggage?"

"If you were my woman, you'd never be traveling alone," he said. "Of course, I guess I can't take much credit for that. Knowing my woman as I do, she'd simply assume that I *should* accompany her and then insist that I do."

"She's a little domineering?"

"Cessy takes the bull by the horns on every occasion, and I am the bull she is most familiar with," he said.

"Most men wouldn't like that," Queenie told him.

"I didn't like it much at first either," he admitted. "But you know what I think now? I think that a woman like that can sometimes bring out the best in a man."

The train had come to a full stop in front of them. The porter jumped out from a door two cars up and put down the steps. He was obviously in a rush and urged them forward.

"Let's get you on board right away, ma'am," he said. "We're already running sixteen minutes behind and we'd hoped to make it up on this stretch."

The man reached for Miss Queenie's bag and Tom held it out to him.

"Wait!"

Queenie's cry was so startling both men momentarily froze in place.

"What is it?" Tom asked.

"I'm not going," she said, firmly. "I'm sorry, I'm not going."

She turned and began deliberately walking away.

Tom and the porter exchanged perplexed looks.

"She's not going," Tom told him with a shrug.

"Women!" the porter complained as he put the steps back on board and waved the engineer forward.

Tom, still holding the woman's traveling bag, hurried after her.

"Miss Queenie, you forgot your satchel," he called.

She stopped and he hurried to hand it to her.

"What is going on, ma'am?" he asked her.

"I'm taking your advice, Tool Dresser," she said.

"My advice? You're the one who was giving advice, Miss Queenie."

She smiled up at him. "Well, Tool Dresser, I'm going back to being the woman that I once was. The woman who could do anything. And I fully intend to bring out the best in my man."

*　*　*

Cessy had intended to spend most of Thursday afternoon by herself. Gerald had promised to send the telegram and attend to some unstated business. She deliberately held herself back from questioning him too closely. They were husband and wife now, and it was her duty to allow him to freely pursue his interests without her interference. She had to bite down her lip to let him do so, but she was determined.

She had hardly begun to direct Howard in the reorganization of the carriage house when Muna surprisingly arrived.

Cessy washed her hands and face and hurried to meet her friend.

"And where is Mr. Bashara this afternoon?" she asked, giving her Muna a warm hug.

"Making his living selling knicks and knacks, I suppose," Muna answered. "And your husband, is he out-of-pocket also?"

"He's gone downtown on business," Cessy answered. "So it's just us once again."

"We can sit in for a real gossip!"

The two giggled together like girls and then took seats in the front parlor.

"I came to tell you that we've set the date," Muna began.

"When?" Cessy asked.

"September twenty-eighth," Muna answered. "That will give all my uncles and cousins a chance to be here."

"So you are still determined to go through with it," Cessy said.

"He is a good man, Prin," she told her. "He is unfailingly honest and he works very hard. He is gentle and kind. He's very funny, too. And he's not afraid to laugh at himself. It's hard to live in a place so strange, to not understand all that people are saying to you, to always be the foreigner, the butt of the joke.

But he is philosophical about it. He is sweet and caring and . . . and tender."

"But does he care for you? That's the question, Muna. Does he care for you or is it only your father's business that he wants."

"Prin, I've thought about it," she said. "I've thought about it a lot since that day we talked in the store. I tried to get to know him. I've tried to give him a chance. I tried to see what kind of man he really is and what kind of life he could offer for me. And I've tried to determine if he has any interest in me, just as myself."

"And what did you decide?"

"I've decided that I like him," she said. "More than that, I think that I care for him. I . . . I believe that I have fallen in love with him."

"Oh, Muna!"

"Perhaps I'll never know if he truly wants me or just my father's store. And if a store was all he wanted, I am just going to go on with our life together, grateful that my father had one to offer him."

"You love him?"

She nodded.

"But it just seems so . . ."

"Don't say anything against him, Prin," Muna warned. "I know you don't like him, but I do. I love him and if you love me, then you will respect my feelings."

"Oh, Muna," Cessy said. "We are both so lucky to get the men that we love."

The two laughed and giggled together. It was almost as they had been before, before a peddler came halfway across the world to marry a storekeeper's daughter, before Cessy had seen a Rough Rider in uniform who she had waited all her life for.

They joked about Cessy's father's initial reaction to her marriage. They discussed the latest gossip around

Burford Corners. They speculated on when and who would bring in the first oil well out on the Topknot.

They talked gardening and bonnets, social reform and the exceptional rearing their future children were sure to receive.

Cessy told her about Gerald's very rigorous schedule of times they should spend together.

Muna related a secret of her own.

"Maloof has . . . has given me a gift," she said.

"What kind of a gift?" Cessy asked.

"A very inappropriate one," Muna answered with a secretive whisper.

"Tell me," Cessy insisted.

"He bought me a pair of black silk drawers," Muna said.

"Oh my heavens! Does he not know how . . . how risqué such a thing is? For an unmarried woman."

Muna grinned impishly. "I think he knows more than he lets on," she said.

"So what did you do?" Cessy asked. "Did you give them back?"

"Absolutely not," Muna replied. "And I never fail to quietly mention to him when I happen to be wearing them."

Cessy screamed in feigned shock.

The two nearly choked with wicked, unmaidenly giggles.

"So, dear Mrs. Crane," Muna teased. "Now that you are married, you must tell me everything."

"Everything about what?" Cessy hedged.

"Don't be coy," Muna chided. "We always said that the one who married first would reveal all the secrets."

Cessy hemmed and hawed for a moment or two.

"What exactly do you want to know?" she asked finally.

"I want to know what is it like?"

"Being married?" Cessy was deliberately obtuse.

"Well, we have meals together and take walks together and we work in the garden and . . ."

"Not that."

"What then?"

"Oh, you!" Muna said in exasperation. "What is it like . . . in the marriage bed."

"Oh, that."

"Yes that."

"You'll find out," Cessy teased. "September twenty-eighth."

"Prin!"

"All right, all right." Cessy lowered her voice to a more secret tone. "It's not at all as frightening and uncomfortable as we've been led to believe."

Muna sighed, relieved.

"Well, it's sort of . . . sort of . . . well, it's sort of wonderful."

"You're joking?"

"No, it's really, really quite nice."

The two young women looked at each other for a long moment and then both broke into red-faced giggles.

"But isn't it so . . . so embarrassing?" Muna asked.

"At first, yes, at first it is quite embarrassing," Cessy admitted. "I thought, How will I live if this man sees me practically naked!"

"How indeed!" Muna agreed.

"But now he's seen me actually naked and it was really very natural," she said.

"He has actually seen you naked!" Muna's words were a horrified whisper.

"Believe me, it is not nearly as strange once you are married as it must seem now. It's like we are bonded," Cessy said. "We are truly one person. There are no secrets between us."

The words warmed Cessy as she said them. She knew that they were true, completely true. She loved

Gerald totally. And he loved her, too, despite all her faults.

Almost as if her thoughts had conjured him up, she spied her husband through the front window.

"My goodness, Gerald is home already," she said.

"Oh, dear, I don't know how I'll face him," Muna said blushing.

"If you ever breathe a word of what I told you, I'll invite you to dinner and cook it myself," Cessy threatened.

The front door shut noisily and Cessy hurried to meet her husband.

"Home so soon?" she called out to him from the doorway.

"Cessy, we have to talk," he said.

His expression was serious and determined. Cessy was immediately certain that some terrible calamity had befallen them.

"Oh dear, what has happened?" she asked, her tone reflecting that fear.

"Nothing!" he answered hastily. "I didn't mean to frighten you. Nothing has happened. We . . . I just need to talk to you."

"Muna is here."

He stood now at the parlor doorway and could see the occupant inside.

"I must go anyway," Muna said gathering her things.

"Oh, no, please don't hurry on my account," Gerald said. "Do sit down, sit down. I'm sorry, Cessy, I never thought about your having company. Please. Our discussion can wait."

Muna resisted for another moment and then reluctantly returned to her seat. Obviously she felt in the way, but politeness demanded that she stay at least until it would seem more natural to leave.

Gerald set upon himself to entertain Muna. His

conversation was light and cheery. Cessy enjoyed watching him at his charming best, but she could not quite dismiss the expression she had seen upon his face when he walked through the door. Something was very wrong.

The tinkle of a bell captured her attention and Cessy looked out the front window once more to see a delivery boy on a bicycle stopped in front of the house.

"Oh, we've got a message," she said, rising to her feet. "I'll be right back."

Cessy hurried to the boy and traded him a nickel tip for the paper he brought. Opening it, she read the words, first with surprise and then with disappointment. With a shrug she returned to the parlor.

"Not bad news, I hope," Muna said.

"Not good news, either," Cessy said. "I was hoping it was a telegram from Gerald's parents. We still haven't heard from them and I am on pins and needles wondering what they will think of me."

"I'm sure they will love you," Muna said. "How could they not?"

"Who is it from?" Gerald asked.

"Reverend McAfee, the poor dear," Cessy answered. "I have simply got to get someone to go out there and help the old fellow so that he can retire. I fear that he is slipping."

"What does he say?"

"He has sent us our marriage license and a note," she said and opened the small paper to read aloud. " 'My dear children, I hope that all is well with you and that your days of newly wedded bliss are a heaven upon this earth.' "

"Isn't that sweet."

"Very nice," Gerald agreed.

" 'I have had the marriage papers filed for you at the county courthouse as I had promised. The enclosed is your copy. I hope that it contains no errors or surprises. I filled the form out as completely and as accurately as I knew how.'"

"That doesn't sound as if he is slipping too badly," Muna said.

"That's because you haven't read the marriage certificate," Cessy said, laughing ruefully. "He has the bridegroom's name listed as Thomas Thursday Walker."

SEVENTEEN

He had meant to tell her. Truly he had. And if Muna hadn't been there when he'd gotten home, he certainly would have. But she *had* been there. And then the marriage license came from Reverend McAfee and he realized even more clearly how humiliating it was going to be for Cessy. She was going to have to face all her friends with the truth that she had been tricked into a marriage with a man whose real name she didn't even know. She would be a laughingstock. Tom simply lost his nerve.

But Friday morning he was determined to tell her all. He headed into breakfast with that firmly in mind. He would explain to her that he loved her. That he wanted her and needed her. And that he had lied to her.

When he entered the kitchen, King Calhoun was already there, gobbling down his biscuits and eggs. He barely glanced up to nod suspiciously at Tom before returning his attention to his plate.

Cessy was waiting for him. When she saw her husband, however, her face flushed vivid scarlet and she lowered her eyes. Tom knew what that demure behavior covered, and grinned.

He had meant to make slow, tender love to her the night before. He had thought that as his last night as

Gerald, he would use all of his technique and expertise, playing the virtuoso with her body his musical instrument.

He hadn't even allowed her the privacy of the screen to undress. He'd begun disrobing her even before they'd got the bedroom door shut. But as he was kissing and caressing her, he realized that she was deliberately holding back. At first it spurred him on. He tried to push her to relinquish her restraint.

Then as if blinders were lifted from his eyes, Tom understood that her self-bridled fervor was for his benefit. His lovely, sweet wife, Cessy Calhoun, was domineering in all aspects of her life. Like her tendency to want to lead on the dance floor, she wanted to guide the movements in his arms as well. She held herself in tight control because of her love for him.

Tom rolled from her embrace and got out of bed.

"Gerald, what are you doing? Come back to bed."

"In a minute," he promised.

He lit the lamp and began rifling through her dressing table.

"What on earth are you up to?" she asked. "Why are you looking through my things? Come back to bed."

Tom opened the second drawer on the left and found what he was looking for. They were soft and smooth in sweet pinks and blues, startling chartreuse and periwinkle, and stately maroons and purples.

"Ah, these will do nicely."

"What is it?" she asked.

Tom reached in the drawer and grabbed a handfull of what she had stored in there and eagerly joined her on the bed.

Cessy was sitting up now. Beneath the covering of the sheet that she held demurely to her neck, she still wore her camisole and stockings.

"What on earth are you going to do with those hair ribbons?" she asked him.

Tom smiled at her and then placed them firmly in her hands.

"I'm not going to do anything with them, Cessy, but what about you?"

"Me?"

"Could you think of something that you'd like to do with these?"

Cessy looked down at the brightly colored pieces of satin in her hand and then back up at him, puzzled.

"Whatever would I do with them?"

"Well, of course, you could always dress your hair," he said. He hesitated a long moment. "Or you could tie my hands to the bedposts."

"What!"

"Do you think you would like to do that, Cessy," he asked, leaning closer to whisper the words upon her neck. "Would you like to have me totally at your mercy. You could do whatever you want to me, whenever you want to me. And I . . . I wouldn't be able to stop you."

Her eyes widened as she discerned the implications.

"I don't know, I . . ."

"Wouldn't you like to say what and when?" he asked her. "Wouldn't you like to be totally in control. Isn't that what you like?"

"Well, yes, but . . ."

"Then tonight, let's do something that you like."

She hesitated, still unsure.

"Don't worry, Cessy, you won't hurt me," he said. Then his tone became one of feigned pleading. "You wouldn't hurt me, would you Cessy? Please don't hurt me."

Tom watched her expression turn from stunned shock to speculative appreciation as she held the ribbons in her hands, stroking the smooth satin.

"Lay down!" she ordered.

Now at breakfast with her father at the far end of the table, she was considerably more demure.

"How is my *extremely bossy* wife this morning?" he asked as he bent down to plant a husbandly kiss upon her cheek.

Cessy rolled her eyes, indicating the presence of her father at the table.

Tom took his seat beside her and leaned closer to whisper for her ears alone.

"We are husband and wife," he told her. "There is no cause to be embarrassed. And anyway, I believe that I am the one who has the most reason to blush this morning."

She began to giggle almost naughtily, and Tom joined in. They were still grinning at each other when King Calhoun's booming voice interrupted their secret reminiscences.

"I understand from Princess that your parents have still failed to answer your telegram and acknowledge your marriage," he said.

Tom was momentarily caught off guard. He had vowed to come forward with the truth this morning, but he couldn't very well blurt it out with Cessy's father here.

"Seems to me that's pretty dang rude," King continued argumentatively. "Princess and I are just plain folks, but at least we've got the good manners to respond to a message."

"Daddy, please—" Cessy began, determined to defend her husband and his erstwhile and mythical kindred.

Tom couldn't let her do it alone. "I . . . ah . . . I did hear . . . ah yesterday," he interrupted.

Cessy looked at him, astonished.

"You received a wire from your family and you forgot to mention it to me!"

"Ah . . . no, not from my family . . . from . . . from their lawyer," he said.

"Their lawyer!" Cessy almost squealed the word. "My heavens! Are they going to try to have our marriage dissolved?"

King Calhoun had obviously jumped to the same erroneous conclusion.

"Who the hades do they think they are?" he bellowed.

"No, it's not that," Tom said quickly. "No, it's not that at all."

The kitchen quieted perceptively at that. Tom even managed a light chuckle at his new bride's hasty conclusion.

"Don't be silly, sweetheart. I told you they are going to love you," he said. "I heard from their lawyer because they are not at home."

"What do you mean they are not at home?" Calhoun asked.

"They've gone for a trip, an excursion . . . ah, to the continent, Paris, London," he said. "They should be gone for ah . . . about six months."

"Six months?" Cessy was astonished.

"Why go to Europe if one has to rush," he said. "So we'll just have to wait to let them know."

"Can't you send them a cable?" her father asked.

"Ah . . . no, I mean not yet, they are still on the ship, of course," Tom said.

Calhoun's brow furrowed. "Isn't that the reason they invented the wireless?"

Tom was saved from having to come up with an answer for that by a frantic knocking upon the front door.

"Mr. Calhoun! Mr. Calhoun!" a young voice called out, not waiting to be let inside. "Oil! They've struck oil on the 'P.'"

An instant of complete and total silence filled Cessy's fine yellow house. Then everything broke loose.

"Wahoo!" Calhoun hollered, rising to his feet in such a rush that his chair clattered to the floor.

Tom felt the same surge of excitement course through his own veins.

Cessy was on her feet as well. Hastily grabbing her hat and handbag, she was right behind her father as he headed out the door. The messenger, Mrs. Marin, and Howard were already in the backseat of the Packard when they got there. Everybody was talking at once, the excitement a palpable thing.

"Crank her up!" Calhoun called out to Tom, and he obliged.

The loud, shaky Packard sprang to life almost instantly as if it, too, could not wait to get there.

Cessy scooted over next to her father, leaving plenty of room in the front seat beside her.

"Sit here," she told him.

"No, I'll just stay here," he said.

"What? Don't you want to see the newest well?"

"I'll just stay here," he repeated.

"Get in," Cessy told him. "You can't miss this!"

"Yes, I can," he assured her. "Please go on without me. Enjoy yourself."

Cessy stared at him in disbelief, but Calhoun couldn't wait for another word. He slipped his growling automobile into gear and they went roaring out of the yard in a great rush. Cessy turned around in the seat to look back at him, her expression incredulous, until they were out of sight.

Tom stood alone in the silence of their noisy departure for a long moment. Then he jumped straight up in the air, screaming.

"Wahoo!"

He began dancing around the yard, singing a tune of his own making at the top of his lungs.

"The 'P' came in, the 'P' came in, the P. Calhoun Number One came in! We did it! We did it! We did it!"

He spread his arms wide and turned in a half-dozen circles, screaming his delight toward the sky, and then fell back in the grass, laughing.

The "P" had come in. All that hard work, all that sweat and grease and mud, all that heat and heartache, it had all paid off.

The crew, his crew, had been first.

Tom sighed.

He wished so much that he could have been there. He wished he could have been standing on the derrick floor when the rumble became a roar. He wished he was there now. There with all of them. Everyone who was a part of it, all of them together.

He sat up on the grass and shook his head. He just almost had to be there. He hated watching them go, watching Cessy and King and even the servants go while he had to stay behind. It was *his* well, not solely his of course, but he'd been a part of it. And as the boys had said, the first well is like the first love, a man never really forgets it.

Now that it had come in, his first well, he was relegated to sitting quietly at home.

He couldn't stand it. Tom rose to his feet and began walking the large expansive lawn as if he were a prisoner and this were his cage. He had been part of this well. Bringing it in was as much his victory as it was King Calhoun's. Not being there to see it sat bitterly upon him.

It was as if it were his birthday and he was the only one not invited to the party. But there was no way that he could show his face at the "P." Or rather there was no way that he could show Tom Walker's face.

Cedarleg and Ma would both be there, as well as the entire crew and all the drillers, pushers, and dressers that knew him as Tom.

King and Cessy would be there, too. And they knew him only as Gerald.

Tom finally took a seat on the porch and gazed in the direction of the Topknot. He couldn't see a thing. He couldn't hear a thing. He simply could not bear it another minute. He would lose himself within the crowd. No one who knew him would even realize that he was there.

Convincing himself that it could work, Tom hurried back into the house to get his coat and hat. Then, eager and excited, he headed out in the direction of the "P."

The slick black fortune was still spewing up high as the crown block and obscuring the top of the derrick when the Packard pulled up at the site. In the early days of oil drilling, before they'd developed control values and occasionally now to show off to investors, gushers were allowed to run for days and waste thousands of barrels of oil that way. But the experienced men of the "P" were already busy trying to clamp down the flow and directing it into the tank pipes.

Cessy was charged with energy and excited as always. Her father had been bringing in oil wells since she was a little girl, but the excitement never failed to thrill her.

Mrs. Marin was clapping as if it were a theatrical performance. Howard jumped from the automobile while it was still moving, seeming to forget all his hard-won dignity as a household servant and ready to share the enthusiasm of the good old days with his former compatriots.

"Ain't she something!" King exclaimed with pride.

"Really something, Daddy," Cessy agreed. "I only wish that Gerald were here."

Her father gave a less-than-sympathetic shrug and hurried away from the automobile and up to the rig.

Cessy left the Packard and followed him through

the crowd. It was an almost carnival-like atmosphere. All the workers from every rig had temporarily shut down their operations to come and watch the "P" being brought in. Their wives and families had eagerly joined them and many of the townspeople as well.

Everybody was talking at once. Everyone offering their own version of the exciting events.

"They hit pay sands at just under seven hundred feet," one young man reported to her.

"At the rate it's pouring out of there," another told her proudly, "this one is sure to make five thousand barrels a day just on its own."

"The Five is almost at the same depth and it's along the same rock strata, they'll be breaking it wide open tomorrow if I don't miss my guess."

"I knew this one was gonna make good," one old fellow assured her. "All that salt water and stink in the beginning, it's the perfect omen, to my thinking."

Knowing most everybody, Cessy offered smiles and greetings at almost every step. And to her dismay found that in her current circumstances as newly wed, she was commanding almost as much attention as the oil well.

"We heard you got yourself married up."

"What's your name now that you're wed?"

"It's hard to believe, our little Princess, married at last."

"I remember when you were toddling around these wells, fat-cheeked and rag-bottomed."

There were words, well wishes, and congratulations all around. Cessy had not thought about herself being the center of attention. But the gusher being named for her, and the subject of her recent hasty marriage being the main focus of local gossip, it was natural that her name would be very much on everyone's lips.

"And where is this husband of yours that we've all heard about but none of us have ever seen?" Ma asked.

"He is . . . he is otherwise involved this morning," Cessy heard herself lying and was not at all pleased.

She didn't want to make excuses for Gerald, but she could hardly tell these people, whose very lives were punctuated by moments like these, that her husband had no interest in her oil well or its success.

"Well, that's too bad," Ma commiserated. "I know how Cedarleg would hate to miss something like this. And it wouldn't be half the fun for me if that old man wasn't here with me."

Cessy nodded and gave the older woman a loving hug.

"Come up to the derrick with me," Cessy begged her. "You know how I hate being the only woman up there."

Ma chuckled. "But you never hate being the one in charge."

Cessy shrugged with unconcern. "But I'm so good at it," she declared.

The two women worked their way through the crowd, speaking to one person here and another there, until they reached the area of the rig and masculine hands helped them up to the derrick floor.

Control of the oil flow had been established. The wet, black soup poured directly into the sump tank behind the rig. Cessy had never minded losing a dress to oil splatter, but the unpredictable force of the underground pressure was dangerous. At Sour Lake an unrestrained well had blown the crown block off the top of the derrick.

Acting immediately, Cessy took control of the festivities. A speech would need to be made, the workers recognized. She began lining the men up in the way she considered most appropriate. The driller

and the tool pusher would stand on either side of her
father. The crew of rig builders to his right, the tank
builders to his left. Various pipe fitters, haulers, and
roughnecks were positioned according to Cessy's
interpretation of their importance and value.

"Where is your tool dresser?" Cessy asked Cedarleg.

"The feller quit me," he answered. "Just days ago
he quit me to marry up some local gal."

"He's probably here," Ma said, her eyes scanning
the crowd. "As hard as he worked and this being his
first, I know for sure that he could never stay away."

"You talking about that Walker?" King Calhoun
asked. "Get him up here. He deserves to take his bow
as much as the rest of us. And I've been looking all
over town for him."

"You still trying to find refinery money?" Cedarleg
asked him.

"It's that or leave this oil in the sumps indefi-
nitely."

Cedarleg tutted with disapproval. "That's too dangerous for my blood," he said.

The earthen pits known commonly as sumps were
dug out to serve as oil reservoirs. A foot or two of
water at the bottom prevented the oil from seeping
into the ground. And planks laid across the top kept it
from evaporating. But the air space below the planks
was often a trap for volatile gases.

"Too dangerous for me," Cedarleg repeated. "The
whole dang Topknot would be about as safe as a
tinderbox. A machine spark, a careless cigarette, or a
strike of lightning could set it off in a twinkling."

"I don't like sump storing any more than you do,
Cedarleg," King told him. "But it's store it or pump it
back into the ground. Without a way to process it, it's
not even worth trying to carry it away."

Cedarleg chuckled. "Mr. Calhoun, I watched you

strike it rich a couple of dozen times," he said. "But I swear to gumption, this is the first time I've ever seen you, or anybody else *strike it poor*."

"Well, maybe if I can find your friend Walker, I can talk him into helping us out," King said. "He's young and if he's smart as you say, he'll be looking for a way to get ahead in this world."

Cedarleg whistled. "You don't know the half of it. That boy's got dreams that are frightening to behold."

"Big ideas, huh," King said.

Cedarleg nodded. "He puts me in mind of you, Mr. King Calhoun, when you were of a similar age."

Calhoun laughed. "That bad? Well, I got to find this fellow for sure."

Cedarleg turned to peruse the crowd himself. "He's got to be here somewhere. This is his first well, you know a fellow can't stay away from that."

"Yeah," King agreed. "He's out there somewhere, the whole town's out there, except for my new son-in-law, of course."

"There he is," Ma said, spotting the man in the crowd. She began waving him forward.

"Where?" Cessy asked.

"Doggone it," Ma complained. "I thought he saw me. But he's like ducked down or some such. Do you see him out there, Cedarleg? Near that scraggly growth of cow vetch?"

All four of them followed her direction, looking from face to face.

"He's got on his nice coat, the one he bought from the Nafees' peddler man," she said.

"I don't see him," Cedarleg said.

"I don't see him now, either," Ma said. "But I'd swear he was there."

"Maybe he's embarrassed to come up," Cedarleg said. "I was pretty hard on him."

"Hard on him about what?" Ma asked, and then answered her own question. "You mean about wanting to steer clear of us?"

"I was really put out with him at the time," Cedarleg admitted.

"I told you that wasn't him," Ma said. "He'd never been like that, it must have been his wife's doings or he'd have never talked that way. I know that young man and he's better than that."

"Better than what?" Cessy asked.

"Oh, Tom was thinking himself too good to bring his new town gal around to meet Ma," Cedarleg explained.

Cessy's eyes widened and she took immediate offense on Ma's behalf.

"Well, then we are definitely not holding things up a moment longer waiting on such a fellow," Cessy declared. "Daddy, get everyone's attention."

King Calhoun nodded to her in agreement. He turned and raised his hands, causing the boisterous, milling crowd to still and quiet.

"My dear friends," he greeted them. "And I call you my friends because after all that we've been through together, that is what we are."

Applause erupted though the crowd.

Cessy couldn't help but smile. These people worked hard under dangerous conditions and in places where they were neither welcomed nor appreciated. They often complained about the lack of amenities, the rootless life, and the hardships endured by their families. But King Calhoun, oil millionaire, seemed willing to share those hardships with them and they loved him for it.

Cessy loved him, too. Her father was a fair and honorable man and he always made her so proud.

"The day I saw this crusty little knoll up here," he announced to the crowd, "I said to old Marv Hotch-

kiss, the geologist, I said there's oil under that
ground, Marv, I can smell it from here."

He cocked his head slightly and gave a slight rise of
his right eyebrow. "I know a lot of you wondered
why God would give a man a nose this big, well that's
why."

There were hoots of appreciation for the fine joke.

"Well, you all know Marv," King continued. "We
been friends for a lot of years. But he don't trust my
hunches no better than he trusts me at poker."

Several of the men offered their opinions on the
same subject.

"Marv, he don't believe nothing that he can't prove
by science," King said.

Nods and murmurs of agreement swept through
the crowd.

"So when he made his sampling and said this hill
was one of them salt domes like Spindletop"—her
father shook his head—"I told him, well if it's good
enough for Patillo Higgins, it'll suit King Calhoun just
fine."

The shouts and cheers that greeted his words were
nearly deafening.

Cessy clapped right along with them, happy,
proud, excited.

From the corner of her eye, she caught sight of
someone. For an instant she thought that it was
Gerald and her heart lightened. She wanted him
here. She wanted him with her now and always.

But of course, she was mistaken. Gerald hadn't
come to the well and certainly if he had, he wouldn't
be out in the crowd but standing at her side where he
belonged.

EIGHTEEN

He hadn't been able to stay away. And he was not sorry. The excitement and the sense of belonging and accomplishment that Tom felt that morning out at the "P" was something that he would never forget. Tom Walker had a part in that. It was Tom Walker who'd helped to make that happen. It was a sense of his own value that he couldn't quite adjust to. He couldn't quite accept it.

Which was one of the reasons he found himself alone the following afternoon on the river road that led to the Methodist Indian Home.

It wasn't the only reason, of course. The house was overrun with people. Two more wells had come in. He heard Calhoun estimate that he'd be pumping 25,000 barrels a day by the end of the week.

The pace and talk were frantic. Apparently a refinery needed to be built right away. Tom was puzzled as to why they hadn't built it already. The plans were drawn and the workmen ready, but something seemed to be holding them up. The only person truly in motion was Calhoun himself, who spent long days running up and down the roads and scattering telegrams across the globe like they were so much confetti.

Deliberately, Tom kept to his room, frequently

claiming a headache complaint that obviously worried Cessy. Twice he had caught sight of Cedarleg. And he actually heard Ma talking to Cessy from one of the parlors.

He was going to be found out, and soon. And he didn't have the first idea of how he was going to handle it. And that was part, if not all, of the reason that Tom Walker returned that afternoon to the place he grew up.

No one was around as he passed through the entry gate. The place was completely deserted. It was eerie seeing the place deserted. He had always imagined it as it was the other day, brimming with young boys and hectic with activity.

He followed his nose to the kitchen and found the cooking woman and her two children. She was surprised to see him, but very friendly, having remembered him from the wedding.

She offered the explanation for the inordinate quiet of the place. The boys were making hay up in the north meadow. Tom remembered well the hot, hard work. There were tasks for even the youngest boy. But with each year the labor and responsibility increased. He had never appreciated the lessons that he'd learned there.

Given a free run of the place, Tom wandered about, refamiliarizing himself with the things, big and little, from his childhood. He walked through the small, sparsely furnished dormitory where he had slept six thousand nights. And on many of those he'd dreamed of his future.

His bunk and wardrobe were kept very much as they had been when he lived here, only neater than he had kept them himself. He wondered briefly about the young boy who dreamed from his bed these days. Was he anything like Tom had been? Was he as anxious to grow up and get away? Probably not.

He made his way into the little building that sheltered Reverend McAfee's schoolroom. It looked smaller than he remembered. But the smell, a mixture of library paste and chalk, was exactly the same. The desks were lined up, as ever, in crisp precision. The smaller ones in front, the largest at the back of the room.

With a smile Tom recalled how grown-up he'd thought himself to be when he was finally ensconced in the last row. He had thought himself far too adult to still be in a schoolroom.

Tom perused the brightly colored globe that sat in a stand next to the teacher's desk. With a bit of looking he found Cuba on it. He'd never heard of the place before he went there to fight. It was not nearly as big as he'd expected it to be. But then lately nothing that he thought seemed to be entirely correct.

"Ah, Mr. Crane, what a surprise."

Tom turned, startled and even a little guilty, at the sound of Reverend McAfee's voice.

"I was just looking around," Tom told him and then wished he could take the words back. Tom was obviously too successful a man to steal anything and it was only the guilty little boy inside him that would make him believe that the teacher would think he would do so.

Reverend McAfee nodded. "So what do you think of our school, Mr. Crane?" he asked.

"Why are you calling me that?"

The reverend raised an eyebrow. "That *is* the name that you are going by these days."

"But that *isn't* the name that you put on our wedding certificate," he pointed out.

The old man nodded. "The marriage license is a legal document. It requires the use of legal names. Have you legally changed your name?"

"No."

"Then your legal name must be used in order for it

to be a legal marriage." he said brusquely. "I do not believe for one moment that your intention was to deceive that wonderful young woman into believing that she was being married when she was not."

"I meant for the wedding to be legal," Tom said.

"Well, it is."

The two men stood staring at each other silently for several moments before Reverend McAfee moved over to his chair. With a puff of pure exhaustion he seated himself and Tom wondered briefly exactly what age the old gray beard actually was.

"How have you been?" he asked finally.

"Tolerable, son, thank you. I have been quite tolerable."

"Good," Tom said.

"And *where* have you been?" Reverend McAfee turned the question around. "After all this time, where have you been?"

Tom stood looking out the window as he answered. "Everywhere, nowhere."

"Everywhere and nowhere," Reverend McAfee repeated and then made a tutting sound of disapproval. "You have always answered the most civil questions in such an annoying way. What exactly do you mean, 'everywhere, nowhere'?"

Tom turned to look at the man, a little surprised. He had not really thought that the reverend honestly wanted his itinerary for the last eight years.

"Everywhere means that I have traveled a good deal," Tom answered. "And nowhere means that none of those places is . . . is my home."

The old man's brow furrowed as he studied him more closely. Tom turned back to face the window, unwilling to put himself under the reverend's scrutiny.

"I joined the Rough Riders," Tom continued. "I went to Cuba."

"Ah . . ." Reverend McAfee made the sound as

meaningful as a long-winded oratory. "And how was that?" he asked.

Tom shrugged. "It was a lot of noise and sweat and blood. I killed men there," he said, then he turned to face the reverend once more. "But I saved a man's life, too. An important man. A man whose family would have missed him dearly. I put myself in front of his body. I deliberately took a bullet for him."

"You say it almost angrily, as if you regret it."

"I don't. I don't regret it. Do you remember how you used to say that each man's life had a purpose and that we may never know what our purpose is for being alive."

The old man was thoughtful. "No, I don't recall saying that, but I think that it's probably true."

"I think, Reverend McAfee, that my only purpose for being born was to take the bullet meant for Ambrose Dexter."

"Why would you think that?"

"You should see his house, Reverend," Tom said. "If you put every building on these grounds together, including the barn, his house is bigger. And it's in the middle of Bedlington. His family has been there since New Jersey was a colony. He is his father's only son, the last man of his line. He has four sisters who worship him and two dozen cousins who think him funny and dear. His grandmama dotes upon him, his father counts upon him, and he is the apple of his mother's eye."

"A very fortunate young man," Reverend McAfee said.

Tom nodded. "If he had been killed in Cuba, there would have been wailing and moaning and grief in that house," he said. "Oh, how they would have missed Ambrose Dexter."

Once more Tom turned to face his teacher. "If Tom Walker had died in Cuba, and he should have, no one would have cared. Why should they? No one ever cared that Tom Walker lived."

"Is that what you think?" the old man asked. "That your existence is important to no one."

"That's exactly what I think. Who am I important to?"

"Well, correct me if I'm wrong, but I got the impression that you are pretty important to that young woman that you just married."

"Cessy?"

"Is that what you call her?" the reverend smiled. "I rather like it. Much preferable over Miss Princess. Princess sounds more like the name of dog than a young lady."

Tom shook his head and chuckled humorlessly. "I thought the very same thing when I first heard her name."

The old man nodded. "You may not share my blood, young man, but I've made my mark on you all the same."

Tom gave him a rueful glance. But his thoughts remained heavy.

"If I could just know," he said. "If I could just know who they were and why . . . why I was of so little value to them that they could give me away and never look back."

"I'm sure they thought they were doing what was best," Reverend McAfee said.

"Why are you sure of that?" Tom asked, his tone almost angry. "What kind of evidence do we have to even suggest that? Don't you know that I spent years waiting for them to come get me, and then more years thinking up excuses for why they couldn't?"

"Yes, of course I know that you've done that," he said. "All of the boys here do that. Even the ones who know their parents to be dead will lie awake at night imagining that it was all a mistake, and that dear

mother and father will be coming to retrieve them the
very next day."

"You can't tell me anything about her?" Tom asked.

"Nothing that I haven't already said," he answered. "She was a young white girl, not yet twenty
I'd guess. She'd brought you in a fine cambric cloak.
Much nicer than anything she wore herself, so perhaps she was only the nursemaid or the hired girl.
She undressed you and took the cloak with her when
she left."

"She didn't even tell you my name," Tom said.

The reverend shook his head. "I asked her what
you were called and she said she only called you 'the
baby'."

Tom sighed.

There was a long silence between them, both men
alone with their thoughts.

"I named you Thomas because that was my father's
name. He was a fine man, as generous and kind as
any that I ever knew. If I'd had a son of my own, I
would have given him that name. I called you Thursday, because that's the day you came into my life.
And Walker, well that was for Francis Amasa
Walker."

"Who?"

"Francis Amasa Walker," Reverend McAfee answered with a slow smile. "He was an economist. Ask
your wife about him."

Tom mentally vowed to do just that.

"Thomas Thursday Walker," Reverend McAfee
said aloud. "Perhaps you never cared for the name,
but I thought it the finest I could come up with."

"I never said I didn't like it," Tom told him.

The old man chuckled. "You never had to say it,
the fact that you wouldn't use it spoke volumes." He
shook his head reveling in his recollections. "I didn't
mind so much when you called yourself Geronimo or
Abraham Lincoln, although it worried me quite a bit

when shortly thereafter you decided you preferred being John Wilkes Booth. But I thought that it was something that you would eventually outgrow. Apparently, Mr. Crane, I was quite mistaken."

"It was a game," Tom said quietly. "It began as just a game."

"Did Miss Calhoun realize that it was a game?"

"No, I didn't mean it was a game with her," Tom said. "Being Gerald was a game. It was just something I did to make the fellows laugh. The ladies always loved Gerald. He had so much more to offer them than Tom did."

"So when you decided to offer for Princess, uh . . . Cessy, as you say, you thought to present yourself at your best. And you thought your best was Gerald."

"Yes," Tom said, nodding slowly. "That *is* what I thought. But you know, I believe now that she would have loved me as Tom."

"Why do you think so?"

"Because the things that she loves about me . . . well, they are not Gerald's things. She isn't interested in Gerald's fancy heritage. In fact, it sort of worries her. And she's not impressed with his aristocratic ideals, she spends a good deal of time trying to talk him out of them. And if she is even vaguely interested in his money or social position, well, she has yet to ask questions about either."

"I don't find any of this particularly surprising," Reverend McAfee said. "She is not at all the sort of young woman that would marry for any reason other than love."

"Yes," Tom agreed. "She would only marry for love. And I really do believe that she would have loved Tom as easily as she loved Gerald."

"Probably so," the reverend told him.

"But can she now?" Tom asked. "Can she love Tom now, after discovering that she has been seduced by lies and married in deceit. Can she love Tom after

learning that? After learning that he sought her out
and willfully pursued her because he fell in love with
her money?"

The reverend shook his head and sighed sadly.

"She is a fair and forgiving woman. But you are in
great need of much forgiveness. I don't know that any
woman could have enough."

He looked exhausted. Worse than that, he looked
beaten. Queenie couldn't remember a time when
she'd seen him look worse. She refused to let it affect
her even slightly.

All around the room there were trunks and crates
and stacks of household goods. Queenie was dili-
gently sorting and packing.

She was a hardbitten, determined woman who'd
made her way in the world against all kinds of odds.
She'd had no choice. In business she'd never failed to
go after what she wanted. To push when other
women would have been content to settle, and to
carve out her own security in the best way she knew
how. That was how she operated in business. It was
only in her personal life that she'd held back, waited,
and done without. That was at an end.

Comfortable, convenient Queenie was about to
make demands.

"Well, it's all over, Queenie," King said sadly. "I
did all I could do and it was for nothing. It's all over."

"What's all over?"

"The well. Royal Oil. *King* Calhoun," he shook his
head. "I'm busted Queenie. Flat busted."

She shrugged almost with complete unconcern.

"Isn't that what you've always told me about the
oil business. Boom and bust, boom and bust. When
things are going well, plan for the worst, and when
life looks its blackest, there is a fortune to be made
on the next hill."

"That's mostly true, but for the life of me, I never saw a oil man go under while pumping 25,000 barrels a day," he said. "I swear, Queenie, I want it etched on my tombstone, IT WAS BANKS THAT DONE HIM IN."

"So you still haven't found anyone to back you?"

"No," he said. "And I've propositioned every bank from here to blazes. I offered a fifty-percent share at the last one. They couldn't even be bothered to hear me out."

"What about Tom Walker?"

"Tom Walker? I don't know a dang thing about any Tom Walker," he said. "I've asked in every bank and barbershop and even every church in Burford Corners. Nobody ever heard of Tom Walker, nor this Prin family that he's supposed to be married into. None of it even exists."

Queenie was thoughtful. "Well, Tom Walker exists because I talked to him day before yesterday."

King looked up startled. "You talked to him! What did he say? Would he be willing to loan me the money?"

"Well, truth to tell King, I didn't ask him for money," Queenie explained. "We had other things to talk about. I just told him that you were looking for him."

"Was he going to find me then?" King asked. "Why the devil hasn't he?"

"I don't know," she answered. "Honestly, he didn't seem to be particularly interested, but I mentioned you just the same."

"Dang it all, Queenie, why didn't you buttonhole the fellow?" King complained. "You know how important this is to me."

"Well, I have a few things on my mind, too, thank you very much!"

Her tone was such that it startled King out of his

lethargy and he looked up at her, wide-eyed with question. He appeared to notice the trunks and crates for the first time.

"You going somewhere, Queenie?" he asked.

"Why, yes, I am," she told him.

He was silent for a long moment. "Are you going up to Denver to see that doctor I told you about?"

"No indeed," she answered. "I don't need a doctor. I saw one this morning and my health is perfectly fine."

King blanched. "You mean you've already . . ."

"No," she answered. "I mean that I am in fine health for a woman bearing a child at my age. He says that everything appears to be all right at this juncture. And if nothing untoward occurs, I should be giving birth in the latter part of February."

She watched his face light up with pleasure and she knew that she was not wrong about him. He came to his feet and pulled her into his arms and kissed her.

"Queenie, I'm so glad about this," he said. "Truly, I think you will be a wonderful mother. And the Palace is not a bad place to grow up, he'll—"

"My child," Queenie stated flatly as she jerked out of King's embrace, "will not be raised in a saloon."

The adamant nature of her tone obviously took him off guard.

"You're not raising him here?" King asked.

"My child will grow up in a sweet little house with a big yard and a picket fence," she said. "He'll walk to school every day in clean broadcloth kneepants and a Saratoga cap from a nice neighborhood with all his young friends. He'll have a pony cart and a puppy. He'll play baseball and ride a bicycle."

Inexplicably she burst into tears.

"Darling, oh darling," he said, sitting her down upon the bed and taking his place beside her. "What is this all about? Why are you so unhappy?"

"I'm not unhappy," she sobbed. "I've never been happier in my life." Unfortunately, she punctuated this declaration with renewed tears.

"Don't cry," he pleaded. "Please don't cry."

"The doctor said that the crying is like the nausea," she told him, hiccuping. "It's just a symptom of being in the family way and it will pass."

"Well, I certainly hope so."

They sat together on the bed. He kept his arm around her, comforting her as she pulled herself together and regained her self-control.

"I am very happy about the baby, actually," she said. "I don't mean to cry about it. I think it may well be the best thing that has ever happened to me."

"And I am happy about the baby too, darling," King assured her. "I am, too."

"I've sold the Palace," she said.

"Sold it? To whom?"

"Tommy Mathis," Queenie answered.

"Tommy Mathis? That painter? Where did he get the money to buy this place?" King asked.

"He's hasn't got it, but I've sold it to him just the same," she said. "Frenchie's going to run the place, but Mathis is going to count the money. He's going to pay me over ten years from a percent of the profits."

"That's crazy, Queenie," he said.

"Not as crazy as trying to simultaneously be a mother and the proprietor of a saloon," she said.

"Where are you going to live?" he asked her.

"In that house with the white picket fence," she said.

"And where is it?"

"Wherever you build it, King."

"Wherever *I* build it? You want me to build you a house?" King was clearly surprised. Queenie never asked him for anything.

"I want you to build *us* a house, King," she said. "All of us, you, me and the baby."

"What are you talking about?"

"I want us to get married," Queenie told him. "No wait, let me say that over again. Because I've always *wanted* us to get married. Now I'm *demanding* that we do."

He looked at her for a long moment and then grinning without much humor he began shaking his head.

"Whoa now, let's slow this old horse down a bit," he said. "What's all this talk about marriage? Is this another one of those symptoms you get from eating for two?"

"Maybe it is," Queenie said. "Maybe that's exactly what it is. But I'm determined to put my old life behind me and start over for the sake of this little child. And that means a husband and a home. I'll start with the husband first and worry about the home thereafter."

"Queenie, darling, you can't be serious about this," he said.

"I have never been more serious in all my life," she said with such solemnity it was sobering. "This is what I intend to happen and I won't settle for anything less."

King's expression had changed from being sympathetic to being annoyed.

"Queenie, now this is silly," he said. "I don't think it's even something to joke about."

"That's good, because I am not joking. I intend for you to marry me, King Calhoun, and I intend for it to happen soon."

"Queenie, darling," he cajoled. "Let's not talk about this right now. You're all het up and my life is falling around me like a house of cards. I couldn't possibly think of anything as serious as marriage in the middle of my business going bust."

"Poor men get married every day," Queenie said.

"And since I know you are going broke, it should give you some reassurance to know that I won't be marrying you for your money."

King swallowed hard and was struggling for the right words to say.

"Marriage is a very momentous step, not done lightly," he told her. "It's the type of decision best entered into after long and thoughtful consideration. It is irrevocable, Queenie. You and me, we wouldn't want to make a mistake."

"A mistake? King, the mistake has already been made," she told him, shaking her head with disbelief. "The mistake is my getting pregnant with no husband."

"Now, we've talked about that, darling," he said. "I don't see how it follows that we should make matters worse by marrying up."

"You are the father of this child, that's the simple fact," she said. "I fail to see how that truth makes anything better or worse, and I don't believe that there is anything much further that needs to be considered."

"You know perfectly well that I am not a marrying kind of man," King said. "I'm undependable and I'm unfaithful."

"That was with your first wife," Queenie said. "We have been quite exclusive for some years, I see no evidence that that is about to change."

"But it would change, I'm sure of it," King said. "The minute I'd promise to keep myself only unto you, I'd be itching for the next pair of pretty ankles that came along."

"Then I would just have to keep a very close eye on you. If a wife can't trust her husband out of her sight," Queenie said with confidence, "then the wife doesn't let him out of her sight."

King was clearly flabbergasted at her words.

"I just can't remarry. I simply can't do it, nor do I think I should. It was not something that I was ever good at."

"Then I suppose that you will just have to change," she said.

"I don't want to change," he insisted.

"What you or I want is no longer important," she told him. "All that matters is what is best for the baby."

King Calhoun was beginning to lose his temper.

"Queenie McCurtain, I never, by any word or deed, ever suggested to you that I would marry you."

"I'm not saying that you did, in truth I am very sure that you did not, but this is our child we are considering now and that changes everything."

"It doesn't change everything for me," King bellowed. "Queenie, you know I would never want to hurt your feelings, but the truth is, a man like me doesn't marry a woman like you."

She raised her chin bravely, refusing to take offense. "You mean a man like you, who has clawed his way to the top of the heap by hard work and sheer determination, does not marry a woman who has done the same?" Queenie asked. "Perhaps that is why your first marriage was such a failure, King. You picked someone that you *should* marry over someone truly suited to you."

"You know that is not at all what I meant," he said. "A man just does not marry his . . . his . . ."

"Are you having trouble finding a word for it?" Queenie asked. "Maybe because you are looking in the wrong direction. You are thinking *whore* or maybe *mistress*, but neither of those words are right. Both suggest that money has changed hands. That never happened. I did it with you for love from the very start. Where you were concerned I was as bad a businesswoman as Frenchie."

King ran his hands over his face. And shook his head with regret.

"I never asked you to fall in love with me," he said.

"We often don't ask for the things that can really change our lives," she said. "I do love you and I'm glad I do. And nothing you can say will convince me that you don't love me as well."

"Queenie, I don't want to hear anymore about this," King said, firmly rising to his feet. "It doesn't matter who loves who or even what you think might be best for whom. I am not under any circumstances going to marry you. It is ridiculous of you even to suggest it."

She looked up at him, willing him to change his mind. Willing him to reconsider.

"I really hope that you don't mean that," she said. "Because if you do, then that is your loss, King. That is your loss of both of us."

"What do you mean by that?"

"I fully intend to get away from this life and to get my child away from it," she said. "If you do not marry me, if I can't be your wife, then I must pretend to be your widow."

"My widow?" King laughed without humor. "What do you plan, Queenie? To murder me?"

"In my heart you will be dead," she said. "I will raise this baby alone and I will tell him that his father is long dead. You will never see your child, you will never know him."

Queenie's words were soft and thoughtful.

"I'll be disappointed for him, because I already know you to be a fine father," she told King. "But that's the way it has to be. If you won't marry me, then that's the way it has to be. He will survive it, of that I'm sure."

She looked King straight in the eye and spoke brutally.

"I'm not so certain that you will. Good-bye, King."

"What do you mean, good-bye?"

"I mean, get out of this room and don't ever come back here again," she said. "There was a time that I needed a friend and a lover. You were those things to me then, and I thank you. Now I only need a husband and a father. If you are unwilling to be that, then there is nothing more to be said. Good-bye."

"Queenie, you're being stubborn and unreasonable."

"I am being a mother. I will protect my child. I will protect him even from you if I have to. King Calhoun, either get marriage on your mind or get out."

"I'll get out! I'll get out all right," he said jerking the door open. It went all the way back on the hinges and slammed noisily against the wall.

"I'll get out of this room and out of this place," he yelled angrily. "There are twenty women on this street alone younger and better looking than you, *Miss* Queenie. And there ain't a one of them who wouldn't drop her drawers in the street for King Calhoun."

"I don't doubt it," she agreed quietly. "But there isn't one of them that carries your baby, either."

NINETEEN

They were lying together in the bed, warm and sated. She loved being in Gerald's arms. The lovemaking was wonderful, but equally as good was the time spent just lying with their bodies next to each other, their limbs entwined.

There were simply not enough hours in the night, she decided. In the daylight they were now so often separated. And she missed him, she realized. He'd spent the previous day lying in the darkened bedroom with a sick headache. Today he had mysteriously disappeared after lunch. At least he hadn't left without word. Thankfully no repetitions of that first awful day when she had almost doubted him. He'd told Howard that he was taking a walk. Considering how long he was gone, she thought, he might well have walked to Tulsa and back.

She missed having him at her side. But it was not Gerald's fault of course. Her father's business concerns had wormed their way into her own life and now no one talked of anything but the refinery. It was imperative that her father find financing for it in a hurry. And each day that went by, it seemed less and less likely that it would happen.

She wished she could talk it out with her husband. She wanted to hear Gerald's views. And in truth, she wanted to have him express his thoughts to her father and Cedarleg and everyone else. Perhaps she was partial, but she believed he might have ideas or insights that the rest of them didn't have. More than that, Cessy believed that he might well have contacts that they did not. Certainly in the exalted circles of society frequented by the Cranes of Bedlington, there were bankers that might be amenable to refinery construction on a proven well.

Cessy mentally chided herself. It was very selfish to want to use her husband's connections to help further her father's business. It made her seem no better than Maloof, marrying to get a store.

But the difference was, she reminded herself, she loved Gerald. That was primary and anything else was merely another consideration. Of course, Muna seemed to believe that Maloof was in love with her, also. Would Gerald worry that she had other considerations when choosing to marry him?

It seemed that it was not going to matter. Gerald was clearly uninterested in the oil business in general or the problems of Royal Oil in particular. Every time someone from the field showed up at the house, he found some excuse to be elsewhere. It was annoying, but what could she do? The oil business might be the livelihood of her father and her friends, but it obviously meant nothing to Gerald.

He moved languidly beside her and gently kissed the wild mass of her unbound hair that lay on her pillow.

"You'll make a rat's nest of it," she stated without much complaint.

"Then I shall brush it free of tangles," he said. "Would you like that, Cessy? I could light the lamp and you could sit naked in front of the mirror while I tend your hair."

Cessy giggled. "Where do you get these ideas?"

He leaned closer to whisper in her ear. "The mind is the most potent sexual organ."

"Well the mind may be willing, sir," she said. "But the flesh seems a little weak."

"Ah, well, with a bit of attention to your wifely duty, my *weakness* will surely be *overcome* and my resolve will certainly *harden.*"

"Oh, how you Yankees do talk!"

They laughed together as he continued to tease her.

"Just hold me for now," she told him. "I'm far too tired to want anything more."

"Holding is nice," he agreed.

She fitted herself in the crook of his arms, laying her cheek against his collarbone. She ran her hand along the sparse hair of his chest and the wickedly ugly wound at his pelvis.

"Hold me and talk," she said. "I miss your voice almost as much as I miss your arms. Do you think we could just barricade the door and live in this bed for a hundred years?"

"We might get hungry," he said.

"Maybe we could build a dumbwaiter to the kitchen and Mrs. Marin could send up victuals to keep up our strength."

"That sounds wonderful, Cessy," he said. "Truly it does. If we could just be here without all the world and the past and . . . and everything out there."

She sensed a strange, sad longing in him and she brought her hand up to the curve of his jaw, lovingly caressing him.

"Cessy," he asked her quietly. "Have you ever heard of Francis A. Walker?"

"Well, of course I have. What a question."

"Who was he?"

"Don't tell me that you didn't learn that at Yale, either," she teased. "I am becoming more and more determined that our children never go there."

"Who was he?" Gerald asked.

"Well, he was an economist and statistician mostly," she said. "He developed our modern census. But his work that has naturally been most interesting to me were his theories and methods in education."

"Education?"

"Yes, he was the president of Massachusetts Institute of Technology. He believed that in training young men in trades and technology, and broadening that with a grounding in history and political science, he could prepare them for the challenges of the modern world."

Gerald nodded thoughtfully.

"His philosophy and his methods had a strong basis in class reform as well," she said. "He believed, as I do, that determined, motivated students could better society by bettering themselves."

"He wanted them to have a chance at something besides being sharecroppers or livery hands," Gerald said.

"Exactly. Why do you ask about Walker?"

"I . . . I was named for him."

Cessy looked up at him, momentarily puzzled, and then laughed out loud.

"Gerald Tarkington Crane was named for Francis Amasa Walker?"

She was still giggling when he sat up in bed. She couldn't see his face in the darkness but her laughter faded at the stillness that suddenly pervaded the room.

"Gerald?" she asked.

A tremendous eruption like distant thunder shook the house and stunned them both.

For a moment, both of them chose to ignore it. They continued to look across the bed at each other. Then a flurry of confusion and hollering commenced downstairs.

The commotion could no longer be ignored. Cessy

had just grabbed her wrapper from the end of the bed when her father began pounding upon her door.

"Princess!" King Calhoun called from the hallway. "There's a fire at the tanks."

"Oh, my God!" she exclaimed.

She rushed to the doorway, covering herself as she ran. Her father was gone from the door by the time she got there. But she called out to the deserted hallway.

"I'll be ready in five minutes!"

Cessy began grabbing up clothing and dressing with careless efficiency.

"What the devil are you doing?" her husband asked.

"I'm getting dressed," she said. "And you'd better do the same if you don't want to have to walk out to the wells. As soon as Daddy is dressed himself he won't wait another minute."

"I am not going anywhere," he stated firmly. "And neither is my wife."

"There's a fire in the oil tanks," Cessy answered him, genuinely surprised at his strange behavior.

"I don't see how that concerns us," Gerald said. "Your father has crews of men in his employ. Neither you nor I have been hired to work for him."

"Gerald, if there's a fire, then there may well be injuries," she said. "I'll need to be there to help."

"You can't go out there, Cessy!" her husband exclaimed. "As your husband, I expressly forbid it."

"You *forbid* it?"

"I do indeed," Gerald said. "Oil fires are dangerous."

Cessy looked at him for a long moment in total disbelief. He didn't understand. He didn't understand at all. Did he truly believe that she could lie here, even sleep the night unconcerned, while her friends and neighbors, even her own father, risked their livelihoods and even their very lives out on the Topknot? Perhaps he could do that, but she could not.

"Yes, indeed, oil fires are very dangerous," she agreed with him. "So perhaps you should stay here, Mr. Crane. I'm sure no one would wish you to risk your life. But my friends and my family are there and I will be with them."

"Cessy . . ." he began once more. But she didn't wait to hear more. She was decently covered and had her shoes in hand. Mrs. Marin could do the buttons up the back of her dress.

She hurried down to the porte cochere.

Neither Howard nor the housekeeper were yet quite ready, so it was Cessy herself who loaded the car with the basket of emergency supplies that was always kept ready. Accidents in the oil fields were as common as snakes. And although physicians were always sent for immediately, medicines and bandages were rightly provided by the company.

She heard her father's boisterous voice, and then everyone was climbing into the crowded Packard. It was already chugging to life. She was offered a hand up into the front seat. She assumed the hand to be her father's until she saw him seated behind the wheel.

She glanced back to see that it was her husband Gerald who aided her. And it was Gerald who took the seat beside her.

"You're going to help us," she said quietly to him.

"I'm going to protect my wife," he answered.

It wasn't exactly what she wanted to hear, but it was close enough, Cessy decided.

The Packard shot off in a burst of dust, swung a turn in the yard and was out on the road almost before she had time to catch her breath. Beside her Gerald was solid and warm and reassuring. She was so grateful that he was there. She was so grateful that he was willing to share her world.

The whole town of Burford Corners was waking up as they whizzed by. News of the fire was spreading quickly. And, Cessy was sure, those opposed to the drilling and distrustful of oilpatch folks were already nodding self-righteously and saying, "I told you so."

Cessy couldn't be bothered by their bad opinion. There was no way on earth to suit everyone or to do things perfectly. People simply had to do the best they could with what they had and let heaven take care of the rest.

As the Packard found the ruts on the wild ride down the river road, Cessy closed her eyes and fervently prayed that tonight, as oil was burning, she would do what she could and heaven would indeed take care of the rest.

The ferry crossing was as far as they could go. The heat and fumes from the fire made the whole Top-knot hill area too dangerous for anyone not absolutely necessary to fight the fire.

The injured were laid out on the soft sands of the riverbank, with Ma to watch over them.

She was out of the automobile in an instant. Calling to Gerald to follow her and bring the medicines. Hugging Ma briefly, she was grateful that the old woman was already there.

"We're going to have to evacuate the camp," Ma told her. "Leave the medicines with me. And get over there as fast as you can. The smoke is blowing straight into the camp. With their menfolks all in danger and their children underfoot, the women will be running around like chickens with their heads cut off."

"You think I can help?"

"There ain't a soul in the world who can do a better job of getting folks organized and in the right direction. It's the kind of thing God created you for, Princess. If some people weren't by nature meant to take charge, the human race would still be sitting around cold caves wishing they knew how to build a cookfire."

"Can you take care of the injured by yourself?" Cessy asked her.

"Ain't much here," she assured her. "Lots of singeings and skin peels, but nobody's near to dying, I don't think. You take Mrs. Marin with you and leave Howard with me. I've sent for wagons to carry them to the doctor in town. He can help me load them."

"Just these few injured? Thank God it was not worse," Cessy said. "And no one was killed."

"Not yet, but there is a lot to be done before this night is over."

Ma glanced past Cessy then and her face alighted with obvious pleasure.

"Well, praise the Lord!" Ma said. "I'm so glad you're here. Get across the river and lend a hand. Bob and Clifford are both among the burned. Cedarleg will be needing every hand he can get."

Cessy turned to see who Ma was talking to and was surprised to see her words directed to Gerald.

Ma wanted to send *Gerald* to help Cedarleg? It was ridiculous, and Cessy fully expected that Gerald would tell her so himself. Her husband had made it clear that he was not interested in her father's oil business and he would not have even come along tonight had he not been concerned for her safety.

No, he would not be going to help the other men. Cessy knew that. She just hoped that his refusal to accept Ma's direction would not be condescending.

"I'd better hurry or I'll miss the ferry," he said.

Cessy was so stunned at his words, she didn't even speak. He was hurrying away without even giving her a chance to say good-bye.

"He's a fine young man, that one," Ma said.

"Yes," Cessy agreed proudly. "Yes he is." She turned to call out to the housekeeper.

"Mrs. Marin, come with me," she said. "We've got to evacuate the oil camp."

Tom had never seen or imagined anything like it. Thick black smoke rose in the air higher than the eye could see. And the bright orange flames leapt up from the surface of the open tanks thirty feet high.

Calhoun halted the Packard on the far side of the river. Those injured, at least a dozen men, had already been ferried across. Tom spotted Ma kneeling among the victims. Cessy apparently saw her at the same moment and hurried out.

"Bring the basket!" she hollered back to Tom.

Tom turned to relay the order to Howard, but the fellow was already gone. There was no choice but to carry it himself.

Keeping his head down, Tom followed in Cessy's wake. With any luck at all, he hoped that the two women would be so busy that Ma wouldn't even glance in his direction.

Even this far away, nearly a half mile, the black smoke swirled and scented the air, burning his throat. The men on the ground were blackened with it, only their eyes clearly visible in the darkness.

"Tom," a voice called out hoarsely. Hurriedly he knelt next to Bob Earlie.

"How you doing?" he asked.

"I ain't bad," Bob assured him. "Just burnt enough to hurt like hell."

"Can I get you anything?" Tom asked him.

The man attempted to smile and offered a joke. "How about a feather bed and a half-dozen whores?" he suggested.

Tom grinned at him. "Thought you were a family man," he said.

"Oh, yeah, it slipped my mind," he said. "With my luck I'll get what I'm asking for and spend the whole dang time saying, 'Ouchee! Gals, please don't touch me!' Then the wife will find me in the morning and make me wish I'd died during the night."

Tom left him grinning and made his way on through the injured. Many of them he knew by name and they knew him, too. They knew him as Tom.

He stood just behind Cessy and Ma as they divided up the night's work. He tried to keep his eyes elsewhere and his face averted. But when he heard Cessy ask if anyone had been killed, he forgot himself for one instant and looked up toward Ma to hear the answer.

"Not yet," she said. "But there's a lot to be done before this night is over."

It was at that moment that Ma glanced past Cessy and looked Tom straight in the eye.

He froze, expecting shock and anger. Fully expecting within the confusion of the moment to have his scheme unmasked and the truth revealed. He expected Ma's face to register anger and shame and disappointment. What he saw on her face, however, was relief.

"Well, praise the Lord!" she said to him. "I'm so glad to see you're here. Get across the river and lend a hand. Bob and Clifford are both among the burned. Cedarleg will be needing every hand he can get."

Tom hesitated. Not knowing what to do. Not knowing what to say. Cessy turned to him. She seemed surprised to see where Ma's remarks were directed, but Tom was certain that it was not a good time to explain.

"I'll have to run to make the ferry," he told her.

And then he did just that, as if the demons of hell were on his heels.

The ferry had, in fact, already taken off, and he had to leap to make it aboard. He stumbled on the landing and fell on his knees upon the boards at the feet of his father-in-law.

"What are you doing here?" Calhoun asked him.

"I've come to help."

King Calhoun snorted. "Oh that's just what we need, snoopers and gawkers."

Calhoun walked away as Tom came to his feet. As they neared the shore, the heat from the burning sump intensified. Tom could see in the distance the "P" still standing. The fire was contained within the inground oil tanks. The only immediate danger surrounding the land and inhabitants was from fumes and smoke. Still, a fortune was burning and without intervention the other tanks would likely catch fire also.

The ferry had only bumped up to the shore when the men aboard disembarked. In the wake of King Calhoun, Tom scrambled by the steep path now heavy with the scent of smoke.

Calhoun stopped and turned to glare at him.

"Get back to the boat," he ordered.

"Aren't you going to need every hand?" he asked.

"Every experienced hand," Calhoun corrected him. "A useless blueblood like you will only get himself killed."

"Maybe you wouldn't mind seeing that happen?" Tom suggested.

Calhoun raised an eyebrow. "No, my Princess seems to have feeling for you, though God only knows why. I wouldn't hurt her for anything in this world. Get on back to the ferry. They'll be plenty of help to be given among the weary and wounded. You can tote and carry for the womenfolk, you won't have to risk yourself by fighting the fire."

"Mr. Calhoun," Tom told him. "I heard that you need every hand. I think you'll be surprised at how well I acquit myself."

He might have said more, but in that moment Cedarleg apparently spotted them and called out.

King hurried to him and Tom followed right behind.

"Can we drain it to tank two or three?" King asked, even before he was truly close enough to hear the answer.

"Not a chance," Cedarleg told him. "I sent a couple of fellers around to scout it out. Fire's so bad on that side, can't even get close enough to put in a line."

"We'll have to pour it into the river then," King said. "I hate to lose it all downstream, but there's no time to dam up the river and nowhere else for it to go."

"What are you trying to do?" Tom asked.

Calhoun looked ready to berate him for the interruption. But Cedarleg looked over at him and grinned.

"Glad you two finally found each other," he said. "We need to pump the oil out from the tanks from underneath the fire."

Tom nodded. "If there's no oil the fire goes out on its own."

"That's it," Cedarleg said. "We can lay pipe in from the side to pump it out, but we've got to have someplace to go with it."

"The river isn't the best," King Calhoun said. "But it's the only choice we've got."

"Maybe not," Tom said. "There's a cut-off meander on the north side of this hill from a bad flood when I was a boy."

"We ain't got time to run pipe all the way down the hill," King said.

"Maybe we won't have to," Tom said. "It's such a steep ledge, nobody ever goes that way. We can run a length out into nothing and let the oil just pour out like a waterfall."

"How far out in the air would that pipe have to go?" Cedarleg asked.

"Ten feet at least," Tom said. "Fifteen would be

better, but a four-inch pipe would do the job. We'd lose some to evaporation, but not nearly all that we'd lose if we pour it into the river."

King Calhoun was looking at him strangely, but Tom couldn't concern himself with that now.

"Let's see this cut-off meander of yours," Cedarleg said.

The three of them hurried off to the far side of the Topknot. The area was heavily grown up in short bush and somewhat distant from the drilling site, but it was thankfully at a sloping angle all the way.

When they got to the edge, it was almost straight down.

"That's it there below," Tom pointed out.

The low place that had once been part of a bend in the river was indistinguishable from the land around it except for the verdant growth of grass and plants.

"The water table is only inches below the surface. The sides aren't much, but if we get it pouring in there, we'll still have time to reinforce them. And in complete safety for the men."

Cedarleg looked hopefully at Calhoun.

Tom looked at him, too.

Calhoun's eyes were narrowed and his assessment accusatory, but his words were what was best for the company and the men who trusted him.

"Get your crew of pipefitters to lay it down as quick as you can. With Bob injured, do you have somebody to pump the tank?"

"Tom can do it," he said.

"All right, you and *Tom* do it and I'll get the roustabouts to building some sides reinforcing the low place as best they can."

Immediately, they went into action.

Tom and Cedarleg hurried back up toward the burning sump. Tom's thoughts were whirling. His scheme was up. King Calhoun had called him Tom. It was all over in a fraction of a second. All his plans, his dreams, his foolish, high-handed aspirations. They were all gone.

But right now was not the time to think about it. There was a hot, choking oil fire that had to be managed and people were counting upon him to help manage it.

As they got closer to the fire, the intense heat, choking fumes, and thick smoke grew worse and worse. Cedarleg quickly explained the plan to the gang pusher and he gave his two best men to Tom and ordered the rest of them to start running pipe to the north side of the hill.

The two pipefitters were sturdy, muscular types chosen for their physical prowess. The type of men known in the oilfield as "forty-four jacket and size five hat." They followed Tom and Cedarleg as they began trying to locate the drainpipe to the sump tank. It was so close to the tank that it was obscured by smoke. They were to go near the edge of the fire to find it.

Tom tied the rope around his waist.

"When you find the pipe, jerk once on the rope and we'll send up the length to connect on it. If you can't hold your breath no longer, jerk it twice and we'll pull you out."

He nodded and dropped to his hands and knees. With his face as close to the ground as he could keep it, he began to inch forward on his belly into the smoke.

He could hear the strange, almost swishing sound of the burning oil. The heat of it lay upon his back like a painful weight as he moved forward. When he'd made a couple of yards he would stretch out his arms in all directions, blindly seeking the pipe. Then he moved forward once more. He moved forward and he thought about Cuba.

In his mind he could see it again. The shimmering heat upon the grass, the smoke of cannon, the smell of death and of dying. Cyril Upchurch lay in a pool of his own blood, his empty eyes staring up into nothingness, almost surprised as he was done in by a ricochet.

He killed a man and the reality of it made the bile rise in his throat until he thought he would vomit. A half hour later, he'd lost count of the men he'd sent to heaven or hell, he only wanted it to stop. He only wanted it all to stop.

He paused to reload. *Kill me, kill me!* he dared the world around him. *Kill me!* He almost said the words aloud. He almost prayed them. *Kill me!*

And then he saw Ambi, standing fighting, proving himself as he had always dreamed. And he saw the rifle aimed in Ambi's direction.

"No!" he screamed aloud.

His friend turned to look at him, shocked.

Perhaps it was his own death wish, or to protect his friend, or a simple reflex reaction under fire. Tom's gun was empty. He couldn't save the man with a shot. So he threw his body in front of that of Dexter's.

The swirling sound of fire was closer now and it scorched him almost as surely as the Spanish bullet had that day. He was too close to the tank. He was sure of that. The ground was already beginning to slope upward.

His breath was so close to the ground he was inhaling dirt. Tom stretched out his hands and off to his left he found metal. He found the drainpipe where it came out of the tank and eagerly followed it backward to its opening.

He yanked once on the rope at his waist and a second later he could feel the tug as the pipefitter clung to it while he crawled forward. He dragged the length of pipe with him and his tools at his belt. It took a good deal of time and Tom almost succumbed to the heat and the fumes.

Finally he was there. They had to get upon their

knees to attach the pipe. The air at that level was intolerable. So they did it in shifts. The pipefitter would hold his breath and work until he could not and when he fell to his face, Tom would go up to take his place. It took at least twenty miserable, uncertain minutes before they had it secured. Then they grinned at each other as they drew desperate breaths and jerked upon their lines.

Immediately they half-scrambled and were half pulled away from the fire, the heat, the smoke.

By the time they hit fresh air, both were coughing, but both were proud and hopeful. At the end of Tom's line a hand was extended to help him up. It was only after he'd accepted the assistance that he looked up into the face of King Calhoun.

"As soon as the pipe's laid and the pump's hooked up, it will be ready to go," he said.

His father-in-law nodded and the work commenced again.

Within an hour the drainpipe ran the quarter-mile distance to the north edge of Topknot hill. A motorized pump had been scavenged from Number Fourteen. There were several false starts, and problems with bad fittings and uneven sights. But just as dawn began to silver up the eastern sky, the oil began to run through the hastily constructed pipeline. Tom, Cedarleg, and Calhoun followed its progress. Out of the smoke and heat that surrounded the sump, across the drilling yard, throughout the length of Topknot and then off the side of the hill.

It came out first in fitful spurts with bursts of air and dirt exploding from it. It was a mix of oil and water, but the two would never blend. As soon as they settled into the tank, the oil would rise to the surface once more. It settled into a strong even flow. A flow that should drain the tank in a day's time perhaps.

The roustabouts working to shore up the edges of

the makeshift storage tank looked up and cheered as
the *oilfall* poured down into the site.

One musically inclined fellow burst into song:

"Showers of blessing. Showers of blessing we need.
Mercy drops 'round us are falling,
But for the showers we plead."

It was a moment for singing. Few were hurt, none
killed, and the worst, it seemed, was over. It was a
moment for thanking God and hoping for the best.
As Tom glanced at the town of Burford Corners, now
visible in the distance, the town where his wife
waited for him, he did both.

TWENTY

Cessy had evacuated the Topknot oil camp to the only place in Burford Corners where she was sure they would be accepted, her yard. The beautiful new lawn and just-beginning-to-flourish garden were now a studded tent city with families so thick upon each other that they looked like a military bivouac. It had been wild, chaotic, nerve-racking, and down-right explosive. Everyone had to be evacuated, but nobody was willing to leave anything, fearing, probably with just cause, that everything left would be scavenged away.

So every piece of everything that anybody owned had to be loaded up on carts and horses and mules and the backs of women and children.

A headquarters of sorts had been set up on the front porch. For Cessy it proved best to simply be a dictator. It was her yard, therefore what she said was law.

When one woman complained that another's son, age thirteen, should be out working the fire with the men instead of playing with the children, Cessy made the youth the official messenger boy. He was sent out to the ferryman every hour to get the news and bring it back.

Several of the women protested the presence of the

340

Topknot saloon girls. Although they obviously had to be evacuated, they could not expect to take refuge in the same yard as decent families. It was Cessy who decided that they, having no tents, could camp under the porte cochere.

It was a general source of unhappiness that some of the campsites had no acceptable places for cookfires. Cessy expressly forbade the lighting of any fires. Meals would come from the kitchen only and Mrs. Marin was encouraged to draft several women of her choice to help with preparing the meals.

By midafternoon when Ma showed up, Cessy felt dead upon her feet. The burn victims had been treated by the doctor and sent home. Since they did not now have homes, Ma had brought them all to Cessy's yard.

For the sake of keeping their wounds clean, Cessy declared that they and their families would be housed inside. All the bedrooms and parlors would be utilized for this purpose.

Ma gave her a long perusal as the two began scouring the linen closet for sufficient sheets.

"You look like Moses did *after* the Red Sea crossing," Ma told her.

"Moses must have had it easier than this," Cessy answered.

"I don't know," Ma said. "There were more of them, and the more folks you got, the more opinions you got to contend with."

"You're right about that," Cessy agreed. "I have never had my ear bent by so many people with so many complaints in all my life."

"It's always that way," she said. "I'm so sorry, honey. And poor old Moses. He was eighty years old at the time they say."

"Poor Moses? At least he didn't get the curse right in the middle of the evacuation."

Ma tried to look sympathetic, but couldn't help laughing. "Oh, I don't know, honey," she said. "Maybe that's why they called it the *Red* Sea."

The two extremely tired women started laughing and simply could not stop. They received a number of speculative looks from other women. That only made it worse.

When they finally began to get control of themselves, they talked about the fire.

"They've shot a pipe right off the side of the hill and are pouring the oil into a pit below," Cessy told her.

"Does it seem to be working?" Ma asked.

"Apparently so," she said. "As the amount of oil in the tank decreases the fire has been getting smaller. When it gets down to just the skim on the water they can let it burn itself out and throw dirt atop it."

"Thank God," Ma said. "And thank God that no one is hurt."

"And your young man it seems had no small part in that," Cessy told her.

"My young man?"

"The messenger boy said that the whole idea of going off the side of the mountain came from 'Toolie Tom,' the tool dresser who lived with Cedarleg. And that it was Toolie Tom himself who crawled to the fire to set the pipe."

"Toolie Tom?"

"That's what they are calling him," Cessy said. "Everybody here is singing his praises and remembering when they met him and spoke to him. He's a regular hero of the day."

Ma smiled proudly. "He's a fine feller, that Tom," she said. "I wonder what his new bride thinks about him working up at the fire all day long."

"She's probably spent much of her spare time thinking exactly what I'm thinking," Cessy said. "Please be careful and I'm oh-so-proud of you."

"Is your man up there at the fire?" Ma asked.

"Of course he is," Cessy answered, looking at Ma incredulously. "You sent him there."

"I sent him there?" Ma was astounded. "Honey, I wouldn't know your man if I should stumble across him in the street."

"But don't you remember . . ."

The sound of the Packard honking as it came down the street cut the conversation short and the two women hurried out to the front porch.

Her heart flew to her throat with thanks as she saw Gerald sitting between her father and Cedarleg. She hadn't realized how worried she had been until she saw him safe and sound at last.

The crowd began to gather around the automobile. They were waving and cheering and shouting. They were grateful to the men, glad to see them home. Cessy was, too.

It was when they took up the chant that Cessy's smile began to waver.

"Toolie! Toolie! Toolie!"

The cheering was louder and louder and Cessy watched as her husband was urged to his feet by her father and Cedarleg. He waved to the crowd as they called out to him.

Then their eyes met. Hers and her husband's. They met and held for a very long moment.

"So that is Tom Walker," Cessy said to Ma.

"That's our Tom."

Cessy turned and walked into the house. She went to the sun parlor and opened her desk and began rifling through the drawers. It only took her a couple of moments to find it. She opened up the marriage certificate that Reverend McAfee had sent and stared at the name written there once more.

Thomas Thursday Walker.

From the secret compartment she pulled out the handwritten note he'd sent and looked at it. It was obviously a note from an oilfield toolie, not from a Yale alumnus.

A sound at the doorway caused her to glance up. He was standing there as she knew he would be.

"Cessy?" he asked quietly. "Are you all right?"

"Am I all right? That is an interesting question," she said. "I am not the person who has been up on Topknot hill fighting fire all day, risking his life, and becoming a hero. I am not the person who has been doing that. I am not *that* person. But then what person am I?" she asked. "Am I Cessy Crane? No, apparently there is no such person as that. Perhaps I am Cessy Walker, but maybe I am still plain old Princess Calhoun. A slightly used Princess Calhoun, but Princess Calhoun nonetheless."

"You are legally my wife," he said. "You are legally Mrs. Tom Walker. Reverend McAfee used my real name so that it would be legal."

"You told him your real name?"

"He knew it. He knew me. I . . . I was raised at the school, Cessy," he said. "I am one of the boys from the school."

"Ah," she said, nodding. "You must have been left there while grandmama ran off with the gondolier."

"Cessy, I don't know how to explain," he began. "It started when I was in the Rough Riders. I pretended to be one of the rich boys from back East. They thought it was a great joke. And when I went to town or to parties with them, the ladies just loved Gerald. The same women who would not give Tom the time of day, crowded around Gerald as if he were a prince. After I left the army, well, sometimes I would still pretend. I'd meet some woman and I'd be Gerald and she . . . and she would fall for him. It was kind of a joke."

"So this . . . this Gerald is a cruel, dishonest amusement that you perpetrate on women," she said. "Do all of these women marry you?"

"No, of course not," he said. "No one has married me but you. I met you and I thought that you would fall in love with Gerald. So I pretended to be him. Women always love Gerald. He is so debonair and charming. I knew you would never fall in love with Tom. Tom is simply too ordinary. I knew that Tom would never catch the attentions of a woman like you. There are a hundred men around you exactly like Tom. You would never notice him."

"That you speak of Gerald as if he were someone else I can understand," Cessy said. "But you speak of Tom as if he were only a character also. Who is it exactly who inhabits your body?"

"I do, Cessy, your husband. The man who loves you." His words were soft and sweet and coaxing, but she heard them through a cold and bitter heart.

"And why were you so desperate for me to fall in love with you?" she asked. "Were you enamored of my delicate charms, my winning ways? Or perhaps you are inordinately fond of women who are mostly flat chested and wear eye spectacles? Maybe those weren't the delights that lured you. More likely it was my beautiful, beautiful oil wells that so incited your lust."

"Listen to me," he insisted. "I admit that my motives were impure at the start. I admit that, Cessy. I was thinking of bettering myself, improving my life. I was thinking . . . well, I was thinking all wrong. But as time went on I realized that I genuinely cared for you. That I could be happy with you and that I could make you happy."

"You think that *you* could make *me* happy? What an incredible conceit! A liar. A cheat. A seducer. A fortune hunter! You think that kind of man would make me happy?"

"Cessy, we were happy," he said. "Think about this last week, we were intensely happy and we can be again."

"I think you've made fool enough of me, Tom Walker," she said. "I cannot, I will not, listen to another word. Please leave."

"Cessy, please, I . . ."

"Do not persist in calling me by that ridiculous name. My name is Princess, but you will call me Miss Calhoun."

"Your name is not Calhoun, it is Walker," he said. "Mrs. Walker."

"Not for long," she snapped. "I am going to divorce you."

"Please don't . . ."

"Now get out of my sight."

"Cessy . . ."

"Must I have someone to throw you out? Do you want to make an uncouth scene on the day of your big triumph?"

"I don't give a damn about that. I only care about you."

"If you care about me as you claim," she said. "Then you will walk out of this room, out of this house, and out of my life forevermore."

Cessy turned her eyes from him. Unwilling to look at him once more. There was a long hesitation and then she heard him quietly close the door as he left her.

The evening meal did not go at all as well as many would have hoped. Without Cessy to tell everyone what to do and how to do it, chaos reigned, feelings were hurt, and the last to eat complained of cold food in insufficient quantities.

Cessy was much needed and much missed. But gossip burned faster than oil fires and everyone knew exactly why Miss Princess Calhoun was not there. Her new from-back-east husband, it had been revealed, was actually no other than their own Toolie Tom. It was more intriguing than a two-cent serial.

Cessy wanted only to be alone. To collect her thoughts and salve her wounds. She had only left the sun parlor after it became occupied by Mrs. Deadum and her injured son Lyst.

She couldn't go up to her bedroom, which was now occupied by Mr. Earlie and his family, and she was afraid to sit in the kitchen where the group of cooking women were intent upon quiet, speculative gossip, or upon the porch where it seemed everybody was watching.

She thought about seeking out Ma and Cedarleg, only to worry that perhaps *he* was staying in their tent.

With no place safe to sit or stay, Cessy grabbed up her parasol and left the house. It seemed the only solution when one's home was overrun with well-meaning people who love you.

He had lied to her. He had betrayed her trust. He had made a fool of her. And she had let it happen.

How could he have fooled her so easily? Only because she wanted to be fooled. Only because she wanted to believe that she had found the man of her dreams at last.

As she walked alone down the empty afternoon sidewalk, she recalled in painful, humiliated memory how she had thrown herself at him, right from the beginning. How she had worn her heart so fully upon her sleeve. How she had fallen in so eagerly with her own ruin.

She was certain that it was love at first sight, destined love, perfect love, and that he felt exactly as she had. It was pathetic. She was pathetic. And the worse place to be pathetic was in front of the person whom you care about most.

He must have laughed at her. He must have laughed and laughed at how gullible and malleable she was.

Plain, bossy Princess, she always tells everybody

what to do. But if you spark her a little bit, give her a few kisses, you can make her dance to your own tune.

She might have lived with the humiliation, the public embarrassment, even the scandal. But how could she live with the knowledge of what it felt to love him and then never to love again?

Tears sprang to her eyes. How could she stand it? How would she stand it?

The horn on the Packard honked loudly, startling her as it pulled up beside the curb. She almost screamed in frustration. Why couldn't she have time for herself? Surely she had earned a good cry.

"You need a ride, Princess?" her father asked. "Get on in here."

"I'd rather walk," she told him.

He nodded. "And I'd rather just keep on driving and come back when all your troubles have settled themselves out on their own. But I'm your father and you're my daughter, and I guess we're going to have to figure this thing out as best that we can."

With a sigh of resignation, Cessy agreed and took a seat in the Packard.

"How's the fire?" she asked him.

"It's out, pretty much. We got a small crew up there watching for flare-ups, but the oil has been drained out considerably. Once we let the dang thing cool off, we'll be storing in there again, I suppose."

She nodded.

They drove in silence a bit further. At the far edge of town he pulled to a stop under the shade of a huge oak at the side of the road. They sat silently together for a few moments merely listening to the drone of bees and the wind rustling through the trees.

"I know you just found out about this, Cessy," King said. "And it's sure hard to think about at first."

"How long have you known?" she asked him.

"Since the middle of last night, I guess," he said. "You know, he could have kept his secret."

"What do you mean?"

"Well, he could have stayed home, like he did the day the 'P' came in. Or even when he got there, he could have held himself back, blended into the background. There were so many people there and so much going on. Nobody would have noticed him too much. I even told him myself to go back and help you. He could have done that and kept the secret."

"Maybe so," she said.

"But he didn't," King said. "He knew he had something to offer. He knew that he could help and he was willing to do so. If he had not helped, at best all that oil would be flowing down the river right now, or at worst it would still be burning and maybe another sump on fire by now. Bad for us, but for him . . . well, no one would know that Gerald Crane was really Tom Walker."

"Tom Walker." Cessy repeated the name.

In memory she could hear his voice in their bedroom, so soft and dear. *I was named for Francis Amasa Walker.*

"He was going to tell me anyway," Cessy said. "He'd already tried at least once."

Her father raised an eyebrow at that and nodded appreciably.

"That's in his favor then, Princess," he said. "That's much in his favor."

"He believed I wouldn't notice an ordinary man like Tom Walker," she said. "He thought that it would take a fancy man like Gerald Crane to attract my attention."

"Guess he didn't know you too well in the beginning," her father admitted.

"I suppose I really didn't give him a chance to," she admitted. "It was love at first sight for me. I knew that he was the one the minute I saw him. I . . . oh, that was just such foolishness."

"Foolishness?" Her father tutted in disagreement. "Princess, I've always known you to be as level-headed and strong-minded a woman as I've ever met. You are a lot like me. And I have to admit I've always been proud of that. But in this you are like me, too. And I can't help but speak against it."

"What are you talking about?"

"Love, Princess," he said. "The kind of love that hits you from clear across a room and knocks you for a loop. That's so rare, it's so very rare. This fellow is not at all what you thought he was and your marriage is not at all what you thought it was going to be. But Princess when you meet someone and violins start playing in the back of your head, I don't think a reasonable person should ignore that."

"Oh, Daddy," she said. "What if he is simply not the right man? What if he is a liar, a cheat, a seducer, and a fortune hunter?"

King looked thoughtful and shook his head.

"I'm not sure if I can tell you for certain," he said. "I was in love once, like that. And she was the wrong woman. She'd lived a hard life and had a shady reputation. She made no secret of her past and I knew it as well as anybody. Marriage to her would have done nothing to enhance the image of King Calhoun and in fact, she might have even tarnished it a little. She was not at all the kind of woman I'd have chosen for a wife. But when I was with her, Princess, I was happy. And when I looked at her and knew that she was mine, I was proud."

"But you walked away from her?"

"I did," he said. "And I would be remiss as a father if I didn't tell you honestly that I regret it."

"Oh, Daddy, maybe it's not too late," she said.

"It may well be," he answered. "Things were said,

words meant to wound that can't never be taken back. I don't know if it's ever possible to get the milk back in the bottle. But yours ain't spilt yet, Princess. It's teetering for certain. But it ain't seeping along the floor. I'd hate for you to be so hasty like your father that next week or next month or next year you'll be sitting around regretting the way that I am."

"I don't know, Daddy," she said. "I trusted him so. I believed in him so. And now I think I might never be willing to trust him again."

"Trust is important," he agreed. "Trust is very important, maybe as important as love. But trust can be gained and trust can be earned. Love is either there or it's not. And when it's not, all the trust in the world is empty without it."

"I do love him," she said. "I can't seem to help that. But I can't just placidly agree to still be his wife."

"In honesty, Princess, I'm having a hard time being angry with him about this," her father admitted. "Oh, I don't like him lying to you none. But in truth I think that Tom Walker is a man much more suited to your nature than some fancy eastern blueblood."

"He married me for my money, Daddy," she said angrily.

King Calhoun chuckled. "Then the joke's on him, ain't it. 'Cause without a refinery we are flat busted, and that's a fact."

Cessy turned to look at him. Her eyes widening in appreciation.

"You're right Daddy, that is a fact. It is really indisputably a fact," she said.

She was quiet, thoughtful, and staring sightlessly into space.

"Lord, Princess," her father complained. "I can hear the gears clanking in your brain clear over this way."

"Daddy, I have to talk to him," she said. "You'd

better take me home. No, no there is no place at home where we can talk. Take me someplace where we can talk."

"Where?"

"I don't know, but turn the car around. We've got to go back and get him."

"He ain't at the house," King said.

"He's not there?"

"You told him to go away, so he did."

"But where did he go?"

"Out to that Indian School, that's where he said he was going, though I doubt he's had time to walk all the way out there."

"Get out, Daddy, I'm taking the car," she ordered.

Her father did as he was bid but looked at her askance. "Princess, you don't know how to drive an automobile."

"Oh, Daddy, you know me, when I set my mind to it, I can do anything."

TWENTY-ONE

Tom had not had time to make it all the way to the school. Cessy, who had lurched and sputtered all the way down the river road, came to an abrupt halt beside him, not a half mile from the Shemmy Creek turn off.

His eyes alighted with hope at the sight of her in the Packard, but she wasn't ready to give him hope yet.

"Get in," she ordered.

Without question he followed her instruction.

"I didn't know you are an auto driver," he said.

"There's a lot of things you don't know about me," she said as she took her foot off the clutch, causing the car to jerk forward, nearly knocking Tom dramatically into the windshield.

He put his hands upon the door and the dash to brace himself as several more lurches ensued, but then the annoying Packard sort of got its footing and went barreling down the road once more.

Cessy glanced over at him. He looked handsome, dashing, as desirable as ever. He looked strong, forceful, masculine. She marveled that she had ever believed him to be the delicate gentleman that was Gerald Crane.

He also looked tired. She was tired, too. They'd been awake for nearly thirty-six hours. The best decisions were probably not made under those conditions. Deliberately she kept that in mind.

She careened the Packard to a stop at the special place, the picnic place. She got out and began walking into the cool glade without so much as a word or glance back.

Cessy heard him hurrying after her, but she refused to wait on him. She refused to take any notice.

This was their place. It was a place so dear to her. It was where he had asked her to wed him. He had claimed to be in love with her, but it was the love of money that had fueled their rush to the altar. Now it was to be the lack of money that would save their marriage.

It took her a few moments to find the rock, but she did and she knelt down to put her hand upon it.

"Still cold?" he asked as he came up beside her.

Slowly she looked up at him.

"Someone told me that there is an underground spring here," she said. "A small river of cold water just below the surface."

"*Someone* told you?" His gaze was questioning.

"*Gerald* told me," she said, more specifically.

He shook his head.

"No, not Gerald," he said. "Gerald couldn't have told you that. Because he wouldn't have known. He's lived all his life inside, warm and protected. It was Tom who was with you at this place before. It was Tom who got you Queen Anne's lace and cattails. This is Tom's place."

"And who am I here with this evening?" she asked.

He smiled at her. "With your husband, of course."

She nodded.

"My husband, who married me for my money."

He did not reply. He sat down on the grass across

from her and took her hand in his own. It was warm, so very warm. A stark contrast to the coldness of the rock.

She broke from his grasp and lay her hand on the cool surface of the stone once more.

"Do you know that wealth can be like this?"

"Like what?"

"Like your underground creek," she said. "Wealth can be hidden from view. Sometimes the people that you would never believe have money have it in cartloads. And the people that you think are rich as Croesus turn out to be surprisingly insolvent."

"Yes, I suppose that's true."

"And that's what has happened," she said.

Tom nodded. "Yes, I guess so. As Gerald, I appeared to be quite wealthy and in fact I had nothing."

"Oh I wasn't thinking of you, or of Gerald," she said. "I was thinking of myself," she said.

He was sitting cross-legged in the grass, a sprig of broomsedge extending from the corner of his lips.

"What do you mean?" he asked.

"Well, you see, you seem to think that you married a very wealthy woman and that you will get to live in luxury all your life. You see those big oil wells coming in and you think they are money in the bank. But they are not at all."

"I don't understand what you're saying."

"King Calhoun looks very prosperous, very wealthy. It's how an oil man must look if he ever expects to have backers. Backers are one of the most key elements to success in the oil business. Even Sinclair or Rockefeller cannot amass enough money for a project like this on their own."

"I suppose not," Tom agreed.

"Certainly it is a good thing to strike oil. And we do have all of that flowing into those sump tanks. But without a way to process it, it's worthless."

"Worthless?"

Cessy looked at him and shook her head. "You may be Toolie Tom, the hero of the day," she said. "But I'm afraid that you still have a lot to learn about the oil business."

"I'm sure I do," he agreed.

"Crude oil, the so-called black gold that we get out of the ground, has no value in itself," she said. "It has to be refined into products. Mostly we use it to make lamp and heating oil, although if those contraptions like my father's Packard really catch on like he thinks they will, it can be used to make gasoline."

"I agree with your father," Tom said. "It's clear that the internal combustion engine is the future and it runs on gasoline."

"Perhaps so," Cessy agreed. "But that is the future and this is the present. Did you ever wonder why no other oil company has come to Topknot?"

Tom's brow furrowed thoughtfully.

"I guess I never thought about it," he admitted.

"It looks very strange here, you know, if you've been to Jackson or Corsicana or Spindletop," she said. "At all the other major fields, and I truly do believe this one is going to be major, there are a half-dozen oil companies cramped up against each other, trying to drill out of the same zone."

"This is my first oil field," Tom told her. "How would I know that? But it's better, isn't it, if your father controls all the oil here?"

She nodded.

"Yes," she agreed. "It's theoretically better. But the reason that no one else is here is not because no one but my father thinks that there is oil here. It's because there is no refinery in this area and no pipeline to one at all."

Tom began to twirl the sprig of broomsedge in the corner of his mouth as if pondering deeply.

"Unfortunately for Topknot and Burford Corners,

there is no way to get the crude oil from the well to anyplace that can make it into something usable and marketable."

"Then why did your father drill here?" he asked.

"Because he believed that there was oil here and he believed that he would get the financing to build his own refinery. That is what he wanted. To be first and to own the refinery and therefore to control the field."

Tom nodded with appreciation. "It sounds like a good strategy," he said.

"Yes, I think it was a good strategy," she said. "But it was a risk. And a risk that has not paid off. Daddy has not been able to get the financing. He has gone to virtually every oil-friendly bank in the country and been turned down again and again. The banks believe that there is more than enough oil in production already. The supply of it currently exceeds the demand. And that bringing new fields into production will only drive down the value of the fields that they are already invested in."

"But that is only in the short term," Tom said. "These bankers are simply not looking far enough ahead."

"They are looking at their pocketbooks today," Cessy told him. "And they have decided not to loan my father the money that he needs. My father must build a refinery to get the value out of the oil. And as each day goes by it becomes less and less likely that it will happen."

Tom was silent, thoughtful for a long moment.

"I'm sorry," he said finally.

"Yes, I am too," she said. "When I told Daddy that you married me for my money, can you imagine what he said."

"No, I can't."

"He said that the joke was on you, because there is no money."

Tom nodded slowly, as if deep in thought.

Cessy raised her chin and kept her tone falsely bright. "I think that you should keep our current poverty clearly in mind when you make your decision," Cessy said.

"My decision?"

"About whether you wish to continue our marriage," she said.

Tom's mouth fell open in surprise. The sprig of broomsedge fell to the ground.

"You said that you were going to divorce me," he pointed out.

"I was very angry at the time," she admitted, swallowing no small amount of pride. "But I'm not sure that divorce at this time would be the best thing to do."

"Are you saying that you still love me?" he asked softly.

"No, I am not saying that at all," she assured him hastily. "I am not sure how I feel about you, or if I can ever care for you as I did."

"But you want to stay married to me."

She hesitated only a moment.

"I . . . fear that I may be with child," she said.

"Already?"

"My . . . my courses were due this week," she said. "It is early, of course, to know. But it seems I am late. If it were true, if I were in a family way, then I would not wish to try to raise a child without a father, even if that father were a lesser man than I might wish him to be."

She saw him blanch and knew her words had wounded him as sorely as she had intended.

"We are both without sleep and just now learning the truth about each other," she continued. "I suggest we meet here at this time, one week from today. By then I shall know if I am with child and you will know whether or not you are willing to take on a wife who not only cannot support you, but who will expect you to support her.''

Once the smoke and fumes had cleared, the oil camp was reestablished in its old location. It was amazing how much longer it took to set things back in order than to disorder them in the first place. The evacuation had taken hours. Most of the work week was spent getting everyone moved back into their campsites.

And a changing neighborhood was also evident. As the wells came in, many of the men from the drilling crews were packing up and moving on. It was pumpers that were needed now. And they arrived, unwilling to spend anymore time than necessary in the camp. They would be living in Burford Corners for some time to come. They were ready to build shotgun shacks and foursquare houses.

While the genteel society of Burford Corners, such as it was, did not welcome the pumper families with open arms, the merchants were as excited and enthusiastic as if they, too, had struck oil on the crest of Topknot hill.

All of this happiness and prosperity, however, hinged upon the Royal Oil Company and rumors about company troubles were beginning to surface.

Where indeed was all this oil going to go? How much could be held in sumps for how long? Was there to be a refinery in Burford Corners or not?

The man who could have answered those questions boarded a train on Thursday with his new son-in-law, Toolie Tom, at his side. He was more now than the hero. King Calhoun had clearly singled him out for better things. There was talk of letting the young man be driller on the next well or perhaps even making him a pusher. Whatever, it was quite an honor even if he was King's son-in-law, although how that was working out no one could really tell.

Tom, it seemed, was back living with Ma and Cedarleg.

The train was an express, but it still took a good while to make its way across half the country. They boarded at dawn and were in Chicago past suppertime. In the darkness they slept through the cornfields and cottages to awaken to a Pennsylvania dawn. It was midafternoon when they freshened up at the Elvira Hotel in downtown Bedlington.

"Just let me do the talking," Tom suggested. "I know these people. I believe that I can trust them. And I hope that they will trust me."

"Lord, I ain't going to say a word," King assured him. "The dang bellboy even looks down his nose at me."

Tom laughed and straightened his father-in-law's collar. "That's because you don't look like you are an oil baron," he said.

"I'm the brokest oil baron you ever saw," King said.

"You're not broke," Tom assured him. "You're merely lacking in financing."

The two walked the length of Broad Street commenting on both the quaintness of the hundred-year-old buildings and the cleanliness of the brick streets.

Tom mentally prepared himself. He held his head high as he glanced around, nodding politely to a matron here, a businessman there. He was as good as any of them. He was a man of his own making.

Dexter Savings Bank was on the corner of Philpott and Broad. The two stopped in front.

"Are you ready?" King asked him.

"I suppose I'm ready as I'll ever be," Tom told him.

"Don't feel bad if they turn you down," King said. "They are bankers. Bankers and oil are just one of those combinations that never quite mix."

Tom sighed heavily and cracked a grin. "I'm just

hoping that a little gunpowder in the stew will make it blend a little more nicely."

Inside they found fine marble floors, well-polished, dark walnut paneling, a chandelier overhead with real electric lighting.

Tom walked directly up to the balding man at the front desk.

"I am here to see Mr. Dexter," he said.

"Which Mr. Dexter, sir," the man said. "There are two."

"Mr. Ambrose Dexter," Tom replied.

"Do you have an appointment, sir?"

"No, I do not," he said.

The man gave only a cursory glance toward the book beside him.

"Then it will be absolutely impossible to see Mr. Dexter today," he said.

Tom sighed, deliberately keeping his fear and disappointment in check.

"Then I will speak to the elder Mr. Dexter, please," he said.

The clerk gave a snort of annoyance and rolled his eyes. "Impossible, the elder Mr. Wheeling Dexter sees only a very select group of our bank's depositors."

"Perhaps I can make an appointment with Mr. Ambrose Dexter for sometime next week, sir."

Beside him Tom heard King Calhoun sigh and from the corner of his eye he could see the older man's shoulders slump. He couldn't allow Calhoun to give up. He simply couldn't allow it. It was too important. They were much, much too close.

"Do you know who I am?" Tom asked the question just a little bit too loudly.

"I have never seen you before in my life," the balding man answered with the conceited self-assurance that anyone who it would be important for him to know he would recognize on sight.

"I am, sir, for your information Ger—" He covered his gaff with a hasty cough. "I am Thomas T. Walker," he said.

"Very nice," the clerk said, clearly unimpressed.

"Go tell Mr. Ambrose Dexter that I am here," Tom said.

"I told you that Mr. Dexter has no—"

Tom slammed his fist down upon the clerk's desk. Every human in the bank jumped at the unexpected sound.

Tom kept his voice soft, quiet, and extremely civil. "Apparently you did not hear me," he said. "I told you to tell Mr. Dexter that I am here. So do it."

The clerk, now clearly rattled, hurried back to the glass-paned doors at the back of the bank.

Inside Tom was shaking. So much depended upon this. So much was riding on the coattails of a long-ago war. But not everything, he reminded himself. Cessy was still willing to marry him. She was willing to live with him, to be married to him even if he were only an out-of-work tool dresser. That's what really mattered. She and he. The rest of this was just . . . it was just money.

"Tom! My God, Tom!"

Ambi came exploding out of his door. He stopped only an instant to open up the one beside his.

"Father, Tom Walker is here," he said.

Then Ambi was there, cranking his hand as if it were a pump handle and talking a mile a minute in that oh-so-clever and sophisticated tone that he had.

His father was there, too, patting him on the back and expressing how glad they were to see him.

"Come on back into the office," the older man said. "We have so much to catch up on."

Tom was almost led away when he stopped and turned to the man behind him.

"Mr. Dexter, Ambi, please allow me to introduce my father-in-law, Mr. King Calhoun of Royal Oil."

"Mr. Calhoun, a pleasure," the elder Mr. Dexter said.

Ambi repeated the greeting.

They made their way into the corner office where Ambi's father still held sway, although it seemed most of the business had been turned over to his son.

The clerk was sent for tea and the four were shortly enjoying an afternoon respite.

"You're married, Tom?" Ambi said.

"Yes," he answered. "Just recently."

"It's been almost two years since I tied the knot," Ambi said.

"You're married also? To anyone I know?"

Young Dexter blushed vividly. "Why Diedre, of course."

"Diedre Willingham?"

Tom was shocked.

"Why, yes, of course, who else," Ambi answered. "You must have known . . . well, I wore my heart on my sleeve for years. Surely you knew that I cared for her."

"I had no idea."

"Why else would I have made such a mess of our friendship," he said.

Tom was dumbfounded.

Ambi turned to a curious King Calhoun. "After the war, your son-in-law stayed with us to recover from his wound," Ambi explained. "He met many of our friends. He is such a cutup, as I'm sure you know. And we all loved him. My wife, who was just past her coming out at that time, became interested in him. He mentioned that he was thinking of marrying her. I had been waiting for her to grow up for a very long time."

Ambi turned back to address the rest of his words to Tom.

"I said some terrible things at that time," he admitted. "Things that I did not mean. And things that I would have taken back a hundred times. But then you were gone and no word all these years. I thought I would never see you again."

"No need to worry about that," Tom said. "Like the bad penny, I always turn up."

TWENTY-TWO

It was a riot of a party. The perfect send-off. Every loose-living oil man in Topknot was there. The other saloons had closed their doors. Only the Palace was open for Miss Queenie's good-bye.

The chaos of the evacuation and then the headache of moving back in had delayed her departure considerably. She couldn't leave Frenchie and Mathis without trying to insure that they made a go of it. After all, it was their payments that she was counting on to live.

They were not about to change the name. Oil field people knew Queenie's Palace. She had a reputation for fair dealing and unwatered alcohol. With her name upon the sign they would continue to flock to the place.

Since Queenie herself would not be there, Mathis had taken it upon himself to paint a huge mural of her on the wall behind the bar.

The likeness was a fairly good one. He'd given her more hair than she could actually ever grow. And the feminine silhouette he portrayed was so generously curvaceous that it must have been in the eye of the beholder.

But all in all Queenie was proud of it. It did look like her and perhaps when King came in here, he would see it and remember her. Maybe he'd remember her as she truly was and maybe he'd remember that he'd once loved her.

"Where are you going to go?" one of her longtime customers asked her.

"Someplace where they ain't heard of me, I guess," she answered, causing a general outpouring of laughter.

"It's just time for me to retire," she explained. "I'll go to some little farming or ranching town where they've never heard of the oil business, let alone Queenie McCurtain."

"Lord almighty, Miss Queenie," a bright-eyed rig builder with a southern accent commented. "Them farmers get a look at you they'll be leaving their wives faster than hot sugar turns to syrup."

Queenie smiled at him, knowing he meant his words to be a compliment, but hoping full well that they would not come true.

She was going out into a new world, but she wanted to hide from it, not be a part of it.

The nausea that had plagued her early on was much improved. But the crying got worse and worse. She had thought that she could make King marry her. That he loved her enough that she could demand that he do it. Apparently he was determined to prove her wrong.

This is what she was determined to do. She refused to feel sorry about it. Still the thought of never seeing him again, never holding him, never having him in her life, reduced her to tears at unexpected times.

He hadn't darkened her door. And if the rumors were accurate, he wasn't even in town. Maybe that was for the best. Perhaps it would be easier to leave knowing he wasn't around than knowing he was there but didn't care enough to even say good-bye.

Of course, King would probably say that she had

made her feelings on that subject perfectly clear. Marry me or don't come back. He had simply chosen the latter course.

Tommy shouted for quiet until he had everyone's attention and offered up a toast.

"To Miss Queenie," he said. "A woman who has stirred lots of whiskey, served lots of beer, and put smiles on a lot of men's faces."

Hoots of laughter came from all over the room.

"You tell it, Tommy!" one fellow encouraged.

He turned to face her. "May you find happiness where you will and smile to yourself in secret when you think of your old friends."

"I will," she promised.

"Cheers!"

"Cheers!"

"Wahoo!" someone shouted.

The piano player picked up the tune again and within a half minute the room was loud and noisy and boisterous once more.

Frenchie was leading a young fellow to the stairway. Mathis hurried over to get his money in advance.

Queenie sat down at the bar and plastered a smile upon her face. She smiled and smiled and smiled interminably. She was drinking spring water with a touch of mint and learning a fact that many before her had discovered. A party of drinkers is pretty boring unless one is suitably drunk.

She wondered how much longer she would have to stay. It was her good-bye party. How quickly could she go upstairs, lay down in her sleepless bed, and wait for the morning train.

It was then that she noticed a sudden strange change in the volume of noise in the place. People were quieting and hushing others to do the same. There was an expectation that was growing and

Queenie looked around to see that everyone was silent and watching her. As the crowd parted between herself and the doorway, she saw him.

Her heart began to pound. It was all she could do not to run toward him and throw herself in his arms.

King Calhoun stood there. Still dressed in his traveling clothes, a candy box tucked under his arm.

Smiling and nodding to those around him, he stepped forward.

"'Evening Queenie," he said. "Is this a party going on?"

"Yes," she answered, her voice cracking. "Yes, it's my good-bye party. I'm leaving on the morning train."

"Just come in on a train myself," he said. "Been back East all week."

She nodded noncommittally.

"If you're leaving in the morning, then it's a good thing I came by here tonight," he said. "I brought you a present."

He set the box down beside her on the bar.

"It's those chocolates that you like," he said. "Brought them all the way from Pennsylvania."

"Thank you, King," she said. "It was very nice of you to come and say good-bye."

"Aren't you going to open them?" he said.

"I'm not really hungry right now."

"Open them up anyway," he said. "There's a surprise inside."

She looked at him askance. "You mean like in the Cracker Jacks."

King smiled. "Yes, ma'am, just like in the Cracker Jacks."

Carefully she untied the ribbons and opened the box. There among the sweet cremes and nougats was a small paper box that said on the top of it: TIFFANY'S NEW YORK-CHICAGO.

Queenie's hands were trembling as she picked it up. She removed the top to find a slim, single gold band lying in a puff of tissue.

She raised her eyes to the man beside her. Her voice was soft as a whisper. "It's a wedding ring."

For fifty years thereafter old timers in the oil field would still laugh and wonder and shake their heads as they told the tale. The day big, proud, King Calhoun dropped to one knee in the middle of a Topknot saloon to ask Queenie McCurtain to marry him.

He had not come. She had waited at their special place near Shemmy Creek for over an hour, until darkness was almost upon her and then she'd returned to the surrey and asked Howard to drive her home.

She had to bite back the tears of hurt and disappointment. He had not met her at the appointed hour.

"Have you heard anything of Tom Walker?" she asked finally.

She heard the hesitation in Howard's voice. "They say he took a train on Thursday, Miss Princess," he answered.

Thursday. He'd been out of her life since Thursday and she hadn't even known it.

She did cry then. She made no attempt to hold back the tears. And she didn't even care if Howard heard them. Her pride was gone. Her man was gone. Her heart was broken.

Howard wordlessly handed her his handkerchief and she cried into it copiously. She could not recall ever allowing herself to lose such control. It was important always to stay in command of oneself and of everything else around.

Only Tom had the power to take that control from

her. He took it from her in his arms through tenderness and passion. And he took it from her now as he broke her heart.

Her shaking sobs had lessened to a grim sadness by the time Howard pulled the surrey into the porte cochere. He helped her alight. And she walked into the house with leaden steps.

Mrs. Marin hurried up the hall to meet her. She didn't want supper. She didn't want sympathy. She just wanted to be alone and silent and miserably unhappy.

"Visitor in the sun parlor, Miss Princess."

"I don't want to see anyone," she said. "Send whoever it is away."

"It's Mr. Walker."

"Who?"

"Mr. Walker."

"Mr. Walker, my husband Mr. Walker?"

"Yes ma'am, he's . . ."

Cessy didn't wait to hear more. She raced to the sun parlor.

"You're here!" she said.

"I am so sorry I was late. The train was delayed in Kansas City and I swear I would have stepped outside to push if I'd thought it would get me here any faster."

"I waited for you at the picnic place."

"I should have gone out there, but it was so late, I was certain that you'd returned home already."

"No I . . . I waited a very long time."

"I'm sorry," he said. "Here, I've brought you some candy." He handed her the fancy box, tied prettily with ribbons.

"Thank you."

"Cessy, I've been thinking about what you said last week," he said. "I know that I was wrong to do the things that I did. I was wrong to marry you for such a reason as mine was. I want you to know that I do care about you. Indeed, I honestly love you and I believe I have told you many times. I don't deserve to be your husband. But if you can find it in your heart to forgive me, I am prepared to make it up to you."

"To make it up to me?"

"I have a job now, Cessy, a good job, I think. I can and will support you. Nothing need be supplied by your father. I will provide for you and any offspring that we might have."

"You have a new job?"

"Yes," he answered. "And we can live here, in your house, if you are so inclined. Can you forgive me, Cessy? Can you take me back?"

She raised her chin haughtily. "I don't know if I can forgive you. But it seems that I must take you back."

"You must?"

"It is not certain yet, of course," she said. "But it seems that perhaps I am with child. For that consequence, of course I must give you one more chance."

"Thank you, Cessy, thank you," he said. "I promise you that you will not be sorry."

"Well, I certainly hope not," she said. "I suppose most women, however, would consider it quite a comedown to believe that one is marrying into a wealthy family only to discover oneself married to a tool dresser."

"Oh, I'm not a tool dresser anymore," he said.

From inside his breast pocket he pulled out the silver card box that he always carried. He removed a card and handed it to her.

Cessy glanced down and read the words written in raised gold lettering. ROYAL-WALKER REFINING COMPANY, T.T. WALKER, PRESIDENT.

"What is this?"

"Construction begins tomorrow," he said. "Your father has made me a partner and the head of this part of the operation."

"How can this be? Where did you get the money?"

"Not everything you know about me is lies, Cessy," he said. "I did go to Cuba. And I do have banking friends among the fine families of Bedlington in the New Jersey."

Her mind was awhirl.

"Then . . . then . . . then I'm not poor anymore. I'm rich again and you knew it before I did! You're marrying me again for my money."

"The partnership in the refinery is my own," he said firmly. "I earned it by getting the financing. You are a rich woman again. And you can thank me for that any time."

Cessy didn't feel like thanking him.

"You . . . you . . . you're not going to suffer at all. You are getting everything that you want!" she complained.

"And you are, too. You love me and want me and you are going to have me."

"I . . . no, I told you that I could not forgive you," she said.

"Yes, I know, you're only letting me stay because we have a child on the way."

"Yes, yes, that is the only reason."

"Now I find that really interesting, because that is not at all what I heard."

"What did you hear?"

"Well, you know how Ma can't resist repeating a joke a dozen times," he said. "Poor Moses. The *Red Sea*, indeed."

Tom walked over and lifted her up into his arms.

"I do hope that when we eventually do have children, lying will not be the only family trait they inherit from us."

He kissed her then. Sweet and long and languidly.

"I love you, Cessy," he whispered to her. "And you'll just have to trust me that I am telling the truth to you when I say that."

She looked up into his eyes and she believed him.

"Where are you taking me?" she asked as he began carrying her across the room.

"Up to bed, of course," he answered. "It's been a whole week since I've made love to my wife. And I've developed a voracious appetite for things married and sexual. Grab that candy box."

"The candy box? Married and sexual includes chocolate these days?"

"I wasn't thinking of the chocolate," he told her. "I was admiring those pretty ribbons. I believe tonight it's your turn to wear them."

EPILOGUE

*Methodist Agricultural & Mechanical College
   at Burford Corners
November 18, 1929*

She looked as beautiful as she had ever looked and he couldn't have been more proud of her. Her dress was a delicate confection of ivory silk, beaded and adorned with lace. The long frothy veil enhanced her dark hair and her handsome eyes. She was obviously nervous and kept picking at her fingernails.

He stopped to peek through the doorway into the sanctuary of the McAfee Memorial Chapel. It was crowded with people dressed in their best finery, all looking back toward the doors expectantly.

"They've seated your mother," he said.

"Thank God," the bride complained. "I think if I had to hear one more word out of her I would have started screaming. She always knows exactly what should be done and spends her every waking minute telling everybody what to do."

Her father smiled. "That's just the way your mother is, Sina. She was born bossy and nothing short of the grave is going to change that. In fact, I wouldn't put it past her to have an earful of advice for Saint Peter when she arrives."

The young woman nodded in agreement.

He peeked through the doorway once more. "Your groom has come into the room," he said. "And I see Phillip has made it."

"Hail the conquering Cornell Law student," she complained. "Why did Joe have to choose him as best man?"

"They are the closest of friends."

"It's just not fair that anyone should have an uncle who is only a year older than she is," Sina complained. "If he starts calling me T.T. in public again, I think I will plant my fist right in his face."

"Oh Sina, you are more like your mother than you think," he said. "And if she were here I'm sure she'd tell you that starting a fistfight at your own wedding is not quite de rigueur for brides these days."

The young woman sighed heavily and put her hands together in front of her in a prayerful clasp.

"Oh, Daddy, should we really be doing this?" she asked.

Her father stilled, looking worried. "Are you having second thoughts about getting married? I like the young man, you know that. And his parents are old friends. But I'll go out there right now and tell everyone to go home if you're not sure."

"Oh, I'm sure about Joe," she said. "I'm just not sure about having this big wedding. With the stock market going bad like it has and you and Grandpa losing so much . . ."

"Now, Sina, neither your grandfather or me is likely to take a jump out of a window. The oil business has always been boom and bust. Filthy rich one day, dirt poor the next. If there is one thing that I have learned in this world is that money doesn't matter all that much. As long as I have your mother beside me, I've got good reason to be grateful."

"That's just how I feel about Joe," she said.

He smiled at her. "Then let's go inside there and get you married, shall we?"

They walked down the aisle together. He was proud to walk beside her, but she only had eyes for the young man waiting at the altar.

He stood in his place and spoke his part.

"Who gives this woman to be married?"

"Her mother and I do," he answered.

Then he stepped away from the young couple and took his place beside his wife and grasped her hand, squeezing it lovingly. They shared a hasty look and felt their own love swell up inside them with a tenderness that was forever new.

He glanced past his wife to his in-laws. King and Queenie, such a perfectly matched pair. They'd spent the last several years traveling in Europe, but he was glad they were here to see their eldest granddaughter get married.

Across the aisle, he heard the groom's mother sniffling quietly. He knew that they were as happy about this wedding as he was.

In a booming voice, the minister had come to the vows.

"Do you Thomasina Thursday Walker take this man, Joseph Maloof Bashara to be your lawfully wedded husband? For better for worse, for richer for poorer, in sickness and in health, til death do you part?"

"I do," she answered.